DRAGON'S FURY SERIES

SERIES

VOLUME I

D1548304

COMING SOON BY
JEFF HEAD

DRAGON'S FURY VOLUME II – TRODDEN UNDER
APR-MAY 2002

DRAGON'S FURY VOLUME III – HIGH TIDE
SEP-OCT 2002

DRAGON'S FURY VOLUME IV – THE LONG MARCH
APR-MAY 2003

DRAGON'S FURY VOLUME V – EAGLE'S TALONS
SEP-OCT 2003

DRAGON'S FURY
-
BREATH OF FIRE

JEFF
HEAD

ALPHA CONNECTIONS
IDAHO, USA

www.dragonsfury-breathoffire.com

Published By:
Alpha Connections
530 W. Idaho Blvd.
Emmett, ID 83716

ISBN 0-9715779-1-9

Printed in the United States of America

DEDICATION

This book is dedicated to lovers of liberty everywhere, and to the principles upon which true liberty rests: faith, morality, virtue, honor, free will, commitment, valor and eternal vigilance. Most especially, this book is dedicated to all of those Americans and their families who have served in defense of liberty and sacrificed their time, their efforts, their very lives and the lives of their loved ones for that cause, whether at home or abroad.

In particular this book is dedicated to those victims of terror and tyranny whose lives were so ruthlessly and brutally cut short on September 11, 2001, and to those selfless emergency personnel, firefighters, police, national guard and volunteers who worked so selflessly to help and save many. It is also dedicated with great respect and humility to the passengers and crew of United Airlines Flight 93. On that ultimate day of infamy, these heroes resisted their hijackers and fought back, resulting in the crash of that aircraft and the death of all involved before it could reach its target, thus saving hundreds if not thousands of more American lives.

It is dedicated with great expectation to those committed and professional service men and women who will be called upon to bring about a just and lasting retribution for the attack that killed and injured so many. May we honor all of these sacrifices and be prepared to make our own for liberty and for our Republic.

ACKNOWLEDGMENTS

Special thanks go to my family for their faith and patience with me while producing this book. In particular to my dear wife of 23 years for her love, patience and forbearance in putting up with and helping me, and to my two sons, Jeff and Jared for their proofs and input to their "old man." In addition, thanks to my father, A. L. Head Jr., a combat veteran of World War II, my father-in-law, Ralph Woodmansee, and my son-in-law Nathan.

I cannot have a section on acknowledgements without personally thanking those who collaborated with me on this project.

Thanks to Joanie Fischer of Pennsylvania, for her reviews, her masterful edits, encouragement and patriotic input.

Thanks to Christopher Durkin of Pennsylvania, for his edits, reviews, writing contribution regarding the Cuban terrorist, Hector Ortiz, and for his invaluable engineering input.

Thanks to Bruce Elmore of Illinois, for his writing contribution regarding Ahmed Haddad, and his input as a Marine (there are no "former" Marines).

Thanks to Matt Bracken of California, for his reviews, for his ideas regarding the overall strategic scenario, and for his ideas regarding methods Red China could use to quickly build and mount a credible amphibious capability and for his input as a former U.S. Navy Seal platoon commander.

Thanks to Arthur Hines of North Carolina for his strategic input on the overall scenario as someone who served so ably on the point of the sword in the U.S. Special Forces in Vietnam.

Thanks to Matthew Riley of Connecticut, for his reviews and edits and his knowledge as a veteran regarding military logistics, combat and equipment.

Thanks to Luis Gonzalez of Florida, for his ideas on writing in a more personal style and his sample in a draft of the introduction to Jien Zenim.

To each of these and all others, who have encouraged me and put up with my ramblings, I say again, heartfelt thanks.

PERTINENT NEWS

Watching for Changes in the Relationships with Taiwan
Enhancing the Awareness of Military Leadership
Distributed to all senior PLA Commanders
Obtained by US Intelligence and translated, Spring 2000

[snip] Taking into account intervention by the U.S. and based on the strategy of our country, it is better to fight now than in the future -- the earlier, the better. The reason being that, if worse comes to worse, we will gain control of Taiwan before full deployment of the US troops. In this case, the only thing the U.S. can do is fight a war with the purpose of retaliation, which will be similar to the Gulf War against Iraq or the recent bombing of Yugoslavia as far as operational objectives are considered ...

Our principle is: "we are willing to sustain major losses of our armed forces to defend even just one square inch of land." If the US forces lose thousands of men, the anti-war sentiment within their country will force them to take the path they took in Vietnam. Unlike Iraq and Yugoslavia, not only is China a big country, but it also possesses a nuclear arsenal.

China has experienced prolonged warfare against foreign invasion, and the People's Liberation Army (PLA) can safeguard the peaceful production activities by the people of all nationalities in China during the war. We do not want to fight a prolonged war, but this is because our country's basic principle is preserving peace and developing economy, not because we are afraid. Prolonged warfare enables us to defeat the enemy. [snip]

Asian giants hold talks
Friday, April 28, 2000

India and China have begun talks to resolve border disputes that have hampered relations between them for many years. Senior foreign ministry officials are holding the two-day exchange in the Indian capital, Delhi.

The talks come ahead of a visit by the Indian President, to Beijing, to mark the 50th anniversary of diplomatic relations between the two countries, and come as relations between the two countries show signs of improvement after India's decision to carry out underground nuclear tests in 1998.

China/ US Defense
August 16, 2000

Chinese military experts have warned that US missile defense plans could spark a global arms race and sour Sino-US relations. China's flagship English newspaper, the China Daily, published articles quoting high military officers, who warn US missile defense could undermine stability.

The article strongly criticized US Theater Missile Defense, which the US wants to deploy around its Asian allies - including Japan, Taiwan and South Korea. China's main concern is Taiwan, considered a renegade province.

The article argued this would strengthen US- Taiwan military ties - a violation of Chinese sovereignty. A researcher at the Academy of Military Science, was quoted saying the new system could pit China against China.

China acquires Russian aircraft carrier, for scrap
August 30, 2000

BEIJING — China has acquired a decommissioned Russian aircraft carrier for scrap metal, Chinese state media reported Wednesday.

The 25-year-old carrier Kiev, stripped of engines, weapons & communications equipment, docked at Tianjin Tuesday.

The Tianma Shipbreaking Co. Ltd. of Tianjin paid $8.4 million for the Kiev, the newspaper said. While some want to renovate the Kiev for tourism, the China Daily quoted Tianma general manager Wang Yucai as saying the purchase contract requires the carrier be dismantled for scrap.

U.S. Navy Missile Defense program completes 2nd flight
August 25, 2000

The Navy moved closer to Theater Ballistic Missile Defense with a 2nd successful test flight of the Standard Missile 2, Block IVA at the White Sands Missile Range. The flight evaluated the flight performance envelope and provided engineers with guidance, autopilot, and stability data.

The test flight was launched out of a land based Vertical Launch System and flew a pre-programmed trajectory within the national range. The test was strictly an evaluation of flight performance and did not require a target.

Today's test was the second in a planned series of eight engineering and manufacturing test flights. Once developmental flight-test series is complete, the program will conduct technical and operational evaluations at the Pacific Missile Range Facility in 2002.

Secret torpedo test 'blew sub apart'
August 27, 2000

Sources report that two civilian experts from a Russian military plant were conducting secret tests aboard the Kursk submarine, which sank after the hull was ripped apart in an accident. Western military experts believe a test fire ignited highly flammable propellant and detonated torpedo warheads.

Western experts say the Russians were upgrading a Squall, a torpedo that can reach speeds of 200 knots while traveling in a super cavity, which reduces friction with the water.

"The weapon uses propellers to boost it out of the sub, then a rocket fires at a safe distance, burning liquid propellant," said one British expert. "If the second stage ignites too soon, that is all."

Further support for this theory came from Alexander Rutskoi, governor of the region. Rutskoi, a former Russian vice-president, said he was told by two high-ranking military officers that civilian experts were aboard the Kursk to test new torpedoes, but he declined to give any further details.

The Russians were still insisting that the likely cause was a collision with a foreign submarine. Western experts have unanimously rejected this.

Chinese Diplomat Woos India
January 14, 2001

NEW DELHI, Jan. 13 Li Peng of China's Parliament, urged India to join with China to form an economic order to represent the developing world.

In a television interview, Mr. Li, the most senior Chinese to tour India since New Delhi's nuclear tests in 1998,said that New Delhi and Beijing opposed a "unipolar world. A multipolar world is more conducive for development,"

Mr. Li's visit is expected to pave the way for a visit by the Chinese prime minister, Zhu Rongji, later this year.

Power of U.S. Draws China and Russia to Pact
January 14, 2001

BEIJING, China and Russia are working on a friendship treaty, the strongest sign yet of their unhappiness with the supremacy of the United States and its plans to build a shield against ballistic missiles.

The effort to craft a more formal "strategic partnership," as the Chinese describe it, reflects the intensity of their concerns about American power and about the proposal for a national missile defense, which Russia and China fear will put them at a military disadvantage. It is a sign of the complex landscape facing the Bush administration, which vowed to forge ahead with missile defenses and treat China as a competitor.

Iran and Jordan move closer
Sunday, January 21, 2001

The Speaker of the Iranian parliament, Mehdi Karrubi, began a three-day visit to Jordan in the latest sign of improved relations between the countries. He is the highest-ranking Iranian to visit since the 1979 Iranian revolution.

Mr. Karrubi told the Jordanian parliament that there was now an historic opportunity to improve relations on the basis of peace and security.

The Iranian Speaker is accompanied by a large business delegation and the two countries are expected to sign trade agreements.

In his speech to the Jordanian parliament, Mr. Karrubi expressed support for the Palestinian uprising in Israel, calling for an independent Palestinian.

Iran wants more cooperation with India, Russia and China
April 12, 2001

TEHRAN - Iran's leader called for more cooperation between Iran, India, Russia and China Thursday while meeting with the Indian Prime Minister.

Ayatollah Ali Khamenei said, ``colonialist countries" were opposed to such cooperation, making it imperative for Eastern countries to strengthen ties.

US Resolute on return of EP-3 Aircraft
April 18, 2001

A Pentagon delegation was meeting Wednesday with Chinese officials to discuss events surrounding the midair collision between a U.S.

reconnaissance aircraft and a Chinese fighter. The delegation made clear that the United States expects the prompt return of its aircraft.

"Our position going into this is very clear. That EP-3 is American property and we want it back," Pentagon spokesman Rear Adm. Craig Quigley told reporters Tuesday at the press briefing.

The aircraft was on a reconnaissance mission in international airspace when a Chinese F-8 fighter came too close and collided with the U.S. plane, forcing it to make an emergency landing. The fighter crashed into the sea, killing the pilot. The 24-member American crew returned to the United States on Saturday after being detained by the Chinese for two weeks.

Supercavitating Weapons – Warp Drive Underwater
April 2001

Naval experts believe that supercavitating systems will alter undersea warfare, changing cat-and-mouse stalking contests between submarines into something resembling aerial combat, with noisy high-speed battles among small, short-range "subfighters" shooting underwater bullets at one another .

Others speak of the possibility of long-distance, multistage supercavitating torpedoes fitted with nuclear warheads. Such devices could navigate in from the sea, pop out of coastal waters, and launch before defenses could react.

Chinese Foreign Minister in Moscow
Friday, April 27, 2001

The Chinese foreign minister, Tang Jiaxuan, has arrived in Russia for a visit aimed at strengthening bilateral relations. Mr. Tang and his Russian counterpart, Igor Ivanov, will attend a meeting of foreign ministers from Kazakhstan, Kyrgyzstan and Tajikistan.

He's also expected to sign a friendship treaty between Beijing and Moscow.

Mr. Tang's trip is expected to pave the way for the visit of the Russian president, Vladimir Putin, to China later this year.

China deploys warships
June 26, 2001

Chinese military forces are increasing naval activity at disputed islands in the South China Sea, deploying a dozen warships over the past weeks. According to reports, twelve Chinese ships were in the Spratly island chain.

The Chinese navy also sent ships to Scarborough Shoal, where the Chinese are building a permanent military site like the one on Mischief Reef.

In addition to a military structure on Mischief Reef, China has also erected installations on Fiery Cross Reef, Cuarteron Reef and Johnson Reef.

The Chinese occupation of the disputed Spratly Islands, claimed by the Philippines, China, Vietnam, Malaysia and Brunei, is part of a strategy of expanding sovereignty using "island chains".

The strategy involves a gradual expansion of control further and further off of China's coast in a bid to establish Beijing's hegemony over the South China Sea, which is important for trade and commercial links in the region.

Coordinated Terror Hits United States
September 11, 2001

In an coordinated attack against the United States, four passenger jets crashed on Tuesday, three into important structures..

- American Airlines Flight 11, carrying 81 passengers and 11 crew members, slammed into the north tower of the World Trade Center in Manhattan shortly before 9 a.m. 15 minutes later, United Airlines Flight 175 from Boston to Los Angeles, with 56 passengers and nine crew members on board, crashed into the south tower. Both towers eventually collapsed in a storm of debris.
- A half-hour after the second crash, American Flight 77 from Dulles Airport en route to Los Angeles, California, carrying 58 passengers and six crew crashed into the Pentagon.
- Less than an hour after the third crash, United Flight 93 en route from Newark, New Jersey, to San Francisco crashed near Shanksville, Pennsylvania, with 38 passengers and seven crew.
- The FBI indicated all four planes were hijacked.
- All government buildings in Washington were evacuated. All U.S. forces around the world were put on alert THREATCON DELTA.
- All federal agencies implemented Government continuity plans.
- President issued a statement from Barksdale AFB near Shreveport, Louisiana. "Make no mistake: The United States will hunt down and punish those responsible for these cowardly acts."
- The FAA halted all flights nationwide at their departure airports.
- Two aircraft carriers and five other ships deployed along the East Coast, and two aircraft carriers to New York, all from Norfolk, VA.

- U.S. stock markets closed and remained closed for several days.
- U.S. borders with Mexico and Canada were closed.

Excerpts from President Bush's Address to Congress
Thursday, September 20, 2001.

Tonight, we are a country awakened to danger and called to defend freedom. Our grief has turned to anger and anger to resolution. Whether we bring our enemies to justice or bring justice to our enemies, justice will be done.

On September the 11th, enemies of freedom committed an act of war against our country. Americans have known wars, but for the past 136 years they have been wars on foreign soil, except for one Sunday in 1941. Americans have known the casualties of war, but not at the center of a great city on a peaceful morning. Americans have known surprise attacks, but never on thousands of civilians. All of this was brought upon us in a single day, and night fell on a different world, a world where freedom itself is under attack.

The evidence we have gathered points to a collection of affiliated terrorist organizations known as al Qaeda. They have been indicted for bombing American embassies in Tanzania and Kenya and for bombing the USS Cole. Its goal is remaking the world and imposing its radical beliefs on people everywhere. The terrorists practice a fringe form of Islamic extremism rejected by Muslim scholars and the vast majority of Muslim clerics; a fringe movement that perverts the peaceful teachings of Islam.

The leadership of al Qaeda supports the Taliban regime in controlling most of Afghanistan where we see al Qaeda's vision for the world. Afghanistan's people have been brutalized, many are starving others have fled. Women are not allowed to attend school. You can be jailed for owning a television. Religion can be practiced only as their leaders dictate. A man can be jailed in Afghanistan if his beard is not long enough. The United States respects the people of Afghanistan but we condemn the Taliban regime. By aiding and abetting murder, the Taliban regime is committing murder. And tonight the United States of America makes the following demands on the Taliban:

-- Deliver to United States all leaders of Al Qaeda hiding in your land.
-- Release all American citizens you have unjustly imprisoned.
-- Protect foreign journalists, diplomats and aid workers in your country.
-- Close immediately every terrorist training camp in Afghanistan.
-- Hand over every terrorist and their support structure to authorities.
-- Give the United States full access to terrorist training.

These demands are not open to negotiation or discussion. The Taliban must act immediately. Hand over the terrorists or share their fate.

They hate the democratically elected government they see in this chamber. They hate our freedoms: our freedom of religion, our freedom of speech, our freedom to vote and assemble and disagree with each other. They want to overthrow existing governments in many Muslim countries such as Egypt, Saudi Arabia and Jordan. They want to drive Israel out of the Middle East. They want to drive Christians and Jews out of vast regions of Asia and Africa. These terrorists kill not merely to end lives, but to end a way of life.

We will pursue nations that provide aid or safe haven to terrorists. Every nation in every region now has a decision to make: Either you are with us or you are with the terrorists. From this day forward, any nation harboring or supporting terrorism will be regarded by the United States as hostile."

Islamic Demonstrations Rock Pakistan
ISLAMABAD, Pakistan, Washington Time, Sept. 20, 2001

Tens of thousands of demonstrators took to the streets of Pakistan's cities yesterday, burning effigies of President Bush and screaming opposition to their government's support for the U.S. campaign against terrorism.

In Karachi crowds swelled to 40,000 in demonstrations called after Gen. Musharraf backed U.S. efforts to apprehend Osama bin Laden and to break up his suspected terrorist network operating from Afghanistan. Demonstrators vowed to fight U.S. forces if they attack Afghanistan.

U.S. special forces move near Afghani borders
September 21, 2001

Pakistan - U.S. Special Forces are moving into countries bordering Afghanistan to begin covert missions to capture or kill Osama bin Laden. Teams of three to five soldiers are expected to deploy into Afghanistan's mountainous regions to locate the elusive bin Laden, Pakistani officials say.

Talks also are under way with Uzbekistan and Tajikistan, Afghanistan's northern neighbors, for the use of their military facilities US military aircraft land in Uzbekistan: Uzbek source.

DRAGON'S FURY
-
BREATH OF FIRE

www.dragonsfury-breathoffire.com

PROLOGUE

November 28, 1970, 20:35 local
Naval Headquarters, Research Center
Hanoi, North Vietnam

Lu Pham rolled back from his workbench and set his slide rule down and swiveled his stool around. Placing his elbow on the desk and his hand under his chin, he sat reflecting.

"So", he thought, "it can be done! ... the secret is simply maintaining the wave form to keep the cavity stable once it has been achieved".

Lu had been working on this problem for over a year, spending uncounted off-duty hours creating the mathematical models, which would prove or disprove his theories. In his capacity as a naval research officer, Lu was working to reduce the noise signature of North Vietnam's coastal craft by studying the cavitation the propellers created and finding ways to reduce it.

He was being funded in the endeavor through Soviet monies, the USSR having become aware of Lu's remarkable mathematical abilities. In the process, Lu had become obsessed by the cavitation itself. In the environment of his official research, cavitation was a bad, dangerous thing. Cavitation of that sort meant sound, sound that the detection devices of the imperialist U.S. Navy could detect and use to either destroy the craft of his nation, or to avoid them.

But the cavitation that Lu had succeeded in predicting was a far different matter. Such stable cavitation could only be created at extremely high speeds, and only by a proper, sleek body moving at those speeds ... towards the ships of the U.S. 7th fleet. Lu had only to document these findings and present them to his superiors. He was sure they would jump at a chance to deliver any decisive blow to their enemies ... to his enemies.

In his mind's eye, as so often occurred when he contemplated delivering a blow to the Americans, he could see the fertile undergrowth, the wetness and the denseness of the forest. Yes, there! he could just see the huts ... and as soon he saw them, he always caught the same faint, sickly, coppery odors on the wind. In his mind, as he proceeded towards the village, he came into the clearing where he could see more clearly … the bodies of his father and his mother. They were in the center of the village, lying on the ground where the US Special Forces "Phoenix" Team had left them after disposing of a particular Vietcong coordinator whom their intelligence had correctly identified as an instrument sent there by the North.

December 9, 1970 15:30 local
Commandant's Office, Naval Research Center
Hanoi, North Vietnam

"Comrade Lu, let me understand, you have developed a mathematical model which leads you to believe that a weapon can be developed to attack the US 7th fleet off our shores and inflict severe damage on them, potentially even damaging or destroying their aircraft carriers?"

"That is correct", replied Lu Pham to Captain Ho Chien Thom, who was the Commandant of North Vietnam's fledgling Naval Research effort. "The device I contemplate would travel at 300-400 kilometers per hour and could reach the imperialist's ships before they could respond to it. One of the key difficulties will be designing the shape of the weapon. The leading edge of the device must be precise in order to create and maintain the cavity through which the weapon moves. Another difficulty will be the propulsion system, which must be adequate to achieve and maintain the speed to create this cavity. Finally, we must find a way to deploy the device".

"Lt. Lu, have you considered that these difficulties make it impossible for our nation to produce such a weapon? Have you forgotten that we rely on our comrade socialist nations for every modern article which we employ?" Now raising his voice, Captain Ho continued, "Have you forgotten that the very slide rule you use to make these calculations was not created here!!!"

"No, comrade Captain, I have not forgotten these things; but, respectfully, I believe that such a weapon can be developed. I also believe that those nations assisting us in this struggle would be more than willing to provide the resources once they see the potential of what this slide rule has produced." was the only way Lt. Lu knew to respond.

Unfortunately, at 23 years of age, the young lieutenant was still very naïve and was not savvy, or experienced in the politics of the so-called "People's struggle" in which he was involved. Capt. Ho, far more experienced in such realities, understood that to propose such a use of resources in the current circumstances would be damaging to his own standing, not to mention the barely adequate funding they were currently receiving.

"Lt. Lu, I need not remind you that most of your associates are involved in this struggle in a far different manner than you. The party leadership and our friends in the Soviet Union have recognized your capabilities and have employed you in research of great import. The effort to which you must employ ALL of your time and intellect is to reduce the sound signature of the propellers of our existing craft, while allowing them to operate more efficiently. Such improvements will not only help our small navy, they will please our socialist brothers who will use it on their ships and will be thus motivated to send more funding, and more weapons to our navy."

"Instead of considering these facts, you have spent considerable amounts of the People's valuable time in researching an effort not related to your primary assignment. Comrade, despite your considerable talents, and despite the noble sacrifice of your parents, you are failing the people."

"So, let me make it very clear to you ... if you do not want to be transferred to the forests and mountains of Cambodia, or to the rebel provinces to the south, I suggest you immediately redirect your efforts to your primary assignment. Is this understood? In the mean time, leave the results of your research here and I will find a way to mention it to the party leadership. "

"Yes, comrade, I understand." Lt. Lu Pham replied as he stood, saluted, handed over his documents and then retired from his commander's office.

December 9, 1970, 3 hours later
Commandant's Office, Naval Research Center
Hanoi, North Vietnam

The old man carried out his janitorial duties as he did every evening in the Naval Research Center. Stooped and moving slowly due to the inevitable arthritis of old age, he cleaned the floor and then emptied the garbage from each of the small bamboo wastebaskets into the trash bag on the cart which he pulled. He had been doing this - day in and day out - for years.

... and, as he had also done for years, he insured that the waste from the Commandant's office, which tonight included the Lt. Lu Pham's discarded computations, was placed in a separate, cleverly concealed bag on his cart.

Late that night, the contents of the bag were en route to the old man's true employer ... the intelligence services of the People's Republic of China.

March 23, 1994, 19:00 local
Corporate Headquarters COSCO (China Ocean Shipping Company)
Beijing, China

Chin Zhongbaio, President of one of the largest shipping companies in the world, and a member of the Politburo of the Chinese Communist Party, watched as the General and his aide entered and stood in front of his desk.

"General Hunbaio, please sit down. Is it true? Have your people in COSTIND (Chinese Commission of Science, Technology and Industry for National Defense) located Lu Pham and brought him here to Beijing? "

The General, who commanded his nation's weapons research and development efforts, knew that Chin was aware not only that Pham had been found, but that he was here waiting to meet the President of COSCO as they spoke. As the General took a seat in front of Chin, he replied,

"Chin, as you know, we found him teaching in Hanoi two years ago and approached him. After developing a friendly relationship, our operative showed him a copy of his long lost research documentation on cavitation. From there it was a simple matter to recruit him into our services as he has a long-standing desire to work against the Americans. All arrangements were made for him and his family. The importance and secrecy has been explained to him along with the consequences of betrayal. He has accepted and he is waiting outside in your reception area as we speak."

Chin pondered the General's words for a moment. Then, without further conversation, he simply said,

"Please, General, have your people bring him in"

The General motioned to his aide standing at attention by the door, and the aide immediately left the room. Presently he returned with a spectacled man in his late-40's and whose face and build showed his Vietnamese heritage.

"Mr. Lu, or should I say, Captain Lu? How nice to finally meet you. I hope that your family is well"

Lu Pham, recently made a Captain rank in the People's Liberation Army Navy, entered the room and walked resolutely to Chin and bowed slightly,

"Thank you, sir, my family is still adjusting to being here, but we have all been warmly received. I must say, I am honored to meet the man who has helped make the Chinese shipbuilding industry the third largest on the planet and the fastest growing. As you are well aware, maritime applications, particularly naval applications, have always been my singular interest."

Chin had been engineering this moment for two full years. Ever since the first meeting with General Hunbaio concerning super-cavitation, its possibilities and Lu's amazing computations from over two decades ago, he had dreamed of developing and deploying such a weapon, with all of its capabilities, for the People's Republic of China. Since that initial meeting, Chin had made it his personal business to be aware of every like and dislike of Lu Pham. He walked around his desk and surprised Lu with a warm embrace; and then guided him and the General over to a warm grouping of plush chairs in a corner of his office, with a magnificent view of the city. While motioning for the others to sit with him, Chin continued,

"Well, Captain, we have a clear mutual interest, although your words regarding my personal contributions are too kind. More to the point, I believe we are in a position to supply the resource, manpower and overall funding to a project you first contemplated many years ago ... almost 25 years ago in fact. Simply put, we would like you to begin work immediately with General Hunbaio's agency and a staff of the best researchers, designers and manufacturers available, developing and producing these super-cavitating weapons for the PLAN. How does that sound?"

Lu was as absolutely thrilled at the prospect, and he wanted to let Chin know. But there was an issue nagging him he felt he had to get in the open,

"It sounds almost too good to be true sir, and something I have dreamed about for many years; but, one question if I may?"

"By all means", Chin replied.

"You have had this information for many years. Why do you require me?"

Chin thought for a moment, then motioned to General Hunbaio and said,

"Well, General, why don't you let Lu know why, after all of these years, we require the assistance of the man who designed these remarkable models?"

General Hunbaio spoke up without hesitation,

"Lu Pham, sometimes there are individuals who are given great insights. All of our researchers, those who have had the clearance to look at your work ... and there have been quite a few ... agree that the principles are accurate, but they have not been able to bring the work forward into reality.

Quite frankly, all of their efforts have failed. Several years ago, it became apparent that we needed to find and turn to the man who had developed the models themselves, and now here you are. It is as straightforward as that."

"Of course, I want to stress again that once this work begins, you and your family will live in the utmost security. You will be working in a facility that is very self-contained, in a town specifically built to house this facility and its workers. No breech of security can be allowed. Any deviation from areas of research or lines of work specifically associated with your task will be viewed most severely. I know we have covered the security with you and your family, but I wanted to re-emphasize it to you this evening."

Hearing this again did not faze Lu Pham. He expected as much, and expected he would hear it over and over again in the future.

"General, I do understand. I understood 25 years ago. I kept quiet regarding this for all of those years. I can do so as I work on it now."

May 13, 2000, 18:30 local
Tianammen Square
Beijing, China

As they walked out of earshot of staff, away from the press, and surrounded by a "wall" of electronic security, President Jien Zenim patted President KP Narayannen of India on the back and said,

"These talks have been gratifying. I am pleased we have been able to come to an understanding between the two us, which will ultimately allow our peoples to embrace the " Three Wisdoms" we have discussed, and which will set a pattern for the peace-loving, socially-minded people of world".

Reflectively, President Narayannen paused and turned towards the President of the People's Republic of China and replied,

"Ah, it is just so Mr. President. Our understanding, rooted in the fundamental principles of the Three Wisdoms, will move our nations towards the realization of goals which will improve the lives of our people and catapult them to their rightful place on the stage of world affairs. Our current discretion and the arduous road ahead will ultimately lead to the emergence of an economic and social order that will sweep the entire earth."

After a moment of thoughtful consideration, President Jien answered,

"As the leaders of the two most populous nations on earth, it is past time that our people began influencing affairs rather than being influenced by them. We shall employ the same methods that have worked so well to our benefit with the undisciplined and decadent American national leadership. Who would have thought that we could make so many gains in such a short period of time? They have literally given us the keys to produce this vision, and at such low cost. By starting early with decadent leaders in other areas, we will guide them in like manner over the next five or six years."

"In the meantime, China will patiently delay plans reunifying our nation, giving the rebel province time to come to its senses. We will also wait to excise, the corrupting influence of the Americans; not only from the South China Sea, but from all of eastern Asia. While we do this, we will continue to encourage them to pour resources into the "economic development" of our own nations which they believe will bring them great profit, and which they hope will corrupt our people. But they will be sorely disappointed."

President Narayannen knew that America had been penetrated to the highest levels. He had his own operatives working to affect similar outcomes in other regions. Just the same, to hear it so bluntly put ...

"You are to be commended, President Jien, for both your vision and your forbearance. Now, what a beautiful spring day it is in Beijing! After further reflection, I believe I will enjoy some of that Earl Gray tea you offered."

President Jien Zenim laughed and again patted President Narayannen on the back while directing him back towards the buildings housing their "official" discussions of "improving relations" and "border disputes".

January 20, 2001, 12:08 local
Capitol Building
Washington, D.C.

"So help me God", declared President Bush as he finished the oath of office and officially became the 43rd President of the United States. In doing so, and by winning the most divisive presidential election in American history, he brought an end to the most scandal-plagued administration in its history, where the sitting President was impeached but not removed from office.

President Bush's administration focused on reversing the largest military downsizing in US history. That downsizing saw the following retired, decommissioned, or mothballed since the 1991 Desert Storm victory:

- 709,000 regular soldiers; 293,000 reserves, Eight standing army divisions;
- 20 air wings with 2,000 combat aircraft, and 232 strategic bombers;
- 13 ballistic missile submarines w/3,114 warheads on 232 missiles;
- 500 ICBMs with 1,950 warheads;
- 4 aircraft carriers, 121 combat ships and the bases to sustain them;
- Plans to scrap all heavy armor in the US armed forces by the year 2012;
- Severe curtailment of F/A-18E/F, F-22, B-2, & Ballistic Missile Defense,

As a result of the terror attack of September 11, 2001, and his stated policy, Bush revitalized the military in some areas. These improvements included:

- Reinstatement of the M1A1 tank as the long-term armor for the Army;
- Deployment of the 1st squadrons of the new Comanche attack helicopters;
- Deployment of the USS Ronald Reagan nuclear aircraft carrier;
- Deployment of 12 new Arleigh Burke Block IIA class Aegis destroyers;
- Reactivation and conversion to SSGN's of 4Ohio Class SSBN's;
- Successful testing and funding for the initial Ballistic Missile Defense;
- Successful deployment of the initial F/A-18 E/F and F-22 fighter wings;
- Full production funding for the Joint Strike Fighter (JSF);
- Deployment of the third Sea Wolf class nuclear attack submarine;
- Deployment of the last two Wasp class amphibious assault ships;
- Deployment of the first two San Antonio landing ship docks;

In addition, the Bush administration sold and deployed significant, military hardware to The Republic of China on Taiwan, including:

- 4 Kidd class guided missile destroyers (DDG's);
- 8 advanced class diesel/electric submarines;
- 12 P-3 ASW aircraft;
- MK-48 torpedoes for the foregoing;
- Surface, air and sub launched Harpoon missiles for the foregoing;
- PAC-3 Upgrade to Taiwan's Patriot missile system.

These ROC arms purchases resulted from the April 2001 incident where a US EP-3 surveillance aircraft was damaged by a Red Chinese fighter, causing the Red Chinese fighter to crash. The American aircraft was forced to land on Chinese soil and the crew was detained for two weeks. The outgrowth of the incident resulted in the additional arms sales to the ROC.

When Usama bin Laden died at the hands of US special forces in 2002, and with the almost complete destruction of his El Qaeda terror network by mid-2003, it appeared that President Bush was assured a second term. Then, on the eve of primary elections, he surprised the world by announcing he would not seek a second term as president. Most thought this was a death knell to Republican hopes for consecutive presidencies and gains in the House and Senate that would result from President Bush's coattails.

This was particularly true when, the Senator from New York, ex-wife of the former President, began doing so well in the Democratic primaries.

But fate had a different path for America, her leadership and for the world.

CHAPTER 1

"All warfare is based on deception." – Sun Tsu

November 3, 2004, 10:00 local
Politburo
Beijing, China

The figure seated at the head of the table had not moved for the better part of an hour. The only detectable motion came from the flickering lights cast by the two-dozen television monitors on the wall on the opposite side of the room as they danced across his features. President Jien Zenim still personified the "new" China of his creation. Having risen through the ranks, having been the "mayor" of the Capital, having beguiled and wooed the West with the promise of wealth and influence, it was as if he had been born to rule. As a result, Jien Zenim was long used to wealth and power, and he was in possession of both right now.

He whispered a few words into the microphone attached to the tiny headset he wore, and there was discernible motion in the darkness along the side of the great conference room. A few seconds later, a navy-blue suited aide appeared by the Chairman's side.

"Tea."—Said Jien Zenim.

The aide rushed away and moments later the rustle of curtains was heard as the aide returned with a cup of tea. President Jien's preference was Earl Grey tea over the local fare; a taste acquired while attending Oxford years ago. Only his most trusted advisors knew of the secret "passions" the President had for things from the West. Earl Grey tea was not the only one.

On the screens, all of the major U.S. networks were covering the same story. It was always like that on Presidential election night. But this time, the East Coast voting booths would close in an hour, and results would not start coming in until four hours later. The timeworn tradition of exit polling had been one of the casualties of the 2000 Presidential election. As a result, the media was directed by law to only report the official State Board of Elections results. Those results would not be released until after the last precinct shut down in the West. The pundits on the screens sat and made empty talk while doing a re-hash of the two major contender's campaigns.

A soft, electronic chime drew the President's attention to the arm of the soft, custom-made Natuzzi chair. He pressed a button and spoke into the microphone with flawless English.

"Good evening, David - how are Jennie and the kids?"

"Fine, Jien! Everyone's great. And your family?"— the voice on the other end of the line was perhaps one of the best known and trusted voices in America. It was a voice millions heard nightly coming from their televisions, a face they associated with every major news story reported for the last two decades. Some called him "The Conscience of America" for his rousing and thought provoking commentaries.

"Fine, David, thanks for asking. So, do you have money on the Packers again this year, or are you finally getting smart?"

The two men laughed.

"No, Mr. President. As you know, I've decided to back a winner for a change."

Jien Zenim's face registered a hint of repugnance. There were few things he detested quite as much as a traitor; but, they certainly had their uses. And the higher placed the better for Jien's needs. If you promised them money, they take it in the belief that it will make them more powerful in the "new" world, and help them maintain a certain lifestyle. They never realized that money would mean very little in the wake of "The Time of the Three Wisdoms", at least not for them. They could not fathom that in the one world to come, only power mattered; and that the power of the largest army in the history of the world was Jien's to command, and all of their money would bow to that power.

"The Time of the Three Wisdoms" was the campaign Jien had designed many years ago to prepare the Chinese people for the coming conflict. It consisted of:

1. "All men and women are equal."
2. "All share equally in the bounty of a working and industrious society."
3. "One goal, one thought, one people for World peace."

He couldn't believe that these methods still worked. Even after all these years, the "Chairman Mao" method of propaganda was still the best way to manipulate the "people" into action, even if the message had changed somewhat. That Mao's propaganda had been so effective in manipulating the masses to the near bankruptcy that the People's Republic had experienced was a testament to the success of those methods ... but not as great a testament as the near bankruptcy had been to the failed Maoist economic policies themselves. That's why the message had to change, and that's where Jien had been able to change things ... and he wasn't finished yet, not nearly so. As the Americans might say, "he was only just beginning."

He spoke again.

"So, David, what do you hear?"

"Jien, it looks like our projections were right on the money, so to speak. In a few hours we are going to be calling it for the old man, and by a wide margin. Unlike the last election, this one left no doubt about the winner. The General got almost three votes to every one of hers ... it's a landslide. The Right is in ecstasy over the victory. After the surprising announcement by President Bush that he would not seek re-election, they are calling General Weisskopf's entire campaign a "Phoenix-like" come back from the brink of disaster."

Jien mused on this. After that Presidential announcement by Bush late last spring, the television pundits played nightly dirges for the GOP, and the written media hinted at scandals and vices as possible reasons for the decision. In fact, Jien's deepest moles had a part in the misinformation that contributed to the sitting American President not running for a second term. On the heels of this, they had all quietly laughed at the old General of Desert Storm fame when he announced he would be coming out of retirement to run for the Presidency so late in the race. They were not laughing now.

It was an unexpected complication for Jien, and he was not pleased. He never was when things didn't go as planned. It had reminded him of his displeasure and unease when bin Laden had prematurely attacked America in 2001. Like then, through the last summer, Jien had experienced growing concern and anxiety as the General gained support, and the Right rallied around him like moths to a flame.

In the past, it had never really made any difference to him who actually won the American election because, as far as he was concerned, all of them were weak ... though Bush had surprised him with his successful prosecution of the "War on terror". Actually, that had also relieved him, because it allowed him to further develop and prepare the greater plan.   But this man, Weisskopf, he was something else again. He commanded the great respect of the American troops. And so now there was going to be a real Warrior in the White House when the plan which had been set in motion so many years ago, entered into its final stages.

"Mr. President, we believe that the incident with his opponent's husband won the election for the General. I know that the Senator probably wished her husband had been struck dumb when he made that insulting remark about the General's age.   We really believe that the General's response to that was the key. The last thing any one of us expected was for old Weisskopf to challenge him, over an open microphone to a wrestling match, "I'll take your sorry butt on anytime you're game" will go down in history as the most effective campaign challenge of all times. When you add to this his selection of the first African-American as a VP candidate, Alan Reeves … well it turned into quite the coup."

Jien could not stomach any more of this at the moment, so he politely ended the conversation by saying,

"Well, David, I have a meeting to prepare for. Thanks for the call. As always, your views, advice and information are most helpful. Say hello to Jennie for me. And happy Thanksgiving if we don't get to talk before then. Tell her I miss her oysters and wild rice stuffing."

Jien Zenim had visited the United States on many occasions after the 1978 recognition of the PRC by the Carter administration. Some of those visits had helped set the stage for the unbelievable influence the People's Republic had developed in Washington, D.C. during the 1990's. During one of those trips, he had been a Thanksgiving Day guest of David's. It was then that Jien acquired another of his western "passions": American cooking. Thanksgiving day, the Chairman would have his chefs prepare a turkey dinner with full trimmings, including Jennie's famed oysters and wild rice stuffing.

"I will pass the compliment on Mr. President.   Thank you again, and goodbye." —the line went dead.

Jien stared at the television screens for a few more seconds and then spoke to those sitting in the darkness.

"Gentlemen, what are your impressions about the new President?"

The room lights came on behind the President, and illuminated twenty men seated around the great conference table. Some were wearing western-style suits, the rest military uniforms. A surprising number were relatively young and in their early to mid-fifties. One by one, they spoke into their headset microphones or read from prepared reports.

"His experience in foreign affairs appears relatively light as he handled strictly the military operations of Desert Storm while the head of their Joint Chiefs and the former President's father handled the foreign affairs and cemented their coalition. We believe his statements regarding his intentions with the American's relationship with us are principally geared at solidifying his conservative base."

"It is unlikely that the American congress and business community will allow him to go too far at this time. Remember, in 2001 with the EP-3 incident, the efforts to develop and maintain any kind of boycott or more severe trade policies against us were just so much chaff in the wind. They have no stomach for it. "

"As to his health, for a man of 70 years he is in remarkably good health. He still carries out an exercise regimen each day and appears very alert..."

Chairman Jien stood up abruptly and turned to face the members of the politburo over whom he presided, many handpicked from among his most trusted and committed allies. His face remained impassive, but there was a deadly look in his eyes.

Some members of the politburo shrank back into their seats preparing themselves for one of the Chairman's infrequent flares of temper.

"You tell me no more than what I can see for myself on WNN!! I want more! Find leverage, find influence which we can use on this American General. He may potentially be an adversary of great virtue and strength, but we shall see if we cannot "convince" him to recognize the inevitability of what is coming."

"So, our plans go forward. Our official economic alliance with India will be announced in April, and this will certainly give his new administration something to think about. In the meantime, please arrange an official conversation between myself and the new American president as soon after his inauguration as possible."

December 16, 2004, 19:30 local
Jiangnan Shipyards
Shanghai, China

Sung Hsu had worked for the COSCO commercial shipbuilding operation his entire adult life. Although he was mildly envious of the sleek and elegant lines of the two aircraft carriers that his sister Chinese company was building in the yards adjoining those in which he worked, he still took great pride in the commercial shipping he helped his own company produce. He was very proud of the fact that his company had grown to be the world's dominant commercial shipping company over the last 3 or 4 years.

The completion of these shipyards in Shanghai, and many others like them around the nation, had allowed China to out-produce the Koreans and the Japanese both quantitatively and qualitatively. Originally these yards were meant to produce up to six of those sleek carriers at a time by the Jiangnan Shipbuilding Company, but a decision had been made to build only two such vessels. This meant that COSCO Container Shipping had been able to "lease" the additional capacity from their socialist brothers in 2002 and thus Sung had relocated with his family here.

Sung's responsibilities as a production crew chief in the modular design bay area, meant he had been instrumental in getting a prominent feature to market for these fine container ships for which COSCO was becoming known. COSCO was touting the robust nature of the modular design of its Container vessels all over the world; a robustness that was focused on multiple uses, either as standard container ships, or, depending on the modularity ordered, as any variety of "RORO" (Roll On – Roll Off) carriers.

Sung was one of several such crew chiefs employed in each yard producing these ships. He was amazed at the various designs. The new modular design bays were set into three separate areas along the almost 300 meter length of the hulls of these great ships. In the normal container ship mode, these bays were filled with the standard container ship ballast and equipment that would allow the containers to be stowed securely on the ship and be handled in loading and unloading. In the various bulk modes, the modules consisted of special "holds" where various commodities like grain could be carried and economically loaded and unloaded from the ship. In the "RORO" mode, the modules represented areas where various types of mechanized equipment, from automobiles to tractors, could be stored with the special ramps that allowed them to be driven directly onto and off the ship. With all of this modularity and ingenuity, the ships' structure, electronics and propulsion had been significantly upgraded over normal container ships. This made the ships very valuable to both Chinese and foreign shipping concerns.

Sung had spoken often of his love for this work to his family. His wife, and the pride of his life, his 12-year-old son (Yan), along with his parents and grandparents, knew how much he enjoyed his work, and the pride it gave him in his own contribution, and in his nation as a whole.

But there was one thing Sung had not talked about with his family, or with anyone else until today. It had started off as a nagging suspicion through the construction of the first ship from these yards. Since then, with the completion of the next two, it had grown into something Sung was fairly certain about. Clearly, the modular designs he had been told of, and for which his crews prepared these ships were not the only modular designs available. It was something he planned at long last to speak of with his superior this evening.

So, as he entered the office of Xien Lin, the foreman for all of the shipbuilding activities for the ship upon which he was working, Sung said,

"Thank you Xien for taking a few moments to see me this evening before I go home. May I sit down?"

Xien had been a faithful employee of COSCO for over 25 years. He had grown with the company and was in an enviable position, one of great trust. He viewed his subordinates as critical cogs in the machinery of COSCO and in particular, was very impressed with Sung Hsu.

"Certainly Sung, please be seated, how can I help you?"

Now that he was actually in Xien's office to discuss his intuitions, he suddenly wished he'd just ignored the feelings. Nonetheless, he continued,

"Really, it is only a matter of interest I suppose. I have been involved, as you know, with the shipbuilding efforts of our mother company, COSCO, for well over 15 years. I have been involved from the beginning with the manufacturing portion of the new modular design we are employing in our container ships ..."

At Sung's hesitation, Xien tried to encourage his subordinate by interjecting,

"Yes, Sung, I am well aware of all of this, and am well aware of the fine job you have done in getting your crew not only up to speed on the manufacturing aspects required to produce the designs, but also in their proficiency under your management. What is it you need to bring to my attention? "

Having unconsciously sought, and now obtained, reassurance, Sung continued,

"Sir, I have always thought I was one of those most familiar with the modular aspect of our designs. However I have begun to realize, as we produce this third ship from this line, that there are many aspects of the modular design with which I am not familiar."

"It seems to me, from observing, and then investigating with some of the adjacent work crews, that there must be modular designs which we are not implementing here. If this is so, then I would like to learn about those modules and perhaps train crews in their implementation."

This statement got Xien's attention and caught him off guard. His surprise must have been evident as Sung again paused, this time with an apprehensive look on his face, hoping he had not over stepped his bounds. These very areas of discussion were what Xien had been told by HIS superiors to be on guard for. Having regained his composure, Xien asked,

"What aspects of the design, or what criteria have you seen that has led you to believe this, Sung?"

Now, completely unsure of the terrain upon which he had embarked, Sung could see no other course but to let his concerns spill out in full.

"Well, uh, sir, at first it just seemed that some of the adjoining structure was perhaps over-designed for the modules we employ here. Then, I took a more detailed look at the wiring harnesses and cables, as well as the structure and realized that there were provisions for corridors and electrical and mechanical functions which are not at all necessary to the modules we are building."

Xien sensed that this talented crew chief was professionally interested in the things he had clearly gone out of his way to look into. He hoped for Sung's sake that "professional" interest was all that it was. In that hope, he sought to diffuse the tension that had developed in the room and again reassure Sung.

"Well, Sung, you must keep these thoughts and speculations to yourself. I will raise your questions and see if there is anything to this, and if so, whether there is any role in it for you. In the meantime, I again caution you to keep these thoughts to yourself. We are not the only shipyard building these ships or adding the modules. Critical state economic secrets, or even national security interests could be involved. Your current position carries a lot of responsibility and you are well aware of the security concerns, so I am sure that I can count on you to be completely confidential regarding this. I will let you know at a later date what, if anything, I find out"

Sung knew the discussion was over and that he would have to rely on Xien to "get back" with him. Still, he felt better for having relieved himself of the concern and genuinely hoped his interest would ultimately be satisfied. Therefore, he made every effort to relay his appreciation and sincerity to Xien,

"Sir, confidentiality will not be an issue. I will gladly comply and I await your further word on this issue."

Relieved at Sung's demeanor and tone, Xien now dismissed his inquisitive subordinate,

"Fine, Sung, fine. You may excuse yourself and go home to your family".

As Sung left the office, Xien immediately picked up his phone and dialed the number he had been instructed to dial if anyone ever raised such questions. Questions regarding the modular designs were outside the considerations of an individual's job function, and were beyond that which the company and the state felt were appropriate. As such, they were a matter of national security.

December 16, 2004, later that evening
COSTIND Headquarters
Beijing, China

General Hunbaio reviewed the records of Sung Hsu, which had been placed before him. His subordinate had taken the call from the supervising foreman on the shipbuilding line in Shanghai earlier in the evening and the General had immediately been called. Although he rarely became personally involved in the review of potential security breaches, the importance of this project and its ties to other military projects under his organization's development made this particular issue of utmost concern.

The General had also never been a man to let even a single blade of grass grow under his feet or to hesitate for the slightest instant. Turning to the head of security, the General said,

"I see nothing here that would indicate that this Sung Hsu is anything more than a loyal worker for the people. Yet we cannot risk the slightest exposure regarding the line of questioning he has raised. It is apparent that we have many fine crew leaders performing the standard modularity on our container ships. Therefore have Mr. Sung contacted tomorrow during work and interviewed in depth. If it is apparent that he is desirous and capable, we will transfer him to one of the shipyards preparing for the special modules. He and his family will of course have to be made aware of and committed to the security measures necessary for such work. If any information is discovered that would indicate that Sung Hsu is disloyal to the people, then handle the situation accordingly and dispose of his remains in such a way as to implicate the gangs which are known to frequent the areas surrounding the shipyards."

"In any case, any necessary measures which would fully contain the information are authorized. Just insure that they serve to contain the situation, not draw attention to it."

January 12, 2005, 21:45
National Reconnaissance Office Headquarters
IMINT Directorate
Chantilly, VA

Tom Lawton squeezed his eyes shut and opened and closed them a couple of times. He was trying to keep from developing eye fatigue as he looked at the images on his screen. He cross checked and compared his figures again and continued to come up with the same conclusions.

"Bill, would you come over here and take a look at this? I have six separate airfields here in Southern China, all within 100 miles of the coast, where the PLA has installed what appears to be some kind of new carrier take off and landing facility ... take a look".

Bill Hendrickson, Tom's superior at the Imagery Intelligence Office (IMINT) got up from his desk and walked over to Tom's terminal,

"Ok, Tom, show me what you've got."

As Bill pulled a chair behind Tom's and sat down looking at Tom's 27" color monitor, Tom started in,

"What I have is dual runways installed at these airfields where the Chinese are practicing takeoffs and landings. This is a configuration I have never seen before, and the "landing decks" are set into the ground so SU-30's make their approach and landing just as if they were approaching a carrier deck. If you look here", and Tom pointed to an area on the screen with the cursor from his computer, "you can see what can be nothing other than arresting wires."

PLA (Chinese) SU-30's

Bill held Tom's capabilities in high regard. Over the last several years, dating back to the EP-3 incident off Hainan Island in 2001, Bill had found he could best stimulate Tom's critical thinking by playing the "devil's advocate". On that occasion, Tom had been the first to observe that the Red Chinese were carefully taking apart and then reassembling the various electronic components of the US naval surveillance aircraft.

"So, it's no secret that the PLAN is building two large deck carriers in Shanghai. We are watching that closely. Of course they would be training."

Tom, anticipating Bill's "devil's advocate" posture, responded,

"Yes, but the configuration of these decks doesn't match what's taking shape there in Shanghai. In addition, look at the close-ups and markings on all these aircraft (which Tom proceeded to show him through various images he called up on the screen). They appear to be training six to eight carrier wings here ... not just the two needed for those new carriers. ... and it's more than the "Flankers". They are using some of those new "Frogfoot", SU-25, attack aircraft they purchased and are now license manufacturing too."

Although reflecting on the potential enormity of this data, Bill continued his role of critic and countered,

"Those "landing decks" look for all the world like an "X" ... maybe they have them crossing like that to maximize the landings and takeoffs for wind conditions. I have to admit, though, I am concerned about what certainly appears to be the training of additional squadrons. Still, I do not believe it is any secret that the Chinese are intent on building several carriers. By the way, what's the latest projection on the completion of those two in Shanghai, and when are they expected to be commissioned?"

Tom appreciated his superior's knack of getting him to think on his feet by challenging him; nonetheless he knew he had Bill hooked.

"They say they will launch those two sometime early next year and then will spend a full year getting them qualified and into the fleet ... so we are looking at 2007 or so. ... But, come on Bill, they are gearing up for something here. Why train quadruple the air wings needed, when they haven't even announced, let alone laid down, any additional carriers yet? What do you think? Should we go ahead and forward this to the Navy's analysts with our comments and see what their read on it is?"

Bill had been hooked from the moment he saw that there were six airfields involved.

"I'll do more than that, my friend. I want us to meet in person with them. In addition, I am going to pass a note over to that NSA Weisskopf is bringing on. The new administration is going to be anxious to analyze this info as they face off the ChiComms. Prepare a presentation of your findings, analysis and concerns, along with the data, and be prepared to comment on them when we meet. Before I forget to say so - OUTSTANDING job digging this up, Tom!"

February through March 2005

It was two weeks before Bill Hendrickson and Tom Lawton were able to hold their meetings with the Navy and the new administration's National Security Advisor, John Bowers. The result was a flurry of activity as the new administration and the Navy began to make further requests of the NRO for more satellite photography, and for over-flights by the NRO's most highly classified surveillance aircraft. The satellite imagery began pouring in and the first over-flight was scheduled for late March, to be followed up by a joint NRO, NSA and Navy meeting in early April, which the President himself indicated he would attend.

As the new American administration pointedly indicated its desires to further bolster the US military, it was viewed as extremely hawkish, not only by potential adversaries, but by many of its allies as well. Some of those allies, particularly in Europe, were concerned about the potential for confrontation. In stark contrast, America's allies in Asia, particularly Taiwan and South Korea, viewed such straightforward defense posturing with relief, and a sense of bridled optimism.

In Red China, President Jien Zenim prepared for his meeting with the new US President which was scheduled for late April, after his joint announcement with India on their economic alliance. He intended, in no uncertain terms, to leverage that announcement to let the American President know that the era of US hegemony in the Western Pacific was drawing to a close. He hoped that the two nations could work together to insure that the transition to the new "reality" in the region was conducted in as smooth and non-belligerent a way as possible.

During this same period, the Chinese shipyard production crew chief, Sung Hsu, having successfully answered all of General Hunbaio's security personnel's questions, was transferred to the COSCO shipyards where the military modifications for the Container and RORO ships were taking place under the tightest of security. Sung was introduced to these three "new" modules and immediately assigned to be a production crew chief. His specific responsibilities became the installation of new LRASD (Long Range Anti-Shipping Device) systems on the decks of the Tactical Attack ships and the Amphibious Assault ships. As these systems were newly tested and now deemed production worthy, Sung Hsu was required to work very closely with those who designed the systems to develop comprehensive manufacturing training materiel. This would allow the conversion process to be implemented in a "mass production" environment at several Chinese shipyards simultaneously. In order to accomplish this, Sung attended meetings to develop the strategies and materiel necessary to implement the training. The LRASD planning session was led by Lu Pham, the Vietnamese scientist, who would later be credited with the most revolutionary development in naval warfare in more than a century.

March 25, 2005 19:35 local
Over the South China Sea

Colonel "Mac" Mendenhall studied the multifunction display (MFD) immediately in front of him. He was approaching the coast of Red China from the northeast of Taiwan. His navigation or "way " points were all programmed for a run down the Chinese coast, passing just to the east of Hainan Island. From there, he would turn away from the coast towards the interior of the South China Sea where his aircraft would begin the long journey back to Nellis Air Force Base in Nevada. As the airspeed indicator passed into the Mach 4 range, and his altitude cleared 100,000 feet, he addressed his electronics defense and surveillance officer (EDSO) and said,

"Ok, Larry, we're cleared for the ingress. We'll be hugging the coast and getting our "view" of those installations. On my mark, we'll be positioned and you can commence your run ... three, two, one ... MARK!".

With that, Captain Larry Jenkins activated his surveillance package, which would be looking directly into Red Chinese territory at several of their air bases using light, radio and other electronic wavelengths and bands.

The SR-77 "Pervador" (or "Aurora" as it was mislabeled by many in the public) was a flying wonder. It was the replacement for the aging, but by most nations' standards, still very "space age" SR-71 "Blackbird" that the United States National Reconnaissance Office (NRO) had retired nine years earlier. This aircraft could cruise at Mach 4 at very high altitude and was designed with the radar cross-section of a sparrow, employing radar-absorbing material directly into its surfaces.

The aircraft employed every sensor imaginable, from devices which would pick up any telltale signs of radioactivity, to devices which would detect and categorize any radar emissions, or any conceivable light wave length, and all VHF and UHF communications, whether clear air broadcasts or simple "leakage" into the atmosphere. It also had the most sensitive encryption software and hardware available on the planet, and could communicate real time with satellite relay stations and devices on the ground, or in space. At full speed, it could outrun almost any anti-aircraft guided missile, though in its eight years of active service, none had ever been fired at it.

For potential use against those nations developing detection and missiles defense capabilities which could reach the SR-77 (and Red China was one such nation), the aircraft could also be coupled with the HR-7 "Thunder Dart" hypersonic reconnaissance aircraft.

The HR-7 could be carried "piggy back" by the SR-77 and then launched at a standoff distance. It could also launch on its own from a suitable airfield. The single seat HR-7 carried a similar surveillance package, but would use its turbojet engines to achieve a speed at which its new technology Pulse Detonation Wave Engines (PDWE) could be activated.

Those engines would then boost the aircraft to Mach 7+ and an altitude approaching 200,000 ft. Its endurance was more limited, but the HR-7 could, by virtue of its speed and operating altitude, circumvent even the most heavily and technologically advanced defenses, allowing those installations that they defended to be analyzed.

On this mission, the additional defensive capability was not deemed necessary to take a good look at all six airfields. As a result, this SR-77 had been sent aloft, without its HR-7 companion craft to conduct this mission. Captain Jenkins had just activated a special package of sensors to complete that mission at the first of the suspected airfields Tom Lawton had discovered from the satellite images a couple of months earlier.

Nine minutes later, and 450 miles down the coast, Larry noticed a red indicator on his defense MFD, just as he heard the warning tone in his headset.

"Mac, I've got an "S" band air search radar painting us from 45 degrees off our nose … range about 80 miles. It's coming from the target airfield just to the north and east of Hong Kong. They haven't made us … but once that operator notices that those intermittent "sparrow" size images are moving across his scope at about mach 4, I bet he sits up and takes notice."

"Do you think there's any chance they'll get a lock on us?" Mac asked.

"Very doubtful. Although latest intelligence reports indicate that with new software upgrades, and other refinements they developed over the last couple of years, they'll be close soon … still, I don't know what they have that can shoot at us even if they do get a lock," Larry replied.

After thinking this over for a minute, and checking his course relative to the people he now knew were looking for him, Mac said,

"Well, you can bet they are working on it. They won't improve their acquisition and targeting without also improving their weapons. Just keep me informed. We'll be past those folks in a minute, and we need another eight minutes to get that last airfield on Hainan Island covered."

Five minutes later, and still some 150 miles from Hainan Island, Larry said,

"Okay, someone's been talking. We are now getting multiple radar, multiple bands all down the coast. There's a "Top Plate" signature 30 miles off the coast of Hainan Island too. Looks like one of their new Haizhou class out there".

Hurriedly checking their course relative to these new threats, Colonel Mendenhall quickly saw what he needed to do to complete his mission, while protecting his ultra secret and sophisticated national asset.

"Damn! It looks like he's sitting within about eight miles of our flight path, and we'll be there in about two-and-a-half minutes. No way we can fly that close. That KS-2 derivative AAW system they installed on their DDG's has a 42 km range with a ceiling of 25,000 meters and that's just too close."

"I'm adjusting our approach and putting us about 30 miles off that ship. You'll still get a good look at Hainan, but not as good as we planned. If you need to make adjustments, do it now. I'm plugging the new course in on my mark …. mark".

With that, Larry quickly studied the information on his MFD, made some quick calculations to determine the optimum settings for his equipment, given the new parameters. Then, as he was keying it in, he replied to his flight commander,

"Wilco Mac. I'll just crank up the "gain" on a couple of these packages and we'll be ready to go. About ten seconds, no biggie".

March 25, 2005, That Same Time
48 kilometers off Hainan Island
On Board PLAN 136 Haizhou

Captain Xinhua Zukang, the CO of the PLAN 136 Haizhou, one of his nation's most sophisticated warships, watched his defense operations officer retrieve the latest information on the fast approaching, unidentified aircraft.

"Lieutenant, there is no doubt, what we have approaching is an American surveillance aircraft, and not the slow, lumbering EP-3 aircraft which we

have seen so often in the past. No, this is not like the one our national hero, Wang Wei, forced to land five years ago. This is their best. We can tell more about this aircraft by what we cannot find out about it, than if the Americans had contacted us and told us it was coming. It is clearly one of their high-speed, high-

PLAN Haizhou Class Destroyer

altitude, stealthy, "NRO" surveillance aircraft. Be sure to record everything you can about it, and attempt to lock onto it with every piece of acquisition and targeting equipment we he have on this ship."

The Lieutenant, who had been in contact with other radar sites along the coast, including the airfield outside of Hong Kong which had initially discovered the target, understood the gravity of his Captain's words. The "Top Plate" radar was of the latest Russian design. Although the "target" had not come within its range, it was capable of taking feeds from other systems and selecting targets and firing at them, as if though its own radar had acquired them.

All of the information feeding into his computer system was now indicating that the "Unknown" was approaching at something just in excess of Mach 4 and was flying at about 30,000 meters and was still some 160 km distant. Clearly, what the Captain said was true ... irrespective of the intermittent nature of the contact ... the Americans had significantly raised the stakes by employing their best surveillance aircraft on a mission over his homeland.

"Captain, the approaching target has just entered our acquisition range at 100 km, but has adjusted its course and will pass some 45 kilometers to the east and south of us at an altitude of 30,000 meters."

"Very well.", Captain Xinhua said. "Keep trying to acquire the target as it passes. The only thing that I would like more than acquiring that American aircraft with our radar and locking on to him, would be to have a weapon that could reach him and bring him down."

"What I wouldn't give for a battery of those new KS-2+ land based anti-air missiles that I have heard rumors of! Just the same, we are going to be privileged to gather a wealth of information on one of our principle adversary's most sophisticated aircraft ... information our researchers and developers will put to good use".

March 25, 2005 19:50 local
80 kilometers South and East of Hainan Island, PRC

"Alright!, We are now egressing the area. What kind of look did you get, Larry?" Mac asked as he completed the turn that would take them away from the coast of Red China and out to sea.

After directing his system to encrypt and send, Larry responded,

"Looked good. Would have been nice to be closer, but I am afraid that Haizhou got about as good a "look" at us as anyone ever has. I tell you, every piece of equipment they had was trained on us trying to lock on to us ... but, they got a definite "no joy" on that. Just the same, I don't relish getting that close to another belligerent if we can avoid it. By the way, the entire "package" has already been encrypted and sent on its way."

March 27, 2005, 17:00 Local
Tianjin Shipyards, Secure Training Facility

"Therefore, comrades, these conversions must be completed in a minimum of time once the modular components are manufactured, and once the processes are defined and in place."

Turning to the presentation screen, where the slides for the presentation were being presented, General Hunbaio continued,

"Just to reiterate, please direct your attention to the next slide on the screen which summarizes the conversion schedule goals for each conversion type:"

PLAN Modular Training		Status: Top Secret
GOALS FOR TIMELY MODULAR CONVERSION		
SHIP TYPE	**FROM STD VESSEL**	**TIME**
Tactical Attack	Container Ship	6 weeks
Amphibious Assault	RORO Ship	8 weeks
Sea Control Carrier	Container Ship	10 weeks
Tianjin Training Facilities		**General Hunbaio**

"I cannot emphasize enough how critical these goals are for your successful fulfillment of the high responsibility your nation has placed upon each of you as foreman and crew leaders. In addition, our motherland and our ability to secure our national security will depend on your success."

"Remember, you will be spread out over 12 different shipyard facilities. Confidentiality will be an absolute requirement. Our most vital and most advanced national security assets will help maintain security. We will commence within the next three to four months. At that time, we will begin work on three Sea Control Carriers, five Amphibious Assault Ships and four Tactical Attack ships. It is our intent to commission the Sea Control Carriers in the late September time frame, and discreetly deploy the others into their intended area of operations."

General Hunbaio, about to complete his introductory presentation, paused as he looked across the audience. It was made up of over 120 crew chiefs and foreman, numerous COSCO and COSTIND executives and many military.

"We will now have the lead weapons engineers from each system present to you the basic requirements and specifications for installing and supporting their various systems. These presentations are expected to require the next four full days, during which you will need to direct you utmost attention to them. We will cover everything from the Vertical Launch Systems (VLS), to the Close in Weapons Systems (CIWS), to aircraft, guns, and, most importantly, the LRASD and Ballistic Missile requirements. The basic location of each weapons system is provided in the plan and profile view of each ship which accompany your handouts. For convenience, I will now display them on the screen."

"Please review these layouts and familiarize yourselves with them and the location of the various components relative to your own areas of responsibility. You will be referring to them often over the next four days, and then for the following ten days, as you develop operational plans and procedures."

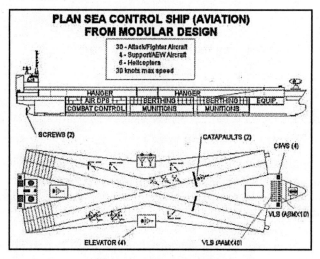

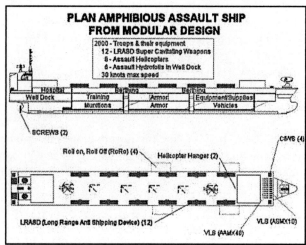

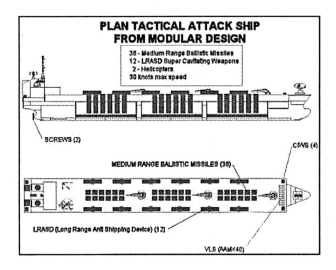

"Unless there are questions, we will take a fifteen minute break before starting the presentations on the LRASD by Commodore Lu Pham."

Before the General could leave the podium, he noticed a hand raised in the audience. Apparently there was at least one question. Thinking that this individual was a hardy and brave soul, the General recognized him and said,

"Yes, Comrade. Please stand up. Utilize the microphone at the end of your aisle. State your name and function, and ask your question."

With that, a relatively young man stood up, picked up the microphone and spoke:

"General Hunbaio, thank you very kindly for recognizing me. My name is Sung Hsu, I am a modularity crew chief for COSCO from our Shanghai facilities. Here is my question."

"Clearly these modules are for warships for our Navy. I am concerned regarding the overall hull integrity for combat operations, and the decidedly smaller number of watertight bulkheads and compartment hatches as compared to military specifications. Is there a retrofit planned in that regard?"

As Sung sat down, the General thought, "Here is a young man unafraid to ask the difficult questions which most of the crew chiefs avoided." The General responded,

"An excellent observation and question. The answer is no. We will be able to produce these vessels, and modernize them, well within the cycle time of any adversary's response, and quickly enough to make up for any shortfalls."

"Are there other questions? … If not, we will reconvene in fifteen minutes."

March 28, 2005, 19:00 Local
Tianjin Shipyards, Secure Training Facility

"Concluding, we have reviewed the structural requirements based on both the static and dynamic loading for this system. We have reviewed the rotation requirements for bringing the weapons to bear, and we have reviewed the access requirements for reloading and maintaining all components of the systems."

"Again, I cannot impress on you enough the need for absolute secrecy regarding this. You will all be living, from this moment on, in the most strict of security environments. The very success of our efforts to secure vital national interests will depend on your ability to insure that this security is maintained both collectively and individually. Failure in this regard will not be tolerated. Success will establish you all as heroes for our cause."

Recently promoted Commodore Lu Pham looked out over his audience. He would never have imagined the realization of his dreams, or the magnitude to which it was being employed … yet here was living proof before his eyes. He found it difficult to believe that he was managing over 150 scientists, engineers and military planners in the design, test and deployment of these weapons. But he took great contentment in the realization that soon, as a result of his doing, America would reap the gruesome harvest of what they had sown. As he contemplated this, he committed it to the memory of his long-dead father and mother. With hundreds of very qualified manufacturing personnel, like the young Sung Hsu whom he had just met, he could now insure the deployment of these revolutionary devices on the necessary vessels, thereby satisfying the needs of the People's Republic of China … and his own. Having reflected on all of this, he concluded,

"This concludes our presentation and discussion of requirements for these systems. In a few days, we will begin the ten days of detailed planning and procedure development, which will produce the final manufacturing plans for the modular conversions requiring this system. Thank you. You have been a most attentive and respectful audience."

April 4, 2005, 13:00 Local
Classified Briefing Room, The Pentagon

John Bowers looked around the room and mentally surveyed the participants in this meeting. As the newly appointed National Security Advisor to President Norm Weisskopf, Bowers would be chairing this meeting. He thought briefly of the family farm back in Kansas and the cornfields his father and brothers were tending as he sat in this meeting. It was to protect those cornfields and the many people like his parents and brothers and their families that meetings like this were necessary.

John Bowers had elected to leave the family farm. He had answered an internal call to serve his country, and for the last twenty-three years he had been doing so in roles of increasing responsibility. He had served well as a Captain in the 1st Brigade of the US Army's 3rd Armored Division during Desert Storm, commanding a platoon of Abrams tanks. His command had been one of the principle units to take on, and literally slaughter, an Iraqi armored division on February 28th and 29th, 1991 in the Iraqi desert near Kuwait.

The resulting medals, and the ceremonies associated with them, had led to his first direct contact with the "General". A close relationship had developed, and now spanned the fifteen intervening years. After retiring as a full colonel three years earlier, John had been called back to "duty" by General Weisskopf. The General had simply and directly asked John to serve as his National Security Advisor and to help him insure that American interests were not only protected, but clearly proclaimed throughout an increasingly threatening world, particularly in the Western Pacific.

So, here he was, surveying the attendees of a meeting, which would prepare a presentation to the President of the United States and the Joint Chiefs the following day. The assembled group included Tom Lawton and Bill Hendrickson from the NRO, Captain Toby "Skip" Pendelton from US Navy Intelligence, Major Tim Lawrence from the US Air Force, and Susan Theigold from the US State Department.

"Okay, let's get this show on the road, shall we? It is my understanding that the photographs and data from the over-flight have been analyzed by everyone here and that preliminary notes, concerns and projections from that analysis by the NRO, the Navy and the Air Force have been copied to and reviewed by you all. Is that correct?"

John looked around the room, receiving either a nod or a simple "Yes" or "That's correct" from everyone there.

"Alright then, that's excellent. Let's go ahead and start with the NRO and proceed from there right around the table, having the Navy, the Air Force and the State Department make their statements in turn. Please try to keep each of your opening comments to 3-5 minutes. We'll have plenty of time for detailed interaction after we hear from each of you. We'll wrap up the meeting with an hour-long session of developing final thoughts as to the meaning and ramifications of this info and what we believe we should do about it, beginning at 3:30 PM. Bill, will you or Tom please begin?"

Bill nodded to Tom and indicated, according to their prior decision, for Tom to "take point" in this discussion.

"Okay, Mr. Bowers, I will be presenting our thoughts on the over-flight. As you all know, on March 25th local time, March 24th here, we conducted and over-flight in international airspace off the coast of Southern China. Our aim was to take a hard look at six airfields where our satellite assets had shown us pictures of what appeared to be the PLAN training large numbers of naval aircraft."

"What was intriguing were two things: first, the number of apparent airfields being used for this activity, and second, the configuration of the airfield facilities so employed".

"Simply stated, in terms of SIGINT and visible data, our over-flight absolutely confirmed the existence of these facilities and the way in which they are being employed. The data also indicates that the Red Chinese are indeed training between six and eight mixed carrier wings consisting of fighter, strike and even what appears to be a new "Airborne Early Warning" (AEW) aircraft in addition to the two wings they are training near Shanghai. Also, it is clear that they are training these air wings with a deck configuration that is not similar to the layout of the two carriers they are building in Shanghai. We will save our thoughts on ramifications and on reasoning for later in the meeting".

As he sat down, Bill Hendrickson quickly interjected,

"I would like to interject here what Tom is too modest to let you know: that is, that it was his own analysis that led to the discovery of the installations which led to the over-flight itself. Our analysis, particularly after the mission, indicates many more air wings being trained than conceivably necessary for the carriers the Chinese are building."

As Bill sat down, John looked directly at Tom while stating,

"Okay, okay. Thanks very much to our friends from the NRO. Tom, you did a fine job in ferreting this out. Oh, by the way, I would like the two of you, Bill and Tom, to be in attendance at the meeting tomorrow for backup when we discuss all of this."

Then, looking over to Toby Pendelton, John continued,

"So, without further pause, let's continue. Please Toby, what are the US Navy's thoughts on the data?"

For the next three hours, the Navy, the Air Force and the State Department first made their initial statements, which to one degree or another basically concurred with the NRO, and then discussed the issues in detail. The fallout of the entire discussion was simply that:

1) The Red Chinese were training a lot more Naval Air capability than would be indicated by the capacity of the carriers they were building.
2) The configuration of the training facilities targeted by this surveillance was strange, and not understood, as it represented a somewhat shorter deck in an "X" configuration, as opposed to the longer and more traditional angled configuration building on the new carriers in Shanghai.
3) The only possible conclusions, given the investment in the unexplained efforts, was that the Chinese were planning on building additional carriers, without divulging any indication of the same.
4) The recommendation was to conduct further surveillance, to consider bringing up the question through diplomatic channels and to consider using human intelligence (HUMINT) assets within Red China to determine what was "afoot," though Ms. Theigold from State strongly disagreed with actively employing HUMINT on the ground in Red China.

"I believe this is a good summary, and I concur with both the conclusions and recommendations. Folks, we are playing a cat and mouse game that is every bit as critical as any of those played during the "cold war" with the Soviet Union ... perhaps more so. I believe it critical that we understand what is going on with these developments. Given what we know of the Red Chinese ambitions in Asia, I will not be surprised if your involvement with this, and the ramifications that evolve from it, do not eventually come to require prolonged, full-time commitment. "

"Bill and Tom, the meeting is scheduled for 3 PM tomorrow afternoon in the situation room at the White House. Let's meet at my offices at 2:30 and go over together."

With these comments by John Bowers, the preparation meeting for the next day's briefing was concluded.

April 5, 2005, 15:35 Local
Situation Room, The White House

President Norm Weisskopf had "that" feeling. He had experienced similar feelings from time to time throughout his life and military career. One had occurred several days before the Iraqis had attacked and taken the small Saudi town of Khafji in Desert Storm. Because he trusted such feelings, and had issued practical general orders accordingly, the US Marine and Saudi forces in the area, although initially surprised, had quickly taken the town back and driven the Iraqis off. The result had been, as he stated at the time, "about as significant as a flea on an elephant's butt."

A more recent occurrence had been just a few months earlier, when an almost overpowering feeling had caused him to come out of retirement and unexpectedly run for the Presidency.

Norm the "Storm" Weisskopf had learned to trust such feelings over the years, and he was having an unusually uneasy one now concerning the information regarding the Chinese naval air training.

"Okay gentlemen, from your presentation and our discussions, it is clear to me that the Red Chinese are significantly building up their naval air in a way we do not understand. I want to understand it."

" So, I would like to ask the following four questions. Mitch, what does the CIA have in terms of options on the ground in China? General Stone, what more can we find out through the use of our strategic surveillance assets? Admiral Crowler, what is the Navy's assessment of the possibility of the Red Chinese deploying more carriers than we are aware of? And finally, number four, Fred, what can we do diplomatically? Should I raise this issue with Jien Zenim in my meetings with him later this month? "

"We have less than an hour gentlemen. Let's hear your responses in turn".

With that, the President sat back and let the Director of the Central Intelligence Agency, the Chairman of the Joint Chiefs of Staff, the Chief of Naval Operations (CNO) and his Secretary of State take the floor in turn.

"Mr. President", began Mitch Foley, the Director of Central Intelligence, "ever since the intelligence fiascoes of the late eighties, and additionally those of the nineties, particularly as regards the Red Chinese, we have been building our assets in this regard. We have highly-placed operatives in their industry and within the PLA. Our penetration of their Navy and strategic missile forces is somewhat less impressive, as is our penetration of their Political Apparatus, although we do have a couple of people close to two of their junior politburo members."

"I believe we can set up an operation to delve into these matters, but it will be necessarily risky for those involved."

In response, President Weisskopf simply stated, "Comes with the territory Mitch, as with any job associated with facing down your enemies, whether overtly or covertly. Make it happen, and be prepared to discuss the details with myself and with John Bowers ASAP. I'll sign off on any directive that makes sense, and that is compartmentalized to the point of protecting our involvement."

"Mr. President, I must object!", interjected Fred Reisinger, the Secretary of State. "Please do not sign off on any such directive without allowing us in State, at least at the highest levels, to review and respond to possible implications."

"Fred, your turn in this is coming. Rest assured, if I believe there are any possible holes or ramifications, I will get your read. In the end, I have to make the call, however, and my threat gauge is pegged over on this. Okay, Jeremy, your turn. Shoot."

Jeremy Stone, a thirty-five year professional soldier and four star General in the United States Army was the current Chairman of the Joint Chiefs. He was committed to strengthening the military technologically, and was also committed to insuring that the Army's heavy armor remained an integral part of the fighting force in the foreseeable future. This stance, with respect to armor, ran counter to the efforts of the last two CJCS and to the former Secretary of Defense. Nonetheless, President Weisskopf agreed, and he had selected both Jeremy Stone, and his Secretary of Defense, Timothy Hattering, who was present in this meeting, for their agreement with his positions on armor, among other reasons.

"Mr. President, the Chinese reacted quickly to our latest SR-77 over-flight. No weapons were fired and they did not lock on, but our crew was uncomfortable with their ability to track and communicate the whereabouts of their aircraft so quickly."

"I would recommend that we pick our targets carefully and employ the HR-7 on the next mission. If we can get HUMINT or SIGINT from satellites to point us in a direction regarding potential new naval construction, or any other relevant facility or region, we can quickly employ an HR-7 in a surprise over-flight to acquire more information".

"Bill Hendrickson and Tom Lawton are sitting in with us today from the IMINT Directorate at NRO. Tom is the analyst who discovered this activity from some routine satellite photographs. Do either of you have any comments regarding the best use of NRO surveillance assets in this regard?"

Bill stood up somewhat nervously to address the room full of the most powerful people in his government,

"Gentlemen, we have analyzed the data extensively. As has been stated here already, it is painfully clear that the Chinese are planning something, of which we have no knowledge or intelligence, with respect to their naval air capabilities. Our estimates indicate that they would have to be building four to five more carriers to handle the aircraft they are training. Our thought is to focus our attention on all of their military shipyards and see if we can find any indication of activities in this regard. Tom, have you got anything to add?"

Tom Lawton was even more nervous than his boss. While used to making presentations on sensitive and very classified material to important audiences, he never quite imagined he would be in a position to stand before the President of the United States and make such a presentation. Nonetheless, Tom had nagging suspicions, so he dove right in.

"Just this: It is clear that the Chinese have announced what they want us to hear: the building of large deck aircraft carriers and training of air wings sufficient for them. The fact that they are training many more air wings at these other facilities without divulging such information, clearly indicates their intention to build more carriers. I would set up a schedule with our satellites and examine every shipyard that the Chinese have, military or otherwise, and then use the HR-7 for detailed looks at wherever that leads."

As Tom and Bill sat down, Jeremy Stone began wrapping up his comments.

By the end of the meeting, it was agreed that John Bowers would coordinate efforts to potentially utilize three national defense resources to aggressively delve into the mystery of the Red Chinese naval air training efforts. These included a covert CIA mission, more NRO satellite and over-flight assets, and, based upon Admiral Crowler's (the CNO) recommendation, to use the latest Sea Wolf class SSN for a covert mission near the shipyards. Any actual mission had to be signed off by the President, but the okay to plan such missions and present them to him for a decision was approved.

In addition, Secretary of State Fred Resinger got a commitment from the President to hold off on any actual CIA or Naval missions until the President met with his Chinese counterpart later in the month and raised the issue as judiciously as possible, and then reviewed and analyzed the results.

After closing the meeting, while everyone was filing out, the President motioned for his long time friend John Bowers to join him for a moment.

"John, find out if Tom Lawton can accompany you and join the first lady and me for dinner next week. I am interested in an "unofficial", after-dinner discussion with that gentleman on his feelings regarding these moves by the Chinese. Let's tentatively say next Wednesday, the 13th. If it's going to work, I'll have the Chief of Staff arrange it and pick you both up."

John was never surprised at the President's ability and willingness to "get right down in the trenches" when he felt it necessary. After all, this was how he had come to know the General himself. After he indicated his intention to contact Tom Lawton, John smiled, shook his head and exited the room.

April 11, 2005, 8:00 AM Local
WNN Broadcasting Studios, New York

David Krenshaw was not an early riser; he never had been. But the early morning (4 AM) call ... and, even more so, its content ... that he had gotten from China had gotten him out of bed and over to the broadcasting studios. Several calls en route had gotten the major editors, production crews and general management apprised of the story on which WNN (World News Network) would be getting an exclusive.

Calls had also gone out to their local camera teams in Beijing, New Delhi and Moscow, and they were all standing by now for simul-casts.

"It's good to know, and it's even better to be known," thought David as he sat down for his final makeup as the production crew was hurriedly making final preparations. His ability to find out about and even (at least in his own mind) influence events to the benefit of his network, and more importantly to the benefit of himself, was moving him straight towards the top of his field. In fact, he was convinced he would pull in some type of serious award for this very story and his involvement in it.

Now the production people were queuing him up ... 3, 2, 1 ... ON AIR!

"Good Morning." This is David Krenshaw in the WNN newsroom, interrupting with a Special Report. We have camera crews standing by in Beijing, New Delhi and Moscow for exclusive coverage of an unexpected announcement by all three governments. Our sources indicate that an historic economic pact between the People's Republic of China and India is going to be announced momentarily by the Presidents of those two nations. It is also expected that the President of the Russian Federation will announce an involvement with these two Asian giants in projects associated with the Sino-Indian announcement. ... Okay, I am told that we are ready in Beijing and New Delhi ... We take you now to Beijing for a Special Announcement by President Jien Zenim of the People's Republic of China."

On his monitor, David saw the picture of the Red Chinese flag, screened over an evening shot of Tianammen Square, which was now appearing on tens of millions of TV sets around the world. The block writing across the screen in both Chinese and English stated,

Special Announcement
President Jien Zenim
People's Republic of China

Momentarily, the picture faded to a press conference room where the WNN camera crew was showing a podium in front of a picture of Mao. Standing at the podium was President Jien Zenim. In the lower right hand corner of the screen, another, smaller shot was superimposed, picturing a similar scene in New Delhi, where the Indian president, President KP Narayannen, stood at a similar podium. Although both men began speaking, the words of the Chinese President were carried by WNN,

"Good evening. We are very happy and gratified to announce today the creation of a new economic pact between the nations of India and the People's Republic of China. This pact has been more than five years in the making and will establish open and free trade between our two countries. It also establishes many agreements on the utilization of our mutual work forces, which, as most people know, are producing a large majority of the products for the various peoples of the world."

"We are calling this pact the "Coalition of Asian States," or CAS for short, and we invite all Asian countries to review the basis for the agreements and how they apply to our mutual benefit. It is our sincere hope that more nations will join with us as we proceed with our future hope and prosperity, based on what we call the "Time of the Three Wisdoms". They are:

1. "All men and women are equal."
2. "All share equally in the bounty of a working and industrious society."
3. "One goal, one thought, one people for World is peace."

We hope to set an example for the rest of the world with these high ideals, showing by example how they can serve as the basis for peace and mutual prosperity between nations. A press and diplomatic package has been prepared for any network or nation wishing them. Thank you, good night".

The picture faded back to David Krenshaw in WNN's New York studios.

"We have just witnessed an historic announcement by the People's Republic of China and India, announcing a new "Coalition of Asian States" based upon an economic foundation with strong ideological overtones. The governments of the two largest work forces and populations on earth have apparently worked out what were perceived, until today, as considerable differences. I am now told that an announcement from The Russian Federation is ready. We take you now to Moscow".

Again, the picture faded, and David saw President Vladimyr Puten sitting behind his desk in his presidential office, facing the camera. After no more than a second had elapsed, he began to speak,

"This evening we have witnessed an extraordinary economic agreement between two great nations for peace and prosperity. Their ability to rise above their differences and unite in friendship and prosperity has energized our own Russian government, and will do the same for our people."

"It is therefore with great enthusiasm that I announce today the Siberian Economic Development Treaty. This treaty is made exclusively with the Coalition of Asian States for the economic development of our vast Siberian resources. We look forward to its impact on the people of our mutual regions as we build or economies and our prosperity upon the principles of equality and social justice outlined in the CAS 'Time of the Three Wisdoms' which we in the Russian Federation endorse completely."

"This ends the announcement. There will be no press questions at this time. A full Press Conference will be held tomorrow in the Kremlin at 10 AM. Thank you, and good night."

Coalition of Asian States and
Siberian Economic Development

As David Krenshaw faded back onto the screen, the enthusiasm in his eyes and demeanor were self evident,

"That was President Vladimyr Puten of the Russian Federation announcing a Siberian Economic Development Treaty between his nation and the just-announced Coalition of Asian States, made up of The People's Republic of China and India. For those of you watching on TV, or listening via the WNN radio network, let me say these are historic and momentous times. What we have witnessed this morning is nothing short of the largest potential economic development in the history of the world. As our correspondents gather more information, and as our analysts review that information with the documentation provided, we'll broadcast updates. Please stay tuned to WNN for more developments throughout the day, and on your nightly news. This is David Krenshaw reporting, and this has been a WNN Special Report."

April 12, 2005, 10:00 AM Local
The Oval Office, Washington, D.C.

"Okay, you've each had time to review these announcements and the diplomatic information handed out with them. Let's start with State and proceed to National Security, Defense and CIA. What are we seeing here folks? What's the impact to us, economically and diplomatically? What does it mean to our allies, and to other nations in the region?"

As the President finished, he turned to Fred Reisinger and waited.

"Mr. President, this announcement caught us completely by surprise. The Chinese and Indians began having more serious talks, which were geared towards settling border disputes, back in 2000. It was generally agreed at the time that they were making good progress. But an economic agreement of this nature and magnitude did not appear to be on the table, particularly after the closer ties we developed with India during the entire campaign to defeat bin Laden and El Qaeda. Clearly China and India have been working behind the scenes and very confidentially to put this together. The announcement by the Russians was clearly coordinated and also indicates considerable prolonged behind the scenes activity."

"As to what it means to us diplomatically, a lot depends upon how serious they are about these agreements, particularly regarding their workforce. Basically, they are going to be charging huge tariffs to utilize their workers in factories within their borders, for corporations that are not part of the CAS. If they implement this as written, it will have the ultimate effect of nationalizing the assets of foreign corporations, without overtly doing so. Basically, those businesses will no longer be able to profitably operate their own facilities and will be forced to look elsewhere. In the meantime, the idled factories, if not paid for, will revert to the nations wherein they exist."

"Normally, this would be economically devastating to those countries, as they lost the contracts with those companies. But apparently both Red China and India feel that they will be able to continue producing product under a different name, and offer them even less expensively to the western markets. The pricing structures and trade formulas in the CAS agreements accomplish this. In addition, with the opening of unprecedented exploration and exploitation of the Siberian oil, gold, timber and other resources … they apparently feel they can live with whatever sanctions we care to place on them … and they may be right. If so, this is going to put enormous pressure on our friends and allies in the region: most notably Japan, South Korea, Australia, the Philippines, Thailand, Singapore, Malaysia and the ROC."

As the Secretary of State finished, the President experienced that same unsettling feeling he'd had almost a week earlier when talking about the Chinese issues. Turning to John Bowers and Timothy Hattering, he asked,

"Okay, John and Tim, what are we getting ourselves into here? I have to believe that the naval air issues and these announcements are related. What other surprise announcements can we expect from the Red Chinese?"

John spoke right up,

"Well Mr. President, although we haven't determined exactly what the Red Chinese are up to in that regard, we do have the three operations we discussed last week ready for you to review."

Before the Secretary of State could interrupt, John continued,

"Don't worry Fred, we aren't going to be stepping on your toes. Based on last week's meeting, none of these require any kind of approval before the President meets with President Zenim in Beijing later this month. However, Tim and I both agree that you should at least review them, Mr. President, and be prepared to act based on the outcomes of those meetings."

"My personal feeling is that either the Chinese are developing something on their own which they will announce in due course, or they are working with someone else, maybe the Indians ... although I find that difficult to believe ... to do the same. The intent would be to establish more military force projection in the South China Sea and surrounding areas."

At this, the Secretary of Defense spoke up,

"Mr. President, I believe we would be smart to increase our military presence in the Western Pacific at this time. These developments are disturbing as the Red Chinese continue to build up their forces across the strait from Taiwan, and in general throughout the South China Sea. Their bases in the Spratleys have been well established and garrisoned for some years now, and they still have that satellite monitoring station on Tarawa Island that was handed over to them under Clinton. They have beefed up their electronics there, as well as the dock facilities and airfield."

"In light of what State just said, I believe it prudent to get another carrier in the area, and perhaps a Marine Expeditionary Unit (MEU), and have them temporarily stationed out of Guam, while we monitor developments."

The Secretary of State interrupted,

"Oh come on Tim, that will be viewed by everyone in the region as provocative and an overreaction. I do not deny that the developments are disturbing and that there may be a military overtone to them. For that reason we should be prepared to deploy. But I believe deploying prematurely would be playing into their hands, and may even force the issue. I would recommend holding off, Mr. President."

President Weisskopf listened to all of this, and made up his mind quickly.

"Alright Fred, we'll hold off on any deployment; but, Tim, get the orders issued that will insure that we are logistically ready to deploy from a provisioning, fuel and armament standpoint. We'll set it up to base them out of Guam in support of the Kitty Hawk group out of Japan."

"In addition, John and Mitch, I will review those three operations. The NRO and the Navy operations are probably going to be a "go" as is, but Mitch, I want to scale back the HUMINT operation and not risk any of our highly-placed assets at this point. What are your thoughts?"

Mitch Foley was actually very relieved. First, the operatives he had placed in the Chinese industrial sector and at the foreign ministry were not something he was anxious to risk. Second, he had expected much more heat to be directed at CIA in this meeting regarding this matter since his Chinese operatives and his other intelligence officers had been taken by surprise.

"Mr. President, I understand and concur regarding those assets. They may be much more valuable to us later. This announcement by China and India was not discussed at their level, but implementing it certainly will be. Regarding finding out more about their naval shipbuilding, I have some ideas and will have our Director of Operations work out the details."

"Great, Mitch, I look forward to the updated plan. The fact that the Chinese surprised both State and yourself is very disconcerting. Something major is going on over there and we need to know what it is. John, we can start on the final review of the other two operations after dinner tomorrow night."

"Finally, Fred, let's finalize the team that will be going with me to Beijing for the summit with Zenim. I want to talk to him directly about these "labor" arrangements and about the Naval Air facilities we have been monitoring. In the meantime, I'd like you to get a read from our allies before the trip so we can factor all of that into the discussions."

April 13, 2005, 22:00 PM Local
Along the Potomac, Washington, D.C.

It was beautiful clear night along the Potomac. Even though the Secret Service was arrayed as inconspicuously as possible around them, and even though the two younger men who had dined with them were clearly there in some official capacity, Linda Weisskopf was glad to be out with Norm. Leaving the "stuffy" and very official Limousine behind and using the black Suburban for this "outing" had been a nice touch, she thought. As she watched Norm walking and talking casually with John and Tom, the young analyst from Virginia, she reflected on Norm's disposition the last few days.

Linda had been with Norm far too many years to not recognize the hints and telltale signs of apprehension and concern. She had seen them when he left for a tour in Vietnam and had then lived with the apprehension that accompanied his return home. She had seen them when he was the deputy task force commander for the invasion operation in the Caribbean. That had been a success, but there had been a cost; as there always was, for any honest and virtuous officer making life and death decisions for his soldiers.

And among his many attributes, Norm was honest and virtuous. He was perhaps a little gruff on the outside, but as she had said so many times, despite that gruff exterior so necessary in his profession, he was a true "burnt marshmallow." Rough and crusty on the outside, but soft and caring underneath it ... caring for his soldiers, caring for his country, caring for her.

She had seen the same signs of apprehension before Desert Storm and on the TV screens, she had felt it over telephone lines during that epic conflict which had thrust him upon the national stage. She had seen it during his candidacy for the Presidency ... and she saw it now.

Norm was troubled. He was probably having another of "those" feelings. And though he hadn't shared it with her yet, he didn't need to. She knew it instinctively ... and he would know she knew it, and take comfort in the thought that she shared it with him.

As if though sensing her thought, he turned away from the young men and came and took her by the hand.

"It is a beautiful night, sweetheart, and I apologize for not being able to spend more of it with you. What I would give to be able to just hold your hand and walk along the river here and properly enjoy this evening. Look at those stars! Even around all these lights they so bright this evening".

Linda knew he could not stay much longer and did not want to make him be the one to break it off. She knew he truly wanted to stay with her and that was enough. She was content with that knowledge.

"You better go on now, Norm. These young men have important business with you, and there is little time left this evening to accomplish it. Let's go back to the "house" and I'll wait up for you."

April 13, 2005, 23:00 PM Local
The Oval Office Washington, D.C.

They had talked for almost an hour about specific technical details of the surveillance regarding the six airfields and the makeup and capabilities of the aircraft that were training there. Finally, the President felt the time was right to ask the pertinent question.

"Tom, I brought you here tonight because you were the one to notice these airfields and were perceptive enough to recognize their potential significance. In addition, John here has recommended you highly. I hope you will speak freely. As an old war-horse, I know that sometimes it's critical ... even essential ... to hear the unvarnished truth from the ranks. It's a lesson I learned and took to heart long ago. What do you feel is going on there with the Chinese and these naval airfields and training?"

Tom was amazed at the President's disarming, open nature. It begged one's trust and confidence to a degree Tom had seldom felt. Instinctively, he knew that this President was one of the rare ones who put duty, honor, and country above his own personal feelings and aspirations, and who would lead you right into the jaws of hell if necessary, with himself on point. Knowing this was the case, Tom did not hesitate to tell him,

"Mr. President, I cannot prove this at the moment, but I believe the Chinese are putting something together somewhere that will carry those air wings they are working so feverishly to train. I don't know where. I don't know when ... but I believe it will be soon, though we have no evidence of it outside of those curious training facilities and the aircraft themselves. They are building carriers, lots of them."

The President glanced at John, who nodded his agreement and approval.

"I tend to agree with you Tom. I want you and your people to work closely with John. You can trust him implicitly. At the same time, always insure that your superiors at NRO are kept completely within the loop. I am afraid that, if the Chinese have been able to keep this from us, there are any number of other things they are bringing together to move their plans forward. We have to find a way to get out in front of it or I am afraid the surprises will not bode well for us. I hope I can make progress in that regard when I visit and speak directly to President Jien Zenim."

"Now, if you two gentlemen will excuse me, it's past my bedtime, and I am going to rectify that."

April 26, 2005, 21:00 PM Local
Government Conference Center
Beijing, The People's Republic of China

The décor had been tremendous and exquisite. The food and entertainment had been marvelous. The pleasantries had been genuinely respectful. Many of the peripheral issues had been discussed and plans had been set in motion for hopefully amiable solutions. But now, the time had come for the two leaders to speak man-to-man, and place upon the table the true issues between them. President Jien Zenim was prepared, even eager, to do so.

He sensed he had the upper hand in these issues, and although he had personally researched the General's exploits and character, and been briefed by experts psychologically on him, still the feeling persisted to be wary.

"Mr. President, let us, as you Americans say, "Cut to the chase." The announcements we have made with India and the Russians must be uppermost in your mind. I am sure you desire to know our intentions."

President Weisskopf was relieved to hear his Chinese counterpart speak directly, and was anxious himself to address this central issue.

"Yes, President Jien, you have, as we say, "hit the nail on the head." This is a principle concern ... particularly the details of the labor arrangements and the new tariffs. To be blunt, we believe this is a move by your government to force our companies out of the factories they have built in your nation."

"It is good to hear an American who will speak directly to principle issues. I respect you for that and hope our conversations can always be so sincere and understood. In fact, we are looking for a significant return on investment. Our workforce has been used by the West to reap unimaginable wealth for the capitalists in your society who own those businesses. We are serious about the ideals and tenets expressed in our 'Three Wisdoms,' Mr. President, and we mean to put them into effect throughout our society."

President Weisskopf could scarcely believe that President Zenim was so bold and direct. His intuition told him that the Chinese President meant every word he was saying, but he also felt he had to be extremely wary; there was much more to this somehow ... much more.

"President Jien, while I respect your forthrightness, I must tell you that the United States would view gravely any attempt, even a veiled one like this, to unilaterally foreclose on American interests within your country. It would lead to severe trade restrictions and perhaps even a trade war. Surely there is some way we can accommodate the interests of your people, and the agreements you already have with our business community."

President Jien Zenim did not hesitate. Though other Americans may have been wholly unlikely to speak so directly and to risk so much, from Jien Zenim's perspective, the Americans were caught in a trap of their own making, despite their newly-elected leader.

"We have accommodated those business interests for many years, Mr. President, at extremely low wages for our workers. We want them to now enjoy a higher standard and believe there are those, even in your own business community, who will pay it".

Again, somewhat taken aback by Zenim's direct and challenging speech, and all the more wary, President Weisskopf proceeded.

"This is a troubling attitude, Mr. President; one that will unavoidably lead to severe economic strain between us, and potential damage to our diplomatic relationship. When we couple this with your extraordinary Naval Air buildup, we are extremely concerned".

This train of thought and dialog was unexpected by Jien Zenim. As such, it upset him and he allowed a little of that emotion to creep ever so slightly into his tone, as a warning to the American head of state.

"Of what Naval Air buildup do you speak, Mr. President? We have made no secret of our efforts to build two aircraft carriers, and are openly training them.. Why is this such a threat to you? Do you honestly believe that the US Navy is the only Navy entitled to such equipment?"

Norm Weisskopf detected the challenge in Jien Zenim's tone and sought to diffuse it in some way without giving up any initiative.

"No, Mr. President, I do not believe this. However, it is clear that you are training many more air wings than are necessary for the number of carriers you claim to be building. We therefore naturally believe that somewhere, unannounced and unnoticed, you are building more. Such secretive plans concern us. We would like to know you intentions."

Now it was clear to Zenim that the Americans had detected the significance of the training going on at the other airfields. His intelligence people had warned of this possibility and it would be good to confirm it to them.

"Mr. President, our only intention is to protect our interests. We intend to build a force, whether ground air or naval forces, adequate to that task."

"With our new Asian coalition, and with the interest many other nations are showing in it, I believe it is clear that those national interests of ours are growing. We sincerely hope and are in fact confident that the United States and its navy will respect those interests rather than violating them".

Well, there it was, thought President Weisskopf. He might as well have warned us to back off of the Western Rim altogether.

"We will respect any legitimate interests of your nation, Mr. President. But we expect our interests to also be respected, along with those of our allies. In that regard, we maintain a right of free passage on the open seas ... whether in the open Pacific Ocean, the Philippine Sea, or the China Sea. We hope that your intentions do include a plan to restrict that passage."

"I trust on these issues, as well as the others we discussed earlier today and yesterday, that our respective trade and diplomatic missions in July will be able to make progress and resolve these differences between us."

"So, the American is done talking", thought Jien Zenim. It's just as well. Clearly Weisskopf has no intention of yielding. Well, this will produce more strain and will eventually lead to conflict. Although unfortunate, it is acceptable. The preparations are almost complete and, unlike the Americans, the Chinese people are ready for it physically and mentally.

"I sincerely hope for that progress as well, Mr. President. I sincerely do."

CHAPTER 2

"Few men have virtue to withstand the highest bidder " –
George Washington

May 5, 2005, 10:00 local
Center of Theological Studies
Qom, Iran

Hojjatolesla Hasan al-Askari Sayeed sat quietly, humbly, as the aging Ayatollah Ol Osam (or Grand Ayatollah) Khamenei approached. The other Grand Ayatollahs sat facing him, and behind them were the many other Mujtahids and senior Mullahs and clerics of the Shia Muslim faith. Hasan knew what was about to happen. The event unfolding today had been ordained several years before. There would be no surprises here.

Putting both of his aged hands on Hasan shoulders, and staring intently into his eyes, Ayatollah Ol Osam Khamenei said,

"My son, it is time."

As Hasan reflected on what was about to happen, he looked into the clear eyes of Ayatollah Ol Osam Khamenei and replied,

"Allah Ahkbar, I am ready"

What was happening was unprecedented in the history of Shia Islam. Hasan was about to receive his authorization as an Ayatollah Ol Osam from the Ayatollah Ol Osam Khamenei, and be tacitly and explicitly recognized by the assembled clerics as Imam Hasan Sayeed, the grand spiritual, political and military leader of the Islamic Republic. He would be the youngest to have attained the position of Ayatollah Ol Osam in many decades. He would be the first true Imam in centuries.

His entire thirty-nine years of life had led him to this tremendous achievement ... but Hasan was far from finished 'achieving.'

Hasan was born in the city of Arak, Iran in 1965 on the 15th of Shaban, the same day as the mystical 12th Imam, Imam-e Asr. Hasan's father, himself a senior Mullah in the faith and an ardent follower of the Ayatollah Ol Osam Khomeini, began his son's teachings early, when Hasan was but five years of age. So effective and strict a course of study had he outlined, and so bright a student had Hasan proved himself to be, that at the unprecedented age of twelve he had been chosen for enrollment in a madraseh for Theological Studies in Arak. There he began his study of Islamic Law in the very place where the revered Ruhullah Khomeini had received similar teachings. His acceptance of, and strict, pious adherence to, the pillars of the Shia faith at such an early age had been a marvel to the older clerics and Ayatollahs who had spent decades obtaining the same levels of single-mindedness and dedication. That such a young pupil could so quickly master shaheda (confession of the faith), nampz (the Shia ritual prayers), zakat (the giving of alms), saum (fasting and contemplation) and Hajj (pilgrimage to Mecca and Medina) was not only unprecedented; it was miraculous. More and more of the clerics and Ayatollahs were speaking of it in those terms as Hasan completed his second year of study in 1979. Many began wondering whether Hasan might represent an actual re-appearance of the mystical 12th Imam, Imam-e Asr (the Imam of the Age) or Sahib az Zaman (the Lord of Time), whom the Shia believe never died, but would one day return as the great Mahdi, or Messiah.

But, the events surrounding the 1979 Islamic Revolution had interrupted all of that speculation, along with Hasan's studies. The conflict with the Shah forced his family into hiding until the Islamic Republic and its Revolutionary Council could establish order. In 1980, the invasion of Iran by Iraq and the resulting war also interceded upon Hasan's education. At the age of fifteen, Hasan had joined the Pasdaran, or people's militia, and marched off to answer what he believed was no less of a 'calling,' joining his fellow Shias in defense of their earthly homeland and heritage.

Missile launch during Iran-Iraq war.

During that war, Hasan had been introduced to another of the seven pillars of Shia Islam: the Jihad, or Holy War, to protect Islam. Even though young, Hasan viewed Iraq's attack as an extension of the infidel Western cultures, and The Great Satan in particular. As such, it was an attack on the pillars of Islam held sacred by his own Shia faith. He therefore practiced and learned war as he had those other pillars. His unwavering trust in Allah and his absolute dedication to the preservation and defense of the Islamic Republic, even in the face of Iraq's military superiority, moved his soul and motivated his compatriots. This uniquely unwavering resolve became glaringly apparent at the besieged city of Abadan, where he and his platoon destroyed six fortified enemy positions by direct assault, bringing honor to his nation and much acclaim among the Pasdaran. By mid-1982, the seventeen-year-old Hasan was commanding an entire company of the Pasdaran.

"Allah Mak! Allah Mak!"

As Khamenei began to officially recognize him before the assembled clerics as the Imam Sayeed, Hasan bowed his head soberly and continued his reflections.

He remembered well the day in late 1982, after capturing an entire Iraqi division intact, when the audible words had made their way, unbidden, into his mind. "These are your brothers. Why do you fight them?". From that time forward, though he was as committed as ever to defending the Islamic Republic and the faith, he vowed to find a way to spiritually, politically and militarily unite his Islamic brothers and break the manipulations of a greater foe.

After the war, Hasan had been given progressive positions of responsibility in the Pasdaran, ultimately being appointed as a commander over a significant portion of that force in 1988. During that entire time, his influence as a spiritual leader had also continued to grow. His strict adherence to the seventh pillar of the Shia faith, to do good and think no evil, was universally recognized by his troops and his superiors alike. Such a commander, they said, could lead them to the gates of Hades and back, returning victorious. No one doubted that with Hasan's influence the Pasdaran would unfailingly fulfill its mission to safeguard the Islamic Republic against any force that would threaten it.

In 1989, when Ruhullah Khomeini died, Hasan, at the age of twenty-four, resigned from his military duties to return to his theological studies. He chose the madraseh at the city of Qom to re-enter the Center for Theological studies, continuing to follow in the footsteps of Khomeini, who had also studied there.

In 1996, he took a three-year pilgrimage and visited many holy sites in Turkmenistan, Uzbekistan, Tajikistan and Kyrgyzstan, impressing many there with his religious knowledge, piety, military expertise and youth. It was during this pilgrimage, while on the southern borders of Kyrgyzstan, that he first heard of the Chinese secular teachings of the "Time of the Three Wisdoms."

Hasan was indeed a pious and a faithful man. He was also a realist. He knew of the rumors concerning his own identity. He recognized, and was wary of, the ambitions of the Chinese. He could neither affirm nor deny the rumors about himself. The One God, Allah, would reveal all in His time. But, that the Chinese were growing in power, wealth and influence was self-evident.

Hasan also knew that it would take a combination of more numbers, wealth and weapons than the entire "faithful" Islamic world possessed to rid Islam of the Great Satan, and his spawns ... and succeed in purging the unfaithful from among Islam's ranks as well. Such numbers, such monies and such weapons were available in China. If he could find a way to make some type of an accommodation with these principles of the "Three Wisdoms," then he could possibly form some sort of temporary, mutually-beneficial alliance of sorts with the godless Maoists, and thereby use them to help him accomplish the greater good.

To that end, in late 1999, near the end of his pilgrimage, Hasan spent three very productive weeks on the outskirts of Beijing in confidential preparations and planning, including several very productive sessions with President Jien Zenim of the People's Republic of China. Hasan had no illusions regarding the magnitude of their differences, but there was no denying that the Red Chinese knew how to manipulate people and systems. It was precisely his desire to benefit from their adroitness at manipulation that had brought Hasan to the table with the sitting Chinese President. The godless manipulations of the Chinese had served to bring about Allah's will with respect to Hasan himself. Those same manipulations would also reveal to him who was corrupted by influence and wealth over faith, and who would ultimately find that such corruption bought them nothing in this world ...or the one to come.

Terror attack on America, September of 2001

Then in September of 2001, Usama bin Laden had surprised everyone with the effectiveness of his terror attack on America. Oh, they had all known something was going to be attempted, still the enormity of it and the successful nature of it had shocked the religious and political leaders throughout Islam.

"And that was just the problem," thought Hasan. That fool bin Laden had been too much the maverick. Committed, dedicated to removing western influence, completely faithful ... yes. But a maverick just the same, with no close ties to the clerics (outside of the fringe Taliban) and no real connections to Islamic political power. As such, the very surprise of his effectiveness was its undoing. No one was positioned or prepared to take advantage of it. Instead, many had to distance themselves from the very success bin Laden had achieved. Hasan himself had counseled the Iranian leadership at the time to distance themselves from him, to walk a tight rope between how they were viewed by the masses, versus how they were viewed by an American and coalition military machine they were not yet ready or able to face.

... and it had worked. When bin Laden ultimately met his fate, when the Taliban was overthrown, and when bin Laden's terror network was rooted out and destroyed, it had left leaders like himself in the perfect position to pick up the reins.

"Imam Sayeed!! Imam Sayeed!!" , chanted the Ayatollah Ol Osams, Mujtahids, Mullahs and other clerics of the Shia Muslim faith, in near unison, as the official clerical recognition was made.

Upon hearing it, Hasan al-Askari Sayeed opened his eyes, nodded humbly and looked heavenward, as if seeking guidance, and his followers led him out of the recognition hall and toward their destiny.

May 6, 2005, 08:00 local
Politburo
Beijing, China

Li Peng, the leader of the Chinese parliament and a handpicked supporter of the president, served Jien Zenim well; not only at home in the "parliament," but as a "quasi" unofficial diplomat. This morning, Li watched as his President absorbed the morning's report regarding progress in Iraq.

"So," President Jien mused, "Hasan has already been named Imam? ... as of yesterday? This is wonderful! We are ahead of schedule. Li, are our "friends" in place, and prepared, in the four former Soviet Republics -- particularly Turkmenistan and Kyrgyzstan? And is there any chance that we can capitalize on this situation in order to obtain an earlier solution in Pakistan?"

Li had worked hard over the last several years nurturing the relationship his nation now enjoyed with India. It had taken a mixture of patience, prodding, compromise and hard negotiating, but he believed that the sterling achievement of his life had been the recent announcement of the formation of the Coalition of Asian States between The People's Republic of China and India.

Now his other major area of focus for the past 10 years was also bearing fruit. A great Islamic coalition, which would find itself very indebted to The People's Republic, now seemed possible. Amazing that it would be so after the campaign by the Americans. But, the fact that it was so in spite of that campaign, was a testament to the effectiveness of their planning.

"President, I believe that we must be patient with Pakistan. The relationship with India is still young, and India's distrust of her neighbor to the west is long standing. Although we have made much progress, we need several more months before the Indian leaders will accept a unified Islamic Republic along their borders."

"I would suggest we proceed as your original plan indicated and insure that the Pakistani agreement occurs after Turkmenistan, Uzbekistan, Tajikistan, Kyrgyzstan and Afghanistan come on board."

"Then, if all goes as we hope with the Sunnis, it will either serve as the impetus for General Musharraf to see the wisdom of unification with the GIR, or it will serve as the spark for an "uprising" in Pakistan leading to the same, as you have envisioned."

Jien knew that Li was right, and agreed with his reasoning. He had chosen well in Li, and was certain of his loyalty and his capabilities. He trusted him, without reservation.

Jien took great personal pride and satisfaction in his own ability to judge the character and capabilities of those with whom he came into contact. As a result, he allowed only those into his inner circle whom he knew to be loyal and committed to him, and to China … in that order.

May 15, 2005, 17:10 local
Lazy H Ranch
Outside Montague, Texas

Jess Simmons climbed down off his old Case tractor that he'd been using to cut hay all afternoon. He was tired and sweaty, but glad he had finished this field before supper. He thought about the fact that the bank had not approved the loan for the new air-conditioned John Deere. At 102 F in the shade, the straw hat and south wind just couldn't manage to fend off the heat; and if it was this hot in mid-May, it was going to be a real sweltering summer.

Now that it was cut, he'd let this hay sit a few days and dry out before he baled it. Later this evening, he'd start cutting that field south of the house. He'd rather work in the evening anyhow, after the heat had let up a little. If he kept after it, he could be finished putting up this cut of hay by "Saturday week" – Texan for "a week from Saturday," which would allow him to finish well before the upcoming training exercises. If the Mendoza brothers came through with their "extra" help from south of the border, he shouldn't have any trouble ... that is, if the weather also cooperated, which was always an "iffy" thing this time of year in north-central Texas. As he wiped his brow and climbed into his ten-year-old F250 4X4 pickup to drive to the house, he thought about how good some cold iced tea would feel on his parched lips right about now.

As Cindy heard the back screen door close, she called, "Is that you, Jess?"

"Sure is, hon," Jess answered, "I'm going to have to go back out this evening for two or three hours after supper and start on that field south of the house. Whew! It was hot out there for a day in mid-May ... what's for supper?"

"Well, I've got fried chicken, mashed potatoes and green beans, darlin'. Come on in and get some of this iced tea I made for you and cool yourself off before we eat. It'll be another five minutes or so," Cindy said as she began to lay out the silverware and place settings. As she thought about Jess going back out after supper, she continued, "You must have finished cutting the field over by Clear Creek then. Did you see Billy? He was over that way with the dog, hunting. He was going to try and get a ride back to the house with you."

"Well," Jess said as he thought back on his cutting, "I did see the dog an hour or so ago. Looked like he was after something. Didn't see Billy, though. I imagine he'll be along in a little while. He isn't going to stay away from the dinner table for too long if he can help it. Doesn't he have any homework?"

With a little exasperated sigh, Cindy chided, "You know I have him finish up his schoolwork as soon as he gets home, along with the watering. He's a good boy and you know it ... takes after his pa. He'd do it anyway without me reminding him. So he was okay. But I do wish you would talk to him about being on time for supper. It's best if we eat as a family, and it makes it a whole lot easier to keep this kitchen clean. Now come on in here and sit down to eat. Food's on."

Jess, who had picked up his glass of iced tea and quickly dispensed of it, walked back into the kitchen from the bathroom where he had washed his hands. As he sat down, he watched his wife of 18 years as she finished putting the food on the table. At 39, he thought she was still the best looking woman he'd ever set eyes on. He couldn't help but marvel at how she kept up with everything while riding herd on a seventeen-year-old boy, not to mention a forty-year-old boy, and tending a large vegetable garden for the family.

As she sat down, he took her hand. Without a word passing between them, they both bowed their heads and Jess said, "Father, we thank Thee for this food and the hands that prepared it. We thank Thee for our freedoms, this home and the land we live on. Help us always be good stewards of the land so it can provide us a good harvest. Please bless the food to nourish us, and bless Billy to come back in safe. In Jesus name, Amen."

As they ate, they discussed the ranch and the prospects that year for their crops and livestock. They discussed Billy, his upcoming graduation, his college plans this fall and his ultimate aspirations of following in his father's footsteps. When the time was right, Cindy asked, "So, you have everything lined up to get this cut in before those training exercises?"

Jess, sensing her apprehension, replied, "Sure do, and since Billy will be out of school, I have no doubt we can get it in. The Mendoza brothers are going to be helping as well. Besides, those exercises are only scheduled for ten days, and I'll be back before you know it. But enough about that. How was your day? When we finish eating, what do you say I help you with the dishes? Then when Billy gets in and finishes eating, I can have him start that field south of the house, while you and I drive over to Bowie and take in a movie or something." .

Cindy, moved to tears by her man's understanding and intuition, could only look into his eyes between bites of potatoes and say, "Jess, I love you!"

Then she got up from the table and moved into the loving arms of her man, Jess Simmons, full-time rancher and part-time Major, U.S. Army National Guard -- a well-trained pilot of his nation's newest and most sophisticated attack helicopter, an RAH-66 Comanche.

As they hugged, they heard the back screen door open and close, quickly followed by, "Mom and Dad, I'm home. What's to eat?"

May 19, 2005, 15:00 local
NSA Office
Washington, D.C.

John Bowers quickly reviewed the two documents he had put together for the signature of the President. Both of the documents were Presidential findings and would be used to "unofficially" authorize the covert missions being planned over the next several weeks to gather more information about the Naval Air exercises in Red China.

The first mission would be an over-flight of the Tanjin commercial shipyards by the ultra-sophisticated and top secret HR-7 (Hypersonic Reconnaissance) surveillance aircraft. These were supposedly commercial shipyards, but CIA HUMINT assets had tied an internal rumor about military applications to them. That over-flight was scheduled to take place on the 25th of May.

The second mission would take place in late June, when the US Navy was scheduled to send the SSN23 Jimmy Carter into the waters near the Shanghai shipyards and, depending on the outcome of the HR-7 mission, to those near Tanjin to conduct a covert mission. The Jimmy Carter had undergone significant modifications during its construction -- modifications which included the addition of a wasp waist, which housed sophisticated underwater launch and recovery technology, suitable for use in SEAL and other classified missions. This launch and recovery technology was made to order for just the type of mission that John and the naval planners had in mind.

Having reviewed the documents and the careful construction of the wording, John was satisfied that "plausible deniability" for the President regarding the specifics of each mission was maintained. Getting up from his desk, which was somewhat cluttered due to the abnormally large number of commitments in which he was currently involved, John put the folder containing the proposed findings in his briefcase and left for his 3:30 PM meeting in the oval office.

May 21, 2005, early evening
Near the Harold Washington Memorial Library
Chicago, IL

Alan Campbell could hardly believe his eyes … but it was true: there went his brother, Leon, into … of all places … the downtown Public Library!

"I wonda what he goin t' do in there," thought Alan. "It jus' don't make no sense! It jus' don't make no sense at all!"

Alan had been worried about his brother for some time now. Ever since Leon lost the vote to lead the "Heat" back in the hood about a year-and-a-half ago, Leon seemed to spend more and more time away. The other bloods were talking, wondering if Leon had just "lost it," or maybe wondering if he was selling them out. Jerome, in particular, was getting a little too full of himself for Alan, even though Jerome was now the leader … and doing a fairly good job at managing both their territory and their "operations."

But still, every other day or so, Leon would just disappear from their "hood" on Kildare, a few blocks from the intersection of Roosevelt and Cisero. At first, several of them had tried to follow Leon, but he was on to them, and just too good at shakin' folks off his tail. That, among other reasons, was why he'd been the "man" for so long in the first place. Well, Alan hadn't given up. He had to know what his brother was doing, and where he was going. Leon had always been his idol and was a good brother, despite their inevitable differences. For them, as their momma had always taught them, the "blood was thicker than the mud."

So Alan had continued to follow, and had continued to get shook. But he'd had a "long term" plan and it was paying off this evening. He simply kept track of where he'd been shook each time. Sometimes a little further east, other times a little further north … but each time getting closer and closer to downtown. Oh, Leon was good, and used different routes, but still the pattern developed -- and it had ultimately led right here to the Harold Washington Memorial Library.

As he waited, Alan reflected. Leon was seventeen years old. He'd dropped out of school at 14, and Alan, always wanting to follow in his big brother's footsteps, had dropped out just a year later when he was twelve. Alan was big for his age, and that fact, along with a lot of exercise, helped establish him in the "Heat" next to his brother. But things weren't the same anymore and tonight Alan was going to confront Leon and find out why.

May 21, 2005, that same time
Inside the Harold Washington Memorial Library
Chicago, IL

Inside the Library, Leon had just finished printing out the most important document to that point in his life. What he now held in his hand was more important than his suspended driver's license. It was much more important than the many citations, tickets, and complaints which he had received. It was more important that the juvenile court judgments he'd lived under while actively being a part of the "Heat."

What he held in his hand now was even more important than the High School Equivalency that he'd earned just eight weeks ago, and which he'd kept secret ... but also kept with him wherever he went. Until today, earning that equivalency had been the proudest moment in Leon's entire seventeen years. But what Leon now held in his hand was, like his High School Equivalency, a "ticket" of a different sort. It was his "ticket" to a new life. It was the paperwork informing him that he had been accepted to Boise State University in Boise, Idaho that fall, and granting him a partial scholarship as well. Leon's excitement was hard to contain. And it was made doubly hard by the fact that he had only shared the source of it with two other human beings.

"Mrs. Jenkins, would you look here? Can you believe it? I'm really going, Mrs. Jenkins. My momma is going to be so proud! She always talked to us about finding a way to knock on opportunity's door. She's told us since we were young that Jesus is waiting on the other side of that door to open it for anyone who is sincere and looking to follow His principles. Well, I finally started knocking on that door and He must have been standing there all along, just waiting to help me. I just wish I'd knocked on it a lot earlier."

Mrs. Nellie Jenkins was an elderly assistant Librarian. She'd been helping Leon for the last several months as he laboriously studied and learned. It had not been easy for him. She never asked about it, but she knew this young man must have come from a very rough part of town; it was obvious from the way he had carried himself, and talked, in those first months. But he had stuck with it, and she had been impressed. Her husband, Charlie, a retired Marine gunnery sergeant, had come in on several occasions and helped, too. He'd taken quite a liking to Leon, and was convinced that the boy had tremendous potential. While he focused on discipline, honor, and the history of America, and the vision of its founders, she focused on English, writing, math and science. Their hours of involvement with this young man had paid off. Right now, Nellie Jenkins was almost as proud of Leon as if he had been her own son.

"Leon, God bless you. You've worked hard for this, and you deserve to take pride in your accomplishment. Boise is a long way from Chicago. But, from everything I have heard and read, BSU is a fine school, and the partial scholarship is a godsend. In addition, Charlie and I want to give you this," Mrs. Jenkins said, as she passed an envelope over to Leon.

Leon took it and looked for a moment at this old white woman who had helped him so much. He remembered the many times her husband had come in and helped him with history and government. There was something about Charlie that Leon recognized and respected. Maybe he had tasted a little of it on the street, although he now knew that those street experiences had been pointing him in the wrong direction. Still, there was no doubting the qualities of leadership and respect and honor that Charlie possessed, and Leon wanted those qualities to be a part of his life as well.

He opened the envelope and read the congratulations card and the personal notes from both Mrs. Jenkins and Charlie ... then he saw the check ... a check made out to him for $5,000.

"Mrs. Jenkins, this is ... I just don't know what to say. You really can't give this to me! How can you afford it?"

"Don't you worry about it, Leon. With Charlie's retirement pay, and what he brings in on the side, and with my own job here, we have more than we can use. Charlie told me that doing this will not only help you, it will help this country; and I agree with him. Just be sure to write to us often once you get settled in Boise. We figure this will help until you find a job and get on your feet."

With that, Mrs. Jenkins gave Leon a hug and pretended not to notice the glistening in his eye ... or her own. When she was done, Leon put his acceptance letter and the notice for the partial scholarship in the fanny pack he carried with him everywhere he went, and walked over toward the stairs. As he started climbing, he turned and waved goodbye to his kindly benefactor.

May 21, 2005, five minutes later
Outside the Harold Washington Memorial Library
Chicago, IL

"Hey, blood! Wha'cha doin in there wit all dem crackers fo' so long?"

Leon would recognize that voice anywhere, and turned in surprise toward the voice coming from across the street. Sure enough, there was his younger (couldn't call him little anymore) brother, Alan, leaning against a street lamp on the other side. Leon crossed over to join him.

"Alan, how did you get here? I know I been shakin' yo' sorry black hide for the last three months. How'd ya do it?"

"Was simple, bro. You shook me every time, but every time we's getting closa to somethin', and I noticed a pattern. All's I had to do was let dat pattern lead me here ... and now here we is. You gonna tell me what's hangin'?"

Leon could hardly believe it. He knew he'd shaken Alan and several of the others. Obviously he'd underestimated the willpower, and the reasoning ability, of his brother. It gave him a lot of pride to see it evidenced here, even if its display meant that he had been 'found out.'

"Well, I guess it had to come out sometime, bro. So here it is. Let's sit down on that bench over there and I'll tell you it all ... but fo' right now, it's gotta be between us. You'll have to promise before I go on."

Alan knew a promise was important on the street. He knew his brother wouldn't ask him for one unless he needed it. He also had gone to a lot of trouble, to find out what was going on. The decision was simple.

"No problem, Leon. You shoulda trusted yo' little bro a long time ago, ya know. So, I promise. Go ahead and spill it."

For the next half hour, Leon explained to his little brother how he'd started thinking more and more about the things their momma had tried to tell them at home about a year-and-a-half ago. At the time, Leon was the man in the "Heat," but he was smart enough to see that too many of the "men" before him were either spending their time in the big house, or they were dead. He didn't want such a future for himself or his brother, and he sure didn't want to see his momma go through that. That had led him to trying to find out what more there was to life. He started spending more time thinking about making some kind of change than about how to sell dope to crackers, or how to keep their rivals off their turf. As time went on, all of those things associated with the "Heat" had started to lose their importance. His change of focus had cost him his position in the "Heat," but it also ultimately led him to confide in his mother's brother, Jack, who worked as a janitor downtown.

"Jack told me to find some books about math, and English, and government and history, and to start reading them. We always kind of looked down on him, ya know? Figured he was some sort of black honkey or somethin' -- workin' as a janitor for all those white people. But you know what? He's got some money and a house of his own ... not some "project" rental. And there ain't no police chasin' him all the time. He also ain't fightin' every other week with his neighbors, an' watchin' his friends get cut."

Alan looked at his brother, he cared for him, but these words were so foreign to him that he was having a tough time accepting them.

"You know what, bro? It looks like Jerome and the others was right. You lost it, bro. You gettin' soft. When you ever worried 'bout all this befo'? What's got into you? You sho' 'nough lost it, bro."

Leon loved his brother. The acceptance and scholarship to Boise State represented what he could do if he put his mind to it. And if he succeeded in breaking out of the trap that life "on the street" had represented, he would be more determined than ever to help his brother do the same. He grabbed his brother's arm with a fierceness that was born of determination. Alan was surprised. He had gotten to be almost as big as his older brother and thought he was in better shape. But the strength of that grip, and the determination in his brother's eyes, brought him up short. All he could do was listen.

"You listen and you listen good, Alan. I ain't lost nothin' but the ignorance I was in. I've been comin' down here to pull myself out of this trap we livin' in. The politicians and all them rabble rousin' folks who always tell us we are owed somethin' been lyin' to us. Bro, they want us here. They want us havin' to count on their programs and handouts. They want us to treat them like some sort of king for takin' other folks' money and throwin' it at us. But, look around! You see things gettin' better? No, they ain't! And thy ain't because they ain't meant to! What those folks really want is us dependent on them."

"I've been readin' about history and how this country was formed, Alan. I've been readin' about how folks, from all over the world, wanted to come here ... and still do. I got on the internet and got me an email account. I've been talkin' to folks from all over. One kid down in Texas I've come to know pretty well is white and his family works real hard on a farm. He's my age and thinks a lot the way I do. Guess what? They ain't rich, but they have things for themselves. He's goin' to Boise, Idaho this fall on a football scholarship. At first I thought it was just 'cause they was white. Then I learned it was 'cause they was willin' to work and learn. Well, I decided I'm willin' to do that too."

At this point, Alan interrupted him. "Yea, bro. But what you got from it all? ... Nothin' but a bunch of hours in a buildin' filled wit books. You know how it is, them white folks, even the poor ones, they can get ahead ... not you, and not me. We got to take what we can."

Leon was frustrated. He knew his brother was just spouting the propaganda of politicians and bureaucrats who wanted nothing more than to keep folks like Alan dependent on their programs, to keep them mired in ignorance and poverty and fighting the "system". But, although Leon was frustrated, he wasn't about to give up on his brother.

"No! Alan, that's the trap. They want you to think it's owed to you. Or, better yet, vote them in and let them take it for you. But that ain't how it is, and you know it. You are only owed what you earn, Alan ... anywhere in life, including the street. Anyone tells you different is a liar and trying to control you. And you know what? The folks that founded this country? Yeah, they made some mistakes. But whatever mistakes they made, they knew what I'm talkin' to you about, an they didn't design it to work to keep folks like us down. Well, for me ... no more. Look here."

As he said this, Leon took his High School Equivalency, and his acceptance to Boise State, out and showed them to his brother. Alan wasn't too good at reading, so Leon read it for him.

"You see, Alan, I did this for myself. Even learned how to talk real English, and learned Algebra and Geometry. There are some folks in that library who took a liking to me and helped me, and I want you to meet them."

"Guess what, Alan? They's white folks, and they treated me the way grandparents would treat one of their own. Now I got some learning, I'm going to college to get more, and I got some honest money. I'm leaving for Boise in six weeks. I'm taking momma with me, and I want you to come too. "

Alan was floored. He was thinking on what his brother had said. He could see the fire in his eyes, and when he thought about it, he could see the truth of it.

"But, Leon, what would I be doin' there?"

Leon looked at his younger brother and knew he was willing, but also knew he was apprehensive. It wouldn't be easy, but he knew Alan could do it.

"Well, we'll start by getting you over to this library right now and helping you learn ... then we'll continue over there in Boise. You may go to school Alan, but I promise, it'll because you want to, not because you have to."

With that, Leon put his arm around his brother's shoulder and they began walking back towards the library to start arranging for Alan's "ticket."

May 25, 2005, 23:05 Local
Over the Yellow Sea

"Well, here we go again," thought Colonel "Mac" Mendenhall, as he checked his mission parameters. Everything looked good, "Except this time it'll be solo," Mac thought, "and we'll be screaming. Talk about the need for speed."

Mac was piloting the ultra-secret and ultra-high tech HR-7 aircraft for the NRO toward another over-flight of Red China, which had been ordered by the Air Force Chief of Operations and the Director of the NRO. He had been carried aloft by an SR-77 from Nellis Air Force Base in Nevada. After several refuelings, he had been released over the Yellow Sea. Following a few minutes of Mach 3 flight, he was ready for his 350-mile ingress and would be igniting his Pulse Detonation Wave Engines in 3...2...1... NOW!

As the turbojet engines idled down and flamed out, the PDWE kicked in. The pulsating vibration was tangible in the cockpit as the sharp, black triangular shape of the HR-7 rocketed to its maximum speed of Mach 7, and to its planned ingress altitude of 180,000 ft. for this mission.

At such speed, the leading edges of the aircraft would fail due to overheating, were it not for the liquid methane coolant circulating through the aircraft's ceramic leading edge. This same coolant was then injected into the PDW engines and ignited as fuel. Nevertheless, at such speed, the aircraft literally glowed from the heat of its passage through what little "air" existed at that altitude. During daylight hours, contrails that resembled "doughnuts on a rope" could be seen behind the aircraft.

Mac monitored his defensive MFD, and tracked the status of his monitoring and surveillance packages, as he approached the turn that would take him between Luda and Chengshan Point and into the Gulf of Chijhli. From there, he would fly on a direct line to Tanjin, finally making a 180 degree turn which would have its nearest approach 20 miles from Tianma Shipbuilding.

His defenses consisted of the inherent stealth of the HR7, its extremely high altitude and speed capability all complemented with a suite of electronic counter measures. There was literally no known weapon in that could challenge him. His most vulnerable moment would be when he slowed to Mach 3 during the turn, and reduced altitude to 150,000 ft. for the surveillance packages.

May 25, 2005, 23:21 Local
KS-2+ AAW Battery, South of Tangshan

Lieutenant Hu Ziyang cupped his hand over the phone and addressed his men, "We have an intermittent inbound contact, approaching and decelerating through Mach 5. We are instructed to take our feed from the principle array at the airfield near Tangshan. Insure that our own guidance is locked out and enable the missiles for remote guidance and terminal thermal lock from their own seeker heads. Quickly now. move!"

Taking his hand off the phone while his men feverishly made adjustments, he listened for any other instructions from the controllers near Tangshan. Things were happening quickly. He had received the call no more than two minutes ago when the first indications of an intruder were relayed. Incredibly, the initial profile was at an altitude of close to 60,000 meters, and an approach speed of Mach 7! Since then, the contact had slowed, and dropped in altitude, but there could be no doubt whose aircraft this was.

The advanced capabilities of this KS-2+ anti-aircraft missile were classified to the strictest top level clearance within Red China. The only two batteries deployed to date were this battery and another one across the bay near the mouth of the Huang Ho River. They were there for the official, "classified" purpose of protecting Beijing from air attack. But the real, top secret purpose was to protect the work that was going on at the Tanjin shipyards.

Using phased array radar, super computing, new software, advanced infrared and optical sensors and a second stage, the KS-2+ land-based anti-aircraft missile was the most advanced system the Red Chinese had. Many felt it rivaled the American Patriot Missile batteries. (In fact, much of the technology to create these missiles had either been purchased, pilfered, or handed over to the Red Chinese by American firms, American politicians and through "exchange" programs established during the mid to late 1990's).

As a result, the missile could be guided to the anticipated area of the target's approach by a controlling facility, by the launching facility, or in a launch-and-forget mode once lock-on was obtained. In any of the ground guidance modes, once the missile got within range of its advanced infrared/optical seeker, it could lock onto the target and destroy it independently.

Lieutenant Hu reflected that, with a ceiling of 45,000 meters and a speed during 2nd stage acceleration of Mach 4, if this American bogey would just continue to slow down and reduce its altitude, there might just be a possibility for his KS-2+ missiles to make an intercept.

"Lieutenant, our weapons are slaved to Tangshan ... we have a missile launch ... now a second!"

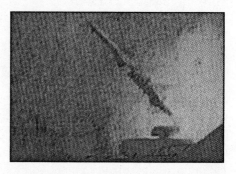

PLA launches a KA-2+ missile.

May 25, 2005, Same time
Over the Gulf of Chijhli

Mac had heard the audible alert tone in his headset... a tone that carried the ominous implication that several radar installations were attempting to acquire him. On his MFD, he noticed that the principle threats were near Tangshan, and across the bay near the mouth of the Huang Ho River. Both were painting him with their search radar, but there was no indication of any lock-on, so he felt relatively secure. At this point, Mac was seconds away from activating his surveillance package.

What Mac was not prepared for was the heightened alert tone that sounded in his headset a few seconds later, accompanied by the bright red "MISSILE LAUNCH WARNING" signal that suddenly lit up on his MFD.

"How in the hell?" Mac wondered as his instruments tracked the two missiles that had just been launched from near Tangshan.

It was decision time. He had been briefed extensively about the importance of this mission. The missiles would be coming at him from the rear. Any significant speed increase on his part to outrun them would take him deep into Chinese airspace. This was something that his plan strictly forbade.

The two missiles appeared to be Chinese KS-2's -- missiles whose ceiling was around 75,000 to 80,000 feet, and whose max speed was around Mach 3. Lower and slower than he planned on operating.

Mac keyed his satellite transceiver and quickly stated, "Red Dragon! Red Dragon! Charlie Mike! I say again, Charlie Mike!"

ThE message was encrypted by his communications systems and sent to a US military satellite in gyro-synchronous orbit over the Philippine Sea.

May 24, 2005, Same time
Secure Video Conference Center, The Pentagon

"Red Dragon! Red Dragon! Charlie Mike! I say again, Charlie Mike!"

Everyone heard the message clearly. Major Tim Lawrence said, "He's been fired on ... but he's indicating that he is continuing the mission."

"Fired upon?" asked John Bowers, "How on earth did they manage that?"

"Can't say. We'll just have to wait for further word, but he should be safe. We know of no capability they have that can reach him," replied Major Lawrence.

"Well, we also thought that there was no way they could even acquire him. Apparently, someone forgot to tell the Red Chinese."

May 25, 2005, Seconds Later
70,000 ft over the Gulf of Chijhli

As their first stages flamed out, the second stages of the KS-2+ missiles ignited and boosted them to their maximum speed of Mach 4, continuing]to increase their altitude.

Then, as the missiles passed through 120,000 feet, their seeker heads scanned the heavens for any optical or infrared source that they could lock on to. 30,000 feet above them, and ten miles in front, they found ample thermal energy from the PWDE and leading edges of "Mac's" HR-7 aircraft.

May 25, 2005, 23:25
Over the Gulf of Chijhli

Mac was getting his share of shocks this evening. The first had come when he had been notified that he'd been fired upon. The next, and greater, shock had come when what he thought were standard KS-2 missiles that his systems were tracking passed right through their supposed 75,000 foot ceiling. That unsettling occurrence had happened only 15 seconds into his surveillance run.

But none of the shocks had been as great as the one that followed a few seconds later, when the audible pitch of the warning tone changed to the unmistakably incessant warning sound of a missile lock, and the message MISSILE LOCK began flashing on his MFD.

Quickly now, Mac keyed his satellite communications and said.

"Combination! Combination ... tip over!"

Mac broke off his carefully-scripted mission profile and began evasive maneuvers. First, he turned to minimize the angle of attack the missiles had on him and force them into a pure tail chase. This evasive maneuver also had the effect of tightening the turn he was already in and allowing him to come around for his egress quicker. He also began to increase his altitude.

As he did this, he was warned of two more missile launches from near the mouth of the Huang Ho River. With four missiles in the air, Mac's "pucker factor" increased significantly along with his anxiety.

May 24, 2005, Same time
Secure Video Conference Center, The Pentagon

Tim Lawrence spun around in his seat and looked in disbelief at John and Bill when he heard the second secure satellite transmission.

"Unbelievable! The missiles have locked on! He's taking evasive action!"

May 25, 2005, Seconds later
140,000 ft over the Gulf of Chijhli

Their second stages already spent, the KS-2+ missiles lost upward inertia and began to turn over at 140,000 ft. Their seeker heads maintained lock on the HR-7 until the missiles began falling towards the Gulf of Chijhli far below.

The HR-7, a mere ten thousand feet higher, and now only two miles in front of the missiles, came out of its turn and began to accelerate rapidly away from the threat of those first two missiles, while gaining altitude rapidly.

May 25, 2005, 23:27 Local
KS-2+ AAW Battery, South of Tangshan

Lieutenant Hu Ziyang hung up the phone and turned toward his men, the crew of the launch and control unit for his battery of KS-2+ missiles.

"We have served our motherland well this night, my friends. The advanced Yankee aircraft escaped our missiles, but we prevented it from entering our airspace, and caused it to break and run like a guilty dog with its tail between its legs! We have faced the best the Americans have and turned them away!"

The technicians raised their voices as one in a deafening cheer. Perhaps now the Americans would learn to not trifle with the People's Republic of China.

May 25, 2005, 23:30
180,000 Feet Over the Gulf of Chijhli

Mac felt the sweat under his arms and on his forehead. That was far too close! And certainly not what he had expected.

Although the second set of missiles also missed, if he had not gained altitude and accelerated to his Mach 7 maximum speed, he could have been easily swimming in the Gulf of Chijhli right now ...or he could have been dead.

Still, he had completed half of his surveillance without a problem. Even though the second half was degraded, he had survived. Now, he was bringing home data about the shipyards near Tanjin and a new Chinese missile system more advanced than anything they had imagined.

Instructing his systems to encrypt and send the electronic data from the night's activities, Mac once again keyed his voice transmission link.

"Mary Chambers wet feet".

May 24, 2005, Same time
Secure Video Conference Center, The Pentagon

"Okay, he's completed the mission and is now egressing. Thank God!"

As Tim said this to Bill and John, there was an unmistakable note of relief in his voice, and on his face.

John Bowers, himself visibly relieved, leaned back in his chair and said, "That's for sure, Tim ... thank God."

Then, after a moment's pause, during which they all contemplated the near-disaster the mission might have turned into, he continued:

"Okay, as soon as you have the data, pour every effort into it. The new missile system is probably as important as what we were looking for in the shipyards."

"Thank goodness they don't have a naval version of this system or Mac would never have completed that flight in March. Tim, you'd better get this one out on the boards as soon as we analyze it and have some definitive information. The Wild Weasel and Prowler crews are going to have a new threat to plan for."

May 28, 2005, 17:30 local
Tianma Shipbuilding
Tianjin, China

Lu Pham was very satisfied. Work was progressing better than he had expected. He had spoken with General Hunbaio just yesterday regarding their progress, and he knew that a favorable report had been passed on to Chin Zhongbaio, the Chairman of COSCO and a member of the Chinese Communist Politburo. New weapons development, particularly the new LRASD weapons, was a huge priority for the entire People's Republic right now, and Lu Pham's team was performing beyond expectations.

After the conversations of yesterday, Lu had determined to come to the shipyards today to convey the thanks of their superiors to the individuals who were making the full production deployment possible, and to review the progress being made in the technical and logistical facets of the work.

He was currently in the company of the top-performing production crew chief, Sung Hsu. As they walked towards one of the six dry dock areas where ships would ultimately be fitted with the modular changes, Lu turned and spoke to Sung.

"You have much to be proud of, Sung. The process improvement plans you have come up with for the placement and onboard maintenance of the LRASD stations are proving to be successful beyond our expectations. When the materiel pipeline for the modifications are ready, we will be able to stay well ahead of schedule with this portion of the refit. Both General Hunbaio and Chairman Chin send their regards and their appreciation."

Sung took the compliment in stride, although it still was incomprehensible to think that his name was being spoken of in such high circles.

"Thank you, Commodore Lu. It is humbling to have such influential men take note of our efforts. Truly, we are only doing our job."

Lu smiled knowingly. Although Sung was being very reserved, one only had to look in his eyes to know of the pride this bright foreman took in these accomplishment ... "and he has every right," thought Lu.

"Sung, you honor your forefathers with your humility and dedication. Nonetheless, the ideas for the additional pivot points on the traversing unit, and the automated reloading mechanism you suggested, are going to make the ability to install, maintain, and reload these systems much easier and more efficient. You have done your homeland and all her citizens a great service."

"... and that's the clear truth," thought Lu Pham as they continued towards the dry docks. With his innovative production processes, Sung Hsu had reduced the time required for the refitting of each Amphibious Assault and Tactical Attack ship by seven to ten days. As they approached the stairs that would lead them down into the first of the dry docks, Lu Pham continued.

"The size and scope of these facilities never ceases to amaze me, Sung. One of my chief concerns has always been our ability to "mask" the logistics of preparing, and then actually refitting, these ships from the Americans. There is no doubt that they are becoming increasingly interested in our efforts. The activities of the other night clearly prove not only that they are determined to understand what we are doing, but that they now know where to look."

Sung Hsu reflected on those events. He had been preparing to leave for the evening when the night sky to his east had lit up with the launch of the two missiles. They had been some kilometers distant, but it had been easy to see those brilliant points of light as they quickly climbed higher and higher. Then, from the south and west, two more had followed, also climbing so very high. But there had been no explosions.

Well, thought Sung, what was one to expect? The state security issues had been explained to him. These were military conversions he was working on, and his own assignment was to develop the methods and procedures for installing weapons, awesome new weapons, on these ships for his nation. The Americans and other countries should just let them alone ... but apparently they wouldn't.

As they continued their descent to the first of the dry docks, Sung Hsu continued.

"Comrade Lu, you can see here in the upper reaches of the dry dock the first of the new logistic delivery systems we are installing. These "channels," or tunnels, lead back several hundred meters to entry points at ground level where materiel can be offloaded from rail and truck."

"It is going to take time to build them all. But, when complete, all major components will be staged and delivered through them directly to the work area for both the Tactical Strike and Amphibious Assault conversions."

"Cranes and conveyer systems will be constructed to transport the materiel from the delivery platforms at the termination of each channel to the ship itself. This will provide for both stealth and protection for the materiel as the conversions are made."

Reviewing with pride the efforts of those working on the tunnels, along with the progress they had made to date, Lu Pham responded.

" ... and we have the workforce and the will to complete the effort in time for production in September. Sung, again, in addition to the innovations regarding the systems themselves, this logistical consideration will help immensely. It is just too bad that there is no method for doing likewise for the Sea Control carrier decks," said Lu Pham as they continued their descent.

"Once we begin actually installing those decks, despite the large housings we intend to erect for their dry docks, our adversaries will know what we are doing. The components for the decks are simply too large."

Sung Hsu pondered this concern. It was not the first time he had done so, because the problem was apparent to everyone involved. He had an idea regarding it and decided now was a good time to share it.

"Yes, but we will be doing this work at several shipyards. We will have these logistic practices installed at each of those facilities, so the efforts associated with those vessels should be much more difficult to ascertain."

"I know it is not my area of responsibility, but I have an idea for the Sea Control vessels. Perhaps, we could erect the coverings at all of the dry docks being used for these vessels ... except this one. Let the Americans find what they are looking for, but keep them focused here so the magnitude of what we are accomplishing is kept from their view."

As they reached the bottom of the long staircase and began walking across the dry dock, Lu Pham considered his production crew chief's words and suggestions ... and was reminded anew of his dedication and ingenuity.

The two men had begun to associate with one another and their families in the weeks that had elapsed since their first meeting. The social interaction meant a lot to Lu because, despite his contributions, there were not many who would associate socially with a Vietnamese family.

But in Sung, he believed he had found not only talented employee, but also a friend.

"Perhaps such misdirection will help, Sung, but it still does not address the fact that fabrication efforts at each site will be almost impossible to hide."

Sung respected Lu Pham. He was a brilliant engineer. But Sung Hsu's expertise was in production and manufacturing, and he had met many westerners over the years at the COSCO facilities. He believed that such misdirection might work with what he had seen of the western mindset.

"I believe, with the coverings and with these logistical channels for other materiels, that they will be less noticeable at those other facilities. By putting the Sea Control efforts of this facility right out in the open, perhaps they may have no reason to look at the others. Perhaps at this point, the best we can hope for is to keep the magnitude of the effort from them."

As they continued to walk, Lu made up his mind to pass these recommendations on to General Hunbaio.

"Your ideas have merit, Sung. Perhaps that is the best we can hope for at this point. I will pass them on to General Hunbaio and we shall see where they lead."

"Now, let us hurry and view the preparations you are making for those pivot points on the traversing collars. My body tells me it is almost time to eat. We will have to hurry if my family is to be at your apartment by eight o'clock. But I know we can do it. You see, the excellent Chi Ro Mein that your wife makes is calling to me."

June 2, 2005
White House Situation Room
Washington, D.C.

Admiral Crowler contemplated on the import of this moment. The next one or two hours could potentially portend a critical watershed in the history of United States and Chinese relations ... perhaps a watershed in world history. Admiral Crowler had been in the Navy all of his adult life. He had come up through the ranks, starting as a "snipe" on a conventionally-powered aircraft carrier. Ultimately he had risen to command one of the premier surface combatants, an Aegis Cruiser. From there he'd been promoted to a Task Force commander as a Rear Admiral. He rose to flag rank six years later. And, as a result of his personal relationship with, and mutual respect for, the President, he had recently been promoted to command the entire US Navy.

He had cut his command teeth during the "Reagan Years" when the 600-ship navy had become a reality. He had also lived through the "Hell Years" of the 1990's when political correctness, sensitivity training, budget cuts and what the Admiral considered to be insane policy decisions had all but destroyed the morale and effectiveness of his "fighting" navy.

Now, he intended to insure that those times were behind them. They were now in the business of seriously putting the whetstone to steel in order to restore the "cutting edge".

"Mr. President, as you know, we had an over-flight of Red China last week. The mission made some startling discoveries, at least four of which made for a very anxious time for all involved."

"I have reviewed the data and ramifications with your National Security Advisor, John Bowers, with the Director of the National Reconnaissance Office, the Chief over the Air Force, General Livingston, with my own boss, the Chairman of the Joint Chiefs, General Stone and with the Secretary of Defense, Timothy Hattering. Are there any general questions before I begin?"

Admiral Crowler patiently waited while the other attendees, in addition to those whom he had just named, considered his remarks. Those additional attendees included President Norm Weisskopf, Vice President Alan Reeves, Secretary of State, Fred Reisinger and Tom Lawton who was attending with the Director of the NRO at the Presidents express request.

Secretary of State Reisinger cleared his throat and spoke.

"Admiral, the launch of those missiles at our aircraft were seen by tens of thousands. The Chinese have lodged an official diplomatic protest and are having a hay day with the press. It is really a diplomatic nightmare as many nations are sending official inquiries regarding the "incident". I thought we were sure that nothing could either detect, acquire or fire upon our aircraft. I need something to respond to these inquiries with."

Admiral Crowler paused for a moment or two, collecting his thoughts.

"Mr. Secretary, we were all surprised by the capabilities of the new Chinese missiles. We will speak more to that later in the meeting. I understand the difficult diplomatic position it has placed us in. I believe we must stick to our guns and officially deny any involvement. As far as we are concerned, and as far as the evidence shows … the Chinese launched their missiles at a meteor descending into the atmosphere which burned during reentry."

Turning to his boss and the Secretary of Defense, the Admiral inquired.

"General Stone, Secretary Hattering?"

At this President Weisskopf spoke up.

"That will not be necessary. Fred, I am afraid there is not much we can do here explicitly other than stick to the explanation that we were not involved … maybe floating Admiral Crowler's explanation would not be a bad idea. In the mean time, let's continue with the briefing."

With the President's definitive word on the matter, further discussion was unnecessary and Admiral Crowler continued.

"Thank you Mr. President. The agenda will be as follows. We are going to have Tom Lawton review the infrared, electronic and signals data we received as a result of Colonel Mendenhall's flight. Following this, we are going to look at our projections of the capabilities of the new missile system that was fired at our aircraft. Finally, we will discuss the ramifications of both the shipyard data and the new missile systems on our current and future relations with the PRC."

"So, with that said, Tom, would you care to make your presentation?"

Tom was well prepared. With enhanced photographs which were based on infrared imaging and radar imaging, he showed the attendees the significant work going on at the Tianma shipyards.

"They are working three shifts and have a huge number of manual and technical laborers preparing these four dry docks. Historically, at this facility, they have had only two dry docks, and these were used predominantly for shipwrecking. Bringing old hulks in and dismantling them for their metal and wiring and anything else of value that could be obtained."

"If you will direct your attention at these openings in the sides of each dry dock, it is apparent that an intricate system of access tunnels are being constructed which extend back to the surface several hundred meters away. Each of them is in close proximity to a major transportation corridor, either rail or vehicle. The implication that they are ramping up for serious shipbuilding at these facilities is clear ... and in a way that will make it much more difficult for either our satellites or other surveillance missions to determine what is going on exactly once they begin".

"Though no ships were present, each dry dock is capable of handling a vessel 800 feet in length and 100 feet wide ... typical size for their container ships."

"With respect to the signals and electronic data we analyzed, it is also clear that those missile batteries and additional, lesser capable batteries have been set up in very thick matrix around these shipyards, particularly for any approach from the sea. They are clearly intent on defending this site."

With respect to the advanced missiles themselves, I have prepared a summary of data regarding their performance against the HR-7 aircraft we had in the area. Please refer to your handout and to the screen:"

General	Guided, high performance Anti-Air
Guidance	Capable of multiple guidance points and terminal guidance
Range	Fifty to Seventy Miles
Ceiling	140,000 ft.
Speed	Two stage, max speed Mach 4

"We do not know if the missile is capable of self guidance once initial lock on is obtained on the ground. We must presume it can because their other high performance missile, the KS-2 certainly can. In addition, it is clear that the terminal guidance includes at least infrared and probably includes radar."

At this point, General Livingston, The US Air Force Chief, spoke up.

"Excuse my interruption, Tom, but I want to emphasize something to everyone here. These are VERY capable missiles ... perhaps as capable as our latest Patriot missiles, although their performance against a true ballistic threat is indeterminate. Somehow we need to determine their full capabilities, as well as their numbers and production status. As it is, we know that they are one of the most capable missiles, outside of our own, that we have encountered."

The meeting continued, during which time two things were made very clear:

1. The Red Chinese were gearing up for serious shipbuilding at the Tianma shipyards. Taking into account earlier CIA intelligence regarding the purpose, and eventual military significance, of the projects, the speculation that the Red Chinese were going to use those locations to build new carriers, or some other military vessels, began to assume more and more credence.

2. It was clear that the Red Chinese had employed a new, highly capable missile system in defense of these very shipyards, along with an entire multi-layered defense of other, less capable systems. This information served as the catalyst in reaching the determination that Tianma was in fact being converted to accommodate extensive military operations.

President Weisskopf addressed the meeting as it was winding down, and as Admiral Crowler sat down after the last agenda item.

"Ok, I want to thank everyone for their fine input. We will go forward with the Jimmy Carter mission early next month. I believe it is imperative, with the creation of the CAS, and given my own conversation with President Jien Zemin, that we gather as much intelligence as possible. Admiral Crowler, just insure, as we have discussed, that the Commander understands that at no time can his boat encroach into internationally recognized territorial waters of Red China. He is to accomplish his mission without doing so, or he is to abort. General Stone, Admiral ... is that understood?"

Both men responded immediately with a definitive, "Yes sir."

With that, the President concluded.

"Gentlemen, these are momentous and potentially dangerous times. Fred, we need to do everything possible to bolster the morale, and the confidence, of our allies and friends in the Pacific region, and to maintain civility with the Red Chinese. Spare no effort to insure that the foreign ministers from

Japan, to Singapore, to Australia understand this. Pass the word confidentially to our friends in the ROC."

"Oh, and one more thing ... Alan, I would like you to work with Fred at State and Mike at CIA to coordinate a detailed review of events of the last few weeks in Iran. We have not taken a hard enough look at that, in my opinion. I know there has not been a lot of news emanating from there ... and little notice is being paid to what news has been released ... but I want to know more about this Hasan Sayeed. His age, and the unusual, almost worshipful, deference that is being paid to him, has me worried. Too many differing Islamic sects saying too many good things. I have a feeling we need to know more. You guys get together off line and arrange to look a little deeper into this man, and his potential significance, both in Iran, and well beyond her borders."

Alan Reeves liked nothing more than to have a myriad of diplomatic and international state affairs on his plate. It was part of the arrangement that President Weisskopf had made with him before he accepted the invitation to run as Weisskopf's running mate. Given Reeves' prior experience under the Reagan administration, the President let it be known from the beginning that he'd rely on Alan for input, and decision-making, where diplomatic and international trade issues were concerned. Alan had liked the offer, and nothing had since given him any reason to regret having accepted it. Weisskopf was not treating his VP in the traditional figurehead manner. He was putting as much as Alan could handle on his plate. And, without exception, Alan had proven capable of handling everything that was placed before him.

Alan operated best under such pressures, and had a "team" who mirrored his capabilities in this regard. The President had just filled their plates yet again, and Alan was anxious to have at it."

"Mr. President, I will do it right away sir. We'll have a planning meeting tonight if that is okay with you, Fred and Mike, and then prepare a detailed briefing with you within the next few days."

June 6th, 2005, 06:00
Wolf Flight, Training Range
Ft. Hood, Texas

Major Jess Simmons was charged up for this morning's exercises. It was 6 AM and he and his back-seater and their flight of RAH-66 Comanches were on the point of the sword ... and moving forward.

For the last three days he had been in briefings and mission planning sessions in exhaustive preparation for the exercises that actually kicked off in the field today. The exercises would be the culmination of his, and many others', efforts of the last three years regarding the full deployment of the new RAH-66 Comanche helicopter.

In fact, for the last 9 years the program had been coming together, from that first prototype which had flown in 1996, to the six operational machines that had been delivered in 2002, when Jess had first been assigned duty with these amazing military aircraft. That was the year he had opted out and gone into the guard, after fifteen years in the Army. Despite his decision to leave the Army, his record in flying the AH-64 Apache helicopter had been so outstanding that Uncle Sam had immediately put him to work evaluating and testing the Comanche.

That work, and the performance of the aircraft itself, had been so outstanding, and so compelling, that the Army had sought, and received, approval to begin low-level production two years ahead of schedule, in 2004 instead of 2006. As a result, thirty aircraft had been produced in 2004, and another thirty in 2005, the latter delivered in the first half of the year. To date, there were now 65 operational RAH-66 Comanches in service. The exercises kicking off this morning would put 25 of them through their paces for the next four days, covering all mission capabilities from Scout, to Armed Recon, to Attack, to Air Defense, and all of the tactics developed for them.

RAH-66 Comanche helicopter Ft. Hood

Jess was piloting the lead aircraft of his company in the attack role. He would locate and then attack opposing force (OPFOR) tanks and other targets of opportunity.

In some of the heavier units, the Comanches would be operating in the scout and armed recon role, handing off the actual attack to AH-64D "Longbow" Apache helicopters. Jess believed that, in the attack role, the Comanche was every bit as effective as (and, in some ways, even more effective than) the older Apaches. This was because, while with the additional stores pylons the Comanche could carry slightly less ordinance, it could do it more stealthily and more effectively. He was convinced that these exercises would serve as proof of the Comanche's attack-mode superiority.

"Guidepost, guidepost, this is Wolf," Jess spoke into his headset on the division's frequency.

"Go ahead Wolf," came back an almost instantaneous reply.

"We are at point Bravo. Confirm permission to proceed."

The operational plan called for his lead element of Comanches to scout well in advance of the division and the other elements of his flight. Point Bravo was the "kick-off" point after which his blue force expected at any time to encounter the OPFOR. From point Bravo, his flight would begin an armed reconnaissance, looking for the lead elements of the OPFOR.

In this case, OPFOR consisted of Soviet block equipment, including T-80 tanks, BMP-3 personnel carriers, AAW support vehicles, Hokum attack helicopters and air support provided by OPFOR F-16's. The Hokums and F-16's were Jess's major concern. They were very capable of targeting his flight of helicopters and taking them out.

For this reason, his flight of six Comanches included two aircraft operating in the air defense mode, carrying full loads of eight ATAS Block II (air-to-air stinger) missiles. Their call signs were Thresher 1 and Thresher 2.

"Roger, Wolf. You are cleared to proceed".

With that, Jess spoke over his flight's frequency.

"Okay, flight, follow my lead. We'll scout the terrain over the next rise across the valley to our front. I'm on point. Thresher 1 and Thresher 2, take up positions on our left and right flanks respectively, and cover us for any bandits. Respond in sequence"

As he received the responses, Jess dashed across the small intervening valley and hovered just below the summit of the hills on the far side. He slowly bought his aircraft up so his millimeter wave radar system's FCR (Fire Control Radar) could peer over the tops of the trees. Just before the sensors were ready to "see" over the treetops, Jess spoke over the intercom.

"Okay, Todd, keep your mark 20 eyeballs pealed and all of our electronic eyeballs up to snuff."

As his infrared and other sensors got a good look at the next valley, his back-seater, Todd Christensen, was rewarded with a view of five OPFOR BMP-3's. They were sitting in a small clearing at the edge of a line of oak trees on the far side of the valley, nestled between two of the hills that marked the far side of that valley in this part of the Texas hill country.

"Okay, flight, on my mark all shooters ease up to targeting position. There are five BMP-3's on the far side of the valley. I will take the center target. Each of you take targets to my right and left, in order of sequence. I will take a second shot on the far right. Await my mark and then acquire and engage."

Quickly keying into the division frequency, Jess said,

"Guidepost, guidepost. This is Wolf. We have contact with lead scout element of OPFOR. Request permission to engage and fall back to point Bravo, executing plan Lima".

"Affirmative, Wolf. You have permission to engage using OPPLAN Lima."

Now, speaking back on his flight frequency, Jess commanded.

"Okay, gentlemen, on my Mark .. 3 .. 2 .. 1 Mark!"

The four Comanche attack helicopters rose, acquired their respective targets using their FCR, and engaged each with a special training round that simulated a Hellfire missile. The practice rounds left the launch pylons and homed in on their respective targets.

June 6th, 2005, 06:10
OPFOR Lead Element, Training Range
Ft. Hood, Texas

As soon as the incoming fire was noticed, all five BMP-3's rapidly backed into the cover of the woods on the side of the hill. As they did so, their commander, Lieutenant Jensen, spoke to his own divisional headquarters.

"Hightower, Hightower. Vulture one and two execute Pincer three!"

Three of his units, including Jensen himself, made it safely into the trees. But two units were not as fortunate, as the training rounds "electronically" blew them apart, relegating them to "KIA" status in the training exercise.

Concurrent with Lt. Jensen's transmission, two flights of four Russian, KA-50B Hokum attack helicopters rose from behind the hills between which the BMP-3's had been nestled. Each flight angled away from

Ka-50 Hokum rises from cover.

the BMP-3's and up and over the respective hilltops to each side, circling towards the Comanches.

June 6th, 2005, 06:12
Wolf Flight
Ft. Hood, Texas

"Incoming bandits! Coming over the rise from the left and right. Thresher 1 engaging!"

Jess saw the threat immediately. OPFOR had sprung a trap on his flight. It appeared that all of the aircraft were Hokums, and that they were armed for air-to-air combat, carrying two missiles each. These would be simulations of Russian infrared homing missiles similar to the AIM-9 Sidewinder in the US inventory.

Jess knew that, even though the Comanche had been designed to reduce its engine heat significantly, even over that of the very cool running Apache, trying to retreat would involve turning his engine exhaust to the OPFOR helicopters. This would maximize their chance to use those missiles against him.

Thresher 1 and Thresher 2 would certainly give them a lot to think about since, between the two of them, they carried as many missiles as all eight Hokums. On the other hand, leaving the two of them to engage the Hokums alone, while Jess and the remainder of the flight fled, could get them "killed." These thoughts passed through Jess' mind in an instant, and then he made up his mind.

"Thresher 1 and 2, engage immediately and then encircle. Remainder of flight, on my lead, move forward and engage with guns, then fall back."

June 6th, 2005, 06:16
OPFOR Lead Element, Training Range
Ft. Hood, Texas

Lieutenant Jensen could not believe what he had just witnessed. The trap had been sprung perfectly and he'd thought that the blue team was toast when the eight Hokums came boiling over the ridges to his left and right.

He expected the four Comanches to fall back. They were outnumbered and did not appear to be armed for air-to-air combat. But that's not how it went down.

Two more Comanches, loaded for air-to-air combat, came over the ridge to his front, and each immediately shot two "simulated" missiles at the Hokums. Three of these four missiles "scored" on the Hokums, taking those three aircraft out of the exercise. At the same time, two Hokums had fired at those two Comanches, electronically eliminating only one of them.

Then, to his utter disbelief, the other four Comanches charged and attacked with their chin guns! In the resulting "fur ball," another Hokum was destroyed before the Comanches broke off and retreated. As they did so, the remaining four Hokums were able to take out one of the Comanches.

At that moment, the surviving air defense Comanche, which had circled around behind the Hokums, came back into the fight with a bit between its teeth. This Comanche scored "hits" on two more Hokums.

As the last two Hokums retreated back over the ridge, the four surviving Comanches regrouped on station. Two Comanches versus six Hokums had been taken out ... and the Hokum was the most advanced OPFOR rotary aircraft in the world today.

June 10th, 2005, 10:15
Debriefing Room, Ft. Hood, Texas

"Major, I must say that your attack on the Hokum ambush that first day was an extremely gutsy thing to do. It was dangerous, unprecedented and very risky … it also worked, and set the tone for the entire exercise."

"You men listen up. I can not recommend such a move, but I can say that your analytical skills must be top notch to survive on the battlefield. You must know your enemy and their capabilities. You must know how they stack up against your capabilities, without having to "remember" it. It must come naturally."

"If you study, train and live with this in mind, then, when faced with circumstances such as Major Simmons was, you will be able to arrive at the split-second decisions that may well save your command. Equally, and perhaps even more importantly, you will make the decisions that will allow you to complete your mission and save many other commands who are depending on you."

General Jamsion looked over the assembled officers and senior non-commissioned officers who had taken part in Operation No Stars. The training exercise had purposely tested US Forces when facing highly capable OPFOR's, where the US advantage in overall battlefield management through digital and electronic technology had been negated. In other words, the units would be left to coordinate through more traditional radio frequency and verbal methods.

This was a part of a policy statement that had been issued by the President, the Secretary of Defense and the Joint Chiefs of Staff soon after President Weisskopf's inauguration. The policy was to insure that US fighting forces were not overly dependent on the digital technology which had made them so invincible in many of the recent regional conflicts. General Jamison liked the attitude and the challenge. It was part of president Weisskopf's plainly stated "honing" strategy .... and General Jamison believed it was high time.

... and the strategy was proving effective. Facing a numerically superior and very advanced OPFOR, the blue forces had come out on top and achieved every operational goal ... though not without losses, some of them significant.

In General Jamison's estimation, though, this was a good thing. He recognized that some foes that the United States would face would have both the technology and the stomach for a fight. Those enemies had the smarts to put up a counter to America's best advantages, and also had the will to slug it out in a war of attrition they hoped would bring America to its knees.

"Major Simmons, do you have any advice or perspective?"

Jess Simmons did not like to be singled out, or held up on a pedestal. He did, however, like to take any opportunity to help train younger and/or less experienced personnel

"I can't really add much to what the General said except to confirm it."

Getting warmed up to the opportunity to teach, Jess continued,

"You know, folks, we didn't have our "God's unblinking Eye," Joint Surveillance and Target Attack Radar (JSTAR), up there giving us the advantage these last few days. We were all briefed on why."

"I can tell you that it is good to train for such contingencies. It is good because it is real. In Desert Storm, the Iraqis may not have been able to do much about such an advantage ... and we see what happens when an enemy can't or won't. But, think back to the Serbs in Kosovo. They did not have any extraordinary electronic countermeasures. What they did have was creative minds and a resolve. The result was that we were bombing ox carts with small engines in them, and other decoys that our "God Almighty" systems couldn't differentiate from the real thing."

"I was involved in both conflicts, gentlemen, and can tell you right now that there are folks who don't like us who are a lot more capable than the Serbs. I hope we never forget it. Study your enemy. Know his strengths and weaknesses. Live them, breathe them ... then be prepared to get right down in the mud and slug it out with him because that is what he is going to be trying to do to you if he can. Thanks, General, for the opportunity to share that."

Jess knew he had said enough, so, to a rousing ovation due to his performance and that of his team, Jess sat down. As he did so, he thought about Cindy and Billy and how the preparations for that next cut of hay were coming. In three days he'd be home and know.

June 18th, 2005, 09:00
Penthouse Suite, Park Avenue
New York City

The unique tones from his "personal" satellite cell phone immediately got David's attention. His wife, Jennie, who was reading the morning paper, glanced knowingly over the top of the "Lifestyles" page she was reading.

"I'll take it in my study," said David over his shoulder as he got up and walked across the marble floor towards the double French doors that led into his "sanctum."

As he entered the six hundred square foot "study" and stepped onto the plush Italian carpet, David plugged the phone into its desktop receiver and quickly sat down and wondered about this call. It was EXTREMELY rare that Jien ever used the cell phone that they had presented to him on one of his many visits to China. Something important must be up and it would be best to get right to it. David pressed the answer button and spoke.

"Hello, Jien! What a surprise, and on a Saturday morning no less. What can I do for you?"

On the other end of the phone, and half a world away, but connected at the speed of light over the secure and encrypted satellite link, President Jien Zenim spoke.

"David, good to hear your voice. Yes, it is Saturday morning there, but late here. I have a few critical items to pass on to you -- things I am sure our friends at WNN will love to have an exclusive on."

Amazing, thought David. Another exclusive!

"Outstanding, Jien! Please fill me in and I will get right on it. Oh! … and before I forget. Thank you so much for the exclusive tip on the CAS announcement, and the corresponding Russian announcement that Li passed on. I know that I am personally in your debt, as is WNN."

Jien continued.

"David, on the 30th of June, you will want to have camera crews on hand at the following national capitals: Kabul of Afghanistan, Ashgabat of Turkmenistan, Tashkent of Uzbekistan, Dushanbe of Tajikistan, Bishkek of Kyrgyzstan and Tehran, Iran. We have arranged for your crews to be in each place to cover the stunning announcements that will be made that day."

"It would be helpful, if as a run up to those special news breaks, you did a favorable piece on Hasan Sayeed of Iran … perhaps a few days before. He will figure greatly into these announcements, and will be making one of his own. We will handle the "arrangements" for your Swiss account as we normally do, and in fact will be transferring double the normal amount for this coverage."

David was dumbfounded. Twice the normal amount? $100,000?

"Not a problem, Jien. I know I can arrange it. We have done a few stories on Hasan, but they have all been relatively light, as we are getting very little information about him, and how he came to power in Iran.

"Would it help if I forwarded you some information, Dave?" asked Jien.

"Absolutely!" exclaimed David, "What I would really like is to interview him one-on-one and at length. No one has done that yet."

This was precisely where Jien had hoped to lead the conversation. He knew that David would now be maneuvered into reporting things as Jien and his planners wanted.

"David, I will make an arrangement with you. If you broadcast a decent piece on Hasan, and then follow that up with live coverage of the announcements, I will arrange for you to have that exclusive interview, along with another double funds transfer. How will that be?"

David literally leapt at what he considered to be another tremendous opportunity to get an exclusive on a huge story, and to further enhance his own reputation as America's preeminent news anchor.

"I would move heaven and earth to be there for such an interview. Jien, you just tell me when and where."

David couldn't believe how fortunate he was, or how lucky WNN was to have him and his "contacts." He wondered how long it would be before he would be in a position to take his place in the upper management of WNN. From David's perspective, it could not be too soon. Perhaps the next time he was in Beijing, he could raise the topic with Jien.

Jien, for his part, knew he had David Krenshaw right where he wanted him, and he was prepared to maximize the advantage. Such power and influence over the information being presented to the American public, and to so much of the rest of the world, was easily worth several Army groups to Jien.

"Very fine, David. I knew I could count on you."

For the next five minutes the two men conversed, with David taking many notes in preparation to plan the news coverage. Their discussion covered everything from recommendations concerning the camera crews in each of the capitals, to details regarding the production efforts at the broadcast studios in WNN headquarters.

When they hung up, Jien smiled … it had gone even better than he had anticipated. Turning to his long-time friend and confidant, Jien said.

"Li, tell our friends that operation "Imam Tiger" has my approval, and should proceed according to plan."

Back in the penthouse apartment in New York City, an exuberant and soon-to-be significantly wealthier David Krenshaw exclaimed to his wife as he exited his study, crossed the floor, and snatched the paper from her hands.

"It's GREAT being me!"

CHAPTER 3

" A sly rabbit will have three openings to its den. " – Confucius

June 25, 2005, 22:00 local
South China Sea
USS Jimmy Carter (SSN-23) 40 miles off Shanghai

"Hold her at one two zero feet, steady as she goes, creep at 2 knots. What are the latest threat indicators?"

In answer to his Captain's question, the officer on the deck informed him that no military traffic had been detected in the area and only nominal commercial shipping and air activity could be identified, all of which was a minimum of twenty-five miles distant.

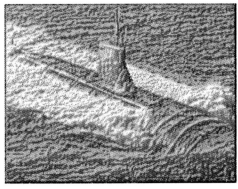

SSN-23 before submerging.

"Very well Conn, get Lieutenant Commander Sheffield."

Captain Simon Thompson was impatient at the moment. He was sitting one hundred and twenty feet below the surface, creeping along at two knots, only twenty-eight miles from the internationally recognized waters of Communist Red China in his nation's quietest and most sophisticated attack submarine. The problem was, the Chinese claimed another 160 miles beyond his current location and would treat him as an enemy if they found him here. He was determined to minimize his exposure in such conditions, and to avoid being located at all costs. He would not feel some measure of comfort until there were another 100 miles between him and that coast, and another thousand feet of water beneath his keel.

"Sir, I have Lieutenant Commander Sheffield."

Captain Thompson keyed the handset the officer of the deck gave him, and then spoke.

"Sheffield, are you and your wild Indians ready to get off my boat?"

Thompson smiled at the chuckle that preceded the response.

"Damn straight we are, Captain. But we'll be happy to hitch a ride out of here with you about twenty four hours from now."

Keying the handset again, Thompson replied.

"OK, we'll rendezvous at twenty two hundred hours tomorrow evening at point Charlie. We'll be there monitoring your frequency from twenty one hundred on. At twenty three hundred, if we have not heard anything, we will clear data and return on the next day for another try. If there are any surprises, we'll contact you with a UHF SATCOM code on the hour per the OPPLAN. You are cleared to exit, Lieutenant Commander. Godspeed, and good hunting. Thompson out."

With that, Captain Thompson monitored the departure of the SEAL (Sea, Air and Land) team under the command of Lieutenant Commander Sheffield. He then took the USS Jimmy Carter (SSN-23), third and last of the Sea Wolf class attack submarines, further out to sea and into the deeper waters that were its natural abode.

June 25, 2005, 21:05 local
South China Sea
On Board ASDS 3

Terry Sheffield surveyed his team and their surroundings.

They were on board an Advanced SEAL Delivery System (ASDS) -- a small, custom-built submarine, designed for the purpose of delivering SEAL teams to their targets along enemy or belligerent coasts. The USS Jimmy Carter (SSN-23), from which they had just exited, had been specifically modified during its construction to carry up to two of these vessels for just these sorts of clandestine missions. The first six of the new NSSN Virginia class attack submarines had similar capabilities. In fact, the first of that class was undergoing sea trials at the current time.

In addition to the crew of two who would pilot the vessel and himself, Terry had seven other SEAL team members for this mission. They and all of their diving and specific mission gear were housed inside the sixty-foot-long vessel. For communications, they were equipped with the SSIXS (Submarine Satellite Information Exchange System) UHF SATCOM communication systems, as well as the ability to receive VLF (Very Low Frequency) and ELF (Extremely Low Frequency) messages. Each ASDS weighed fifty-five tons and could travel through the water on its electric motor at eight knots for distances in excess of 120 miles … and they could do it while keeping their embarked SEAL team dry.

"A far cry from my early days in the SEALS," thought Terry, "and a much needed improvement."

Standing up and getting the entire team's attention, Terry addressed the men.

"Okay, gentlemen. I will review the mission plan again, and then you might as well get a little shut eye if you can."

Pulling down an electronic display board from an overhead slot, Terry directed his men's attention to a diagram of the mission plan depicted on the board.

"Okay, we are en route from point Alpha here, some forty miles off the entrance to Shanghai harbor. We have approximately thirty-eight miles to go before we arrive on station at point Bravo, here. It'll take us approximately four to five hours to get there if we don't run into any difficulties. At that time, Ensign Murdock and Jack will remain on station here at Bravo in a low power mode monitoring communications, while the rest of us exit the vessel and proceed in."

"Once we are in the water, we have a good six-hour swim ahead of us to map and reconnoiter the harbor and set up the gear per the plan. Each swim team will position and activate their eight MUAS (miniaturized underwater, all aspect surveillance) devices at the indicated positions to cover the required area of the harbor. Any need to deviate from the pre-planned position points must be exactly noted for proper correlation of the data. Once back in our little "hive" here, we will head for point Charlie, maintaining a low profile and the rendezvous with the Jimmy C."

"Gentlemen, we have planned and trained for this over the last four weeks. Neither we, nor the Jimmy Carter, would have been assigned this mission if it were not of extreme importance. We are the "A" team, gentlemen. And it is time, once again, to demonstrate why."

"Are there any questions? ... I didn't think so. Well, you know the drill. Catch whatever rest you can. That is all."

June 26, 2005, 6:12 local
Beneath Shanghai Harbor

"There, the last MUAS device is anchored to the floor of the harbor and now it's time to turn it on, arm its security package and get out of Dodge," thought Terry. He had just watched his swim "buddy," Chief Ben Kowalski complete the job of attaching the device firmly to the harbor floor. Kowalski then activated the device, armed the no-tamper circuitry, closed the access cover and joined him.

Utilizing hand signals, Terry indicated that it was time to make their way back to point Bravo and rendezvous with the other three swim teams at ASDS 3. Both of them then turned away from the device and began swimming towards point Bravo. As they did, Terry considered the high tech surveillance equipment they were leaving on the floor of Shanghai harbor.

The devices would monitor acoustic signatures, using a special low-power setting and extremely classified battery technology. When vessels meeting the criteria programmed into the micro-circuitry were sensed, the device would go into "record" mode. This mode would last only a moment or two as each vessel that met the requirements had an acoustical, photographic, electromagnetic and electronic recording made of it.

Each device was capable of making up to eighty such recordings and storing them digitally. The devices used classified material and circuitry that employed the saline ocean water to generate electrical power. This invaluable characteristic provided a service life of over twelve months.

With thirty-two such devices set on the harbor floor, every conceivable approach to the aircraft carrier shipyards in Shanghai was covered. For the next year, or until the capacity of every device was full, any suspicious or combatant vessel coming into the area would be recorded.

The data could be gathered either by sending more SEALS to recover it, or through activating a small buoy device by ELF signal. The buoy would then rise to the surface, orient a low-power transmitter towards the military satellite in gyro-synchronous orbit over the Philippine Sea and send an encrypted and condensed communication burst of the device's memory. When informed of an "activation", the military satellite would orient itself to "watch" the specific location of the activated device to pick up its low power burst. After communicating, the buoy would utilize chemicals to destroy itself as it sank back to the ocean floor. Each device carried five such buoys.

Twenty minutes later, Sheffield and Kowalski were joined by the other three swim teams who had all accomplished their missions. All of them were exhausted from their long swim and prolonged time in the water. They couldn't help but think, as they cycled through the lockin-lockout chamber, how nice it would be to get back into the dry and relatively comfortable, if a little cramped, interior of the ASDS for the trip back to the Jimmy Carter.

June 26, 2005, 19:25 local
East China Sea, 88 Miles off Shanghai
USS Jimmy Carter (SSN-23)

"Captain, I have a surface contact, bearing two-three-seven degrees, heading one-nine-five degrees. Mark it as contact "Sierra"" … make that two surface contacts now, bearing two-three-seven degrees. Now tracking Sierra one and Sierra two."

Captain Thompson swore to himself. That bearing and heading intercepted the course that the Jimmy Carter was taking to point Charlie for the rendezvous with the SEALS. He needed more information and he needed it now.

"Do you have a range on the contacts, speed, type?"

"Can just make out a speed of approximately 23 knots, sir. Looks like the range is twenty miles … okay, Sierra one just went ACTIVE! I say again, I have active sonar from Sierra one on its location. Mark both contacts, Sierra one and Sierra two, as Jiangwei-II class frigates."

The Jiangwei-II frigate was a serious threat. Each carried one of the newer Ka-28 Helix derivative helicopters, which were license built in China from Russia, and which carried dipping sonar and anti-submarine torpedoes. The frigates also carried a variety of anti-submarine weapons from torpedoes to the newest sextuple, medium-range ASW rocket launchers. Their sonar, a multi-frequency, bow-mounted S-07H sonar, was effective, though it had not detected the Jimmy Carter which was below a protective thermal layer and was coated with sonar absorbing materiel. Those frigates, or their helicopters, would literally have to be right on top of the Jimmy Carter to get any kind of return.

"Helm, all slow. Make your speed five knots. Take us down another hundred feet to five hundred. Let's make sure we stay below this thermal layer."

Within sixty seconds, the sonar officer updated the situation.

"Captain, active sonar has stopped, but I now have a dipping sonar. Has to be from a helicopter off one of those frigates, bearing one-niner-six degrees, range of sixteen miles. Contacts Sierra one and Sierra two are also slowing to ten knots and coming to a heading of one-two-five degrees."

"Well, that does it," thought the Captain. "Those suckers are going to hang around our rendezvous area and we just can't risk it at this stage."

"OK, looks like they are in a random search pattern over there in the vicinity of point Charlie. Helm, make your heading oh-seven-two degrees and lay in a course to point Delta. Conn, transmit a UHF SATCOM message to our "friends" at twenty-hundred hours, code "Diane"."

June 26, 2005, 20:00 local
South China Sea, 20 miles from Point Charlie
On Board ASDS 3

"Commander, we 're receiving a UHF SATCOM signal."

Terry knew that he wouldn't be getting any message unless there was a problem. Just as he wouldn't send one unless he couldn't make the rendezvous or had to use an alternate point. Something must be going down.

"Jack, go ahead and decode as it comes in."

After a few seconds Jack looked up at his commanding officer and said.

"From the Jimmy Carter sir, one word: "Diane"."

When they heard this, everyone knew that they would have to revert to point Delta for their rendezvous with the Jimmy Carter. This would mean more time and miles since point Delta was twenty miles further to the southwest.

"Okay, Jack, respond in the affirmative to the message, and you and Ensign Murdock lay in a course for us to point Delta."

June 27, 2005, 01:10 local
East China Sea, Point Delta
USS Jimmy Carter (SSN-23)

As the XO (Executive Officer) of the USS Jimmy Carter reached to hang up the communications handset into which he had been speaking, he nodded to the Captain.

"Captain, ASDS secure and the SEALS are on board. Lieutenant Commander Sheffield reports 'mission accomplished'."

Thompson considered this, thankful that they had been able to avoid detection by the Jiangwei-II frigates. Now it was time to move on to part two of the mission.

"Let me see your commset, XO. I'd like to quickly address the crew."

The XO handed Captain Thompson the handset, and Thompson raised it to his mouth.

"Crew, this is the Captain. We have retrieved our special guests who successfully completed their mission. Great job to all for detecting, identifying and then avoiding those contacts earlier. It allowed us to stealthily and successfully retrieve our friends. I know we have been running silent for the last several days, but we have several more days of the same to complete the remainder of the mission. I want you to know I am proud of your performance and proud to serve with each of you. Carry on."

Handing the commset back to the XO, the Captain continued, addressing him.

"Thanks, XO. Once you get us underway for the other objective in this OPPLAN off of Tanjin, please find Lieutenant Commander Sheffield and then the two of you join me in my quarters. I'd like to review each of your assessments and factor them into the Tanjin operation. The closer quarters up there have me nervous and we're going to have to be at 110%."

June 27, 2005, 19:00 local
WNN Broadcast Studios
WNN HQ, New York City

Looking into the camera with his famous "serious" look, David Krenshaw began the "News Special" regarding the remarkable rise to power of Hasan Sayeed.

"Ladies and gentlemen, tonight WNN news brings you a special broadcast regarding a remarkable individual of whom many of you have heard, but about whom little is known, other than the fact that he has recently come to power in Iran."

"What is remarkable, at least from the Western perspective, is the age of this new leader. Hasan Sayeed is thirty-nine years old and has taken his position at the pinnacle of a religious, political and military hierarchy where most leaders' ages are nearly twice his own. Yet these venerable leaders, including the Grand Ayatollah Khamenei, who was the leader of Iran until early last month, have willingly stepped aside to allow this individual to assume power peacefully, and, by all accounts, very effectively."

"Naturally, we here at WNN are investigating how this came about and why. Tonight, as a result of the type of exclusive sources that you have come to expect from WNN, we believe we can answer some of those questions. Please stay with us for those answers after this break for our commercial advertisers."

David was excited about the next several weeks. This show would kick off the plans he had made with his WNN producers and management, which mirrored the plans he had made with Jien. Over the next ten days, a virtual whirlwind of activity would take place in the Mid-East with the emergence of a greatly-expanded Islamic republic. And David and WNN would be right in the middle of it ... exclusively in the middle of it.

After the break, in a multi-media display that dazzled the viewers, David told bits and pieces of Hasan's life story. David touched on Hasan's birthday and how it fell on the same date as that of the mystical 12th Imam of Shia faith and the strong beliefs the Sunni's had regarding the 12th Imam. He portrayed Hasan's remarkable entry into the religious schools and programs in Iran at such an early age. Using old Iranian military film, he showed live clips of Hasan's death-defying charges at Abadan during the Iraq/Iran conflict. This footage was followed by various still and video clips of his years in leadership positions within the Pasdara, and then some very rare photos of his pilgrimage in the mountains and deserts of the 'stan regions surrounding Iran.

This was all done through various narratives and interviews by other WNN commentators, and a few Islamic clergy who had spoken of Hasan in the past. The segment neared its end with video footage of the thousands of loyal followers who led Hasan out of the Center for Theological Studies in Qom, Iran after the Islamic recognition and confirmation of him as the

Imam Hasan Sayeed. The segment concluded with a video of Hasan boarding a Lear jet, which would fly him to Tehran.

"So, what does this mean to America and to the west in general? This is a question that is difficult to answer at the moment. To date, Imam Sayeed, as he is called, has called for religious unity amongst all Islam, and has preached tolerant and peaceful co-existence with other nations of the world who do not interfere with the affairs of the Islamic Republic. While the message calling for the unification of Islam will give many Americans great unease, reminding us all of the events of September 11, 2001, the message of peace and tolerance is the antithesis of the message preached by those who were responsible for that horrific attack."

"We at WNN are seeking to understand and report the implications of this story. The history of the West and Persia, and particularly the United States and Iran is a history of mixed signals and precarious diplomatic relations. Perhaps Hasan Sayeed can re-open ties with the West, but to date there has been no indication that this is his intention. Inside Iran, the power of the Islamic faith, and the Shia faith in particular, is consolidating and continuing its hold over virtually every aspect of society. Clearly, the source for the most reliable information is none other than Hasan Sayeed. As we close tonight, we at WNN are proud to announce an exclusive interview with the Imam Sayeed that has been scheduled for 7PM EST on August 9th. Please tune to WNN at that time as I interview this dynamic, new leader of Iran."

"This is David Krenshaw, thanking you on behalf of WNN. Goodnight."

As the "live" indicator went out and his producer gave him a "thumbs up," David thought about how well the show had gone. The presentation had come off about as perfectly as possible.

"I wonder what those bozos over at Weisskopf's State Department thought about that," David wondered as he got up and began walking towards his dressing room. "Their jaws are probably hanging down to the floor right about now. Ha! Rank amateurs!"

June 27, 2005, 20:05 local
State Department Conference Room
Washington, D.C.

"Where does this guy get his information?"

Fred Reisinger looked around the room at Mike Rowley, the Director of the CIA, and several of their jointly-assembled subordinates.

"I swear, I feel like we're looking at scenes from Baghdad all over again. I remember back then during Desert Shield, and then Desert Storm, when many of us in the State Department and even over in Defense were getting part of our intelligence from the Cable News of the day."

Mike Rowley was also surprised at the depth of information that WNN had accumulated on Hasan -- more than his own operatives had been able to gather for sure. Perhaps it was time that they started checking into Mr. Krenshaw and his "contacts" ... if for no other reason than to gather intelligence and be able to be working on it before it was announced over the nightly news. Clearly, somehow, WNN was connected.

But Mike Crowley was also peeved.

"That little fart Krenshaw rubbed this in our face, Fred. The very idea of him calling your deputy like that and "advising" us to take a look at 7 PM this evening for 'all we ever wanted to know, but hadn't been able to find out about Hasan Sayeed'."

"If I thought he was a loyal American and that he made that statement out of concern for our decided lack of intelligence, that would be one thing. But of course, in that case he would have shared the information with us earlier. In addition, his commentaries on the President and his clear "longing" for the "good old days" of a couple of administrations ago just don't sit well with me. It was those "good old days" that created the majority of the problems we are facing right now."

Secretary Reisinger nodded appreciatively at the comments of his friend and compatriot in the Weisskopf administration. It was rare that the Secretary of State and the Director of the CIA saw things so similarly ... 'and it was also an indication of the wisdom and capability of the President in putting together his cabinet,' thought Secretary Reisinger.

"Mike, I understand your feelings, but whether it was an intended snub or not does not matter at this point. At least we were watching it and can now get our staffs working on this, instead of hearing about it late tonight or tomorrow morning."

"I'd like to suggest we form a couple of task forces to look more closely at the situation: One can analyze things from a potential religious standpoint as it impacts the people in the region ... that part about the confluence of Shia and Sunni faiths on this 12th Imam. The other can analyze things from a strictly political perspective, to find out how susceptible the surrounding governments are to any unifying influence Sayeed may wield."

June 30, 2005, 11:45 local
Public Assembly Square
Ashgabat, Turkmenistan

Abduhl Selim was seventeen years old, soon to be eighteen. He was not happy about being here in the middle of this hot day in the middle of this big city, waiting for an announcement by his government. Abduhl had been raised in the Kara Kum desert near the Kopet Mountains. What he enjoyed most was being able to sit in the shade of the trees at the oasis in the foothills near his home, watering his father's sheep and looking out over the expanses of the desert. He wished he were doing that right now.

Although raised in a faithful Islamic family, Abduhl had not "taken" to the religious instruction like his siblings and many of his friends. Oh, he believed in Allah and believed that Mohammed was His prophet. He also said his prayers ... when he was close to home. When he was away from home and away from the pious adults, he did not think on religion much at all, preferring to learn about the animals or the desert ... or, more and more lately, about weapons.

But today, his father had insisted that they be in the capitol, Ashgabat, for the important government announcement. His father had indicated that their leader would today announce something of over-riding political and religious importance, and that it would be an historic occasion that they would all look back on with pride. So, they had made the long trip and here he was.

"Allah be praised that the fruit markets are open and have plentiful stock this day!' Abduhl thought as the mid-day heat and the proximity of tens of thousands of others kept him uncomfortable. Actually, his discomfort came more from the pressing crowds than the heat. But the fruit was good, so he ate another slice of the tangerine he had purchased and savored the flavor as he let the juice slowly run down his throat.

As he was savoring the sweet taste, and appreciating the juice quenching his thirst, there was movement on the great balcony of the government building that overlooked the large public square where Abduhl and his family were standing. He noticed the western TV personnel with camera crews off to each side and in front of the balcony. He recognized the President and Chairman of the Cabinet of Ministers, Saparmurat Niyazov, standing with several of the leading members of the Halk Maslahaty and Assembly or Majlis. After a moment, the President began walking towards the podium.

As he did, Abduhl's Father, Muhamet, said, "Son, listen now and pay attention. It is said that this announcement will change all of our lives forever."

"My fellow countrymen. Today we are gathered here in our Capital for an announcement of great import. The proceedings are being televised throughout the nation and the world. My voice is being carried by radio wave to those areas where a television signal is not available."

"As most of you know, or may have heard, Hasan Sayeed became the leader of the Islamic Republic to our south early last month. It is a moment of great import for all Islam as Ayatollah Ol Osam Hasan Sayeed is recognized for his leadership, piety, wisdom and knowledge in all of Islam. He visited our country a number of years ago and shared his views and vision of a truly united Islam with our scholars and religious leaders. I had the opportunity to speak with him at length then, and have done so many times since."

"Early this spring, Hasan and the leading Ayatollah Ol Osams from the Islamic Republic began working with our own Halk Maslahaty and the Assembly or Majlis. As a result, a vote has been cast in both assemblies, and I have expressed my concurrence. On Independence Day, 27 October of this year, there will be a national referendum putting to the will of the people the issue of aligning ourselves with, and becoming a part of, the "Greater Islamic Republic"."

An audible intake of breath was heard throughout the crowd. Almost 90% of the population of Turkmenistan was Islamic. Such a prospect, a truly united Islam, was deeply rooted in the heart of all the faithful. That a true opportunity was presenting itself was both surprising and exhilarating to most of those assembled here. Soon, cries of, ""Allah Ahkbar!" and "Imam Sayeed!" began echoing in the square and growing in volume.

Abduhl did not know what to think. Although he recognized the import of this announcement, to him, one government seemed like it would be pretty much like another. At the oasis and in the deserts, little government interaction was required or expected.

The President let the excitement build for a moment or two, then using the power of his amplified microphone, he continued.

"I am happy to announce, that today similar announcements are being made in Kyrgyzstan, Tajikistan, Kyrgyzstan, Afghanistan and Iran."

With this, the cheers and the calls from the crowd crescendoed. After several minutes, the President was again able to make himself heard.

"In some of these countries, the transition is being made immediately as of today. In others, like our own, referenda of the people will be held to approve the votes cast by their representatives. The target date is for full alignment and sovereignty as a single Greater Islamic Republic, made up of a constitution of these various republic states, by November of this year, with the Imam Sayeed as our leader."

"What it will mean is the creation of a nation numbering over one hundred twenty million, stretching from the Persian Gulf and the Caspian Sea to the Himalayas. A unified nation of Islam with the petroleum, precious metals, agricultural and moral strength to take its place at the seat of the world's great powers! To this I say, Allah mak! Allah mak!"

Despite his previous reservations, Abduhl joined with the tens of thousands gathered in the square as they shouted their assent along with their leader.

"Allah mak! Allah mak! Allah mak!"

June 30, 2005, 3:17 local
WNN Broadcast Studios
WNN HQ, New York City

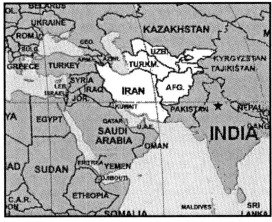
Creation of the Greater Islamic Republic.

"We repeat, WNN has been on the scene in the capital cities of Iran, Afghanistan, Turkmenistan, Uzbekistan, Tajikistan and Kyrgyzstan for the stunning announcements by the respective governments regarding the merger of these nations into a Greater Islamic Republic."

"Each nation, excepting Iran and Afghanistan, has announced referendum votes for the approval of the action being taken by their executive and legislative bodies. It is expected, given the overwhelming majority of Islamic people in each nation, that these referenda will pass."

"One of the surprises here is the actions in Afghanistan. We all remember there the military actions that resulted in the death of Usama bin Laden and the toppling of the Taliban. It was thought that the resulting governing body, which was a mixture of democratic process coupled with more moderate Islamic clerics, would have been more resistant to such a merger. Clearly, that was an incorrect impression."

"If all of these referenda pass, as we believe they will, this will result in a unified nation of Islam numbering in excess of one hundred twenty-five million people possessing great natural resources. The on-screen map we have maintained throughout this broadcast in the inset on your screen to my upper right, is a map of the resulting 'Greater Islamic Republic.' Our understanding is that the capital will be in Tehran, and the President will be Hasan Sayeed, about whom we here at WNN aired a special report several days ago."

"We expect reaction from the surrounding governments of Iraq, Pakistan, India, Kazakhstan, China and Russia within the next few hours."

"The reaction from the United States, Europe, and, in particular, from Israel, should be forthcoming as the day progresses. We will inform you of any such announcements as they occur."

"Again, ladies and gentlemen, this has been David Krenshaw, reporting live on WNN with the stunning announcements which today are creating the new nation of the Greater Islamic Republic."

June 30, 2005, 8:20 local
Oval Office in the White House
Washington, D.C.

"Somebody tell me why it is I feel like a fellow who hasn't been invited to a party that all my friends are talking about. Fred, Mike, what in the hell is going on? First this unprecedented Coalition of Asian States, and now a "greater" Islamic Republic, as if we didn't have a big enough headache with the "lesser" one. Come on guys, we're not living in a vacuum here."

"... and what is this with Afghanistan. I thought the Northern Coalition, which helped us in the fight against the Taliban was leaning our way. What's this with the immediate unification with Iran?"

Clearly, President Weisskopf was upset and frustrated. His own domestic agenda was progressing nicely through both a Senate and a House decidedly in the majority on his side of the issues. His agenda, which included governmental fiscal responsibility, more local control of education, seriously looking at a national sales tax to replace the IRS and the income tax and more emphasis on prosecuting and incarcerating violent criminals while utilizing rehabilitation, detoxification and community programs for the non-violent had broad based support. But achieving success in monitoring potentially dangerous international situations seemed to be an almost futile endeavor for Weisskopf and his cabinet. Fred Reisinger slowly shook his head and looked at his boss and said,

"Mr. President, we have a couple of task forces that are making good progress on understanding Hasan Sayeed and his potential influence in the area. I held a review meeting with them yesterday afternoon before we heard of these announcements. They have indicated a strong possibility, due to Sayeed's religious instruction, the date of his birth and his stated views concerning Islamic unification that both the Sunni Muslims and the Shia Muslims may unite behind him. I was preparing a report for the cabinet last evening when this news broke. We were concerned that Afghanistan would quickly move to align themselves with Sayeed, and, even more disconcerting, we are concerned that at some point both Pakistan and Iraq may also enter into this 'alignment'."

At this suggestion, the Chairman of the Joint Chiefs and the Secretary of Defense began speaking simultaneously.

"Great. That would result in one of our worst fears … a nuclear armed Islamic Republic!" was General Stone's frustrated comment, while Secretary Hattering exclaimed, "Having a much larger and stronger nuclear power on their borders would scare the living daylights out of the Indians."

Secretary Reisinger spoke again.

"Gentlemen, please let me continue. Diplomatically, I believe it is absolutely critical that we consolidate and reassure our allies with all due haste. This must be an effort on two fronts now. "

"We already started an effort to work with the Philippines, Japan, Thailand, Malaysia, Singapore, New Zealand and Australia in the face of the CAS. I might add that we are experiencing good progress, particularly with the Philippines and Thailand, in securing forward bases of operation in those two nations. Secretary Hattering is working closely with me on that. This is occurring in the face of significant protest from the Chinese concerning our efforts in this regard, and over the most recent surveillance flight."

"But now we must redouble our efforts to insure that we do the same negotiating and discussing with Saudi Arabia, Turkey and Egypt in the Mid-East. In my opinion, those three nations are the key to heading off this Islamic fervor. If we can keep those nations strongly "in the fold," I believe we can counter the growth and influence of this new consortium. And it goes without saying that we should work closely with Israel."

The President agreed with what his Secretary of State was saying, but was uneasy all the same. He had met Jien Zenim and could not shake the feeling that his Chinese counterpart was somehow deeply involved in all of this.

"What are the Chinese saying, Fred?"

Fred had expected such a comment, and had come prepared to discuss it.

"Mr. President, they issued a prepared statement this morning, about three hours after the announcements. Basically, they are saying that they welcome the developments. Their official comments were, as I recollect, 'The People's Republic of China welcomes and approves when any poor and oppressed peoples join together in unity and social equity to raise themselves above their circumstances and sit proudly at the table of world events.' Apparently, they plan to change their embassies in these nations to consulates, and then have the main embassy in Tehran serve as their embassy for them all as soon as the referenda are held."

At this juncture, Mike Rowley, the Director of the CIA, spoke up.

"Mr. President, we at CIA are involved with Fred's people in the task forces looking into the potential influence of Sayeed on the governments and people in the area. It is important to note that these countries are peopled by large majorities of Islamic. The largest non-Islamic population is in Kyrgyzstan, where the Russian Orthodox population numbers 20%. "

"Apparently there is some resistance in that nation to this announcement. In fact, there was some violence in Bishkek during the announcement. From all accounts, the uprising has been apparently quickly and brutally suppressed. We have received reports of refugees already heading towards the Kazakhstan border. This is important because Kazakhstan was the focus of heavy Russian immigration during the Soviet years -- which resulted in that nation's population being almost equally split between Europeans and Asians, and between the Russian orthodox faith and Islam. Not surprisingly, the people of European heritage hold most of the power there. We could be looking at a potential trouble spot in the region."

The President had heard enough. His press secretary was due to make an announcement at 9 AM, and he wanted to obtain a consensus on the wording.

"Okay, Mike and Fred, keep on it. I want this situation to be emphasized in the daily briefings. Right now we have to announce something to the world. I am inclined to use the opportunity to suggest we normalize relations with Iran, and insure that American companies and citizens in these other nations are reassured. Fred, please work with my press secretary to come up with wording to that effect and let's review it here at eight forty five."

"In addition, Fred, please move forward with the plans you spoke of regarding our allies and friends in Asia and the Mid-East. In that regard, I would like you to arrange for me to speak with King Fahd of Saudi Arabia, Prime Minister Netinyahu of Israel and President Sezer of Turkey ASAP."

"Tim and General Stone, I would like you to work up an assessment of the military strength of these aligning nations and how quickly they can combine, both logistically and operationally. Include a worst case scenario that takes into account Pakistan and Iraq. Please schedule a meeting for early next week to review and discuss the implications."

July 4, 2005, 21:45 local
University of Wyoming Football Stadium
Laramie, Wyoming

"Whoa, dude, look at that!"

Alan was really getting into this fireworks display.

"It sho' is somethin. I never would've thought to be here. Leon, we got you to thank fo' it. Mmmm, but I love this cool air up here."

Leon Campbell looked over at his mother. They had arrived in Laramie yesterday evening pretty late, and upon hearing about the big 4th of July celebration, had decided to stay an extra day to take it in. He was glad they had. What a great time they were having. In fact, the last week had been the best time he could remember. He, his brother Alan and his momma, Geneva, all traveling out west together, seeing things none of them had ever seen before.

It hadn't taken long either. As they drove west on Interstate 80, they left the city of Chicago behind soon enough. As soon as they got 20 miles outside the city, they reached the furthest extent that any of them had ever traveled. It was such an experience seeing all of the open farmland right there in Illinois. They had never imagined it was like that so close to them.

Then, they had crossed the Mississippi River at Rock Island. They had all heard of the Mississippi and how it was a large river, but nothing compared to driving almost a mile across the biggest bridge they had ever seen, over water the entire time.

The further west they had gone, the more amazing the experience had been to them all. As they traveled across Iowa, they were amazed at the cornfields. Row after row, field after field.

"Now I knows where all dat corn a fixed for you boys growin' up came from," had been their mother's comment after passing by one extremely large field. They had all laughed together at the statement. Surely, they thought, no place on earth could grow so much corn.

Then had come Nebraska. The sheer magnitude of it, the open spaces, the scenery of rolling hills for mile after mile. They had stopped in North Platte and visited the Buffalo Bill Ranch State Park near there and had purchased some souvenirs. Trying to imagine a time when buffaloes by the millions roamed that land was not as difficult when you were driving across its great expanse.

The further west they went, the more the scenery changed. Soon, they weren't looking at all of the green grass or fields of corn. There were more and more wheat fields as the land became progressively drier. There were more and more hills and rock outcroppings.

Although Nebraska seemed to go on forever … soon enough they came to the Wyoming border. Not long after entering that state they got their first glimpse of mountain ranges off in the distance. When they did, Leon stopped the car and got out. As he was gazing into the distance, he spoke to his brother Alan.

"Would you look at that, Alan! Who would have imagined it? Those mountains must be over sixty or seventy miles away. The pioneers must have felt something like this!"

Alan couldn't say he was as excited as Leon, but he had to admit that this first glimpse of the Rocky Mountains was quite the experience.

"I know I feel like a pioneer, Leon. This is all new to me, bro. I never would have thought there was so much open space in the whole world!"

After passing through Cheyenne, they had begun to climb into the mountains themselves and were soon passing by the higher peaks of the Continental divide.

They stopped at the pass above Laramie and spent several hours walking and talking and enjoying the moment. One family from Utah had stopped and engaged them for over an hour in some really pleasant conversation. The family was on their way home from a vacation in Illinois. They had visited a small town of Nauvoo on the Mississippi River. Apparently that town carried some sort of significance for their religion. Upon hearing of the Campbell's story and travels, they had been sincerely excited for them and spoke of how great it was for them to be making such an effort as a family. Before they drove off, the father and son had shaken Leon's and Alan's hand and the wife had given their mother a hug. It wasn't the first time on this trip that people had spoken to them kindly, and had taken an interest in their circumstances. They weren't used to such friendly behavior, but it felt good, and they knew they could easily become accustomed to it.

There on that pass, when the sun had gone down, it got cool quickly and they had returned to their car, driven into Laramie and found a hotel room for that first night. Now here they were, the next day, Independence Day, sitting in a full football stadium watching fireworks.

Leon thought about that., 'How fitting,' he thought to himself.

For him and his brother and mother, this was like their Independence Day. As surely as those colonial folks had thrown off the chains of their English bondage, he and his family were throwing off the chains of their lifestyle and circumstances. The prospect had Leon both humbled and excited.

A local civic organization and a local church had gotten together and organized a choir for the holiday event. Now, as the fireworks continued to light up the night sky, the crowd began to sing patriotic songs in the background. As they sang America the Beautiful, all three of the Campbells were mesmerized by the words ... words they had all heard before, but had never really listened to, or appreciated.

"Oh beautiful for spacious skies,
For amber waves of grain,
For Purple Mountains majesty,

Above the fruited plain."

"America, America,
God shed His grace on thee,
And crown thy good
With brotherhood
From sea to shining sea."

"I never knew it before, momma, but America but sure is a rich, blessed and good land. Talk about your 'spacious skies,' we know that's the truth now don't we? Guess we're going to discover how much more truth we've missed out on. Who would have ever thought it?"

Geneva Campbell looked over at her son. There were tears in her eyes. This boy, this good bright son, he had been their 'explorer,' their 'pioneer.' 'God be praised for the likes of Leon,' she thought.

"Leon, I espect we goin' to find out a lot more. Just like you say. Yo daddy had a lot of good in him, God rest his soul. I wish he could see us now. He would have been proud of you, Leon … and you too, Alan."

"It takes a real man, a real special man, to be able to pull hisself up and break out of a no good mold. Leon, that's just what you are doin, and Alan, you's helpin' and had the strength to see it fo' yo self … and you's bringin' you old momma wid you. We got a long ways to go to this Boise, Idaho … but we got someone special wid us … I do believe the good Lord's along for this ride."

July 7, 2005, 15:30 local
Islamic Republic Government Offices
Tehran, Iran

Imam Hasan al-Askari Sayeed considered his growing inner circle of government, military and religious figureheads. He knew he would be wise to consolidate and keep this number manageable. At the same time, he had to remain careful. He was riding high on a wave of public acclaim and great expectation. His message of Islamic unity and a basic application of the Three Wisdoms to the world of Islam were falling on very receptive ears.

Hasan turned to his closest advisor and friend, Ayatollah Ol Osam Sadiq Shiraziha, whom he had appointed as the foreign minister and asked.

"And what of General Musharraf in Pakistan? Are the overtures continuing?"

Sadiq reviewed the notes on his Palm computer and responded.

"Imam, the Pakistani's are very interested in aligning with us and thus extending the Greater Islamic Republic. They recognize the wisdom in this unification, the power and influence it will bring Islam overall. They marvel at the success you have had thus far. You are receiving widespread approval and support amongst the people of Pakistan and I believe this is fueling Musharraf's overtures."

"General Musharraf is insisting, however, on Pakistan being given a voice equal to the current number of seats in our Parliament, due to the size of their population. He is also insisting that he be named as overall Defense Minister for the entire Greater Islamic Republic."

Hasan considered this. The Pakistani had a point from a representation standpoint, but Hasan was more interested in Musharraf's acceptance of his Imamate. The acceptance of this, and most importantly, the people's acceptance of this, would negate any influence in the Parliament.

Military Minister was another issue altogether. Hasan had no intention of having anyone supplant him in that role, particularly not someone who had made overtures to the west the way Musharraf had during the US action against the Taliban. Hasan understood the position Musharraf had been put in, but it had been a true test of his commitment to Islam, and he had failed when he allowed America to use his airspace and bases. Besides, Sayeed believed that multiple military subordinates could always be used to insure that no individual ever accumulated the power to challenge his authority.

"And what of the Imamate?"

"Imam, Musharraf is indicating that he and his ministers are willing to accept the reality of your Imamate and recognize you publicly as the true ruling Imam for all of Islam, both Sunni and Shia, as you have desired."

Ah! There it was then, a public recognition. Hasan bowed his head and meditated for a moment, awaiting the inner voice. When he was satisfied that he had heard the promptings from within, he lifted his head and spoke to his long time supporter and confidant.

"Sadiq, tell General Musharraf that we will accept his terms regarding the Parliament, but that his request regarding the Defense Minister position will have to be put to the Ayatollah Ol Osams and the collective senior Mujtahids and Mullahs several weeks after the unification in August."

"Sadiq, as you well know, the vote will go against him. Musharraf, in requesting the position of Defense Minister, has shown his lack of faith regarding the Imamate. We will remember this, and deal appropriately with it later. In the meantime, begin making arrangements with the clerics."

"Now, what of Hussein?"

Sadiq did not have to refer to his Palm computer. The question regarding Iraq was a touchy one. It was absolutely necessary to bring Iraq into the fold of the Greater Islamic Republic. Sadiq knew this. But the leader of Iraq, so long a thorn in the side of the West ... while being used by them ... was not willing to surrender his perceived role as the leader of Islamic resistance.

"Imam, Hussein continues to insist that he share power with you. He indicates that without him we will never bring the Palestinians, Lebanese or Syrians into a unified Islam, not to mention, he says, the Iraqis. He feels he is also the key to the intimidation of the Saudis."

Hasan knew that Hussein was a cunning and ruthless leader. He also knew that he was not pious or committed heart and soul to the one faith, outside of using it as a tool to help control his people. It was clear however, that the terror he wielded amongst his own was his mainstay to power, and this was not in keeping with the tenets of the Prophet or of Allah.

"Hussein overestimates his influence in all of these areas, including and especially the loyalty of his own people. It is because his faith is not pure. He uses it only as a tool to rationalize his atrocities against many of the faithful who speak out against his transgressions."

"Very well. He has made his decision, and established the course. Are our contacts and arrangements with the Hamas complete? Are our own operatives in place and prepared to act?"

Sadiq, aware that with this line of questioning the decision to act had been made, affirmed to his Imam that all contacts with the Hamas were secure, and that their own special operatives and sleeper agents in Iraq were in place and prepared to carry out their assignments.

"Very well, my loyal and trusted friend," replied Hasan. "Then I will issue the necessary orders to have Operation Zakat proceed as we have planned. May Allah be with the faithful."

July 15, 2005, 09:30 local
Along the Yenisey River
Krasnoyarsk, Russia (Siberia)

"Нет, Остановка No. там. Не ходите дальше. " (No. Stop there. Don't go any further!)

Colonel Andrei Nosik could not believe his eyes. His battalion of 40 BTR-80 personnel carriers had offloaded here in Krasnoyarsk to "assist" with the Indian and Chinese workers streaming into the Trans-Siberian region. But no provisions had been made for their billeting or maintenance.

So, the Colonel had picked an open "park" area along the Yenisey River near the Trans-Siberian railroad and directed his vehicles and men to park there. But the civilians and the "foreigners" were all getting in the way.

"Какое говно! Это не - ни за что, чтобы использовать Motherlands военный." (What crap! This is no way to use the Motherlands military), thought the Colonel as his company commanders and their non-comms began to organize the mass confusion.

He had forty of the "special" light recon version of the BTR-80, fitted with a crew of two (instead of three), lighter armament and better communications … and capable of carrying eight combat soldiers and their gear. In this case, he would be carrying ten of these filthy foreigners whom the President had seen fit to invite into the Motherland.

The Colonel understood the reasons for this mission. He understood the value of the currency and resources the vast number of Indians and Chinese would bring his financially-strapped nation … but he didn't have to like being the one picked to be the nursemaid for them.

He had six hundred men. Eighty crew members, forty back-up/reserve crew members, a security detachment of two hundred men and logistical personnel numbering two hundred and eighty ... and all of their vehicles and equipment. He also had twenty special trailers to house and transport the research, exploration and initial production equipment they would be hauling into the wilderness.

If all went well, he would be taking the initial load of three hundred engineers and workmen by rail eight hundred kilometers north and west of Krasnoyarsk. There they would disembark and run another two hundred kilometers off road to the west in their BTR-80's to their target exploration and production area.

He was scheduled to make a total of three trips, bringing a total of six hundred of the miserable excuses for humanity to their "base," and then providing for their security, transportation and communication needs.

Eventually, they were ordered to cut a rough airfield out of the wilderness so more supplies and materiel could be brought in by air.

"Это могло быть даже хуже. Дьяволы могли бы побродить вокруг страны безнадзорной." (Well, it could be worse. The devils could be strolling around the countryside without supervision.) thought the Colonel as he summoned his company commanders for a planning meeting.

As he waited for them, his mind wandered to his earlier service experiences in Chechnya, when his personal feelings for foreigners and their influence took root. The Muslims there fought so rabidly. There was nothing sacred, nothing honorable … not that war can ever really be honorable.

Just the same, there are certain lines which, when crossed, turn the combatants more into animals than men … the Muslims in Chechnya had forced that on them … and Chechnya had been too close to home. Far too close to mother Russia to not understand that one had to prevent at all costs such terrors being introduced to ones homeland.

The Colonel was determined to do his duty, to do it professionally, to obey orders, and to insure, at all costs, that the Rodina was defended from such horror. That's what had him worried now. In the Chinese and the Indians, he saw foreigners, with foreign cultures and foreign ways of thinking. More opportunities to unleash the horror on his homeland.

Well, he would help them develop. He would help them pull money and resources out of the ground to secure his nation. He would also watch them. Their "security" ran two ways … like a two edged sword, it was sharp on both sides.

As his commanders entered his tent, which was set up and ready now, Colonel Nosil began.

"Good morning, gentlemen. We have a busy day in front of us, and an even busier tomorrow. Let's review the operation plan as it exists today. Given the godforsaken conditions we found here, we will have to modify things from a logistical standpoint. Once we determine the actual status of our civilian guests and their equipment, we may have to revise it from a personnel and/or operations standpoint as well."

"I expect this information to be available this afternoon by fourteen hundred hours. We will meet then to review it in detail. After that, I want each of you to get back with your teams and develop your final operation plans that I expect to see here on this desk no later than nineteen hundred hours. Understood? Good. This meeting is over."

July 16, 2005, 13:15 local
Along the Trans-Siberian Railroad
50km outside of Krasnoyarsk, Russia (Siberia)

Dr. Buhpendra Gavanker was standing on the flatcar outside of the BTR-80 to which he had been assigned. Even though July, it was cool this far north, at least by his Indian standards.

Dr. Gavanker had been raised in Madras, on the southern coast of India. After a tour of four years in the army, he had completed his undergraduate schooling in Bangalore in Mechanical Engineering and had then gone on to obtain a masters of science in Geology and a Ph.D. in Fossil Fuel Exploration. Those advanced degrees had come while he worked for Larsen and Tubro in Bombay.

While working at Larson and Tubro, he had been approached by the Minister in charge of the Energy Directorate for the Indian government. An offer had been made and Dr. Gavanker, fiercely loyal to his nation, had accepted. For the last ten years, he had worked in analyzing geological formation in India and surrounding friendly nations to search for more petroleum production. He had been quite successful.

So, when the People's Republic of China and India had announced their economic coalition, Dr. Gavanker had been a natural selection to lead the teams of Indian scientists, engineers and workers into Siberia in search of more petroleum. His initial studies had indicated that hundreds of kilometers to the north and west of Krasnoyarsk, there was a potential for a large, untapped reserve of petroleum. Initial samples had been promising and had indicated where the test bores should be drilled. Dr. Gavanker had decided to lead the team that would sink those bores and then set up initial production operations once the reserves were located and being pumped out of the ground. If his calculations were even close to being correct, this find had every chance of being a major oil field, perhaps rivaling the Baku oil field in the Crimea.

"Colonel Nosik, I could not help but notice that all of these personnel carriers remain armed, and that a number of them are fully armed with larger weapons systems. Why?"

Colonel Nosik recognized the intellect of the Indian standing next to him. He had been fully briefed on the Doctor's capabilities and what a large find could mean to Russia in terms of their share of the oil, and in terms of the capital that would be realized as a result of India's and China's royalty payments on their shares. This consideration allowed him to overcome somewhat his aversion to so many foreigners entering his nation.

"Doctor, this country is wilderness. We lose smaller convoys and supplies to bandits and armed insurgents each year. This joint effort to develop these hinterlands is too important to risk to such. I hope that helps you understand. If the bandits see power in overwhelming numbers, they will not think of interfering with us in any way."

Dr. Gavanker had not imagined that such concerns would be his. He knew that in the mountainous Kashmir regions of his own country there were similar problems, but had not thought to consider that anything like that would exist where his government had sent him. On the other hand, he had skipped several of the orientation meetings as he was immersed in his research.

"I understand, Colonel. We have similar problems in the Kashmir in India. How long do you expect it will be before we arrive on location at the base camp?"

Mentally reviewing the schedule, and then doing a little quick math, the Colonel responded.

"The train will be fairly slow. There will be several stops at small towns along the way. I expect we will get off the train sometime tomorrow evening. We will then check our equipment and start out overland the following morning. With no problems, I expect we may arrive late the next day ... that would be the nineteenth ... or, at the latest, early on the twentieth."

Dr. Gavanker did not relish another day-and-a-half on this flat car, followed by a day-and-a-half cooped up in the cramped confines of the BTR-80. But given what the Colonel had described, given the fact that no airfield existed in this country at this time of they year, and given the great potential for his nation represented by the petroleum ... he was content with the schedule and the discomfort ... he had little choice in any event.

"Very well, Colonel. Thank you for the information. I look forward to working with you and your men. I know it is not what military men are accustomed to, or like to do. I served in India's army for four years. Though it was over twenty years ago, I remember what soldiers liked and what they didn't like. I hope you and your men will be patient with us. In the end, it will pay off handsomely for both of our nations."

As the Indian walked over to a group of his own people who were sitting on one of the vehicles, the Colonel thought to himself, "He might be a foreigner, but at least he understands and appreciates our position. Perhaps this duty will not be as unpleasant as I had imagined."

July 18, 2005, 10:00 local
White House Situation Room
Washington, D.C.

General Jeremy Stone pressed the advance button on his hand held controller and went to the next slide in his computer generated presentation. This slide was the key for the entire meeting.

"Now I will direct your attention to the screen and the projected Force analysis for the emerging "Greater" Islamic Republic. As you can see, the numbers are significant, particularly in the worst case scenario where Pakistan and Iraq become a part of this."

Greater Islamic Republic Armed Forces Analysis
Army and Airforce

Country	IDiv	ADiv	Tanks	APC	AHelo	Aircraft
Iran	35	15	1350	900	250	250
Afghanistan	5	3	250	300	100	100
Turkmenistan	2	3	500	800	20	150
Uzbekistan	3	1	200	400	20	100
Tajikistan		1	100	100	10	50
Kyrgyzstan		1	100	100	25	100
Best Case GIR	**45**	**24**	**2500**	**2600**	**425**	**750**
Iraq	40	20	2000	1000	200	350
Pakistan	35	20	2000	900	150	200
Worst Case	**120**	**64**	**6500**	**4500**	**775**	**1300**
Modern Equip	**80**	**35**	**3000**	**2000**	**300**	**500**

Naval

Country	FFG	Subs	Aircraft
Iran	15	3	22
Pakistan	14	9	14
Iraq	3		20
Worst Case GIR	**32**	**12**	**56**

"We expect that these numbers will be pared down as they consolidate to a number closer to the modern and effective numbers you see at the bottom of the first chart. Still, these are significant numbers and they will end up with perhaps as many as ninety-six infantry divisions and fifty armor divisions, with the older units being used in-country for internal security. They can organize this into twelve army groups of approximately eight infantry and four armored divisions each and spread them along their borders and internally. We expect the India-China-Kazakh border, with the real threat there being Russia, and Saudi borders to get two of those army groups each."

"They have a sufficient number of high-quality of airfields that they can disperse their fighter and attack aircraft accordingly in support of the army groups. As I indicated, we expect the two to four Army groups to be dispersed internally in support of their "Home Guard" units."

"We'll have to watch their training and their disbursements, but we are already seeing signs of movement to training areas in the six combining Islamic nations that support these conclusions."

"With respect to their naval assets, we expect that they will be concentrated along their coast at the entrance to, and along, the Persian Gulf, with Pakistani units being stationed along the Arabian Sea in the vicinity of India. Although the total force is relatively small, the subs have us worried. It was bad enough having to worry about those three Kilos the Iranians had, but the Pakistanis have four or five very effective and modern diesel/electric boats in their inventory that we will have to be more concerned about now."

"A force of eight to ten diesel/electric subs could wreak havoc in the Persian Gulf, Mr. President if they ever got the mind to, particularly with the addition of any significant land-based air support out of Iran. They could shut the Gulf down and we would be obliged to go in and clean them out under very difficult circumstances, either from land bases in Saudi, Kuwait and Bahrain, or from carrier-based air."

"All in all, gentlemen, the combined arms of this emerging "Republic" will make them the 4th strongest conventional military force in the world. That puts them behind ourselves, the Russians and the People's Republic of China ... and with the financial and maintenance difficulties the Russian have been having, they could arguably be called the third strongest."

"Strategically, we already know Pakistan has nuclear capability and we have long suspected it of Iran ... if Pakistan joins in, then we will know for sure. In addition, Iraq is constantly on the verge. Bottom line is this: They have theater-capable missiles and doubtless will be able to hit Israel or any of our allies in the region. One of our major concerns is how the Israelis will react. The Pakistani installations are too numerous, and too distant, for Israel to expect to be able to pull off a conventional unilateral strike to take them out.

President Weisskopf was taking all of this in. It was pretty much as he suspected, but nonetheless extremely sobering to hear. In fact, everyone in the room was unsettled, from the Vice President on down. The long-standing and delicate stability that the west had maintained in the Middle East which was only maintained by playing rival Islamic factions off against one another, was being undone by Hasan Sayeed. This was extremely concerning to the President and all of his foreign policy team. In 2001 through 2003, in addition to the clear need for retribution for the terrible attacks on America of September 11, 2001, the message of Usama bin Laden, one of uniting Islam and doing it with terror, had been the compelling strategic reason for stopping him and his El Qaeda. The emerging Greater Islamic Republic provided an even more compelling strategic reason because of the unquestioned success in that unification that Sayeed was having. But Sayeed was not giving them any pointed reason to take action and he appeared poised to upset the entire balance of power in the Middle East. Thinking of this, and what such goals had produced back in 2001, took the president off on a tangent for a few minutes.

"Okay, I want to make sure that all of our security arrangements at the airports and on the flights remain in place, as well as what we are doing for other major infrastructure, water supply and power. I believe with Federal officers running airport security checks and with Marshals on the airplanes, that we have effectively curtailed terrorist attacks using our airlines. But what we have here is a situation where Islamic fundamentalists are coming to power on an unprecedented scale. Before we continue with the discussion regarding the GIR military capabilities, I want to ask Stewart to address our overall Homeland Security initiatives."

Stewart Langstrom had been appointed by the President to Direct the Office of Homeland Security. It was a new position still, having come into being in the wake of the 2001 terror attack, and was only the second person to ever fill the office. Stewart had been raised in the mid-west and was extremely conservative. He had served eight year in the US Army, rising to the rank of Captain. He'd been deployed in Desert Storm, but saw no combat as he led a logistics detachment that supplied materiel to the front. After his service, he had done well in business, running his own small textile business in St. Louis, before running for Congress in 1998. He had been there ever since, being given some fairly plum assignments on Defense and transportation committees, or at least until the General, President Weisskopf, had selected him to fill this position.

"Mr. President, my predecessor was very successful in getting the FAA to control and run airport security and in getting Air Marshals on every flight. As you know, there has not been another successful hijacking of a US airliner since that time. In addition, he worked with the Coast Guard, the National Directorate of the National Guard and with the fifty governors to establish security at our major infrastructure sites such as Hoover Dam, the Grand Coulee Dam and other sites inside our borders."

"Still, we have a long way to go. I am hoping to be able to implement security communications and procedures to the county level, such that the local county Sheriff's work with their own people to establish "Home Guard" units to watch the local infrastructure. There are many relatively small sub stations, dams and other sites that would have large impact on our nation if taken out. I would like to pattern the program after a successful grass-roots program already implemented in Idaho."

The head of FEMA, Curt Johnson, who was also attending, spoke up at this.

"Come on Stewart. you're talking about older men and boys who have no training trying to do a professionals job here. We may spend more money on false alarms and cleaning up after them than we would …"

Stewart didn't flinch. He felt Curt was competent, but also did not particularly like his "us or them" view of the civilian population, the people who paid for his salary.

"No, Curt, I am talking about having this thing controlled at the level it should be controlled, the local level. The Sheriff's know their people and they are the ones best suited to establish the small, volunteer units. If we went they way your tone is indicating, not only could we not afford it, but we would create far too many "Federal Police" interacting with the local people. They would resent it. This way, we have the people who are apt to have the most personal buy-in, involved in the protection of their own communities."

The President didn't want to get too side tracked. He particularly did not want Stewart and Curt clashing here. There were still too many "procedural" issues to clear up regarding command and control of the nation in the event of a wide scale national emergency. Under many executive orders, the head of FEMA accrued significant power in such a circumstance. The President was very committed to spreading that power around, as he felt it should be. Stewart would be one of those, along with the rest of his cabinet, who would lead in such a circumstance, having full executive powers centered on him, the President, also as it should be according to the Constitution. But those things were all in the works and could be handled at a different date.

"I like it Stewart. I'd like you to proceed in that direction, but lets make sure there are enough training dollars at least so that Curt's fears can be addressed. Something the Sheriff's can elect to use or not."

"Now, turning back to the principle topic we were discussing, and forgive me for sidetracking the meeting like that, but General, how quickly before the GIR can consolidate all of these personnel and equipment and become an effective force? The numbers are impressive, but we all know that the logistical and training challenges they face are enormous."

General Stone turned to the Director of the CIA and said.

"If I may Mr. President, let me allow Mike to answer that, as his assets are already in place and reporting on these very things. Mike?"

Mike Rowley looked up from his seat over on the far side of the table from General Stone.

"Mr. President, the fact is we have had people in many of these nations since the wall came down and the Soviet Union split up. We are weak in Iran, Afghanistan and Iraq, but have good assets in place in all of the others. What they are already telling us is troubling."

"Within ten days of the announcements, Iranian military advisors were in each of these nations. They are also already in Pakistan and there has not even been an announcement there yet. They are setting up a rigorous training program for the officers and senior non-commissioned officers that will then be rolled out to their troops in general. This program looks like an

Iranian version of a combined arms tactics course, and it emphasizes increased communications and mobility."

"In addition, they are setting up the training and military infrastructure to allow for fairly dynamic logistical flexibility. In the commercial, or at least non-military sector, we are seeing a similar ramp up in terms of preparing for the civil infrastructure to support this."

"Bottom line? Mr. President, we feel that within twelve months they are going to be fairly cohesive. Within twenty four months, if they continue on the path they are on right now, they will have strong mobility and logistic capability throughout their area of influence."

Fred Reisinger, the Secretary of State, interrupted at this point.

"Come on, Mike. Isn't this forecast a little aggressive? I mean we are talking about desert wasteland and terribly rough mountainous terrain. It would require an effort on their part that would be something equivalent to our effort to get to the moon. I can't believe they have the expertise, equipment or money to pull it off."

"Mr. Secretary, they certainly have the money … and money talks. In order to prevent the realization of this scenario, what we need is to convince our European allies, and even our own corporations, not to help the Islamic effort. We also need the necessary allied negotiations and understandings in place soon, or we need the necessary trade restrictions in place to prevent what you have described from coming to pass. Our major concern is that the Coalition of Asian States will decide to get involved in helping this from an infrastructure and construction standpoint. If that happens, then there may be very little we can do to prevent it."

The President interjected.

"That's exactly my concern, Jeremy. What we are seeing here is a tremendous shift in power and influence in Asia, the subcontinent and the Mid-East. It is one we have little hope of influencing or controlling unless we act very quickly to find some leverage or division that we can exploit and use to fracture it. Fred, Mike and John, we need some answers on this. If it builds up too much momentum, and if somehow this Greater Islamic Republic and the Coalition of Asian States get together … well, with Russia playing footsie with them, we could have a huge problem in Asia and the Mid East. I mean a HUGE problem."

Fred Reisinger had been thinking about just these things.

"Mr. President, I believe that the long-standing enmity between India and Pakistan is one of the keys in what you just mentioned. I believe that the friction between Iraq and Iran is the other one. There are enough ideological differences and long-term animosities in those areas right there, if we exploit them, to fracture this."

John Bowers, who had been quiet the entire meeting, now took this opportunity to speak up.

"I agree, Mr. Secretary. But, Mr. President, we are behind the eight ball on this. Things over there have taken on a life all their own. The religious unity that Hasan is bringing to both the Sunnis and Shias in all of these nations is unprecedented, and is breaking down those animosities. If we expect to capitalize on any of their historical differences, I believe from a diplomatic and economic standpoint we are going to have to do it in a hurry."

President Weisskopf nodded his agreement.

"I agree, John. Ok, here's what I would like to do. Alan, I'd like you to head up a working team with Fred, Mike and John to develop some options here in the next five to seven days. Let's plan to get back together on the 25th with the idea of deciding on some firm options in the diplomatic and economic areas that we can move forward with by the first of August. It's time we had a surprise "announcement" of our own, perhaps by the 28th. Alan, keep me apprised of the group's progress."

"Thank you all for attending, and thank you, Jeremy, for an excellent briefing."

July 18, 2005, 23:10 local
Private Presidential Quarters, The White House
Washington, D.C.

The First Lady, Linda Weisskopf, was sitting up in bed, reading an historical novel about colonial America, waiting for her husband.

"Norm, could you bring me a glass of ice water when you come to bed?"

President Weisskopf had been sitting in his lounge chair in the living room, winding down from the day somewhat, but still reviewing in his mind the developments in the Mid East and the Far East and how they were fitting together. He knew there was a "plan" and that the Chinese were somehow behind it ... but what was the end game?

"Sure, honey. I'm just getting up now and will be in there in just a second."

Linda loved her husband so much. No matter how high a level his career and capabilities had taken him to, he never forgot what she considered to be the "important things." Things like being willing, without question or reservation, to get a glass of ice water for his wife ... or taking walks along the river in the moonlight. She thought, "Norm Weisskopf is as capable a leader, thinker, strategist and warrior as his nation has probably ever produced, but he never lets it go to his head, and he never, ever forgets any of those who have helped him get there."

As the President handed his wife the ice water and then climbed into bed beside her, she sensed his continued unease.

"You're still worried about a potential Zenim/Sayeed alliance aren't you?"

Having discussed his apprehensions with her somewhat on the night of the WNN Special Report on Sayeed, and then again when the various surrounding Islamic nations announced their alignment with the "Greater" Islamic Republic, Norm Weisskopf was not surprised that his wife had taken note. He was also not the least bit surprised that she had pegged his continued and growing apprehension in that regard.

"Alliance? Perhaps not that strong. But am I worried about an alignment of convenience? Yes I am, very much so. Despite the unlikely nature of it, there are just too many unprecedented things happening, and I can't help but feel that they are not coincidental."

"Someone is going somewhere with this, and I believe somehow Jien Zenim and Red China are involved. I just can't put my finger on exactly where they are going. It's clear that our best interest are not a part of that equation, and I am feeling this urgent need to get those interests out front and center, and to make sure they are accounted for as this picture comes into focus."

Linda was not an expert on foreign policy or the strategy associated with all of the economic, diplomatic and military pieces that populated the game board in Norm's mind. She was, however, an expert on Norm. And she knew that, whether she understood the game or not, it was critical to have people like her husband who did understand it in leadership positions -- people who played the game with the understanding that "American interests" served as the game-piece that would not be sacrificed under any circumstances. It seemed to her that Norm was the first President squarely focused on those interests since the early 1980's, almost twenty-five years ago. She also knew that Norm had a basic religious faith, and that a higher power often guided his good heart through those feelings he experienced and the ideas that germinated as a result of them.

"Norm, listen to your heart and the feelings you've been blessed with. They have never led you astray. I believe they come from God."

"Also, listen to the good, honest people you have been impressed to surround yourself with. I have faith in you, honey. If anyone can see clearly how to keep the peace and maintain our nation's interests ... it's you. You're not in this position alone ... or by accident ... and we both know it."

The President regarded his wife's wisdom and forthrightness with awe on many occasions. This was one of those occasions.

"Thanks, sweetheart. What you say is true. I believe in my heart that America is guided by the hand of God. It's just difficult to keep that belief in perspective in the middle of a long day with so many issues mounting. ... Good night."

As he closed his eyes, and laid his head back into his favorite feather pillow ... and before sleep took him, he voiced this simple request in his mind.

"Dear Father, let Linda be right. Just point me ... I'll take it from there."

A few minutes later, Linda finished her small glass of water. She noticed that Norm's breathing had become deep and regular and he was asleep. As she set her book down and turned out the light, she uttered her own prayer.

"Please, Lord. Just show him the right direction ... he can take it from there and, with Your help, accomplish what needs to be done."

July 21, 2005, 02:10 local
Entrance Shanghai Harbor
Shanghai, PRC

The leading escort cut a fine line through the water as it entered Shanghai harbor. It was an updated Jiangwei frigate, the 540 Huainan, and

The Huainan runs toward Shanghai Harbor.

it entered the harbor first and feathered off to one side to stand as a sentinel for the procession that followed. Behind it, in a much tighter group than they had formed during the early evening hours, came three of the most modern and fastest container ships in the world.

The Shenzhen near Shanghai harbor.

Trailing them was a single Luhai guided missile destroyer, the 168 Shenzhen, bristling with modern weapons systems, sensors and two modern anti-submarine warfare (ASW) helicopters. One of those helicopters hovered near the mouth of the harbor as the convoy entered, using its dipping sonar to insure that no unwanted guests were lurking nearby.

As the Shenzhen loitered near the mouth of the harbor, the three container ships slowly moved towards their pre-assigned dry docks. By morning they would be secured in them.

What the ASW helicopter and the escorts did not pick up were the small surveillance devices anchored to the bottom of the harbor. As each of the Chinese ships maneuvered into the harbor, they passed over these devices that were hidden in the silent blackness 40-60 meters below. These were the MUAS devices that the SEAL team from the USS Jimmy Carter had 'planted' almost a month before. Each of them faithfully recorded the presence and movement of each ship that passed close enough to activate its sensors.

The same scenario played itself out several hundred miles to the north/northeast, as a similar convoy of two military escorts and three container ships entered the harbor at Tanjin. There, the faithful MUAS devices activated and recorded the presence and passage of each ship as well.

But what was not recorded by any American surveillance device were the other two, separate convoys that entered different harbors that night. Nor would any recording be made of the passage of convoys, over the next several weeks, into eight other harbors not covered by MUAS devices around the People's Republic of China.

Within twenty-four hours of the passage of the convoys, the first signal was transmitted from the ELF facilities stretching across Michigan to the MUAS devices in Shanghai and Tanjin harbors. That signal activated the release of the first communication buoys from each of the devices. The release occurred on a staggered, thirty-minute schedule between releases. This was a safeguard against detection by the Chinese as a result of too many devices communicating at once, even at the low power setting. Once the buoys reached the surface, they transmitted the information to the waiting satellite.

July 31, 2005, 10:45 local
WNN Broadcast Studios
New York City

"Summarizing then, our guest today on "Meet the Nation" has been Secretary of State, Fred Reisinger. Mr. Reisinger made two surprise announcements regarding diplomatic relations in the Mid East and in India."

"In a startling reversal of policy, the United States has announced that sanctions against Iraq would be lifted, indicating that this administration felt that fifteen years of such sanctions is enough. This is a tremendous irony as the President of the United States today is the General who defeated the Iraqis in Desert Storm of fifteen years ago."

"In an equally important announcement, the Secretary of State announced new proposals for economic, diplomatic and military initiatives with India. This is an announcement of great surprise coming so soon on the heels of the formation of the Coalition of Asian states by the People's Republic of China and India."

"Just how China will respond to the Indian initiative of the United States is yet to be seen. In addition, the reaction of the Greater Islamic Republic and its leader, Hasan Sayeed, is awaited with equal anticipation."

"Speaking of Hasan Sayeed, WNN is proud to announce that the Imam Sayeed's first western interview will be held by WNN's own David Krenshaw one week from tomorrow night at 7 PM EDT. As world events continue to unfold, we know our viewers will not want to miss such an important interview."

"Mr. Secretary, thank you for agreeing to appear on "Meet the Nation." We look forward to the press conference the President will hold regarding these announcements tomorrow. Now, as is our custom on "Meet the Nation," the last word is yours, Mr. Secretary."

From years of experience dealing with on-air interviews, Secretary Reisinger expertly turned and faced the active camera.

"Thank you. Let me just say that the United States is known for its willingness to help the peoples of the world, even its own adversaries, when they are faced with hardship and trial. Today, we have offered to do so with our former adversary, Iraq, hoping they will accept our outstretched hand and rejoin the family of nations."

"At the same time, the United States is known for its ability to enhance a nation's Gross Domestic Product (GDP) and standard of living through trade, technology exchanges and strong diplomatic ties. In the sub-continent region, it is past time that America strengthen its ties with the largest Republic in the world: India. With today's proposed initiatives, we have taken important steps to accomplish this alliance. We look forward to the opportunity to work with our friends in India to make it a reality."

As Secretary Reisinger finished, the host of WNN's "Meet the Nation" turned toward the camera and closed the show.

"Thank you, Mr. Secretary. Folks, that's all we have time for. This has been Sunday Morning's "Meet the Nation" on WNN. Thank you and good day."

July 22, 2005, 13:15 local
National Reconnaissance Office Headquarters
IMINT Directorate
Chantilly, VA

The signals from the MUAS devices were processed from the military satellite in gyro-synchronous orbit over the Philippine Sea and relayed to CINCPAC (Commander in Chief Pacific) naval headquarters in Hawaii for analysis. Simultaneously, they were transmitted to the Office of Naval Intelligence (ONI) in the Pentagon, and to the NRO offices in Virginia.

Tom Lawton had received the information almost an hour-and-a-half ago. He had been waiting for it impatiently. Once he received it, he immediately processed it into an analysis program he had written himself for this very purpose. The program had plotted the location of each MUAS device onto digital images of the two harbors. When the data was processed, the program would plot the tracks of any ships recorded by the devices that fit within the parameters of their sensor algorithms.

Tom Lawton was studying the printout of data from the recordings made early on the morning of July 21st.

"I believe we have something here, Bill. Looks like, that early on the morning of the 21st, we had convoys that appear to have been escorted by military vessels enter both Shanghai and Tanjin harbors. The ships they were escorting were large container ship varieties, and all of them moved immediately towards the dry dock facilities we have been observing at Shanghai and Tanjin."

Bill Hendrickson had assisted Tom in writing the analysis program through which Tom had just run the data. After taking in what Tom had said and considering it for a moment, he knew exactly what they needed to do with this information.

"Have you run that part of the data through the second stage analysis to identify the specific ship types?"

In fact, Tom had just submitted the data for analysis. Once something of interest was located using the initial portion of the program that plotted the time, location, size and basic type of ship, it could be run through a second analysis which compared the acoustical and electronic data against known signatures for various ships. The result of that analysis could deliver specific ship classes, and even the name and designation of each specific ship.

"I just entered it, Bill. Should have the results in a couple of minutes."

"Ok, here it comes now ... we're looking at a Jianwei frigate and a Luhai destroyer escorting three of ... what looks like their newer large container ships. Each of those container ships made for individual dry dock facilities in each harbor."

Bill Hendrickson considered this. Those dry dock facilities had been logistically set up for significant conversion and, from their prior surveillance and analysis, had significant underground storage areas for the materiel that would go into those conversions.

"This looks like it's developing into something significant. We need to continue to watch the satellite imagery, and maybe schedule more time if we see them doing anything to those container ships that could be remotely related to their naval air activities."

"Let's go ahead and document these findings as soon as possible. I'll set up a conference call with the Naval folks at CINCPAC and the ONI. I expect they will come to similar conclusions, but let's go through the motions to make sure. After that, it'll be time to get Mr. Bowers involved again and see where they want to take this."

"It'll be interesting to see what takes shape in those dry docks. Tom, I don't know why I didn't think of it before, but take the deck configuration from those airfields and overlay it on one of those container ships going into the dry docks up there at Tanjin. Let's see what we get."

CHAPTER 4

" He who sells his next life for his life in this world, loses both of them. " –
The Prophet

August 2, 2005, 14:00 local
Presidential Bunker Complex Number A312C
Outside of Baghdad, Iraq

Sahdam Hussein contemplated the meeting that was about to be held. Here, in one of his twenty-seven personal bunkers, fifty meters below the ground, more attacks on the Israelis, the "Little Satan," would be planned. Despite the best efforts of America, and despite their most recent overtures relaxing the long held sanctions against his country, Sahdam would continue funding and planning retribution and violence on the Jews who continued to occupy Palestine and who continued to persecute what he considered its rightful citizens, the Palestinians.

Today, Sahid Ibrahim, the operations officer for the Hamas, one of the principle organizations conducting operations against the Israelis on the West Bank, was meeting with Hussein and his military council. The word "Council" was not really accurate. Sahdam was his own council and these men simply carried out his wishes. The subject of today's meeting would be the funding of the next month's operations for the Hamas. Iraq funded these activities out of accounts which, if ever fully traced, would lead away from Iraq to Iranian off-shore commercial interests.

Sahdam Hussein trusted no one. He had survived for several decades as the absolute ruler in Iraq, surviving the very worst that any enemy had attempted against him, by being cunning, ruthless and completely thorough in his security arrangements.

Anyone gaining access to him had to pass through metal detectors, dogs trained to find explosives and a complete body search, including a thorough x-ray. At all times, when within fifty meters of the ruler, any visitor was covered by no less than three locked and loaded weapons. The guards carrying these weapons were prepared to defend Sahdam at all costs. They were extremely loyal to Sahdam due to their blood lines, their religious fervor, the promotions and favors that Sahdam had showered upon them ... and due to the imminent threat of death that hung over their entire families should there be even a suspicion of disloyalty.

Even those armed and primed guards, whose loyalty was thought completely secure, were themselves under the eye of other hidden and completely compartmentalized snipers whose loyalty was similarly insured.

All of these security arrangements were complemented by the system of twenty-seven presidential bunkers where the same measures were employed. Hussein alternated between each of these bunkers in his daily schedule on a completely random basis.

These multi-level security arrangements had served Sahdam well through attempted coups, attempted assassinations, the war with Iran and, his crowning security achievement in his eyes, the great Desert Storm that had pitted Sahdam and his forces against the Great Satan, America. In that war, seven of his bunkers had been destroyed by the American's specialized deep penetrating weapons. But Sahdam had not been there when any of those missiles had come calling. In fact, leaking where he "might" be had allowed him to ferret out his own traitors and security risks.

In truth, his greatest anxiety had been caused by the protracted "war on Terrorism" that the United States had conducted. During those years, he had spent prolong periods of time in the bunkers again. He had feared that the United States would discover his well-hidden involvement with supporting bin Laden in the initial attack on September 11, 2001. He had spent many sleepless nights expecting them to be his last. He had sanctimoniously and sarcastically offered the Americans "help" in searching through the rubble of their fallen financial symbols. He had feigned no knowledge and openly condemned the loss of innocent life ... while all the while fearing his involvement would be found out. But, somehow, Allah-be-praised, it had not come about and his security held up yet again, and he had survived.

That security held up because it was rigidly enforced. Today, after they were cleared for access to meet with Sahdam, Ibrahim and his aid would not be allowed to bring their own pens, pencils, notebooks or any other article to the meeting. Despite the fact that Sahdam had known Sahid for over fifteen years and had planned many "operations" with him, security could never be compromised or taken for granted.

"No," Sahdam thought, "I have not survived the best attempts of the Americans by being lax on security measures." To date those measures had allowed him to outlive and out-rule all those who had opposed him, including three American Presidents ... and he felt certain they would continue to do so today.

But he was wrong.

Sahdam took notice of the movement at the door. As he watched, Sahid and his aid were brought into the conference room. As the door was closed, Sahdam rose and greeted his longtime compatriot from the head of the table.

Sahdam watches Sahid enter

"Is-salaam maleekum , my brother, keef Haalak ."

Sahid returned the classic Arab greeting as he was guided towards his chair.

"Wa maleekum is-salaam, il-Hamdulillaah!!"

As he was moving towards his seat, Sahid took note of his surroundings. There were ten armed guards in the room, his own aid, eight of Iraq's military council, and, of course, Sahdam. Sahid thought for a moment about his mission and all of the planning that had gone into it ... all of the faith that was vested in it. The truth was, he had always thought highly of Sahdam and the efforts he made to stand up to the west in general, and the Americans in particular.

But, despite this admiration, over the years it had become clear to Sahid, that little if any progress was being made in the holy cause of Islam. In fact, Sahid had become convinced that the Great Satan was using Sahdam. They were using his threats and potential for regional instability to keep the Israelis strong and to keep their own people and industries focused, united, against Islam and blinded to the travails of his people.

Although Sahid had firmly come to these conclusions, until recently he had felt that these difficulties were Allah's will, and he was content to await the hand of Allah in showing how they should fight their enemies more effectively. That "hand," and the long-anticipated answer for Sahid, had finally come in the form of the great Imam Hasan Sayeed.

Faithful Arabs in many countries were calling him the "Great Uniter," the modern messenger of Allah. Sahid believed he was the 12th Imam who had returned to lead Islam to victory over the infidels. Sahid was prepared to sacrifice his all, his very life, to help insure that victory. Right now, that victory required Iraq to join with the Greater Islamic Republic for a mighty Jihad against the unfaithful, and then against their enemies. But Sahdam Hussein had chosen to place his own thirst for power and prestige over the will of Allah, and this self-aggrandizing behavior was thwarting the growth of the Greater Islamic Republic.

This state of affairs could not be allowed to continue.

As he was taking his seat, Sahid thought about the carefully-scripted role he would play over the next few minutes in bringing Islam together, and how what he was about to do would insure his own entry into the great paradise of God. His aid, a good and valiant defender of the faith, would join him there, though the aid was completely oblivious to what was about to happen.

As he dragged his chair up to the mahogany conference table, Sahid began to put pressure on the lower back molars on each side of his jaw. Those molars had been filled and crowned years ago and were taken for granted by the security detachments in Sahdam's facilities. After all, they had seen them on their x-ray machines many times.

Three days before coming to Iraq, the crowns covering those two molars had been removed and the fillings drilled out and filled with small, pressurized cartridges that were coated with the same material from which the fillings were made. The crowns had been replaced, but not glued in. By exerting the right pressure, Sahid could remove the crowns and activate the pressurized gas within each cartridge.

By the time Sahid was seated comfortably at the conference table, he had already removed the crowns with practiced precision. After Sahdam had finished with the introduction, which consisted of his normal railings against Israel and America, he invited Sahid to stand and speak concerning the plans that were to be the object of the meeting.

Sahid stood and looked around the room. He took a deep breath and then, to everyone's complete astonishment, he uttered the following words:

"Sahdam Hussein, on behalf of the United States of America, I find you guilty of murder and war crimes!"

At the mention of the "United States," "guilty" and "war crimes," the guards began to bring their weapons to bear on Sahid. But it was too late. A small cloud of mist erupted from Sahid's mouth and shot towards Sahdam, while diffusing around the room. It was a mist filled with an extremely toxic nerve gas that did not have to be inhaled to produce its deadly effects. It was absorbed into the body upon contact with the skin of the victim.

Even as the subsonic bullets from the guards standing behind Sahid began to rip into his body, the first tiny particles of the mist began to fall upon Sahdam Hussein's exposed face and arms. In an effort to avoid the gas, Sahdam had thrown up his arms to protect his face and fallen back in his chair, but the desperate action proved futile.

Sahdam rolled back in his chair in shocked surprise. A stunned silence fell over the room as Sahid's lifeless body thudded to the floor. Looking around the room, a wry smile appeared on Sahdam's face for an instant as he thought there would be no ill effect from the mist ... but the instant was fleeting.

Suddenly a terrible, almost animal-like scream erupted from Sahdam's throat. His entire body began to writhe in horrific spasms and convulsions as the nerve agent began to destroy his central nervous system. Over a few seconds, the spasms, the convulsions ... and the screams ... got worse, much worse. Similar screams began to erupt from all around the room as others began to experience the same effects.

Two of the guards standing in the back of the room, and three of the council members who were sitting in the back, were quick-witted enough to exit the room at the first hint of any untoward action and with the gunfire. They were able to do so before any of the expanding and diffusing mist particles touched their skin. They proved to be the only survivors.

As the shocked guards who were monitoring the audio and video feed watched, the hapless victims thrashed around in unbelievably violent contortions as their spasms worsened. Horribly, three or four audible "cracks" were heard as convulsions wracked the spinal cords of the victims into unnatural backward aches...so unnatural that their spines literally "snapped." The screams were beyond description; the sight beyond imagination ... and, ironically, every minute of the grotesque human horror was recorded in full by Hussein's own audio and video security equipment.

Within five minutes it was over. All sixteen individuals who remained in the room were dead and sprawled about the room in a most grotesque manner. The five who had gotten out were not allowed to exit the outer room to the conference center for many hours.

Iraqi toxicologists, scientists, medical doctors and investigators would carefully analyze the scene, while protected by full bio-chemical suits, for several days before declaring the room safe for unprotected humans. Eventually they would discover the cartridges in Sahid's mouth from which the gas had erupted. Upon performing a microscopic examination of each of these cartridges, astonishingly, they would find the following letters stenciled on the side of each in tiny script: "MANF. TO US MIL SPEC – 0602."

In addition, the Iraqi investigators, and later independent investigators, would find clear forensic evidence that Sahid's fingerprints had been medically altered. The Iraqis surmised that this had been done with a technology and precision that could only have originated in the west, and which was reserved for the highest level clandestine operatives.

August 2, 2005, 20:00 local
Islamic Republic Government Offices
Tehran, Iran

Minister Sadiq Shiraziha gently knocked on the door to Imam Sayeed's personal office. After a moment or two, during which Sadiq waited patiently, knowingly, he heard Hasan give him permission to enter.

As Sadiq entered the room, Hasan rose from where he had been praying. After exchanging Arabic greetings, Hasan spoke.

"I take it there is news out of Iraq?"

Respectfully waiting for his Imam to make his way to his desk and be seated there, Sadiq then answered.

"Yes, Imam. We have received word. Operation Zakat has been successfully completed. President Sahdam Hussein is dead. Our operatives report that five of his eight ruling military council died with him, along with a number of personal guards. Sahid Ibrahim and his aid were also amongst the dead. God rest their souls."

Hasan thought about the guards and some of the military council in Iraq. Some of those men had been faithful Muslims and would now be with Allah in paradise. A special place was surely reserved there for the faithful and patriotic Sahid.

Hasan also thought of the years of effort on Hussein's part to fight the west and unite Islam. Of course, the principle reasons had always been for the advancement of Hussein himself. It was actually quite tragic that Hussein's ambitions had overshadowed his faith.

"Allah be with Sahid and all of the faithful who entered into paradise today.
"

"Their sacrifice has not been in vain.   Today, with his great act of martyrdom, I believe that the faithful servant Sahid Ibrahim did more for the cause of Islam and its unification, than all of the combined acts of the great Ayatollahs of the past hundred years.   I say this with no disrespect whatsoever meant for those faithful servants."

"But, we must move on.   Sadiq, what of the political and civil situation within Iraq in the aftermath of Hussein's death?"

Sadiq reflected just a moment as he recollected the communiqués and conversations to which he had been privy during the last several hours.

"Imam, as instructed, our agents in the Iraqi Foreign Ministry have announced Hussein's death to the world, along with the allegations regarding the West.   A video of the entire incident that was made as a standard security procedure, has been released.   It will be the major news story in the west in their afternoon editions and their evening news."

"As for the local, civil situation in Iraq: surprisingly, on the streets there is little chaos, and much celebration, amongst the common citizens.   This is perhaps as clear an indication as one could imagine of the true feelings of the people towards Sahdam.   Despite this apparent ambivalence, at best, towards Sahdam's death, as the implications regarding the west are finding voice, there are many anti-western demonstrations forming."

"There is also some indication that Hussein's ruling party and the surviving council are trying to consolidate power.   But our efforts amongst the people are already producing significant progress in developing a popular movement to join the Greater Islamic Republic and face the West in solidarity.   I believe our people in the Foreign Ministry and mounting public pressure will give us the opportunity we need, within the next few days, to formally offer a proposal for alignment, in order to calm the situation and prevent anarchy, chaos and further bloodshed."

Hasan was pleased.   Allah's will for a unified Islam was pressing forward. It would press forward through all obstacles, both those thrown in its path by the infidels as well as by the unfaithful.

"Excellent.   Keep me informed of the developments, Sadiq.   Perhaps I can make this announcement during the upcoming WNN interview.   It would

136

come just two days after the Pakistani announcement and would serve to keep the West all the more off balance."

"Though I have been troubled by the recent efforts of the Americans with respect to Pakistan and Iraq ... those efforts have been seen for what they are, very transparent and belated attempts to divide a solidarity that is blessed by Allah and growing rapidly."

"Nonetheless, it is indicative that the American leadership is awakening to what is happening around them. I believe that the reality of a united Islamic Republic stretching from Syria to the Himalayas will quickly remove any remaining sleep from their eyes. We will have to proceed carefully once they begin to see things clearly."

August 3, 2005, 07:50 Local
News Stand, Central Park
New York City

Herald Post   Special Edition
Sahdam Hussein Assassinated!
Iraqis Blame United States CIA Operation
Video of Assassination Released
Baghdad, Iraq   August 2, 2005

(UIP) In horrific detail, the death of Iraqi leader Sahdam Hussein, a longtime adversary of the United States and Israel, was captured on video yesterday as it occurred in one of the deceased leader's Presidential Bunker facilities. The stunning video captured the final words of the assassin, a terrorist leader in the Hamas organization, which preceded the death. These words, and other alleged circumstances surrounding the killing, have led the Iraqi Foreign Minister to blame America and the CIA for the assassination.

The statement by the terrorist, "Sahdam Hussein, on behalf of the United States of America, I find you guilty of murder and war crimes!" preceded the release of an unknown mist from the speaker's mouth. This mist, which spread throughout the room, killed Sahdam and many members of his ruling military council who were present at the time. The Hamas leader was shot and killed by Iraqi guards before the effects of the mist resulted in the other deaths. Experts speculate that the mist was some for of nerve gas.

"Extra, Extra ... read all about it! Sahdam Hussein assassinated! Iraqis blame the CIA! Get yours news here ... Extra, Extra ... read all about it! Sahdam Hussein assassinated! Iraqis blame the CIA! Get your news here!"

Amazingly, in an era of almost instant news gratification via the internet, email, connected wireless phones and Palm computers ... tens of thousands of people were flocking to the newsstands to pick up their copy of the Special Edition news print.

... and this was not just occurring in America, where the passing of the longtime adversary and enemy was greeted with a surprised relief ... and with a question of what now would become of Iraq. Newspaper stands all over the world were swamped with people anxious to "read all about it." Web sites which carried the story experienced unprecedented traffic. Online newspapers and news service sites were so overloaded that some of their servers could not effectively handle the increased load.

Everywhere, the world held its collective breath, wondering what would occur as a result of the death of Sahdam Hussein. Everywhere, people sensed that great changes in political and ideological alignments were afoot in the world.

In the Arab world, outside of his ruling party and many of the Palestinians, Sahdam had been more feared than liked. Nonetheless, the prospect of a potential assassination of an Arab leader by a western power generated animosity, mass demonstrations and calls for independent investigations.

In the West and Far East there had been more concern about Sahdam's unpredictable and uncivilized nature than respect for his leadership skills. Yet, despite his infamy, people had recognized him as a Mid East icon. His absence, for good or ill, created a vacuum ... and nature abhors vacuums. Inevitably, the void created by Hussein's death would be filled by something as yet unknown....

August 3, 2005, 14:20 Local
White House Press Briefing
Washington, D.C.

"In closing, let me assure you all, that under NO circumstances did the United States government or any of its agencies take part in, plan, or in any way instigate the assassination of Sahdam Hussein. The United States viewed Sahdam Hussein as a rogue leader and an adversary who took advantage of, and persecuted, his own people ... and who was a threat to the peace and stability in the entire Middle East. But, not even under such circumstances does the United States condone assassination as a means of promoting or realizing global political stability."

"If we had a mind to target Hussein, we would have accomplished it during war-time conditions fifteen years ago … and if you remember, I was personally involved with those events. Believe me when I tell you, we could have gotten the job done at that time, had it been our desire."

President Weisskopf looked at the sea of hands that were immediately and impatiently raised as he completed his statement. The chorus began at once.

"Mr. President! Mr. President!"

"Bill."

"Thank you, Mr. President. What is the United States response to the video of the assassination in which the killer specifically referenced the United States.?"

President Weisskopf had asked a similar question earlier in the day of his own advisors, particularly Mike Rowley, Director of the Central Intelligence Agency. The answer had satisfied him, but the explanation offered for public consumption had to remain less forthright for the time being.

"Until we have a chance to analyze this video in detail, and until more information is forthcoming, we will withhold our comment. However, I can once again reiterate that the United States had nothing to do with this."

"Mr. President! Mr. President!"

"Judy."

"Mr. President. You indicated that our government had nothing to do with this assassination. Yet how can you reassure the people that our government is being forthright? In light of past activities, both domestic and international, from presidential activities to the activities of law enforcement and the military, the government has been caught lying time and again. How can the American people believe you, Mr. President?"

Norm Weisskopf did not like having his honor or his integrity called into question. He had learned a long time ago at West Point to personally maintain nothing but the highest standards in this regard. It was an integral part of his character. And one he took seriously.

"Judy, I am not one of the former Presidents to which you refer. My own military record and stance on the issue of integrity is open to the public and well documented. A government that will directly lie to its people in an effort to cover wrong or illegal activity, is a government not worthy to rule a free people."

"I will say it again: the United States had nothing to do with this assassination. ... Now, final question."

"Mr. President! Mr. President!"

"John."

"Mr. President. You have repeated several times, with great emphasis, that the United States had nothing to do with this incident. Can you tell me this, sir ... is the United States government ... or are you personally glad that Sahdam Hussein is dead?"

"Ah! Now there is a fifty-dollar question," thought President Weisskopf ... "How to answer?"

"Well, John, let me just put it to you this way. If there is a half inch thorn stuck in my foot and causing me great pain ... I would be very glad for the thorn to get pulled out and thrown in the trash, without ever bearing the thorn itself any animosity. I hope that helps you understand my personal position on this matter."

"Thank you, and good day."

August 5, 2005, 10:35 Local
Office of the President
New Delhi, India

"Mr. President, the People's Republic of China has every intention of insuring the peace between the United States and the Greater Islamic Republic (GIR) once Pakistan carries out its intention of uniting with the GIR We are willing to sign a treaty with all involved parties to that effect at any time you would desire."

"In addition, we are hoping that at some date in the near future our peoples in the PRC, the GIR and India will come together in an even greater coalition, despite any religious or ideological differences, and in the spirit of the Three Wisdoms. Such an alignment would affect an economic and political coalition that would rival anything the west can put together. Can you imagine it? Having the economy, the buying power, the influence to challenge the United States or the European Union on our own terms, eye to eye, without the need to blink at all?"

President KP Narayannen of India listened with respect to what Li Peng had to say. He knew that Li was President Jien Zenim's closest advisor and spoke for him. He knew that the coalition that he and Jien had announced and implemented was surpassing their economic and political aspirations. Now it was time to invite others to the table ... but the Pakistanis? Could it be true that Hasan Sayeed had so much influence that he could break down those barriers? More importantly, does Jien Zenim believe that he possesses both the necessary trust, and the necessary power, to be able to incorporate Hasan and his minions into his overall plans?

"I believe we will avoid a direct "military" alliance or commitment at this time, Minister Li. However, we are open to expanding the CAS. At the same time, we are concerned about the growing power of the GIR, particularly now that it will be moving to our borders by encompassing Pakistan. Although a nation's name may change, the old rivalries and animosities are still there and are difficult to forget about."

"Still, we feel that we are strong enough to preserve the peace on our own borders and will wait to see how the GIR conducts itself. Becoming a member of the CAS, and committing to the economic and social principles that form its basis, would be an initial step in the right direction, and one we would welcome ... albeit, as I say, due to historical precedence, it is a step of which we would be wise to remain somewhat wary."

"Inasmuch as the PRC is working with us in the CAS towards our mutual goals, we would welcome your efforts as an arbitrator from a diplomatic standpoint with any issues that arise that we cannot mutually resolve."

Li Peng sensed some of the reservation, and had to admit that there was good historical precedent for it. At the same time, he knew that his leader's goals and directions in this regard were critical ... and explicit. The latest US efforts to keep the wedge driven deep between Pakistan and India could not be allowed the slightest prospect of success.

"President Narayannen, allow me to address a critical point, and, with your pardon, let me do so very directly. What of the recent overtures by the United States, and their attempts to draw India away from our developing CAS relationship?"

President Narayannen considered this point carefully. He and his advisors had discussed this very subject in great detail. Some were for opening their arms to the Americans. An alliance with the United States was something many in India had wanted for a long time.

But others, Narayannen included, argued that America's attention was not sincere. They argued, quite convincingly, that American overtures had occurred only as a result of shifting economies and balances which appeared to threaten them. In short: America was fickle, and could not be relied upon.

The counter to this had been that the new administration under Weisskopf was strong, and could be trusted. But the inevitable response to that argument had been that the Reagan administration, too, was a strong and trustworthy one ... and look at what had followed a few short years later.

"Minister Li, we have discussed this in detail in our cabinet meetings. We feel that the American overtures are insincere. We are very happy with, and committed to, our CAS responsibilities and agreements. We view the CAS, and its basis in social equity, to be in the best long-term interests of the people of India."

"Having said that, we will take advantage of any offers the Americans make that do not hamper or interfere with those long-term commitments and responsibilities to the CAS. We will insure that the Americans understand this, and if they wish to make equitable trade agreements and concessions to us in spite of it ... well, we would be foolish to not take advantage of them."

"But, please be sure convey to President Jien in no uncertain terms our commitment to the CAS and to the plans he and I have discussed for the last several years."

This is what Li had hoped to hear. The Indians were not buying the American plans, and with the announcement by Pakistan's General Musharraf on August 7th, now only two days away, it would be clear to the world that the Pakistanis weren't buying them either.

"I will certainly convey that message to President Jien. I know he will be gratified to hear of it. On behalf of President Jien, and on behalf of the People's Republic of China, I offer my thanks for your hospitality and your commitment. May the success, well-being and prosperity of our peoples remain linked through such bonds of friendship and commitment to social equity."

August 7, 2005, 13:35 Local
National Security Council Pressroom
Islamabad, Pakistan

General Pervez Musharraf looked out over the assembled news reporters, heads of state and their representatives, his own eight-member National Security Council and the many others who had been invited to hear this announcement. They were all waiting expectantly in the large pressroom. The announcement he was about to make had been discussed by him and the Security Council (every member of which he had personally appointed after his military coup seized government power in 1999) for many weeks. Every possible angle had been debated.

There was no doubt that Hasan Sayeed represented the best opportunity for Islamic unification since the Prophet himself. The trouble with this was that it was so obvious, and had been discussed so much, that the people themselves knew it and were demanding it.

This left the General in a quandary. He had been successful in his coup. He had successfully played the competing western, eastern and religious influences against one another … even during the Americans terror war that had placed him in such a tenuous position and caused such upheaval. In the process, he had demonstrated to the world the new nuclear capability the Pakistanis had obtained in response to the Indians. He had been able to modernize his military with both American and Chinese hardware. And he had, at least from his perspective, improved the standard of living for many of his people in the process. But the quandary was that the people were now looking to Hasan and not to him.

Trying to walk a tightrope between the competing ideological influences of the west and east had been a dangerous game and a "touch and go" proposition for his governmental position. To go against the will of the Islamic people in his Islamic nation could prove fatal to him personally … he took note of the demise of Sahdam Hussein with special interest in this regard. The various news media around the world might buy into the propaganda regarding the cause of Sahdam's death, but General Musharraf knew better.

Contemplating this precarious situation caused the General to realize again that he had little choice in the matter. He placed his hands on either side of the podium, looked directly into the camera, and began.

"Today we in Pakistan make an historic announcement to add to those of the last several months. We of the National Security Council of Pakistan have reviewed the growth of the Greater Islamic Republic with growing interest and excitement. The prospect of a unified Islam has touched our hearts and our spirits. It is truly the dream of ages ... but one that cannot be contemplated lightly or without serious reflection."

"Therefore, we have spoken with, counseled with and negotiated with the leaders of the GIR, and with Imam Hasan Sayeed himself, over the last many weeks. We have considered the impact of a unified Islam on our people, their security, their potential for growth and prosperity and their physical, social and spiritual well-being. As a result, we have made an important decisions on behalf of our people which we wish to announce today."

"First, we are convinced that Hasan Sayeed represents a true Imamate for all Islamic people. Today we recognize him as such and proclaim to all true believers everywhere that they should similarly consider the meaning of this reality for themselves."

"Second, we announce today the alliance and merging of the Islamic Republic of Pakistan with the Greater Islamic Republic. It is the will of the people. It is the will of Allah ... we can but follow."

"The details of the agreement between Pakistan and the Greater Islamic Republic are provided in the packages you have been given. These same details will be voted on by the people in a national referendum on September 1st. We expect the agreement to be overwhelming approved by the people of Pakistan and will proceed diplomatically on that basis from this date."

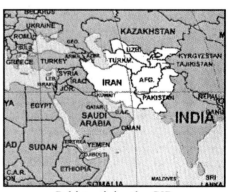

Pakistan joins the GIR

"This completes the announcement. There will be no questions."

August 7, 2005, 09:35 Local
Oval Office, The White House
Washington, D.C.

"OK Fred, let's hear it."

The Secretary of State, understanding full well the gravity of the developing situation, began his comments.

"Mr. President, the unification announcement by Musharraf will create a serious situation in the region. Not only does it significantly add to the size, influence and overall capability of the Greater Islamic Republic, but it exasperates an already delicate situation in the Kashmir bordering India."

"Our efforts regarding India are making progress. They have made clear to us their intent to remain committed to the CAS, but the fact that they are willing to conduct and accept some trade and diplomatic negotiations indicates a potential for making inroads into that commitment. In addition, I believe they want to "hedge their bets" in terms of continued awareness of the growing threat across their eastern border. I believe, if we play our cards right, we can make progress with India and perhaps create a wedge in the CAS, and any potential for development of the CAS with the GIR."

Tim Hattering listened with increasing concern. He believed that the Pakistani announcement was an unmitigated disaster and he could not stand by while it was soft-pedaled to his President.

"Excuse me for the interruption, Fred, but wait just a minute. This thing with Pakistan is a disaster! We have sunk hundreds of millions of dollars, maybe billions, into Pakistan's military hardware and into the research that led to their nuclear capability. Now, all of that, every damn penny of it, is in the hands of a fundamentalist Islamic state that has sponsored terrorism against the United States, and has made its intent clear regarding all of the Middle East. Sooner or later that is going to mean an abject threat to our friends and our own strategic interests in the area."

"The CAS is an equal threat and I appreciate our efforts diplomatically with India to undercut it. But, I am more interested in the immediate threat and ramifications of the ideological and military impact of Pakistan being gobbled up by the GIR. I thought our efforts with India and Pakistan were supposed to help prevent this very thing."

Fred Reisinger was not swayed by Tim's outburst. In fact he had expected it. There was no doubt that the military implications of the growing GIR were weighing heavily on the minds of military leaders around the world.

"Tim, let me remind you that in our last meeting we discussed this very eventuality. We have only had a short amount of time to dissuade and prevent something that appeared to be on the verge of happening anyway. If you remember, General Stone indicated that GIR "advisors" were already on the ground in Pakistan. No, our best bet with respect to Pakistan and the GIR is to keep India nervous and looking to us for help if at all possible."

"But, let's jump to the GIR and talk about that. The Iraqi situation has me very concerned. We are trying to influence Saudi Arabia, Turkey and Syria, but everyone is nervous. The GIR influence is growing and right now, Iraq has almost gone into a state of abject anarchy. There is little we can do diplomatically there at this point. What little political infrastructure remains believes we are guilty of murdering Sahdam."

As President Weisskopf listened, he realized that the unease he had been feeling since before his initial meeting with Jien Zenim of China had continued to grow. It was like an ever-present mole eating away beneath the surface. If you weren't careful, you'd step in a hole and fall and break a leg, or worse yet, eventually the complete foundation of your entire surface world would be undermined and lead to a massive collapse. That's how the President felt as international conditions continued to deteriorate.

"Fred, or Mike, what is the likelihood of any group in Iraq allowing us to help them come to power?"

Fred Reisinger was aghast.

"Mr. President, from a diplomatic standpoint, I have to advise against such a course of action. If we blatantly help any group in Iraq, it will be viewed as an admission of guilt with respect to Sahdam's death."

"Fred, they already think we are responsible for it, and things are going to hell in a hand basket. We cannot afford to allow the GIR to occupy Iraq, and I promise you, that is where this is headed. I wish to God that my own National Command Authority (NCA) would have allowed me to finish this job fifteen years ago, but it was not my call and we can't cry over it now. I am not going to make the same mistake."

"At the same time, I understand we cannot just waltz in there and take over Iraq. I am going to need your help, Fred, to assist me with the Saudis and the Turks especially, so whatever options we have can be accomplished with their support. What about it, Mike? Is there anyone we can work with over there? What about the Kurds?"

Mike Rowley had been polling his CIA assets for days. He had a pretty good picture of the conditions, and the prospects weren't good.

"Mr. President, unfortunately, the Kurds in the North of Iraq and the groups in the south are completely wary of us. Most of this is due to what you just alluded to. We gave them the "green light" fifteen years ago to go after Sahdam and implied we would help. Then we stood back and watched while the army we had just defeated slaughtered them. I can have our folks try, but there is little prospect for success, and tremendous prospect for losing those very people."

President Weisskopf never took his command authority and its potential for mortal impact on those he commanded lightly. But he couldn't shake the feeling … no, the almost sure knowledge, that this entire affair was getting away from them. If they allowed it to do so, the consequences could be much more deadly than even he wanted to contemplate. He simply would not allow the realization of such a scenario.

"I know Mike, but this is one time we are going to have to risk it. Tell our own people to get ready to earn some hazardous duty pay and have the contacts we maintain on the ground in Iraq make the effort."

"John, what's the opinion of the NSA regarding the impact of Iraq coming under the GIR? Give me a best case and a worse case scenario from your people's analysis."

John Bowers had been busier than at any point in his life. The planning sessions with respect to his own combat involvement in Desert Storm had been a cake walk compared to trying to keep up with the CAS and GIR developments and their potential impacts. But he and his people had made the effort, and they had good people in all branches of the military helping them.

"Mr. President, the best case is that everyone in the region is made extremely nervous and that the influence of the GIR is used to impact oil prices, production and delivery to our detriment."

"The worst case is that the GIR continues to grow and that other Islamic states continue to come under their influence to the point where we are totally pushed out of the Mid East."

This what just about what the President had expected, though having it put in those clear, stark terms was like a slap in the face.

"John, let's continue down this path. What is our dependence on Mid East oil at this point, and how long would our strategic reserves last if our Mid East supply were cut off?"

"Mr. President, since we began drilling off the west coast, and added more drilling in Alaska under the last administration, we have cut the dependence down to about 30%, but we are still very reliant on them. Without those measures from the last administration, the current situation would be much more bleak. Even so, my analysis indicates that with no Mid East oil, but continued production from other sources, our ninety-day emergency reserve could be stretched to about six months."

Six months in normal, peacetime circumstances. It's not enough, but is all he could hope for. Clearly, in a wartime scenario, those numbers could only be stretched one way. Turning now towards his Federal Emergency Management Director, the head of FEMA, Curt Johnson, the President said:

"You all know Curt. I asked him to attend this meeting today specifically because I feared these types of developments. Curt, I want you to work with John Bowers and write up and Executive Order (EO) for me to sign which will accomplish the following:

1) I want to be able to quickly treat our energy supply situation as a National Emergency and allow the government to restrict consumption by government agencies and establish quotas for non-critical agencies.

2) I want to open up to petroleum exploration and production all Federal Lands that any of my Executive Agencies manage.

3) I want the Department of Energy to relax requirements on the construction of nuclear power plants. Make it so that they must only adhere to the Nuclear Construction Code at the date of approval of construction only, as opposed to having to retrofit construction to newer codes whole the plant is being built. This act alone will spur the Bechtels and Brown and Roots to immediately look at building more plants here in this country..

"Please have such an order on my desk prepared to be signed within five days. I hate to say this, and it can go no further than this room, but what is taking shape here could well turn into as great a crisis to our nation and its interests as anything since the second world war. It is time we began putting in place some preparations in that regard."

"Tim and General Stone, please work with our friends in Kuwait to arrange for a "training exercise" involving two additional wings of F-15E strike eagles, a Marine Expeditionary Unit (MEU) and all of the logistical support necessary to maintain them there for a six month period at least."

At this point, Curt Johnson spoke up.

"Excuse me for the interruption Mr. President, but while I understand the need for the provisions in the EO for the restrictions and quotas for governmental agencies, why is there nothing in your instructions for the private sector? That is where the vast bulk of the utilization lies. Unless we curb usage there, we will buy very little."

President Weisskopf had expected such a question. The measures he was taking were necessary, but many in government felt that their "duty" would be to extend such provisions to the public. But Norm Weisskopf knew the limits of his powers, and he had taken an oath to abide by them.

"Curt, I am only going to say this once, and I want all of you in this room to understand it completely. We are the servants of the people, not their masters. Our duties and powers are very explicitly laid out in a training manual we all took an oath to bear true faith and allegiance to. It's called the Constitution. I intend to do just that: bear true faith and allegiance to it, so help me God, even when the going gets tough."

"The reason I do not include such provisions in my executive order is that I have no power or authority to do so. I would be violating my oath of office to presume to do so ... irrespective of whatever "Acts" congress has passed, or whatever rulings the Court has made. Simply put, they cannot pass and act, or make a ruling, that supercedes the Constitution any more than I can write an order that does so ... and have it be legitimate. If it's not legitimate, it's illegal and a violation of our oath of office."

"This EO will be preparatory. It is a "just in case," which will allow us to be better prepared as a government should things get worse. If they do, at that time we will work with the governors, the Congress and with the people to extend such provisions as necessary, but we will do it according to what the Constitution dictates. We will not become, in any way, shape or form, suppressors of individual freedom ourselves, irrespective of the bad precedent established by prior administrations. Is that understood? Is that understood by everyone in this room?"

As Curt responded in a quick affirmative, and as everyone else in the room did likewise, John Bowers glanced over to General Jeremy Stone and both men gave one another a knowing, but barely perceptive, nod. John and General Stone both felt, at that moment, that whatever else happened, a real American patriot and hero was in the saddle for this ride, regardless of how rough it got. They would spread the word through the ranks that the "Old Man" had what it took to see them through.

August 9, 2005, 17:00
Presidential Offices
Tehran, Greater Islamic Republic

As the red light flashed and David knew that they were back on the air after the commercial break, he continued.

"Welcome back. We are here in Tehran conducting an exclusive live interview with Imam Hasan Sayeed. We have discussed his roots and education. We have discussed his military experiences during the war with Iraq and his amazing exploits during those years... exploits which established Hasan's bravery and remarkable leadership skills."

"We have discussed his rise in power and influence within Iran and his ultimate recognition as Imam by the Iranian clerics and Ayatollahs. Finally, in the last segment, we discussed with the Imam the amazing growth of the Islamic Republic. Now, Imam Sayeed, we would like to discuss current events and ask for your perceptions regarding them. Let us start with the Coalition of Asian States. What are your views and intentions towards that unprecedented and developing influence?"

Hasan felt that the interview was going extraordinarily well. This American, while clearly in love with himself and his perceived influence, was giving Hasan every opportunity to tell his own story and relate things from his own perspective, just as Li Peng had indicated he would when the interview had been suggested by Li on behalf of Jien Zenim.

"Well, David, the CAS is, as you indicate, an unprecedented coalition. Who would have thought that, with their past differences, the Indian Republic and the People's Republic of China would have bridged their gaps and created such an alignment? But, on the other hand, when one reflects on the basis for that agreement, namely the Three Wisdoms, it is not so unlikely or unprecedented as one would think."

"All men and women are equal."
"All share equally in the bounty of a working and industrious society."
"One goal, one thought, one people for World peace."

"These are tenets that much of your own nation's amazing productivity, longevity and success have been based upon. Is it so surprising then that other nations who embrace these philosophies are also successful?"

"As to the intent and views of the Greater Islamic Republic regarding the CAS, we welcome on our borders a coalition that embraces such views. Islam embraces many similar views. The Prophet taught us that we should treat others as we would be treated; that we should look to do good and not evil. Equality, sharing and peace are all good things that we should all seek. The Greater Islamic Republic can live in peace with any people who truly seek these things."

David Krenshaw had been amazed throughout the interview at how smooth and well-spoken Hasan was. He continued to have that impression.

"Yes, but if I may, I take some issue with what you have just said. In the American system all do not share equally in society. The principles of capitalism are more geared towards the hope that everyone has equal opportunity to share, but that anyone can rise as high as their individual efforts will take them, while others who are either not inclined, or unable, do not rise as high. Also, in the Islamic world it cannot be said that men and women are equal."

"It is true, David, that capitalism -- the system of government in many of the western nations, the United States in particular -- does represent a differing political and social philosophy from the system of social equity that the CAS is focusing upon. But, when one considers the numbers of people in the CAS, and the potential for suffering amongst two billion people, it is a difference that can be understood, and one that can be accommodated."

"Within Islam, we prefer to look upon equality as something that exists within the sexes as opposed to between the sexes. For example, anyone with a perceptive eye can tell that men and women are not really "equal." In this way, the nations of Islam try to follow a path that embraces the best of both systems, while desiring to live in peace with all."

David noticed that his time was running short, and he had saved what he felt to be the most pressing topic until last. If he began now, he felt he had just enough time to have a healthy discussion regarding it.

"Thank you, Imam. As our interview winds down, let us move on to the topic of Iraq. As you know, Sahdam Hussein was assassinated one week ago today. There are serious allegations regarding that assassination and my own government's possible involvement. In addition, Iraq appears to be in a state of anarchy, and what is left of Sahdam Hussein's government is having a difficult, if not impossible, time of ruling the nation. What are your thoughts on this state of affairs? And what, if anything, are the intentions of the Greater Islamic Republic in this regard?"

Hasan had patiently waited for this opportunity. The time was at hand to bring the rest of Islam together, and Iraq was the one major remaining keystone in that effort. With this interview, at this moment, Hasan had been given the perfect audience by Allah to make that appeal, and he intended to seize the opportunity.

"David, the death of Sahdam Hussein has been felt with sadness and remorse throughout Islam. Whatever else you may say about him…and as you know I spent some years of my own life fighting his armies…Sahdam was relentless in his opposition to the west and its unwarranted interference in Islamic affairs. Throughout his life, he also fought what many of us consider to be the corrupting, materialistic and lustful influences of western culture on our peoples. We will miss that strong voice, that relentless effort to maintain our Islamic culture."

"As to the allegations regarding his assassination … they are serious and would be viewed seriously by any nation if they are proven correct. We will not pass judgment in that regard until more information is available, to allow for an informed and sure determination."

"The civil conditions in Iraq are difficult. What little economy was allowed by western sanctions, has been injured all the more by the current circumstances. These dire circumstances affect the children and the widows and the infirm the most. We desire to see such suffering stop. We call on the west to lift all sanctions and send what humanitarian aid they can. We are doing the same."

"As you know, David, there is a significant percentage of the population in Iraq which is calling for unification with the Greater Islamic Republic. Although we make no secret or apology for our stated intention to unite all of Islam, we will not presume to take advantage of such conditions by coercion or deception."

"At the same time, we feel that, in the American tradition, the voice of the people should be heard. As a result, we have met with, and obtained the approval of, various NGO's and agencies in the UN to call for a UN-sponsored referendum in Iraq. Since their own government is not in a position to do so, this will put the option for unification with the Greater Islamic Republic before the people. We are proposing that such a referendum occur on September 1st, in conjunction with the similar referendum in Pakistan."

"The Greater Islamic Republic, outside of proposing to the general assembly such a referendum, will be in no way involved with the actual voting or its administration."

David Krenshaw was dumbfounded. Here was the leader of what was developing into one of the superpowers of the world announcing during his exclusive interview such a politically and diplomatically explosive proposal.

Although he knew he should feel used, his unease was counterbalanced by the fact that he would be remembered as the one who ferreted out such news.

"Imam, I, of course, am not in a position to render official judgment or approval for such a proposal. I am sure my government will respond officially, and that the UN will render its own decision. I can say that this is an unprecedented venue for such an announcement, and I thank you for the opportunity to bring such "news" to the world. That is, after all, the primary purpose of WNN, and the focal point of my own career."

"One more question if you will. Imam, what can you say to the west today, to America in particular, to ease their mind regarding you clear call for a united Islam. Just a few years ago, another very charismatic leader called for the same, and he then proceeded to kill many thousands of America in the infamous attack in September of 2001?"

Sayeed had known that this question was certain to come up. Everyday Americans would indeed be concerned. He meant to put their fears to rest.

"I can simply say this. There are vast differences between the individual and his organization that called for Islamic unification and our current efforts. The foremost is the message of peace and tolerance we not only preach, but practice when it comes to the western nations. Surely the west, surely no one any where would deny us the opportunity to unite in peace and tolerance. We have no intention of attacking anyone as long as our borders and strategic interests are not violated"

David Krenshaw was pleased with the answer.

"Okay, Imam, I must say that what you have stated is a clear difference in message and rhetoric. Unfortunately, we are out of time. I want to thank you, Imam Hasan Sayeed, for this interview, and thank everyone at WNN and within the Greater Islamic Republic who worked so hard to make it possible. This has been David Krenshaw with WNN from Tehran. "

August 15, 2005, 18:20 MDT
Ann Morris Park, on the Boise Rover
Boise, Idaho

It was a warm day, about eighty-nine degrees. But in the shade of the trees by the river and with a steady breeze, it was quite comfortable. Geneva Campbell was enjoying herself in Boise. This park was so lovely and peaceful. The weather was simply grand. Even when the temperatures hovered near ninety degrees, with the low humidity in the western part of the nation, and with shade and a breeze, it was quite comfortable compared to Chicago.

She watched her two sons. Reflecting on fond memories of her deceased husband, a thought came unbidden into her mind. "Lord, Jerome, I wish you could see your boys now." She continued in that vein as Leon and Alan threw a Frisbee back and forth to each other in a small meadow near where she sat, "Maybe you do, Jerome, maybe you do".

"Hey Leon, what time did you say those folks from Texas was supposed to be here?"

Leon made a dive for the Frisbee, caught it in his outstretched fingers, rolled and rose to his feet in one fluid motion.

"Mom, the Simmons said they'd be here about six thirty. I expect we'll see them any time. Billy said he'd be wearing a big cowboy hat and we couldn't miss him."

Geneva was a bit apprehensive. She still wasn't used to meeting all of these people. But Leon had assured her that the Simmons were good folk who worked the land and were God-fearing. Thus far in Boise, the Campbells had faired very well in the people they had met. So many had been kind to them and anxious to help the "newcomers." "So," she concluded to herself, "perhaps it won't be so bad after all." Best to just enjoy this cool breeze and clear dry air until these folks get here.

One hundred yards to the north, along the paved path in the park, Jess, Cindy and Billy Simmons were walking towards the south and looking for the Campbells. They had driven from Texas to Boise, arriving yesterday evening, and it had been a long but beautiful drive.

They left Montague County, Texas on August 12th and drove to the northwest along US Highway 287 all the way through Amarillo to Dumas, Texas. There they had taken US Highway 84, which they followed all the way to Raton, New Mexico. Along that portion of the trip, they stopped for an hour at the Capulin National Monument in northeast New Mexico and viewed the inactive volcano cone there. It was a beautiful view from the top and they could see the Rocky Mountains clearly. It had only been a forty-five minute drive to Raton from the national monument.

At Raton, New Mexico, they had taken Interstate Highway 25 north over the beautiful and historic Raton Pass into Colorado to Trinidad. They spent that first night in Trinidad.

The next day they rose to a cool (by Texas standards) morning and continued their journey. They followed Interstate 25 further north along the majestic "front range" of the Rocky Mountains. They passed through Colorado Springs about noon and ate lunch there and took some pictures with the mountains as a back drop. North of Colorado Springs, they came upon the US Air Force Academy. Both Jess and Billy wanted to stop there, so they had spent two hours touring the campus. As summer cadets and some of the staff there learned of Jess Simmons' military status and his "flight" capabilities, it had led to several interesting and enjoyable conversations. Late in the afternoon they passed through Denver. At Fort Carson, they got back on US 287 and drove across a beautiful mountain pass into Wyoming. At the bottom of that pass they came to Laramie, Wyoming on Interstate Highway 80 where they spent the second night.

The next morning, another brisk one for these native Texans, they followed the same path the Campbells had taken a little over a month earlier along Interstate 80. Around 5 PM yesterday, August 14th, they had arrived in Boise. After staying in a nice hotel right off of Interstate 84 last night, they had found Boise State University (BSU) in the morning, met the coaching staff, who treated them to lunch, just before noon, and then got Billy checked into his dorm by 2 PM.

Now, as they walked through the beautiful Ann Morris Park, they hoped to soon find the Campbells and make acquaintance with Leon and his family. They did not have long to wait.

"Hey, Leon! Look down there. Here comes a big white guy with a big ol' white cowboy hat just like you said. Looks like his parents are with him ... I bet it's your friend Billy."

Leon turned and looked up the path. Sure enough, just coming around the bend were three people, one of them wearing a big white cowboy hat. "Whew," thought Leon, "if that's Billy, he's a monster."

"Momma, let's get up and walk down that way and meet the Simmons. I'm positive that's them."

As Geneva got up from the bench and joined her sons, almost a hundred yards away, Billy noticed the movement and turned to his Dad.

"Dad, that must be them down there near that clearing. Look, I bet that colored guy waving to us is Leon!"

Billy waved back and started to jog towards the three Campbells.

"I hope this works out, Jess." Cindy Simmons said to her husband. "Billy seems real excited, but I'm just a little nervous. I mean this young man was a gang leader in Chicago and has been involved in who all knows what."

Jess considered his wife's remarks. Jess could understand her concern. Fact was, he had been concerned himself. But he had talked to Billy and trusted his son's instincts, his ability to handle himself in difficult circumstances and his commitment to doing what was right.

"Cindy, I know what you mean. I have had similar concerns. But, you know, Billy is eighteen now. He's a man and has to make his own way. I believe we've raised him right, and I believe it'll show. I think, from what I have heard, he and Leon are going to get along just fine.

"Leon's story is quite remarkable, you know. Very few have the strength, or vision, or faith in themselves to pull themselves out of a situation like he was in…let alone to pull their entire family out with them. Some get pulled out of it by parents who have the strength; some get pulled out by a teacher along the way; some come out of it after going through the discipline and structure of the military. I have seen quite a few of those cases myself. "

"Most never come out of it. It's too bad, because it's no secret that many of the government programs perpetuate the conditions … and many of the politicians know it … but they feel their agendas and political careers are empowered by those same conditions, so they keep it up. No, honey, it's rare that an individual like Leon comes along and pulls himself up by the bootstraps on his own. That being the case, I believe Billy and Leon are going to get along just fine."

With that conversation complete, the two families met and introduced themselves. There was a lot of laughter, and back-slapping stories to share on all sides. In this fashion, for the next two and half hours they enjoyed a wonderful and pleasant evening getting acquainted next to the clear running waters of the Boise River.

August 18, 2005, 14:37 local
Jiangnan Shipyards, Special Conversion Dry Docks
Shanghai, PRC

Lu Pham was glad to have Sung Hsu with him on this trip. Sung had developed so many excellent procedures and manufacturing processes in Tanjin that he was now a supervising director over construction foremen for the overall conversion process. As such, he was reviewing the implementation of those practices and processes in the various shipyards where the conversions were taking place. Lu was reviewing the LRASD weapons systems and their logistical preparations at each shipyard.

As a result of the growing friendship between themselves and their families, it made for a much more pleasant trip.

"Lu, we are over a week ahead of schedule at all the other shipyards. But here in Shanghai, we are several days behind. This morning I think I found out why."

"It's simply a matter of the process for installing the LRASD pivot assembly. For some reason the crews here have gotten two of the initial installation instructions reversed. While the systems can be assembled successfully with these two steps reversed, it is causing a work flow issue."

"Materiel that has been logistically staged to be handled last is being retrieved first, before it can be moved into a position to be picked up most efficiently. The extra time in transit, repeated over and over again, is impacting the schedule."

"I spoke with the foreman and had the procedure re-written to the correct sequence. They are going to try to add additional individuals working during the swing and midnight shifts to make up for the time loss."

It never ceased to amaze Lu how Sung fit so seamlessly into the large scale manufacturing role. Of course he had been at it for over fifteen years, but Lu knew others who were outstanding managers, who had been at it even longer than Sung, but who did not have the gift for it that Sung had.

"Outstanding, Sung. You have a way of analyzing, locating, deciphering and resolving issues that would put most doctors of research to shame, my friend. For my part, all of the weapons systems and their logistics are in order. The testing is completed and the systems have but to be installed and integrated into the fire control and PROM (Programmable Read Only Memory) processors on board each ship. All is progressing most excellently!"

"Oh, by the way, Sung. The suggestions that you gave several weeks ago regarding the Sea Control ships have been studied and implemented. A single dock in Tanjin is going to be making conversions in the open, where the prying eyes of the Americans are sure to take note."

"The other facilities will do their conversions under the cover of the housings we have built for those dry docks. In those cases, the landing decks are being cut up to move by rail so they can be delivered to the other sites in such a manner as to avoid detection by the American surveillance satellites and aircraft. The decks will then be reassembled on site."

Sung was very gratified at hearing this. He was extremely satisfied in his new work on these "special" conversions. He was proud to be contributing to the success of his nation in such a manifest way.

"Lu, what decision was made on how to transport the decks on those Sea Control Ships being converted at Tanjin?"

"They will be transporting them by large barges, pulled behind two of our large sea-going tugs. In fact, tomorrow evening, the first deck is scheduled to be loaded up and transported. I expect the Americans will quickly discover the transit with their surveillance satellites and hopefully have their full attention riveted to it. I would love to be a fly on the wall in some of their planning sessions when they see that."

August 19, 2005, 23:37 local
Yulin Naval Base, near Haikou
Hainan Island, PRC

The Yulin Naval Base was one of the People's Republic of China's most extensive facilities. It had originally been built by the Japanese, but had been extensively expanded and modernized on several occasions by the PLAN.

The base was capable of making the most extensive repairs to any ship in the PLAN. In order to accommodate this, it had extensive repair facilities, two large dry docks and ten large crane systems capable of lifting several hundred tons each. Tonight, these cranes were going to be utilized for the largest lift job in the history of the naval base, or in the history of the People's Republic of China.

The special carrier deck had been installed near the airfield portion of the naval base. The deck was two hundred and fifty meters long and forty meters wide. It was constructed of steel and had been strengthened against blast damage. It weighed almost five thousand tons.

Each of the ten cranes would have to lift a little less than five hundred tons. Since they were rated at five hundred and fifty tons each, the system had the capacity. Still, it was a complicated effort. The cranes were positioned along a rail system that had been built so they could move virtually anywhere along the waterfront. They had been aligned on two specially built rails, fifty meters apart. Five cranes were situated on each side of these rails.

The deck had been moved there by a large multi-tracked vehicle, specially built for this purpose, which had been constructed in an underground facility where it had remained until needed. Two days earlier, the transport vehicle had been driven under the deck through a specially constructed access path specifically built with this day in mind. Once under the deck, it had used its own hydraulic lifts ... two hundred of them, to lift the deck clear of the anchoring sub-structure and start it on its way to the harbor. It had taken a full twenty-four hours to cover the two miles.

Once the deck was in position between the cranes, the cranes were attached to the deck at special hoist points and they began to slowly and carefully lift the deck. Once the deck came clear of the transport vehicle, the cranes themselves began to move slowly along their rails towards the harbor inlet where the barge awaited.

The barge itself was three hundred meters long and thirty-five meters wide. It had a carrying capacity of seventy-five hundred tons. Earlier in the evening, at seven thirty, the cranes arrived in position with the deck suspended above the barge.

At that time, the deck was ever so slowly lowered onto it. Once this was done, and the deck was resting on its support points, but still held by the cranes, workers spent four hours attaching the deck to the barge at each of the support points. Once the attachment was accomplished, the cranes were moved away from the barge and the deck was finally ready to be towed away.

Around midnight, two Dinghai class sea going tugs of the PLAN came alongside the barge. Once they were attached, they began towing it out of its berth and out of the harbor. At eight knots, it would take four days to tow the deck to Tanjin shipyards where it would be permanently installed on one of the container ships.

Early the next morning, the tugs and their barge were some ninety kilometers up the coast towards Tanjin, steaming about ten kilometers off the coast. At this point, not long after first light, they were observed by a US reconnaissance satellite as they continued to slowly made their way north, up the coast of China.

The images recorded by the satellite were immediately communicated to CINCPAC in Hawaii, to the ONI in the Pentagon and to the NRO in Virginia, according to the procedures already in place for any reconnaissance coming in from the South China Sea that dealt with the PRC.

August 20, 2005, 09:12 EDT
National Reconnaissance Office Headquarters
IMINT Directorate
Chantilly, VA

"I'd say that about ices it, Tom. Just insure we get a track on that barge and the two tugs and find out where they are going. My bet is Tanjin. Those crafty devils are going to create some conversion aircraft carriers from their friggin' container ships. Who would have thought it?"

Tom was sure his boss was right. Ever since they had overlaid the deck design onto the Container Ship plan view, it was clear that those deck configurations were made for these ships. The only question had been, how were they going to get those decks, or ones like them, fitted onto the ships?

Well, this morning that had become clear as the semi-weekly photographs of the Hainan Island area had captured what appeared to be a small aircraft carrier moving up the coast. Once Tom had analyzed the information, it became clear that two large tugs were towing a barge which had the deck attached to it.

"The photographs of the Yulin Naval Base show that the deck is gone, and we already know where. This is interesting, though. I have checked the other airfields where these special naval "decks" had been installed and the only one that is missing is the one from Hainan."

Bill was not concerned about this fact. The other decks would move as the PRC was prepared to add them to container ships. "Boy, that must be a heck of a conversion," he thought.

"They're probably just biding their time, Tom. Let's go ahead and report on all that we have deduced at our ten AM video conference. I am sure CINCPAC and ONI have seen this and have come to the same conclusions. Anyhow, now that we know how the Chinese are going about it, there'll be no problem keeping track of it."

… or so they thought.

CHAPTER 5

" To command a group requires truthfulness. " – Sun Tsu

August 25, 2005, 03:50 local
Along the Great Zab River
Near Irbil, Iraq

"The insertion had gone almost perfectly," thought Will as his team gathered around him.

Having flown into the northern "No Fly Zone" from Turkey aboard a specially configured C-17 Globemaster aircraft owned and operated by the CIA, the eight-man team had made a "HALO" (High Altitude, Low Opening) drop. The northern "No fly zone" had been maintained by US and RAF aircraft for fifteen years, since the end of the Gulf war, and had provided an enclave for the Kurdish population there.

They had parachuted into a remote wash two hours ago and made their way to their designated rendezvous point near the Great Zab River. Now, they were concealed and waiting for their contact.

Will Peterson was a senior CIA field officer and a former Delta Force Company Commander. He had six special-forces non-commissioned officers and his

CIA Team parachutes into northern Iraq.

XO with him. All of them had spent years in the elite Delta Force and all of them had been recruited by the "Agency" to help conduct America's foreign affairs in places where the bright lights of cameras were never meant to shine.

Will heard the slight sound of someone moving stealthily along the dirt path below them. The sound stopped and after a moment a single phrase was whispered.

"al-Mustaqbal"

Will's point man, and the most fluent in Arabic among them (though they all looked Arabic and could speak fluently) responded.

"Shaheda."

Within fifteen minutes their guide had led them further up the canyon of the Great Zab River where they branched off on a small footpath into a feeder canyon. After another twenty minutes of rather steep ascent, they moved to one side of the canyon where the team waited while their guide removed brush from the expertly concealed mouth of a cave and exchanged whispered identification and greetings with two well- concealed sentries. Upon entering the cave, and after following it through several turns, they found that it widened into a rather spacious, natural room. Several men attired in unremarkable desert dress were in the room gathered around or sitting at a table. One of them looked up as Will and his team entered.

"Will, how good to see you after so many months! Please, bring your friends and join us here at the table."

Will's team looked to him and he nodded his head back to the entry. Two of the team silently walked back and took up positions between the gathering and the entrance to the cavern. Will and the other five team members then walked over to the table.

"Jabal, it is good to see you my friend. I take it Badar bin Sultan arrangements for the delivery have been successfully completed and your people are prepared?"

Jabal Talabari's Patriotic Kurdistan Front had been fighting Sahdam Hussein, his Iraqi intelligence operatives and their army for more than seventeen years. He had known Will for almost eight of those years, since just a few months after the 1996 fiasco in Irbil.

Jabal had great reason not to trust the Americans and be wary of them. Many of his friends were dead as a result of American promises that had not been kept. First one American president and then another had sent men like Will to help overthrow the Iraqis … only to have them pulled out when the heat was turned up … which is exactly what had happened in Irbil in 1996.

Perhaps this time, with Weisskopf as President, with so many new weapons and with the Saudi and Turkish backing, they could be successful.

"Yes, we have the weapons; we have the "ballots;' we have the polling locations and we have made our plans. Kurdistan will not vote to join Iraq in their alignment with the Iranians, and the voting in Baghdad and other areas will not go as they envision. I was reviewing our plans just now with each of these division commanders as you arrived."

At Jabal's direction, Will's team members were paired off with Jabal's division commanders. Will worked directly with Jabal.

Over the next several days their specific operational plans were reviewed and modified and the timing between events and the various elements of the PKF was worked out. Then the entire OPPLAN was relentlessly rehearsed with the division commanders and their subordinates.

August 28, 2005, 11:50 local
In the Knesset
Tel Aviv, Israel

"Summing up then, we must recognize that a tremendous and mortal threat to our very existence is developing in this Greater Islamic Republic. Adding Pakistan's mature nuclear program to Iran's elementary capabilities will add up to as great a threat to our survival as we have faced in our history."

Prime Minister Benjahmin Netinyahu sat down. He had poured out his soul to his compatriots and he was as worried as he had ever been.

"Mr. Prime Minister, while the potential for a threat is real, we have yet to see any clear indication from Sayeed or any of his ministers that they intend us any harm. I believe, if we work with their Foreign Minister and seek to live in harmony with them, we can avoid conflict. They know we are similarly armed and they know we are willing to use those arms."

"If we rattle our sabers in their face, if we provoke them when no reason has been given, then we risk causing the very confrontation you want to avoid."

Netinyahu considered the words of his rival, Isaac bin Ammon, the leader of the opposition Labor party. The words were not new; the logic was as old as history, and history had proven it incorrect on countless occasions.

"You sound for all the world like one of the doves in the American Senate, Isaac. Have we learned nothing? We must send a message of strength and resolution to Sayeed. We cannot afford to allow him to think for a moment that we are weak, or that we fear him. Iran, which is the focal point for the Greater Islamic Republic, has financed and trained many of our worst enemies. I have seen no reduction in that effort."

"Now Afghanistan has joined their ranks and it appears that Pakistan and Iraq will soon follow. All of these "states" have spent untold billions to train and equip those terrorists and themselves to fight and destroy us."

"We dare not forget this. The American President issued us a warning a few weeks ago. He felt strongly enough about it to call and talk directly to me. I believe we should take this warning and his recommendation to establish and maintain our readiness seriously."

Isaac bin Ammon rolled his eyes. He certainly believed in their nuclear deterrent. He believed in remaining strong. He was simply tired of these so called "hawks" who were intent on provoking every nation around them with their "in your face" attitude.

"Benjahmin, we have gone around and around on this over the years. I believe that Hasan Sayeed is reasonable …certainly more reasonable than Sahdam Hussein. "

"Our report from the Mossad earlier today indicates that it is probable that Hasan and his people are behind Hussein's demise. I think we should thank him."

"Save us from the naivete and incompetence of fools," Netinyahu thought.

"While I am glad that Hussein is gone, I feel we have replaced an unreasonable, yet predictable tyrant with a much more rational and dangerous one."

He turned to his defense minister.

"Jacob, increase our readiness, across the board. Also, request more time from the American satellites and utilize our own assets to monitor the Army groups that the Iranians are training near Ahvaz. I want the anti-aircraft missile defenses and our artillery on the Golan Heights strengthened too."

"Let's pray that somehow the "elections" in Pakistan and Iraq do not turn out as our predictions indicate."

August 30, 2005, 17:50 local
Israeli Defense Force (IDF) positions
Golan Heights

Colonel Abraham Eshkol had been monitoring the placement of new AAM batteries all day. It had been a hot day, too. Even here on the heights the temperature had hovered at forty degrees Celsius most of the afternoon.

The new Arrow missile system, developed and manufactured by Israel, was impressive. "Every bit as capable as the newer Block 3 Patriot systems," the Colonel thought, even if the altitude capabilities are a little less. When complemented by the new American system firing the ground-based version of the AMRAAM (Advanced

IDF "HUMMRAM" air defense system

Medium Range Anti Aircraft Missile), the Golan Heights would be as well protected against air attack as possible.

Now the Colonel turned his attention towards the perimeter defenses and the new artillery that was being added to his position. As he did so, he summoned his executive officer.

"Major, I want a report of your progress today on my desk by nineteen hundred hours. Just make sure that our perimeter defenses are completed within the next three days. I want that new line of bunkers dug in below and forward of the existing defenses. As we discussed, also insure that the extra batteries of the 155's and those new MRL's (Multiple Rocket Launchers) are positioned in their revetments. Carry on."

As the Colonel turned and walked toward his command vehicle, he contemplated his latest improvements and orders.

"Threat condition three and significantly increased strength. Must be concerned that this Hasan Sayeed's influence will continue to spread."

Even though he was happy that their long-time protagonist, Sahdam Hussein, was dead, the prospect of a united Islam spreading closer and closer to his homeland was enough to cause him serious consideration and consternation.

As he gazed from his elevated position to the west and north out across Syria, he was reminded of the Masada where long ago his forefathers had been besieged by the Romans. That siege had ended with mass suicide.

"Well, we will not end up in such a position here. Any enemy trying to assault these heights will find their own death waiting here, not ours."

September 1, 2005, 14:23 local
Voting Precinct
Islamabad, Pakistan

The lines went on for hundreds of yards outside of the building housing this precinct's voting booths. Tens of thousands were lined up here and all across the city, as they had been since before the polls opened at this morning.

The same scene was being played out across Pakistan in all of the major cities, as well as smallest villages.

Here in Islamabad, and at a few other high profile places, the camera crews of WNN and other major media outlets were recording it all and broadcasting it across the world. No exit polling was allowed, but it was clear beyond doubt what the results were going to be.

The population and military power of the Greater Islamic Republic would more than double as a result of the events this day. In truth, preparations for insuring this pre-ordained victory, and capitalizing on it, had been ongoing since the announcement by President Musharraf several weeks ago.

September 1, 2005, That Same Time
UN Monitoring Station outside of a Voting Precinct
Baghdad, Iraq

The stooped and crippled old man was in line, waiting his turn to vote like the thousands of others. He was within fifteen meters of the entrance to the building that housed the voting booths, and was just passing the UN monitoring station. The UN had a contingent of officials with side arms at the monitoring station, and several others within the voting facility.

The UN-provided monitoring and light security was backed up by Iraqi Republican Guard troops who manned a security station at the entrance to the voting facility itself. The Iraqi contingent was more heavily armed and was using a UN-supplied metal detector to prevent weapons from entering.

As the stooped old man approached the security station, he noted carefully the position of the alert guards: two men with automatic assault rifles standing to either side of their compatriots at the metal detector, and one UN officer just outside of the station whose hand rested lightly on his side arm.

Underneath the stooped frame and the wrinkles of the old man in line, was the heart of a fighter. Concealed by the robes, and belied by the stooped posture, was the body of a twenty-four year old Kurdish freedom fighter, along with an AK-47 rifle and three hand grenades.

When he was within five meters of the security station, the Kurdish militant armed his first grenade while holding it under his robes with one hand. His other hand had already charged his assault rifle. Pretending to stoop even lower, as though looking at something on the ground, he gently tossed his hand grenade back towards the UN monitoring station while lifting his AK-47 towards the security station.

Grabbing the rifle with both hands now, he expertly pulled the trigger while he swept the muzzle across the security station, cutting down the two guards and one of the Iraqis manning the metal detector. An instant later, the grenade detonated with a thunderous report, directly in front of the UN monitoring station.

In the pandemonium that was breaking out around the voting facility, the Kurdish freedom fighter calmly walked up to the security station and fired a three-round burst into the heads of each of the downed Iraqis and then tossed another of his hand grenades into the voting facility. Hurrying now, he ran back towards the UN monitoring station where several UN officials were staggering out of the ruined doorway.

As the blast of the second grenade tore through the polling place, the young Kurd again pulled the trigger of his AK-47, knocking down two of the UN officials and driving the others back into the building.

Lobbing his last grenade into the UN monitoring station itself, before it could explode, he discarded his AK-47 and disappeared into the crowd that was fleeing the scene in terror.

As he melted into the stampeding throng, he whispered to himself in Arabic:

"For the liberty and sovereignty of Kurdistan!"

September 1, 2005, 19:42 local
Patriotic Kurdistan Front Cavern
Near Irbil, Iraq

"Things have gone as well as can be expected. Here in the Kurdistan area, the referendum has been defeated and our "write-in" ballot efforts will make it plain that we have voted for our own independence."

"In the more southern areas, there has been significant disruption by our personnel, but the vote is overwhelmingly for unification with the Greater Islamic Republic."

As Jabal completed his thoughts and status report, Will felt he had to interject.

"Don't be too optimistic yet, my friend. While the election here has certainly gone as we hoped, and while our efforts at disruption in other areas were mildly successful, you can bet that there are Iraqi armed forces gathering to move against us as we speak."

"… and I'll tell you what I think. Though we may be prepared to take on what is left of Sahdam's Republican Guard … I am concerned about the massive forces of the Greater Islamic Republic. We need to be prepared for them … they will certainly only look at the overall voting totals which will indicate that the Iraqi people have chosen, by a significant margin, to unify with Sayeed."

Jabal considered this analysis. What Will said was true: the GIR would certainly try to get the UN to recognize the overall results of the voting only. Furthermore, even though, thanks to the Americans, there were substantial weapons caches and significant intelligence, reconnaissance and planning assets at his disposal, Jabal was not as optimistic as his friend about standing up to the Republican Guard. After all, they had tried several times in the past and failed.

But, with the death of Sahdam, the morale and commitment of his best fighting unit was weakened, and with the continued attacks by his forces in the south diverting significant Iraqi assets in that direction … perhaps they could indeed hold off the Republican Guard. But the combined forces of the Greater Islamic Republic would be a different matter altogether. The GIR's military capabilities were not something to be taken lightly.   They represented a viable military entity the likes of which Jabal was not eager to reckon with, but he was fairly certain that the day of reckoning was not far off.

"What of your nation's commitment and help, Will? Will your President Weisskopf diplomatically support us? More importantly, if it requires it, will he militarily support us?"

From everything he had heard, Will had no doubts what President Weisskopf's inclination would be. The question was, what would his party … what would the congress … what would the people in America allow Weisskopf to do?

"Jabal, if it goes that far, our intent is to do just that. We must protect your people's sovereignty and we must keep the growing Greater Islamic Republic contained with every means at our disposal."

"Let's review your defensive posture now, and see if we can be ready to repel those Republican Guard columns should they head this way."

September 2, 2005, 14:18 local
Oval Office, The White House
Washington, D.C.

Vice President Alan Reeves could appreciate his boss's special "feelings" that guided his policies and many of his major decisions. The Vice President was in fact having one himself regarding the current situation with the GIR.

"Who would have thought that in the space of a few short months we would be looking at a unified Islamic Republic of this magnitude?" he thought.

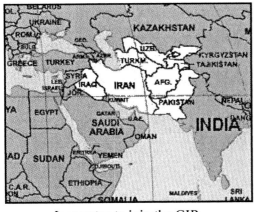
Iraq votes to join the GIR.

"Mr. President, the Pakistani vote was overwhelming. Although only some 70% of the vote is counted, the decision to unite with the Greater Islamic Republic is enjoying and astounding 94% plurality."

"In Iraq the vote is somewhat less impressive, with only about a 68% unification vote, with 62% of the vote reporting. These results are not without incident either. We have at least half a dozen reports, at least two of them confirmed, of violence at voting places."

"The Kurds in the north have voted overwhelmingly to establish their own Kurdish homeland, inviting Kurds from Turkey and Iran to join in. They utilized ballots covertly supplied to them in place of the UN-supplied ballots. Those "new" ballots looked very official, but added the choice to create a Kurdish homeland, Kurdistan. That choice, or option, is passing in those northern areas by 84%."

"Kurds from both Turkey and Iran are streaming into northern Iraq and they are preparing defensive positions against any attempt by the Iraqi army to intervene. In this regard, the Kurdish ruling council, which has been in place since their vote for autonomy in the 1990's after the Gulf War, is already making official inquiries to us and other nations regarding recognition and assistance. Yesterday, they officially declared their independence."

President Weisskopf carefully considered this information. Things were going as they had hoped in the North, but the election overall had not been disrupted and the results were convincing. Recognition of Kurdistan would be a very risky business and most probably a somewhat isolated position. England, Australia and Israel would possibly join in such a recognition, and it was hoped that Saudi Arabia and Turkey, who had covertly been a part of the "help" given the Kurds, would also join in. But the real question was what the reaction of the GIR would be.

"How has the GIR officially reacted, and what are we seeing regarding any troop movements?"

Vice President Reeves turned to the Secretary of State, Fred Reisinger.

"I'll let Fred address the GIR reaction, Mr. President."

"Mr. President, the GIR, as you can imagine, has officially applauded the current results. They have indicated that there would be an official announcement by Hasan Sayeed himself once the figures are final. We expect the final results will be in by tomorrow or the next day at the latest."

"To date, they have been silent on the issue of the Kurds in the north, although the provisional Iraqi government is loudly condemning the vote, and publicly indicating that no attempt to split the traditional Iraqi nation will be tolerated."

"John, what are we seeing regarding GIR troop movements?"

John Bowers had checked with the NRO and with the Pentagon before the meeting regarding this very issue.

"The GIR has had military advisors in increasing numbers in both Pakistan and Iraq since the announcements of the referenda. They have stationed one Army unit and fairly large numbers of aircraft near their border with each country. As of this morning, no movement has been noticed from those Army units, although there can be no doubt that they are logistically preparing to move. A couple of squadrons of attack and support aircraft have flown into Baghdad this morning."

Well, there could be no doubt as to how the GIR would react. Hasan Sayeed had made a mission out of uniting the Islamic world. Incredibly, he had succeeded beyond anyone's wildest imaginings ... and now there would probably be hell to pay. Norm Weisskopf knew that now was the time to make clear America's resolve in the area, rather than to simply allow all of Islam to be consolidated under Sayeed.

"OK, Fred, let's start moving towards an initial diplomatic relationship with Kurdistan. Other nations, outside of Turkey and potentially Israel, are going to await our lead. I'd like a diplomatic mission established in Irbil and an announcement that we are sending a diplomatic team over there to discuss Kurdistan's future amongst the family of nation. Perhaps this kind of pre-emptive diplomacy will forestall the Iraqis and the GIR for a short time."

September 4, 2005, 15:00 local
Islamic Republic Government Offices
Tehran, The Greater Islamic Republic

The GIR announces results of the voting.

"We are pleased to announce the overwhelming results of the referenda in both Pakistan and Iraq regarding the people's choice in those two countries to unite with our Greater Islamic Republic. The voting in Pakistan resulted in an astounding 94.6% of the voters choosing the path of unification."

"In Iraq 72.3% of the people chose to join in our efforts to unite our Islamic brothers and sisters everywhere. Sadly, the voting was marked by some violence and the results would have been higher had extremists and terrorists not attempted to thwart the will of the people. Such interference will not be tolerated and will be ruthlessly put down."

"Nonetheless, the results are clear: the former nations of Pakistan and Iraq have voted, by overwhelming super majorities, to become a part of the Greater Islamic Republic. We will move quickly to consolidate these regions and peoples into our peaceful and prosperous Republic."

"To this end, I have two important announcements to make."

"First, after serious and in-depth negotiations over the last several weeks, we announce today that the Greater Islamic Republic is officially joining the Coalition of Asian States. I must thank our Foreign Minister, the Ayatollah Ol Asam Sadiq Shiraziha, for his unceasing efforts in this regard. We proudly join with India and the People's Republic of China in the tacit recognition of the "Three Wisdoms." Here in the Greater Islamic Republic, they shall be phrased as follows:

1. "All men and woman are created equal in their distinct roles in society."
2. "All share equally in a working and industrious society."
3. "One goal, one thought, one people for World peace."

The Greater Islamic Republic joins the CAS.

"This economic and social coalition is sweeping the world and we invite and urge all to join with us in our commitment to social equity for all people."

"Second, with respect to attempts to break apart the traditional nation of Iraq which has voted to join with the Greater Islamic Republic, we announce our unwavering commitment to the integrity of our borders and our people. Outside interference in this regard will not be tolerated. I have ordered elements of our national defense forces to prepare to put down any attempt to split off a portion of our nation and thereby thwart the will of the people."

"To the Kurdish people we say, join with your countrymen in our quest for social equity. This is not the old regime in Iraq, which I, too, fought against. This is a new day for all Islam ... a day we should mark by living in peace with one another and moving forward in the spirit of Shaheda and Sarum in our Islamic faith. For those who would attempt to subvert our nation and the will of the people, the answer will be the Jihad. There is no independent Kurdish state."

"In this spirit, we announce a moratorium on action in this regard until November 1st. We will work with the autonomous Kurdish region to negotiate a peaceful unification with our Republic up until that date. We will be prepared to enforce the will of the people after that time. We warn foreigners seeking to influence events to their own advantage to not meddle in the internal affairs of our nation. Outside influence and moves toward diplomatic recognition of a break-away state will not be tolerated."

September 8, 2005, 10:25 local
UN General Assembly
New York City, USA

"The resolution passes by a vote of 95 in favor and 12 against."

Ambassador Wong Yingfong sat back with pride and satisfaction. The issue had never really been in doubt, but to have won such a lopsided victory was all the more gratifying. When introduced to the general assembly the day before yesterday, it had taken favors and promises to get the resolution to the floor so quickly, but Wong had been a diplomat for many years and knew the ways of the United Nations. Now, the resolution was passed, "A Resolution recognizing the passage of popular referenda in the former nations of Pakistan and Iraq uniting both nations with the Greater Islamic Republic." An article of that resolution specifically condemned efforts by any portions of the nationalities to ignore the will of the people and break away from their former nations. The Article did not describe specific action that would be taken in response to de-unifying efforts, and there were no binding commitments. It was more of a "sense of the General Assembly."

But, the United States, Turkey, Saudi Arabia, Great Britain, Australia, Japan, Canada, Israel, Brazil, South Korea, Thailand and Egypt had voted against the resolution. The United States, Turkey, Great Britain, Canada and Australia had already made diplomatic contact with the leaders of what they were calling Kurdistan, though this contact had stopped well short of official recognition to date.

With The People's Republic of China, India, Russia and the Greater Islamic Republic voting for the resolution, the growing economic and ideological influence of those combined entities had swayed many nations. Others had been content to remain on the sidelines with Germany, France, Greece, Italy and twenty other nations abstaining.

As he made his way out of the general assembly hall, Wong saw that his counterparts from India, the GIR and Russia were waiting for him just outside of the door where they had agreed to meet afterwards. Shaking hands with the Ambassador from the GIR, Ambassador Wong addressed the others.

"Greetings, my friends! Let's now retire to the conference room in my mission where we can discuss developing some method to give this resolution some teeth."

September 11, 2005, 19:25 local
The Oval Office, The White House
Washington, D.C.

"Imam, I understand that the resolution has passed, and I understand your offer which expires at 12 AM on November 2nd. My point is simply that the Kurdish people are already autonomous and that they have voted to not unite with the GIR. The issue here is an intrinsic change in the nation of Iraq and its people. The people in the "Kurdistan" area have chosen to make their autonomy permanent."

President Weisskopf had agreed to this call at the insistence of his Secretary of State. Normal communications and contacts were not producing any results and time was short. But Hasan Sayeed felt he was holding all the cards and he was communicating accordingly.

"President Weisskopf, with all due respect, there is no Kurdistan. Neither was there any provision for independence for the autonomous regions of which you speak. What there is, is a commitment by the GIR to keep things as they were, with the existing autonomy conceded by the former Iraq within its borders, which is now a part of the GIR. This is all we are willing to agree to, and it is what the UN General Assembly has voted to support."

The President had to suppress his growing ire. Sayeed was determined to have all of Iraq and with the help of Red China, India and Russia he felt he was in a position to force the issue.

"Imam, first of all, as you know, the UN resolution is non-binding. Second, referring to the former ruler of Iraq, Sahdam Hussein, and his "concessions" does not impress the United States. Quite frankly, as you know, Sahdam Hussein was a tyrant. The fact is this: the people of that region have spoken; they have declared their independence. I want you to understand our commitment and firmness in this regard. We, along with several of our allies, intend to recognize Kurdistan as an independent nation."

Now it was Hasan Sayeed's turn to restrain his growing ire. Wasn't it just like these infidels to go against the prevailing feelings of the world and attempt to force their will on entire nations.

"Mr. President, from your time as a youth, you have some background with the people of my nation. You know that, for the most part, we are committed to our faith and to the people of our faith, as well as to the people of our nation. Iraq is now a part of our nation ... all of it. If we are allowed, if we are not interfered with, we are certain that the people in northern Iraq will recognize our commitment and embrace it. It is the interference of other nations, including your own, which has led to the current conditions. I do not mean to debate this with you, or to evoke argument and denials. We are convinced from our own intelligence sources that the irregular ballots in the north, and much of the violence in other areas, was instigated by your CIA and the operatives of other nations. We have said nothing of this publicly, but we insist at this time that such interference cease."

"With respect to your commitments and firmness on the matter, I assure you, Mr. President, we are equally committed and firm. If the Kurdish population persist in their efforts to divide Iraq beyond November 1st, our response will be swift, devastating and decisive. Good day, Mr. President."

"CLICK."

Everyone in the room was surprised at the abruptness with which the call was terminated. Fred Reisinger had hoped that a direct exchange between the two leaders could produce some opening, some chance to avoid confrontation. That hope was now all but gone.

"He's serious. First of all, the CAS is hurting us economically, even more so our allies in Western Europe. The Chinese, the Indians and now the GIR are exclusively exploiting Russia's Siberian resources. American and European efforts in the region have been shut down., contracts have been reneged upon, and hundreds of millions, if not billions, have been lost. Now, we are being faced with an ultimatum regarding the Kurds and Sayeed feels he has the international support and military power to stand us down."

Interjecting at this point, Russell Gage, the Secretary of the Treasury, and leader of the National Economic Council (NEC), whose principle function was overseeing the Administration's domestic and international economic policy-making process, spoke up.

"Mr. President, as we discussed when the CAS first announced its objectives, we are seeing significant weakening in our petroleum, precious metals and natural gas industries. This undercutting is due to the adverse effects that most of the large players in these markets are experiencing as a result of CAS actions and policies."

"As Fred has said, in many cases they have simply reneged on contracts already in place, forcing our firms to eat huge capital investments. This is beginning to have a very real impact on the stock markets in those sectors of the economy, and has every potential of impacting other sectors as well. With the vast petroleum reserves and resources of the GIR being added to this scenario, economic prospects are not good. In a very real sense, we will be vulnerable to economic warfare every bit as serious as the military kind."

Secretary of Defense Tim Hattering considered the Secretary of State's and the Secretary of the Treasury's pronouncements. He agreed with both, but wanted to insure that the meeting stayed on track in focusing on addressing the immediate Kurd situation.

"Excuse me, Russ, but, Mr. President, I agree with the warnings and comments of both Fred and Russ and have to add to it my own with respect to the immediate issue of the Kurds. Over the last several days, we have tracked several former Republican Guard divisions taking up "jump off positions" at critical junctures leading into "Kurdistan." It is apparent they are staging supplies and aircraft to support a quick and overwhelming strike toward Irbil and then Kirkuk, and another towards the west along the Turkish frontier."

"What's of even greater concern is that the GIR is moving two entire Army groups and their air support towards the former border with Iran. We believe one of them will support the Republican Guard units to the north in their plan for keeping Kurdistan in line, while the other will secure their order with Kuwait and Saudi Arabia."

The President took this in.

"What strength are we talking about here?"

Tim consulted his notes.

"Mr. President, I do not have precise numbers, but right now the Republican Guard is amassing fifty to sixty thousand combat troops, two to three hundred tanks, more APC's and two to three hundred combat aircraft. Following behind that are perhaps one hundred thousand GIR combat troops in each Army group supported by six to eight hundred tanks and three to four hundred combat aircraft … that is, that many aircraft for each group."

"They are serious indeed," thought the President. "Such numbers are more than enough to handle the Kurds in the north, and far more than enough to secure their borders with Saudi and Kuwait, unless of course they are assuming we are going to contest this militarily, or …"

"OK, I want everyone to listen very carefully. I'm afraid that there is a very real possibility that the GIR is not just planning to secure their borders with Kuwait and Saudi. They have assembled a force that would be capable of crossing those borders. I want us to start looking at that possibility right now."

Turning to the grouping of chairs where the Secretary of Defense, the Chairman of the Joint Chiefs of Staff and the Secretary of State sat, the President continued.

"Tim, work with General Stone, the Joint Chiefs, John, and Mike to start analyzing and planning from that perspective. General Stone, you'd best look at very inconspicuously calling up the reserve units associated with Central Command and the 24th Mechanized Division to augment the MEU we have already sent over there to train with the Kuwaitis. Get the ready brigade of the 82nd Airborne prepared to airlift over to Kuwait on my order. Jeremy, make sure General Horton of Central Command understands our need to field a force capable of defending Kuwait and Saudi and have him start the planning. I know exactly what he's going through and will give him the full support of this Presidency. Make sure he understands that."

"Fred, begin working with Kuwait, Saudi and Bahrain and get the necessary agreements in place to activate our pre-positioned equipment and allow for the manning of that equipment. In addition, prepare an official diplomatic recognition of Kurdistan and coordinate it with Great Britain, Canada, Australia, Turkey and Saudi Arabia."

"Also, work with Russ and the NEC to analyze the numbers and consequences in anticipation of a possible revocation of Normal Trade Relation Status for all of the CAS, including Russia. I know this can be a potential bombshell to the economy and the markets, but we may have to experience such difficulties to extract ourselves from a very compromising position. We have simply allowed ourselves to become too dependent on a potential adversary. Review this analysis with Alan and brief me on how best to communicate it to our friends and allies. I will make an announcement to the nation regarding all of this on Friday evening, September 15^t, and I want to insure that we coordinate it with whatever similar announcements and actions our allies can take in concert with us."

Finally, turning to his right where his Vice President, Alan Reeves, was seated with his National Security Advisor, John Bowers, the President concluded.

"Alan, please work with Fred, particularly in preparing the way with our allies who abstained in the general assembly vote regarding Iraqi. I'd like to think that we could get at least Germany and Italy behind us on the recognition of Kurdistan. In addition, we want to make sure that Japan, South Korea and the others who voted with us, but are not yet prepared to recognize Kurdistan, don't vacillate.

I also want frank discussions on the potential need to utilize our trade relations with all of the CAS and Russia as an incentive for them to insure continued free trade with respect to the Siberian resources, and in particular the outstanding contracts and commitments that have been unilaterally terminated. We should probably also include in that discussion the CAS policy regarding the labor tariffs. If necessary, Alan, visit their heads of state personally to discuss these issues frankly, or arrange meetings between them and myself."

September 12, 2005, that same time
Presidential Offices
Tehran, The Greater Islamic Republic

"Instruct our 1st and 2nd Army group forces to immediately initiate operation Mongoose and proceed beyond the borders of the former Iraq and take up staging positions per that plan. Make it clear that there are to be no accidents, no provocation. Just move to the staging areas and await further orders."

"Sadiq, arrange personal calls with President Zenim of the People's Republic of China and President Puten of the Russian Federation. I believe it is time we expend further funds on more weapons systems and supplies."

"Then, call for a meeting of the ruling Mujtahids and senior Mullahs within the next three or four days. We must request the faith of our people in this and seek Allah's will in the measures that will be necessary to complete our task of uniting all of Islam. After that meeting, within one or two days, I would like to hold a meeting of the entire military council."

Hasan Sayeed watched his Foreign Minister and devoted subordinate leave to make the arrangements he had directed. The culmination of his primary mission, the unification of all of Islam, was within grasp. But before that mission would be realized, Hasan knew a testing would have to be endured. The time for that testing would begin in earnest appeared to be close at hand.

September 13, 2005, 10:25 local
College of Engineering, Boise State University
Boise, Idaho

Both Billy and Leon had noticed him when he came in. He quietly took a seat in the back row of the lecture hall, took off his cap and sat quietly as the professor explained the essentials of first order derivatives to the class.

School had been in session for just a couple of weeks and Billy and Leon were in two classes together, one of which was this Calculus class that was required for Billy's Mechanical Engineering major and for Leon's Physics major. The two of them had become close friends and Billy enjoyed the opportunity for some home cooking as Leon invited him over to their apartment to eat three or four times a week.

They had talked about everything. From the inevitable talks about girls, to long discussions on cars, to their thoughts about politics and finally to their mutual desire to get into the military. Although Billy's father was in the U.S. Army, both Billy and Leon were more drawn to the Marines, Billy as a result of his studies of all the military service branches (he thought he would like infantry operations, ships and helicopters and he could get all of them in the Marines). Leon was drawn there as a result of his experiences with Charlie Jenkins, the retired Marine husband of Nellie Jenkins, the librarian back in the Harold Washington Memorial Public Library in Chicago who had helped him so much.

The lecture went on. As they took notes and listened to the professor, both boys stole glances to the back of the amphitheater style lecture hall. He was still there. Dressed in what looked like a service "C" Uniform, a Gunnery Sergeant of the United States Marine Corps for some reason was sitting back there in their Calculus class.

When the lecture ended and the professor dismissed class, the Gunny moved to the double exit doors and simply stood there as the students left the lecture hall. As Billy and Leon approached the doors, the Marine looked straight at Leon and spoke while stretching is hand forward for a handshake.

"Leon Campbell? Hi, my name is Sergeant Ken Bennett. My friends either call me deadeye, or just Gunny "D". Sergeant Major Jenkins gave me a call a week or so ago and said I ought to look you up, so here I am."

As Leon shook the firm hand, he had to think a minute … Sergeant Major Jenkins? … Oh! He must mean Charlie!

"You mean Charlie? Well that's great! Charlie taught me a lot about our country and what it is really all about ... he also spoke a lot about the Marines."

"Oh! Excuse me Sergeant … this is my friend Billy. He's from down in Texas and his Dad flies the most advanced attack helicopter in the military."

Gunny "D" turned and shook Billy's hand.

"So your Dad is a Marine? He flies the AH-1Z Supercobra?"

Billy had studied everything he could about every active attack helicopter in the world. He was very familiar with the debate.

"No, sir. My Dad is in the U.S. Army reserve and flies the RAH-66 Comanche. It's a great bird with unbelievable stealth characteristics, and very maneuverable … but it can't carry the ordinance the King Cobra can."

Gunny "D" was impressed.

"Well, Billy, you sure know your helo's. … and from what Sergeant major Jenkins told me about you, Leon, you're anxious to look at how to become a Marine while taking advantage of your scholarship."

"Tell you both what. Why don't you come over to my recruiting office and I'll show you some films. Some of them will knock your socks off because of the neat, intense scenes of our equipment in action … tanks, LAV's, helicopters, jet aircraft, amphibious assault ships, aircraft carriers, etc."

"Others will tell you a lot about the Marine Corps and the various ways to sign up. Either way, you are both welcome any time. How about this afternoon, or right now if you have the time?"

The Sergeant had taken the liberty of looking at Leon's schedule before coming. He knew Leon was free this afternoon and now hoped that his friend, Billy, was too.

"Sounds GREAT to me," said Billy, "I wouldn't miss it and I can come over right now. "

Leon also agreed, and all three left the Engineering building for Sergeant Bennett's office.

September 14, 2005, 20:30 local
Lazy H Ranch
Outside Montague, Texas

"OK, that's great, honey. Glad to hear you enjoyed it so much. …Yes, you bet, I'll be sure to pass that on to your father. Please wait for him to talk to you before you make any final decision. I know, I know … that's the main reason you called."

"Tell Leon and his family hi for us. Good luck in the game this weekend … we hope you get to play. Don't forget your studies … Yes, I know you do. Ok, honey. Bye."

Cindy hung up the phone. Billy sure had been impressed by a Marine recruiter there on the BSU campus. Well, this was no big surprise. He had always indicated a preference for the Marine Corp. But Cindy sure wanted him to take advantage of his education before he joined up. Well, Jess would talk it over with him and give him the best advice possible. She was confident Billy would then make the best decision. As she thought about this, she heard the pickup pull into the driveway and the engine stop. A few seconds later, the front door opened.

"There you are. I was beginning to wonder if you had gotten lost."

Jess crossed the room and gave his wife a hug and then walked into the kitchen with her.

"Nope, just had to dicker with old long-winded Harv Harberson about that hay he wants to buy. In the end that was alright, though, because he ended up settling for more than I was going to ask … sort of talked himself into it. Anyhow, sorry I was late."

As they sat down at the table together, Cindy reassuringly put her hand on Jess's arm.

"Well, it was no big thing. Too much longer and I honestly would have started worrying, though. But you did miss a call from Billy."

Jess had thought a lot about his son over the last few weeks since he and Cindy had returned from Idaho. He wanted to know what was going on … wanted to know how his son was faring … what was the football pro gram like … whom was he befriending …. how were his classes. Jess trusted his son implicitly. He just wanted to share these things with him. Cindy wanted to know all of this too … and even more. But wisely, they knew that their son was off on his own and needed some independence and space to let him stand on his own two feet. He would call them if he needed help or had news.

"Now," Jess thought, "I've missed one of those calls."

"What did he have to say?"

Cindy watched Jess's eyes carefully as she told him of Billy's meeting with the Marine recruiter and Billy's excitement at the films he had watched. She particularly watched Jess as she told of Billy's excitement as he learned of the capabilities of the AH-Z King Cobra helicopter the Marines were deploying.

"He's talking about trying to find a way to join up with the Marines now and get his basic training out of the way after football season or next summer. He says he thinks he can work it out between the school and the Marines to defer his active duty until after graduation, or something like that."

"Jess, he sure sounded excited. I could hear it in his voice. He has the eyesight and the smarts for it. He wants to be a pilot like his Dad."

Jess's eyes never betrayed any hint of disappointment regarding a possible Marine career for his son as opposed to the U.S. Army. There was none. Jess knew it was an honorable thing to desire to serve you nation in any capacity and Jess already had great respect for the U.S. Marine Corps.

"I'll have to look into whether the Marines have such programs and what the particulars are for them. My guess is they will help him with some of his expenses, although the football scholarship is full ride."

"That new Cobra is a nice bird. He could do a heck of a lot worse. I'm glad they are on our side … although the Comanche is still the hottest thing flying under a rotor."

As Jess said this, the phone rang.

"I'll get it, honey."

"Hello. Yes … this is he. … I see. When? Yep, that'll be more than enough. Ok. … Ok. Not a problem, I'll be there. Thanks. Goodbye."

When Jess hung up the phone, Cindy stood and walked over to him. They had been together too long and she had heard too many similar calls to not recognize the inflection in his voice or the types of answers he had given. She could recognize in an instant his "military" voice and knew he had just received some type of call pertaining to it.

"Jess, I already know. When do you have to report?"

"It's a call to active duty. Couldn't go into any details over the phone, but I am to report to Tampa, Florida next Wednesday, the 20th. It's a minimum of three months."

September 15, 2005, 9:50 local
Former Iran/Iraq Frontier
Between Abadan and Basra, GIR

Abduhl Selim was exhilarated as his squad leader announced that they had just crossed into the former nation of Iraq. So much had happened in the last four months since his country of Turkmenistan had united with Iran and helped to form the Greater Islamic Republic.

Abduhl had turned eighteen years old soon after the announcement of that unification. That announcement had changed his life and stirred his soul. It had been almost a religious event for him as he had cheered the announcement of unification and the creation of a greater Islamic Republic. Although not overly religious himself, that event had given birth to a keen desire within his soul to be a part of the historical events unfolding around him. When they had returned to their home after the announcement, he had gone to his father and shared with him his love for weapons and his desire to join the armed forces of this blossoming new world power.

His father had shared much with Abduhl. To Abduhl's utter shock and amazement, his father had not only assented, but had talked long hours with him about Abduhl's feelings, and what his father considered his strengths and weaknesses. It turned out, his father knew more than he would have possibly imagined ... and his father understood him.

From that point, he had gone into the basic training with the former Turkmenistan armed forces. That very training was in the process of being modified and updated by representatives from Iran, now the Greater Islamic Republic. During his six weeks of training, Abduhl had proven so phenomenally proficient with a rifle that he had been recommended and approved for transfer to one of the more elite regular GIR units. As a result, upon completion of his basic training, Abduhl was on his way south into the former Iran and to his new unit, an assault company in the 2nd Army group of the Greater Islamic Republic.

Now, a month later, here he was, traveling as a part of a scout squad for his company, riding in a eight-wheeled BTR-80 armored personnel carrier. Every few moments the sound of low flying attack helicopters or jet aircraft could be heard passing overhead.

Abduhl's BTR-80 crosses into Iraq.

"Abduhl, come forward. It's your turn to take watch."

The BTR-80 had several firing and observation ports through which the embarked infantry could observe their surroundings and fire their weapons in response to combat situations. While in transit, in non-combat areas, the soldiers had been trained to keep a regular watch through a few of the observation/firing ports in an effort to avoid their being surprised by enemy forces or insurgents.

Although many of the soldiers did not like this duty, Abduhl enjoyed it because it provided a break in the monotony of riding in the canvas seats, and it let him see glimpses of the countryside through the clouds of dust raised by other vehicles.

"Yes, sir! Right away, sir!"

The sergeant hid a smile at the enthusiasm and willingness of this young soldier.

"Allah be praised," he thought, "I pray this youngster's attitude is infectious."

"Just make sure you keep your eyes open. As we approach closer to Basra, there will be more buildings and we want to be on our guard. In Basra, our column will be taking the "E" highway to the north towards Baghdad and support of the Iraqi forces preparing to reclaim the regions in the north, should the rebels continue in their rebellious ways. We'll change watch in Basra. That's about two hours from now."

Abduhl smiled as he cradled his AK-74 assault rifle in his arms and took up his position at the observation port. Two hours to Basra! Baghdad by tomorrow evening! And all of it as a part of his nation ... one people, one faith and one leader.

That leader was one Abduhl was coming to trust and respect more as the days went on. He was a leader who had the will to secure their nation's place in world affairs ...a leader who would not let any other power, particularly any western power, interfere in the affairs of their nation. Although Abduhl was mature enough to understand that it would be better for the Kurds to align themselves with their Islamic brothers peacefully and willfully, a part of him hoped they would try to maintain their rebellion. He wondered if the Americans would be inclined to interfere.

Abduhl and the rest of the world did not have to wait long to find out.

September 15, 2005, 19:00 EDT
The Oval Office, The White House
Washington, D.C.

"Good evening, my fellow Americans. I come before you this evening to inform you directly of certain actions your government is taking in response to world events. I believe it is imperative that the people of this nation are as informed as possible regarding the state of international conditions world-wide. It is equally imperative that the citizens are informed regarding our national interests and how we, as your elected representatives respond to them on your behalf. We are a nation governed by the people and for the people, and it is, and will continue to be, this administration's policy to never forget that critical and fundamental principle."

"As most of you are aware, there have been extraordinary developments in world affairs over the last several months. In the Far East a very strong Coalition of Asian States formed several months ago with the idea of uniting dissimilar cultures, governments and peoples along ideological and economic lines that are extremely socialistic at best, and Marxist at worst. They are attempting to accomplish this coalition by entering into exclusive trade agreements with several nations, Russia in particular. These relations have harmed many corporations based in America and Europe, as well as many in Asia, which are headquartered in nations outside of the CAS. This is because in those areas being exploited by the CAS, the arrangements are exclusive to CAS member states and, accordingly, the host countries have canceled contracts and arrangements of long standing with our corporations and many corporations of our friends and allies."

"In addition, within the CAS, a new tariff has been attached to the labor force of the member countries. This high tariff has driven many more American and other firms out of the market, forcing them to abandon significant capital investments which the CAS nations then pick up for pennies on the dollar at best. Many of our companies are going out of business as a result."

"Inasmuch as these practices violate the very essence of free and fair trade, we are taking the following action by way of response."

"First, we are asking the National Economic Council, headed by the Secretary of the Treasury, to examine the impact of removing normal trade status from the nations of India, The People's Republic of China and all members of The Greater Islamic Republic. Unless these nations indicate a clear commitment to reverse these unfair and confrontational trade practices, as President I will recommend revocation of normal trade relations for these countries by November 1st of this year."

"Such measures, if they are implemented, will create hardship for some American companies. We will offset these hardships through short-term subsidies to encourage economic development and the opening of markets in other areas more favorable for US trade. Conditions for said subsidies and areas targeted for companies desiring to qualify will be announced in concert with any suspension in normal trade relations with the aforementioned nations."

"My fellow citizens, it is past time that we step forward in our fair and free trade efforts and insure that said trade is always fair to American firms and in keeping with American national interests. In so doing, we will not impair or impede the free market. We will apply normal trade relation status with all three of these criteria in mind ... free, fair to America and not at odds with American national interests. It will require the efforts of all of us, working together as individual citizens, to insure that these measures work. Send a personal message to these nations with your pocketbook."

"Second, on the agenda tonight, is a matter of utmost importance, and one that strikes at the heart of our most cherished national principles. It is the principle of self-determination and sovereignty. As most of you are aware, the nation of Iraq has virtually ceased to exist. Our long-time adversary, Sahdam Hussein, was recently assassinated, and the nation of Iraq fell into a state of virtual anarchy. The resulting atmosphere in the Mid East has been one of extreme tension, and we have been monitoring that potentially volatile atmosphere closely."

"We have supported the UN initiative to allow the people of Iraq to hold a referendum to establish the direction of their peoples. The results of that election sent two very important and distinct messages to the world."

"First, the peoples of central and southern Iraq voted clearly to unite themselves with the Greater Islamic republic. We support their will in this decision, although we would rather have seen them remain independent."

"Second, the already autonomous Kurdish areas of northern Iraq voted to establish their independence. This is something they have sought since World War I when the current borders of Iraq were imposed upon them. They have never ceased working for their independence and were kept from it by one of the most brutal tyrants of the last fifty years. The suffering of the Kurds has been well documented. Our northern no-fly zone, which we have maintained since the Gulf War until just before Sahdam's death, has provided them with some protection and allowed them to achieve autonomy under Hussein."

"Now these people have voted overwhelmingly for self determination and independence in creating the Republic of Kurdistan."

"Ladies and gentlemen, my fellow citizens and all those listening across the world. Tonight, as President of the United States, and in concert with the nations of Great Britain, Canada, Australia, Israel, Turkey and the Kingdom of Saudi Arabia, I announce the official recognition of the Republic of Kurdistan as a free and independent, sovereign nation."

"In the weeks to come, we will establish our embassy in the capitol of Irbil."

"We urge calm and peace in the region. We especially urge the Imam Hasan Sayeed and the Greater Islamic Republic to honor the express wish of the people of the Republic of Kurdistan. The borders of the Republic of Kurdistan and its sovereignty must be respected."

"To help insure the integrity of this sovereign nation, the United States will present a resolution to the security council and the general assembly of the United Nations calling for the establishment of observers on the border and calling for mediation between the GIR and the Republic of Kurdistan. These resolutions will also propose creating a "buffer" zone between the two forces until a diplomatic resolution is reached. For your information, the map being displayed on your TV screen and on our live broadcast site on the Internet, portrays the location of the new Republic of Kurdistan, the proposed buffer zones, and the final vote counts according to the UN monitoring teams."

"As a precaution against coercion by outside forces, and as a demonstration of our own commitment, I have activated a number of U.S. Army reserve units to be available to support our Marine Expeditionary Unit which is in Kuwait training at the moment. These forces will also be available to support our forces on the ground in Turkey should they require such support for any contingency. The specific units and their function will be announced tomorrow morning at a press conference to be held by the Secretary of Defense, Tim Hattering, and the Chairman of the Joint Chiefs of Staff, General Jeremy Stone."

"We believe these measures constitute an appropriate response to conditions which pose risks and challenges to our national interests and our ability to conduct free and fair trade. We urge the nations of the CAS to carefully consider their economic policies, and to work to meet us half way in developing fair trade policies between the CAS member nations and America and her allies."

"Again, we particularly urge restraint on the part of the Greater Islamic Republic in dealing with the new nation, the Republic of Kurdistan. In the spirit of our own independence, we in America, along with several of our allies, have taken the step to recognize them as an independent nation because of the historical nature of their struggle, and because of the ideals they embrace."

"We state in clear and unmistakable language, to any nation that would attempt to coerce a free people: the decision we have made to recognize the Republic of Kurdistan is not a step we have taken lightly. Nor is it one from which we will walk away."

"Now, my fellow citizens, goodnight, and may God bless our great Republic; may God bless the United States of America."

September 16, 2005, 08:03 EDT
WNN Broadcast Studios
New York city, New York

"Continuing with our top story."

"Reactions to President Weisskopf's dramatic announcements yesterday are pouring in from around the world. Impact on Wall Street has been mixed as the Blue Chips have been steady to higher while the Technology sector is taking a beating. The volatility is due to the large investment in high tech design and manufacturing in the People's Republic of China and the impact that cessation of normal trade relations will have on those investments."

"On Capitol Hill, many on both sides of the aisle are condemning the announcement by the President as being too harsh and too reactionary to the economic build-up of the Coalition of Asian States. Others, predominantly conservatives, are hailing the President's actions as long overdue, given the continued military build-up of the People's Republic of China and its expanding unfair and unfriendly economic influence in the region."

"Reactions from overseas are mixed."

"The most severe reactions, as might be expected, are coming from The Greater Islamic Republic, India and The People's Republic of China."

"President Jien Zenim of the People's Republic of China was quoted this morning in the China News with this response:"

"It is unfortunate that the United States has chosen to react in this fashion. Economically and diplomatically, President Weisskopf has embarked on a path of confrontation and vilification instead of understanding. The People's Republic of China will not follow suit. We will work both with the United States and with our CAS partners and come to as amiable a solution to these difficulties as possible."

"Harsher words were quoted by the Imam Hasan Sayeed, the leader of the Greater Islamic Republic:"

"How dare the United States interfere our internal affairs as a sovereign nation. The people of Iraq have spoken, in the American tradition of democracy, and have voted to unite themselves with the Greater Islamic Republic. The elections were monitored and certified by the United Nations and sanctioned by the general assembly of that body, despite violence that attempted to disrupt and destroy the election, perpetrated by the very people whom the United States claims it is backing. "

"We repeat to the United States and to the world: we will not tolerate outside interference in our internal affairs. We are negotiating with the leaders in the autonomous northern regions of the former Iraq in good faith. We offer amnesty to those involved with the independence movement, other than those we intend to identify who committed violence during, or attempted to defraud, the election process itself. We guarantee the continued autonomy of the region within the Greater Islamic Republic. We urge all citizens in the region, both Kurds and those of other ethnic or cultural backgrounds, to maintain order and avoid outside influence and attempts to divide our nation and our faith."

"We repeat, any efforts, after November 1st, to divide our nation will not be tolerated. We warn those nations establishing diplomatic ties with this break-away region … you will not be accorded normal diplomatic protections should the revolt continue. We do not recognize the rebellion or any of the institutions which are trying to legitimize it."

"Other nations either condemning the moves by the U.S. President, or responding negatively to them, have included, India, Russia, Libya, North Korea, Vietnam, South Africa, and the Western Hemisphere nations of Cuba, Venezuela and Panama."

"Finally, reactions from America's allies and friends are cautious. Support ranging from cautious to unqualified comes from England, Canada, Australia, Saudi Arabia, Israel, Turkey, South Korea and Taiwan. Germany, Italy, France, Greece, Brazil, Egypt and Japan have all expressed their reservations and their intent to await further developments."

"With the response around the world varying so widely, it is highly unlikely that the United States will realize its desires for a UN monitoring force in the region to establish a buffer zone between the former Iraq and the break-away Republic of Kurdistan. We will update our viewers immediately with breaking news from the region."

"Now ... for other news."

September 19, 2005, 15:28 Local Time
COSTIND Headquarters
Beijing, PRC

Seated in the plush corporate management conference room were:

General Hunbaio, the commander of all of The People's Republic of China's weapons development, along with several of his deputies,

Chin Zhongbaio, the CEO of Red China's COSCO shipping company, the largest ship builder in the world, along with his managing directors,

Lu Pham, the mastermind behind, and designer of, Red China's newest and most secret weapon, the LRASD and,

Sung Hsu, the ingenious head of COSCO manufacturing.

The General was addressing the group, and was completing a review of the status of progress on the COSCO shipping military conversion project, and building towards two special presentations.

"I am pleased to announce that as of this morning we have launched the Beijing, our first Sea Control Carrier from the Tanjin shipyards. This is a proud day for the People's Republic of China and her people. We have entered a new era of Naval Power and Naval history for the People's Republic of China. And we intend to continue along that path. We expect to begin launching more of these ships from our more secure facilities by the middle of November.

"In addition, over the next two weeks, we will launch our first Amphibious Assault ship and our first Tactical Attack ship from our other conversion facilities. These ships will not only allow us to extend our capacity to project our nation's foreign policy around the globe, but the new LRASD weapons systems which they carry will also allow us to do so without fear or concern of how our adversaries might attempt to interfere."

"In addition to this review, today we have gathered ourselves together to recognize the tremendous efforts and roles of two of our most talented personnel in the achievement of these accomplishments. One of these two individuals is Commodore Lu Pham, the designer and developer of our new LRASD weapon system. The other individual is Sr. Manager Sung Hsu, the brilliant manufacturing manager who has seen to it that the conversion of these vessels proceeded smoothly and ahead of schedule."

"In recognition of those efforts, Lu and Sung, please stand up."

Sung Hsu was embarrassed, proud, moved and patriotic all at the same time as he stood next to his friend, Lu Pham. He was glad that Lu was here to experience this with him. He only wished his wife and children could also share it with him. No matter, he would spare no description in sharing it with them (at least as much as security would allow) when he got home.

For his part, Lu Pham was proud and richly gratified as he stood. He was fulfilling his dream of creating an extremely complex and revolutionary weapons system that would be used to pay back the United States for its crimes against his family. He had never allowed this underlying desire for retribution to affect or taint his work, but it had been an fundamental motivation for him the entire time, nonetheless.

"Commodore Lu Pham, in recognition of your contributions and command performance, I am proud to promote you to Admiral in the Navy of the People's Republic of China. From this point, you will report directly to me in your efforts on the LRASD weapons system and its integration into the fleet. Congratulations in your new responsibilities Admiral Lu."

As the General shook Lu's hand he presented him with his new insignia.

"I will now turn time to Chin Zhongbaio for the presentation to Sung Hsu."

Chin Zhongbaio stood and approached Sung Hsu. Chin was one of the most powerful men in the People's Republic of China. A member of the politburo with direct access to, and the confidence of, President Jien Zenim, he was also the Chief Executive Officer of the largest shipping company in the world, which he had personally managed the growth of since its inception.

Chin prided himself on the prestige, honor and power his accomplishments brought COSCO and his homeland, and on his ability to recognize and develop talent which served COSCO and the PRC. In Sung Hsu, he had discovered and developed one of the most promising of talents … in truth, with Sung, there was little development necessary. Sung developed himself.

"Sung Hsu, in honor of your accomplishments on the Amphibious Assault conversion project, and further suggestions which have benefited all of our military conversion projects, today I promote you to the position of Senior

Vice President of Manufacturing, Military Conversion Projects. In this position of responsibility, you will report directly to me. Congratulations."

September 20, 2005, 08:15 EDT
National Reconnaissance Office Headquarters
IMINT Directorate, Chantilly, VA

More satellite photos had come in early this morning. What they showed was not a tremendous surprise, but was stunning nonetheless. There, with tugs on either side and moving towards the harbor entrance (and being recorded faithfully by the SEAL MUAS units as it did), was the first Aircraft Carrier to enter the service of the People's Republic of China.

"Bill, you might want to take a look …they've launched her. We knew it was coming anyway, but as of late yesterday China time, she was moving out of the Tanjin harbor."

As Tom said, Bill had expected it would be soon. The Chinese had moved with stunning speed in the conversion of a very impressive VSTOL (Vertical and Short Take Off and Landing) Aircraft Carrier. They had clearly been planning this for several years and had executed the plan almost flawlessly. Bill had to respect that effort, but it concerned him just the same.

"And what of the shipyards?"

Tom and Bill had discussed their opinions of how quickly the Chinese would turn things around and begin converting another ship. The answer had largely been answered several days ago when another COSCO container ship had been photographed pulling up near the dry dock shipyard into a position which would allow it to quickly be placed in the dry dock and worked on. Today, all of that was confirmed through satellite imagery.

"Already in the dock, Bill. In the last two-and-a-half days, they floated the first out and have the second in there ready to go for round two."

Bill had expected as much. It looked like the People's Republic of China was going to be able to launch Sea Control Aircraft Carriers every few months. The question now was how long it would take for them to make these things operational.

"We'd best get this together and get with John Bowers and the Navy. The Navy has already got an advanced LA Class SSN over there ready to track this lady through trials. With everything else that's going on in the Mid

East, though, our ability to focus on this will be impaired. We're going to have to find a way to stay on top of it anyway, between all of these Central Command requests we are getting."

September 20- November 1, 2005

Bill Hendrickson was right. The focus was on the Middle East, and over the ensuing six weeks conditions there continued to deteriorate as diplomatic efforts increased dramatically and military preparations began in earnest.

On September 22, the United States introduced its resolution to the General Assembly of the United Nations for a monitoring force and a buffer zone between the Greater Islamic Republic and the Republic of Kurdistan. This resolution, after two days of heated debate, was defeated by a vote of 47 in favor and 65 against.

Thereafter, visits by the Vice President of the United States and the U.S. Secretary of State proceeded at a rapid pace. The Vice President ably assumed the task of reaching out to allies and friends and putting together a coalition of nations who favored the independence of Kurdistan. Along with Great Britain, Canada, Australia, Israel, Turkey and the Kingdom of Saudi Arabia, by October 10th the Vice President was able to convince South Korea, The United Arab Emirates (UAR), The Republic of China (Taiwan), Egypt, Germany and Brazil to officially recognize the new nation.

In the meantime, the Greater Islamic Republic was able to gather significant support for its position that the Republic of Kurdistan was a region rebelling against the legitimate wishes of the people of the Greater Islamic Republic. The nations of Libya, Syria, Jordan, North Korea, Vietnam and Uzbekistan stood firmly behind the GIR's deadline of November 1st for the use of force. The People's Republic of China, India and Russia did not recognize the new Republic of Kurdistan. But they supported GIR efforts to end what they called the "rebellion." They also made a great show of volunteering to mediate the "crisis" between the United States and the GIR.

Militarily, the United States activated its pre-positioned equipment (consisting of armor, ammunition, fuel and other logistical supplies) in Kuwait, the UAR and Saudi Arabia. The U.S. Central Command, under four star General Lyman Horton, was given overall theater command for what had been labeled Operation "Desert Sentinel" and began beefing up its troop strength. The 82nd Airborne ready brigade, the Marine Expeditionary Unit already in Kuwait, and initial elements of the 24th Mechanized Division's armor and infantry brigades were all deployed. Other reserve and regular units in lesser numbers were sent to Turkey to strengthen the airfields there.

The 9th Air Force began flying in squadrons of F-15E, A-10 and F-16 strike fighters along with F-15 air superiority fighters and all of the supporting aircraft to airfields in Saudi Arabia and Turkey. Turkey augmented the already strengthened U.S. security around the airbases with its own forces.

In addition to the MEU and its supporting ships already deployed in the area, the U.S. Navy also deployed one Carrier Battle Group (CBG) in the Persian Gulf and another off the coast of Turkey as a show of force and commitment, and to support Operation Desert Sentinel. In addition, two Surface Action Groups (SAG's), consisting of one Arleigh Burke class guided missile destroyer (DDG) and two Spruance class destroyers (DD) each, were deployed to the Persian Gulf and the Mediterranean Sea. Four Los Angeles class nuclear attack submarines (SSN) were also deployed to the area.

Most of the U.S. ground strength and that of its allies of England, Australia, Canada, Saudi Arabia and Kuwait, were located along the Kuwait and Saudi Arabian borders as a shield for the Kingdom of Saudi Arabia.

Arrayed against them were the much larger numbers of the GIR 1st Army group, which were augmented by the former Iraqi Army and Republican Guard units in the southern areas of former Iraq, south and west of Basra near the Kuwait and Saudi Arabian borders. These units had continued to pour into Iraq along with the GIR 2nd Army Group. The 2nd Army Group moved north to augment the former Iraqi Republican Guard that had taken up positions along the Kurdistan frontier between Baghdad and Irbil. All units made a point of deploying to staging areas well off the border.

Hundreds of military aircraft including modern SU-27, MIG-29, SU-24 and SU-25 aircraft were also ferried to airfields in, Southern and Central Iraq. As air patrols of the GIR and air patrols of both the U.S and its allies began to fly in proximity to one another, tensions escalated.

In mid-October, Hasan Sayeed issued a general call up for reserves and volunteers to augment the already massive ground forces of the GIR. The answer was unprecedented as hundreds of thousands of young to middle-aged Islamic men flocked to military training facilities in every major town across the broad expanse of the Greater Islamic Republic. Arms shipments from both Russia and the People's Republic of China were arriving daily as the oil wealth available to the GIR was used for expedited shipments.

By October 25th, one week before the deadline established by Hasan Sayeed was set to expire, the entire world again held its breath as belligerent forces were arrayed facing one another in the Middle East.

By that date, more than 200,000 GIR forces were prepared to occupy Kurdistan, supported by 800 tanks, 200 attack helicopters and 500 combat aircraft. In the south, along the Kuwait and Saudi borders, the GIR had an even larger force of approximately 225,000 troops, supported by 1200 tanks, 250 attack helicopters and 800 combat aircraft.

By comparison, the coalition put together by the United States had 200 aircraft in Turkey, supported by 50,000 Turkish troops and 15,000 U.S. forces which were there to act as a final defense for the air bases out of which the U.S., English and Canadian aircraft were operating.

In the south, the U.S. had amassed 50,000 combat troops supported by another 25,000 coalition troops. The ground troops were established in a defensive posture along the border between the GIR, Kuwait and Saudi Arabia, along with their equipment, which included 400 tanks, 200 attack helicopters and 300 combat aircraft. All of these numbers were growing daily and as the days of October dwindled, the feeling of anxiety hung palpably in the desert air.

CHAPTER 6

"Never interrupt your enemy when he is making a mistake." -
Napoleon Bonaparte

October 30, 2005, 06:50 local
Republic of Kurdistan Military Headquarters
In the Cavern Near Irbil, Iraq

With the move towards independence, Jabal Talabari had been appointed the commanding General for all of Kurdistan's military forces. Over the last weeks, in addition to the fifteen to twenty thousand members of Jabal's original Patriotic Kurdistan Front, Jabal, along with help from Will Peterson and his American CIA compatriots, had been able to recruit another thirty thousand personnel. The Kurdistan people were anxious to defend their new nation, but given the time constraints, only very rudimentary training could be conducted. Despite the lack of "formal" training, they were willing to fight for their new republic and Jabal felt they could make up in commitment and desire what they lacked in training. Unfortunately, the only way to do that when facing a well-disciplined and well-trained enemy, was to pay the butcher's bill.

Forty-five thousand personnel, with no heavy armor and only minimal anti-tank and anti-aircraft, were facing over 200,000 trained fighters with hundreds of heavy tanks and hundreds of modern attack aircraft and attack helicopters. The weapons that had been provided to them by the United States were modern and would function very well. Ultimately, the level of support they received from the U.S. Air Force flying out of Turkey and the degree of its effectiveness would be the key to the coming battle. In addition, in the end, it would come down to whether the U.S. and its allies were prepared to commit ground troops to support his new nation should the tremendous numerical advantage the GIR enjoyed overwhelm his forces.

Using his pointer, Jabal began the briefing, indicating the major bridges along the Tigris River within the Republic of Kurdistan territory.

"Will, we are as prepared as we can be given the training and disposition of our forces. The bridges along the Tigris here at Bayji where large number of the former Republican Guard and GIR forces are located, here, here … and here are all ready to be destroyed. This bridge in the city and this one near Bayji will be the most difficult to take down."

"We have our 2nd and 3rd infantry divisions placed between the Great and Little Zab rivers in defensive positions we have indicated. They will protect the Capital and hopefully spring the trap should the GIR take the bait."

"Our 4th infantry division is placed before Karkuk in a defensive mode and we expect them to take the brunt of the initial assault from the GIR units now staging northwest of Khanaqin. Our people will fall back rapidly under what we believe will be a major attack, and allow the GIR to push them hard towards the Little Zab river. Although admittedly a very risky strategy, we plan to allow the capture of two of the bridges over the Little Zab, here … and here as the GIR continues the pursuit of our "routed" 4th infantry division. When they enter these canyons and this terrain here to the north and west of the bridges, the 2nd and 3rd divisions will spring the trap."

"Our reserves consist of the 1st mechanized division, which is located in the hills outside of Mosul. Once the 4th infantry division begins its retreat, the 1st mechanized division will rapidly perform an encircling movement to approach the GIR forces from the rear as they pursue our retreating 4th, about the time they cross the Little Zab River."

Will Peterson reviewed and carefully considered the plan. The whole thing would depend on the U.S. Air Force keeping the GIR aircraft from conducting ground support or reconnaissance to discover the positioning and disposition of the reserve division, and the specific location of the 2nd and 3rd infantry divisions.

It would also depend on the GIR making its primary push up towards Karkuk, which meant the U.S. Air Force would have to located and subvert any other "thrusts" by the GIR, particularly any major push to the west on that side of the Tigris river towards Mosul. Will was certain there would be just such an effort by the GIR in that regard, and U.S. reconnaissance seemed to confirm his suspicions: the GIR was staging its forces at Bayji and on the north side of the Euphrates river near Al Qa'im. Locating and thwarting that western thrust would also be one of the primary keys to the upcoming battle.

Though it had been discussed here in Kurdistan, Will was certain that, other than a few special forces squads for very specific missions, the U.S. would not commit any significant ground forces here in the Republic of Kurdistan … too risky at this point. The missiles - Javelins, Stingers and LAWS -

provided to the Kurdish ground forces would have to do the trick on the battlefield, while the U.S. Air Force destroyed the GIR armor from the air.

"Jabal, the plan looks good, though I remain concerned about any major GIR thrust towards Mosul from west of the Tigris. If our aircraft do not find and stop such an offensive, it could easily catch our mechanized reserves in a vulnerable position. I am in touch with U.S. Air Force personnel out of Turkey and will have my people coordinating air support with each of your divisions. We need to make sure that your forward controllers are tied into my men and that we have multiple backups for that communication. It will be one of the primary keys to success on the battlefield. How are the anti-tank and anti-air defenses distributed?"

Jabal consulted his notes briefly.

"The 4th infantry division at Karkuk has our older Soviet block anti-tank weapons and shoulder- fired anti-air missiles. They have been well instructed in purposely minimizing their effectiveness so as to draw the GIR forces in, while not allowing themselves to be over run. We have about half of our most seasoned soldiers and NCO's in that division. The others are split equally between the reserve mechanized division and the divisions who will represent the jaws of our trap."

"The 2nd and 3rd infantry divisions have almost all of the Javelin missiles and LAWS missiles. I believe we have 100 Javelins and 150 LAWS missiles evenly split between those divisions. They also have roughly half of the Stinger missile systems; 75 in all. The 1st mechanized division has only a few of the anti-tank missiles since they will be depending on their mounted chain guns and light cannons taking the GIR vehicles from the rear. They are carrying the other half of the Stinger missiles for anti-air defense."

Will knew that the strategy was risky, but it was the best he and Jabal could come up with in consultation with the planners back in the states, given the forces at their disposal. Upon this plan, and upon the U.S. support of it, the future independence of the newly formed Republic of Kurdistan would hinge.

"Well, continue reviewing the plan and refining it with your division commanders, and they with their brigade and company commanders ... all the way down to the squad level. We won't have too long to wait. My guess is that the GIR is going to come boiling out of their staging areas tomorrow and be right up on the border on the 1st."

October 31, 2005, 06:50 local
Incirlik Air Force Base Ready Room
Near Adana, Turkey

Brigadier General Wesley Howell, the commander of the U.S. Air Force Expeditionary force in Turkey, reviewed the assembled pilots and logistical officers assembled before him. They were assembled in the largest briefing room on base, not far from the Command Center.

The General had allowed photographers and reporters into this briefing. As a result, he was going to be necessarily vague, to the point, and very upbeat. As the flashes went off on the cameras around him, the general began.

"OK, we're on 24 hour alert status as of this morning. Our operational goals are simple in the event of an invasion of Kurdistan. Our part of Operation Sentinel, as you all know, is simply to:

1. Prevent GIR air from penetrating Kurdistan air space.
2. Maintain air superiority over Kurdistan.
3. Provide air support to Kurdistan forces as requested.
4. Destroy any GIR anti-air assets directed at our forces.
5. Destroy any GIR AEW assets tracking our forces."

"In order to accomplish this operation, we will have combat air patrols increased to an around-the-clock basis starting this afternoon. Three flights of F-15 Eagles will maintain CAP over Kurdistan at all times with two flights of ready air here on the ground at all times. The CAP flights will be directed by two E-3 AEW aircraft which will each be escorted by two F-15's."

"In addition, we will have two flights of Wild Weasel F-16 aircraft up at all times, who will vector in to any GIR anti-air assets encountered."

"Finally, there will be one flight of four F-15E Strike Eagles and one flight of British Tornados airborne at all times with matching flights on ready air here at the  base. These will provide ground support to Kurdistan forces as requested, or be used to interdict GIR ground forces as they cross the border into

JOINTSTAR aircraft near the Turkey border.

Kurdistan. Control for these flights, will be provided by one JOINT STAR aircraft and its escorts which will be on patrol near the border."

"Folks, the pilots and aircraft you will likely encounter out there and the anti-air you are apt to meet are considered several notches above the opposition we faced in Desert Storm almost sixteen years ago. Be cognizant of this at all times. We will have a final briefing at 0400 hours tomorrow morning."

November 1st, 2005 12:00 EST
WNN Broadcast Headquarters
New York City, New York, USA

"As we report the top news at noon, all eyes are on the Middle East where in just an hour the deadline, the "line in the sand" established by Hasan Sayeed, will expire. This deadline represents when the Kurdish citizens in the northern provinces of the former Iran must cease their efforts toward achieving independence, or face military reprisal by the GIR."

"Tensions are running extremely high in the region as the deadline approaches. U.S. President Norm Weisskopf has indicated that the United States and its allies will support the new Republic of Kurdistan. To that end they have been moving troops and equipment to the Middle East over the last several weeks."

"These recent maneuvers have been eerily reminiscent of those which preceded the Desert Shield effort in Kuwait and Iraq almost sixteen years ago. WNN conducted a live broadcast of a briefing from the U.S. Air base at Incirlik, Turkey last evening where the Commanding General, General Wesley Howell, laid out in clear terms what the U.S. Air Force goals will be should hostilities erupt."

"He indicated that the primary goals of his forces are to maintain air superiority should GIR aircraft attempt to enter Kurdistan airspace, to provide air support to Kurdistan forces as requested and to destroy any GIR forces, including airborne early warning craft, which appear threatening to our forces."

"WNN has news crews on the scene in Baghdad, Irbil, the U.S. Air Base at Incirlik, and near the GIR front lines in Bayji. We will update you immediately with any breaking news and will include on-the-spot, real time coverage wherever possible."

"Now, on to other stories around the nation."

November 1st, 2005 23:50 local
GIR Forces
Kurdistan Frontier

The GIR Operation, dubbed "Veiled Sword," had been planned in great detail. At 0500 on November 2nd, from Bayij an entire GIR corps would feint towards Karkuk and then wheel north towards Mosul. With two hundred main battle tanks, four hundred armored personnel carriers, six hundred troop-carrying trucks, two hundred pieces of artillery, fifty attack helicopters and the support of one hundred and fifty fighter and attack aircraft, it was a thrust the Americans and Kurds could not ignore.

Four hours after this thrust began, an even larger mechanized thrust of three hundred main battle tanks, five hundred armored personnel carriers, three hundred artillery pieces and fifty attack helicopters, supported by two hundred fighter and attack aircraft would strike towards Mosul from Al Qa'im in the western desert.

The GIR's operation plans called for Mosul to be taken at all costs, so that any forces protecting Irbil and Karkuk would be cut off. In order to hold those forces in place, a large corps-sized thrust would also be made from the frontier north and west of Khanaqin. This thrust would include one hundred main battle tanks, two hundred armored personnel carriers, five hundred trucks, three hundred pieces of artillery (one hundred of which were Multiple Launch Rocket systems) supported by one hundred attack helicopters and another one hundred and fifty fighter and attack aircraft. This part of the attack would begin coincident with the attack originating from Bayij

In order to neutralize American air, the GIR was also diverting three hundred fighter and attack aircraft from its bases deep within the former borders of Iran. These had been flown to five different air bases in the eastern part of the country and were already taking off to form up into their combat groups. They would be refueled over GIR territory in the former Iran and then would fly nap of the earth through the darkness to the north of Tabriz before turning west into Turkey north and east of Lake Van. From there they would proceed directly to attack Incirlik.

It was anticipated that the Americans would respond strongly to this large force out of the GIR. When they did, Veiled Sword called for half of the fighter and attack aircraft supporting the thrusts toward Mosul to break off and fly directly to Incirlik to attack. It was expected that this massive four hundred and seventy-five aircraft attack on Incirlik would overwhelm the defenses and lay waste to the airfield and other aircraft parked there.

All of the GIR aircraft, would be controlled by three GIR Ilyushin Il-76 "Mainstay" AEW aircraft. These aircraft had been purchased by the GIR from Russia, and were dedicated to the Veiled Sword operation. They were crewed by volunteers Muslims from the Russian Federation as a part of the overall deal for the aircraft.

GIR Mainstay AEW aircraft over Iraq.

November 2nd, 2005 043:30 local
E3 Sentry "Overseer", 35,000 ft over Zakho
Kurdistan Frontier with Turkey

"Bravo flight, Bravo flight, this is Overseer. We have many unidentified aircraft approaching Bayji from the south. Count is forty aircraft and climbing … make it fifty-two aircraft and climbing. Vector two-seven-niner degrees, angels forty to intercept."

U.S. E-3 Sentry AEW aircraft over Turkey.

The controller on the U.S. Air Force E3 aircraft was observing the approaching GIR support air for the GIR 4th Corps thrust north of Bayji. He had just vectored one of the flights of F-15 Eagles to intercept this force and he was in the process of vectoring a second flight F-15's and calling for reserves.

"Aircraft identified as bandits. I say again we have bandit aircraft approaching from the south and entering Kurdistan airspace. Weapons free. Charlie flight, vector one-one-three degrees, angels forty to intercept."

"Homeplate, this is Overseer. Release Delta flight and have two more flights go to ready standby status. It's going to get thick up here."

In answer to a request from Alpha flight to also vector them towards the action, the four F-15's further to the north and east, the controller on board the E3 elected to have them maintain station.

"Negative Alpha flight.   Maintain position and monitor command frequency."

Now eight of the twelve airborne F-15's were converging on the over one hundred fighter and attack aircraft that were supporting the GIR 4th Corp thrust towards Mosul. Each Eagle carried eight missiles, four AMRAAMs and four Sidewinder air-to-air missiles. The AMRAAM - radar guided with a range of about forty miles, the Sidewinder- a close in infrared homing missile, with an effective range of ten to twelve miles.

Very quickly the lead element of F-15's was in range.

November 2nd, 2005 4:42 local
F-15 Eagle Bravo flight, 40,000 ft over Kurdistan
Between Mosul and Bayij, Kurdistan

"Fox-1, Fox-1."

The leader of Bravo Flight launched two of his AMRAAM radar guided missiles and continued in towards the approaching GIR aircraft. At 35,000 feet and about 30 miles in front of him, the initial flight of MiG-29 aircraft was approaching. There were twelve of them

F-15 Bravo flight prepares to engage over Turkey.

and they were all painting him and his flight with their N-019 radar in an attempt to get a "lock on" and prepare to launch their own missiles.

As his wingman and the other members of his flight each launched two missiles, the approaching GIR flight attempted to perform a splitting maneuver to evade the eight missiles launched at them. But two of the aircraft collided and exploded in flames and the other ten had to break their maneuver to avoid the debris. The more deadly condition for the GIR pilots was the oncoming flight of AMRAAM missiles. The AMRAAM was the most advanced radar-guided air-to-air missile in the world. A true "fire and forget" missile that had its own internal radar and homing guidance, the missile had an effective range of over forty miles. When the AMRAAMs arrived, six of the remaining ten MiG-29's fell in flames. At this point the distance had closed to 20 miles and the second flight of GIR fighters, this time twelve SU-27 Flankers, was also approaching.

The four remaining MiG-29's launched two of their long-range R-27 missiles each, and now eight missiles were coming at the four F-15's. At almost the same moment, the F-15's launched another AMRAAM each at the oncoming MIGs. Half of the GIR missiles were the R-27R semi-active radar homing missiles; the other half were the R-27T infrared homing missiles.

"On my mark, break. Mark!"

Upon command, each of the four American fighters performed its breaking maneuver flawlessly and attempted to change its aspect ratio to the oncoming missiles and reduce its radar cross section, while actively jamming the missiles. This worked for the R-27R missiles and only one of those four missiles found its mark as an F-15 took a hit. That pilot ejected safely as he lost control of the aircraft. Not fooled by jamming or aspect ratio changes, two R-27T infrared homing missiles impacted two American aircraft, both of which exploded. There were no chutes. The two F-15 pilots were the first Americans lost in this first battle of what later would evolve into a very long and horrific war. Only one of the Americans, the wingman to the flight leader, was able to employ his infrared defensive flares to draw the heat-seeking missiles away from his aircraft.

Meanwhile, the four AMRAAM missiles had destroyed another three MIGs. Now, one MiG-29 faced one remaining F-15, a mere twelve miles apart..

The last F-15 launched its last AMRAAM at the MiG-29, and then turned away from the oncoming SU-27's in an effort to egress the area as more missile launch warnings appeared on the pilot's HUD.

"Overseer, this is the Jinx from Bravo flight. Be advised we have three aircraft down, bandits still approaching. I am attempting to disengage."

But the warning was too late. The SU-27's had already launched four R-27 missiles at him, and before it could complete its turn it was destroyed.

At this point, the second flight of F-15's, Charlie flight, came within range.

November 2nd, 2005 4:55
SU-27 GIR Flight , 37,000 ft
over Kurdistan
South of Mosul, Kurdistan

"Missile launch! Perform evasive maneuver three on my command ... Now!"

SU-27 goes head to head over Turkey.

The flight leader for the twelve SU-27's, a more capable fighter aircraft than the MiG-29, quickly had his entire flight of twelve aircraft perform their evasive tactics in the face of eight oncoming AMRAAM missiles. The maneuver was performed successfully, but the deadly AMRAAM missiles found their marks and SU-27's fell in flames.

As the remaining eight SU-27's turned to continue their approach, the Americans launched another eight AMRAAM missiles. By this time, the distance had closed to the point where the SU-27's could lock onto the Americans and launch their own radar and infrared-guided missiles if they chose to press the attack. In the face of the deadly threat of the oncoming AMRAAMs, the disciplined and well-trained GIR flight leader made a fateful decision.

"Do not evade. I repeat do not evade. Obtain lock and launch two missiles each at the oncoming targets."

The SU-27 carried a longer-range version of the R-27 missile than the MiG-29, which included a radar homing version, R-27R1 and an infrared version, R-27T1. Quickly, twelve of these missiles were in the air, targeted on the F-15's from Charlie flight.

November 2nd, 2005 05:05 local
E3 Sentry "Overseer", 35,000 ft over Zakho
Kurdistan Frontier with Turkey

"Homeplate, this is Overseer. I am declaring an air emergency! Repeat: an air emergency! We have just picked up many bandits approaching from the east over Lake Zan. Count is over one hundred and growing."

"Alpha flight, vector oh-niner-three degrees, angels 20, weapons free."

"Homeplate, scramble all ready aircraft. We now have a massive raid approaching from the east in addition to those approaching from the south. Bravo and Charlie flights are down. I repeat: both flights are down. Bandits continue to approach."

As the controller communicated this warning, he noticed that twenty aircraft had broken from the formation approaching over Lake Zan, and were vectoring towards his aircraft. Keying the local frequency, he informed the pilot and his own escort.

"Colonel, we have a flight of twenty bandits vectoring towards our position. Our escorts should vector at one-two-five degrees at angles 20 to intercept. We are going to have to evade back towards Homeplate ASAP."

Colonel Frank realized he and his crew were in mortal danger. The GIR was pulling out all the stops to overwhelm their layered defense. Nothing remotely similar to this had ever occurred in Desert Storm.

"OK, I have them. Get strapped in back there. We are headed for the deck. Inform Homeplate and alert Starlight and their escort that they'd best RTB."

November 2nd, 2005 05:20 local
Control Tower
Incirlik Airbase. Turkey

"Sir, we have that large raid approaching from the east and the two smaller groups approaching from the southeast. Overseer is off the air. Alpha, Bravo and Charlie flights are all down, sir; 100% down. Our two reserve flights have engaged and expended all missiles. Of those eight reserve aircraft, two are left and they are attempting to RTB."

"Our strike aircraft are engaging the mechanized columns that are moving towards Mosul, but they are suffering significant attrition due to GIR air in those areas. After their munitions are expended, or when their position becomes untenable, they are going to egress to the Turkish airfield at Diyarbakir."

"Enemy strength remains high and they are continuing to press their advantage. Our current analysis indicates that our own efforts and the two intercepts performed by the Turks have eliminated over eighty of their aircraft at a loss of eighteen of our own fighters and twelve Turkish. In addition, Overseer is off the air and presumed down and we have lost Starlight, the JOINT STAR aircraft. The raid strength from the east appears to be at over two hundred and fifty aircraft, and there are over one hundred and twenty combined aircraft approaching from the southeast."

At this report, General Howell looked grimly at the screens and reports. The loss of the E-3 Sentry and the E-8 were tragic, and would have made the entire GIR effort worth it from their perspective. But the GIR was clearly intent on more than eliminating critical assets over the battlefield. They were intent on eliminating U.S. air superiority altogether in the region. Within twenty minutes all hell was going to break loose at Incirlik.

The general considered his remaining assets. He had his remaining fifteen F-15's up on a barrier CAP forty miles out from the base. His B-1's, KC-135's and remaining two reserve E-3's were supposed to be airborne already, and en route away from Incirlik. His last remaining E-3 was airborne and fifty miles to the west of Incirlik with an escort of four F-15's. That E-3 AWACS aircraft would help control the coming battle.

As the raid approached, the General was trying desperately to rearm his F-15E's and F-16's for air-to-air, but the raid was going to arrive before he was complete. Still, it would be a near thing and if those F-15's could delay things for even a few minutes, there was a chance.

"OK, insure that our airborne F-15's remain well outside the twenty mile free fire zone we have set up for our ground-based AAW defenses. Make sure the Hawk and Patriot batteries understand that they will have free fire authorization from us within the next few minutes. Make sure our ground defense forces understand the same with their shoulder-launched Stingers and their Avenger air defense systems."

"Are the B-1's, E-3's and KC-135's and their escorts away?"

Before replying, the Major checked his notes and information on his palmtop computer. Then replying to the General he said,

"Yes, sir. Those aircraft and their escort have cleared the free fire zone and are en route to Izmir. Izmir is providing a CAP two hundred miles out along the axis of their approach. Between that CAP and their own escorts, I feel they are as safe as we can make them"

"Good, pass the order on to the air defense batteries informing that they are weapons free within the free fire zone … and get everyone into the shelters -- particularly those news people. I'll be down in the command center."

November 2nd, 2005 05:40 local
25,000 ft., GIR Raid,
110 Miles East of Incirlik Airbase. Turkey

General Mahdavi Ardakani, the commander of the GIR raid on Incirlik and the individual responsible for developing the plan, surveyed his accompanying aircraft. The four U.S. Air Force F-15's had taken out five of his MiG-21 and seven of his MiG-29 aircraft, but all of the F-15's had been destroyed in the process. The two Turkish attacks had destroyed another eight of his MiG-21 aircraft and seven of his Mig-27 attack aircraft while all twelve of the Turkish F-16 and F-5 aircraft were destroyed. This left the general with two hundred and sixty-two aircraft for his raid on Incirlik.

He knew that there were approximately ten to fifteen F-15's prepared to meet him, and then there would be the air defense at the base itself. As a result of the heavy jamming from off to the west, it was difficult to tell at this point. For the ground attack, he had twenty SU-24 Fencers, twenty-four SU-27's, twenty-four MiG-29's, sixty MiG-21's forty MiG-27's and forty of his own American built F-5's. Escorting all of these he had a total of fifty-four other MiG-29's, SU-27's and MiG-21's outfitted for air-to-air combat.

It was the latter that he was about to employ against the F-15's that were defending the air base. It was the General's hope to blow a hole through those defenses and allow his attack aircraft to pulverize the base.

"Flights C through G, this is command. Perform pincer three on my mark … three, two, one … mark!"

"Attack flights A and B, and flights L through Q, await my order for execution of OPLAN order four C."

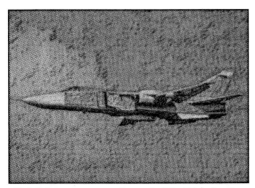
SU-24 prepares to launch Kh-59 missile.

On his order, eight SU-27's and six MiG-29's split to the north while ten SU-27's and six more MiG-29's split south. They all went to full combat throttle and wheeled around to come at the defending F-15's from the resulting pincer positions. As this was occurring, twenty-two escorting MiG-21's went to afterburner and shot ahead of the attack group towards the F-15's. Over two hundred attack aircraft continued relentlessly towards Incirlik.

Each of the attacking SU-24's carried two Kh-59 TV-command guided missiles, which had a range of sixty miles. The General was betting that all of them could get within range of Incirlik and launch those missiles before being intercepted by any surviving F-15's. He had positioned the SU-24's forward, near the center of his attack formations. In the next few seconds, the General would order them to full combat throttle so they could dash forward, launch their Kh-59 missiles and then egress quickly towards GIR territory with an escort of six SU-27's.

November 2nd, 2005 05:45 local
30,000 ft., Barrier CAP F-15's
30 Miles East of Incirlik Airbase. Turkey

Colonel Jim Phillips immediately saw the developing situation. The GIR was trying to run a classic pincer maneuver on him. In addition to the advantageous positioning they were attempting, they had overwhelming numbers on their side. He desperately needed to break through the oncoming fighters so he could get to the attack aircraft and perform some significant attrition on them before they could reach the base.

Things were going to be desperate for their base and they all knew it. The sheer numbers of the oncoming GIR raids were going to inundate the defenses well past the point of saturation. The desperation was beginning to show somewhat in their voices and in their protocol.

"Bob, on my mark take your flight and break left to those bogies coming down from the north. Jerry, take your flight and break right to those bogies coming in from the south. Everyone else, follow me. On my mark we're going to attempt to break through the middle and get to those attack aircraft."

"All units, use Watchtower for targeting and guidance as long as possible. Watchtower, Homeplate ... do you copy?"

The E-3 Sentry did indeed copy, as did the controller at the tower at Incirlik.

"That's a copy, Lonestar. Good luck. Even up those numbers for us."

Setting his resolve and focus, Colonel Phillips concentrated on the timing of his ordered maneuvers.

"… three, two, one … mark!"

"Good shooting, and may God have mercy on us all."

November 2nd, 2005 that same time
WNN Broadcast Studios
New York City, New York, WNN

"We interrupt this program to bring you a SPECIAL NEWS REPORT."

On TV screens across America and around the world, David Krenshaw's face appeared as WNN interrupted normal programming.

"Incirlik Air Base, Turkey. … We have reports of military activity and are cutting live to our on-scene reporter, Maria Gomez. Go ahead, Maria."

The feed cut to a night picture of a young Spanish American female reporter. Her hair was blowing in a gusty wind and she had her ear to her headset. In the background, crews were seen feverishly working on an F-15E Strike Eagle. Maria looked up into the camera and began speaking.

"Yes, David, this is Maria Gomez at the U.S. Air Force base at Incirlik in Turkey. We are about one hundred yards away from the command center here in an area that has been set up for the press to view aircraft as they taxi and then take off. Earlier this evening there was significant activity on the line which we have on video and will share with you later."

"Right now, we are experiencing high tension and frantic action here as many aircraft are being feverishly readied in the background."

"Within the past five minutes we have witnessed the launch of several dozen missiles from what we presume to be anti-air batteries. Several of them were Patriot missile launches. Incirlik base appears to be under attack."

"BLAMMMmmm"

"Joe, get that explosion over to our right, about one half

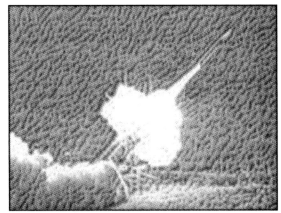

Patriot missile launch from Incirlik.

mile over. Several of the missile launches earlier originated in that area. Apparently one of those batteries was just destroyed after what could only be a missile streaked in at unbelievable speed and exploded."

Short rang anti-air defenses at Incirlik.

"You can hear the sirens in the background which have been going off incessantly for the last ten to fifteen minutes. As they started, we were stopped by Air Force security and asked to seek shelter, but when they had to rush off to another location, Joe and I made our way back here to get as much of the attack as possible on video.

"Oh! Another set of missiles is coming in! Joe, pan left!"

As the camera panned left, two exhaust trails were clearly visible, leading from the ground about a mile distant and trailing up behind two rapidly climbing missiles. As the missiles got higher and more distant, the cameraman expertly zoomed in and videoed the destruction of a GIR MiG-27 "Flogger" aircraft in a tremendous explosion when its fuel and ordinance ignited simultaneously with the impact of one of the missiles.

"Unbelievable! David, did you catch that? Ladies and gentlemen, we are witnessing a live GIR air attack on Incirlik airbase. Quickly, Joe, over there on the runway, there's a flight of four Strike Eagles just taking off."

Again the cameraman panned and caught four F-15E Strike Eagle aircraft as they took off under full afterburner thrust and rocketed almost straight up into the night sky. They had risen no more than three thousand feet when the aircraft on the far left of the formation was hit by a missile and exploded in a brilliant flash of light and burning debris. There was no chute.

"My God! They took out one of those F-15E's!"

The scene became more hectic as the cameraman swung back to catch as much of the action on the flight line as possible. There were numerous explosions on the taxiways where aircraft were being rearmed and several ejection seats lifted off from those positions. Many more didn't.

"Look, Joe, quickly pan towards the far end of the runway. Do you see them? Those are unmistakably MiG-29 aircraft coming towards us. Look,

213

they are releasing some type of missiles or bombs … Joe, are you catching this? Now, they are rocketing almost completely vertical. Oh. No! … Joe, get down, one of those bombs is homing in on the Command Center!"

On the screen, the unmistakable image of a bomb came flying towards the news crew as Joe zoomed in directly on it. The weapon flew off at a slight angle towards the Command Center when suddenly there was an incredibly bright flash, and then nothing but static.

"… Ladies and gentlemen, we seem to have lost our feed from Incirlik. We will try to reconnect with Maria momentarily and continue with the on-scene report of the action there in Turkey."

November 2nd, 2005 06:15 local
Incirlik Airbase. Turkey

Within the thirty minutes, it was over.

Colonel Phillips' force on barrier CAP gave an excellent account of itself. The GIR pincer movement failed to capture and destroy all of the American aircraft before they could engage the GIR attack aircraft formations. All eight of the F-15's sent to foil that pincer maneuver were destroyed, but not before they shot down eight GIR MiG-29's and ten SU-27's. This still left four MiG-29's and eight SU-27's to fly CAP over the attacking forces as at that moment no more U.S. defenders were in the air, outside of the four F-15's protecting the last E-3 Sentry.

Colonel Phillips himself penetrated the main GIR formation with his seven aircraft and was able to get into range before the twenty-two MiG-21's and their R-73 missiles could counter them. Colonel Phillips and his flight launched twenty-eight AMRAAM missiles into the oncoming horde of GIR aircraft. The AMRAAMs were launched just as the SU-24 aircraft, which had surged slightly ahead of the main attack group, launched forty-eight air-to-ground Kh-59 missiles and then turned away. While the American AMRAAMs were flying towards their targets, the MiG-21's came into range and launched eighteen R-73 "Archer" infrared missiles at the F-15's. In the resulting "dog fight," five of Colonel Phillips' aircraft were destroyed, including the Colonel's own. His last living thought had come while sighting on a MiG-29 attack aircraft. He announced "Fox-2" as he launched a Sidewinder missile, just an instant before being destroyed by two "Archer" missiles launched from two of the four MiG-21's that were targeting him.

Altogether eighteen GIR attack aircraft and ten of the escorting MiG-21's were destroyed by Colonel Phillips' attack. His disregard for his own life in the face of overwhelming odds, and while attempting to stave off the attack on Incirlik, would later earn him, posthumously, the Medal of Honor.

As the WNN news crew observed, the longer-range Patriot missile batteries and the Hawk missile batteries engaged the Kh-59 missiles first. These were fast, anti-radiation (or anti-radar) missiles that had been designed specifically to attack anti-air missile defenses. The resulting "engagement" destroyed 50% of Incirlik's Patriot and Hawk missile sites, and caused another 25% to expend their missiles defending themselves. Nonetheless, the remaining Hawk systems and the Patriot systems exacted a heavy toll on the GIR attack aircraft before they reached the base, destroying twelve MiG-27's, eight F-5's and fourteen MiG-21's. At this point, the shoulder-fired Stinger missiles and the Avenger missile systems came into play.

Just as the GIR attack aircraft appeared over the base proper, the first flight of re-armed F-15E strike eagles took off. As related in the SPECIAL BROADCAST, their takeoff and the vivid destruction of one of their number was seen around the world as a result of Maria Gomez's reporting and the live video captured by her cameraman, Joe. These four aircraft, armed with four AMRAAM and four Sidewinder missiles, had to fight their way to altitude in order to launch their missiles. Only three of them succeeded and engaged the first wave of MiG-27 "Flogger" attack aircraft which were making their bombing runs on the runways. These Strike Eagles destroyed fourteen aircraft in a wild, twisting and confusing dogfight, before they were destroyed themselves. These were the last American aircraft to get into the air from Incirlik that day, or for the remainder of the battle for Kurdistan.

The MiG-27's caught twenty F-16's and twelve F-15E's on the ground at Incirlik as they were rearming. Tremendous secondary explosions occurred as GIR munitions exploded amongst these aircraft on the taxiways and runways. Several pilots were able to eject from their aircraft and survived, but most were killed where they sat. While performing these ground attacks, another eighteen GIR aircraft were destroyed by the shoulder-fired Stinger missiles and the Avenger missile systems among the defense forces.

As the MiG-27's completed their work on the runway, two flights of twelve MiG-29's, fitted for ground attack, appeared unmolested over the airfield. These were the fateful aircraft that Maria Gomez described. Each carried one Fuel Air Explosive (FAE) device used to attack the command and control facilities, the fuel dumps, the barracks, the hangars and revetments.

FAE devices create huge detonations by spraying a fine mist of highly explosive liquid into the atmosphere, and then igniting it to produce extremely large, lethal explosions. Such detonations could level almost any structure within hundreds of yards. The resulting twenty-four massive detonations destroyed most of the structures on the base, killing the entire command staff in the command center, including Brigadier General Howell. That same explosion also killed Maria Gomez and her cameraman, Joe, of WNN as they caught their own impending demise on film.

While these ground attacks were going on, the dozens of remaining MiG-21 and F-5 aircraft were making run after run against the ground defense forces and more attacks against the air base's runways. This resulted in numerous US casualties on the ground.

When this large raid from the East completed its attack and departed, right behind it came the one hundred aircraft from the Southeast. These aircraft were completely unopposed, except for the remaining light, but effective, Stinger missiles defenses among the ground forces. These defenses accounted for ten more GIR aircraft, but another dozen FAE explosions and scores of bombing and strafing runs insured the already definitive results of the earlier attack. For all intents and purposes, Incirlik was completely out of commission.

November 2nd, 2005
Republic of Kurdistan

The result of the massive pre-dawn raid on Incirlik was that the GIR, with the exception of some early morning engagements, enjoyed total air superiority in its operations against Mosul and against Karkuk that day. Both assaults on Mosul, the one from Bayji and the one from Al Qa'im, achieved their goals with little impediment, once the initial F-15E's and F-16's had expended their munitions. In these attacks, and the resulting dog fights with supporting GIR aircraft, another eight F-16's and six F-15E's were lost, along with twelve MiG-29 and eight SU-27 aircraft.

The Kurdistan 1st Mechanized Division near Mosul, with no air support, and little chance for effective reconnaissance, was caught out in the open as it made its enveloping move towards Karkuk. Their light armor and APC's could not compete with the heavy armor divisions in the corps-sized GIR assault on Mosul. Well before the end of the day, except for a few straggler units which had been lucky enough to escape, the Kurdish 1st Mechanized Division ceased to exist as a fighting force.

Given the air support the GIR mechanized columns experienced, damage to them was limited to the loss of twenty-two tanks and approximately thirty armored personnel carriers and trucks. By the end of the day, the two assault forces had combined into a massive force that took up positions within, and to the north of, Mosul. GIR aircraft were landing and being refueled and rearmed at the former Iraqi air base there that night.

The GIR assault on Karkuk also enjoyed tremendous success and was carried out completely unhindered by U.S. or allied air forces. Although much of the rapid advance by the GIR was due to the Kurd plan of falling back in a mock retreat, nonetheless, the speed of the advance was so great that it almost caused the "mock" retreat to fail. The Kurd forces were almost overrun, as they could not "retreat" fast enough.

Despite this, the Kurd forces did inflict some damage on the advancing GIR armored columns. These losses added up to a dozen tanks and eighteen armored personnel carriers.

When night fell, except for local resistance in and around Karkuk, the GIR forces had bypassed the city and reached the Little Zab River where they stopped to re-provision. Their plans called for the crossing of the Little Zab to occur very early the next morning using the two bridges they had captured intact, and to proceed towards the Kurdistan capital of Irbil.

November 2nd, 2005, 07:30 local
Situation Room, The White House
Washington, D.C.

It was General Jeremy Stone's sad duty to brief the President and his closest advisors on yesterday morning's engagements in Turkey and Kurdistan. He didn't look forward to it. Quite frankly, he was somewhat shocked by the disturbing content of his briefing, but it was nonetheless his duty and one he was bound to fulfill.

"Sir, we have reviewed what we know and the results are devastating."

"Incirlik has been destroyed. We physically hold the base and there has been no ground incursion into Turkey, but the base is completely non-functional, and anticipating further air attacks tomorrow."

"The first indications of the attack came from large numbers of aircraft coming up from the south, from bases north of Baghdad, in what appeared to be supporting air for ground assaults into Kurdistan from Bayji and Al Qa'im. When our aircraft crossed the border to intercept, roughly half of those aircraft engaged our aircraft."

"When they did, a massive raid of what appeared to be approximately three hundred aircraft was picked up coming out of the GIR over Tabriz and then Lake Van. This group caught our aircraft out of position and was able to destroy both the forward E-3 Sentry and our Joint Star aircraft and their escorts while en route to Incirlik."

"From there, things developed into essentially a two-pronged attack on Incirlik. As the second larger group proceeded towards Incirlik, the first group overwhelmed the twelve aircraft we had sent to intercept them. These two forces then converged on Incirlik, one after another, from two different directions in a massive and well-coordinated attack."

"Regrettably, General Howell was killed in that attack and we lost approximately three hundred and fifty personnel on the ground. "

"Of the over four hundred aircraft used by the GIR to attack Incirlik, we estimate that we destroyed over one hundred and sixty. Our losses amounted to forty-three aircraft in the air and thirty-two more aircraft on the ground. The British lost a total of twelve of their Tornados."

Audible intakes of breath could be heard all around the table. The President's face was impassive. This was the worst day for the U.S. Air Forces in its entire history. It was the worst day for U.S. Air Power since World War II when it had been called the Army Air Corps. Although they had inflicted severe damage on the GIR's attacking forces, the GIR had achieved all of its operational goals and prevented the United States from achieving any of theirs. In addition, a pivotal base had been destroyed and it would take time to rebuild it … a rebuilding that would have to occur under fire. The real loss to the United States and its allies was in their ability to inflict damage on the forces that were occupying Kurdistan, and the loss of time … of which Kurdistan had precious little.

"OK, this is devastating and I will have to talk to the American people this evening. We will miss General Howell. His loss, in itself, is a national tragedy. I want to insure that the sincerest of condolences are passed to his wife and family. Jeremy, please see to this personally, and, if need be, I will also speak with Joan."

"In the meantime, what can we do from the south? Can we send aircraft from the south around the eastern border of Saudi to get at the GIR forces in the north? How about escorted B-52 strikes from Diego Garcia or Carrier strikes from the Reagan in the Gulf? What can the Turks do to help us?

Secretary of State Reisinger took the opportunity to answer the President's questions regarding Turkey.

"Mr. President, regarding the situation with Turkey, I was on line with their Foreign Minister this morning. They condemn the actions of the GIR, and will beef up their air defenses in their eastern provinces to more capably intercept any future GIR incursions. They are moving forces to help insure this now. They are also calling up reserve units and moving ground forces to insure that their borders are secure. But, one thing they will not do is attack GIR forces in Kurdistan. But they continue to fully support our efforts to do so through the use of forces now based in Turkey."

General Stone assessed the military options.

"Mr. President, we could probably put together a package from the Ronald Reagan supporting heavies from Diego Garcia. The problem is, they would be fighting their way through, both coming and going."

"The GIR is not asleep at the wheel. They have significant forces in Theater, and they have proven themselves willing to carry the fight to us. I believe such an effort would suffer terrific attrition, and may not effectively provide the support we desire."

"I recommend that we not bring the Ronald Reagan any closer in towards the Gulf. In fact, I believe we should move the Reagan and its battle group away from the Gulf and give them more room to maneuver in the Arabian Sea. With the number of aircraft the GIR is apparently willing to lose, it is not worth the risk."

"We are putting up a significant CAP over Incirlik and believe we can have planes launching from there inside of three days. They would be controlled by portable facilities on the ground and from E-3 Sentry AWACS flying out of Izmir, until the runway is sufficiently repaired to allow for the larger aircraft ... that's about three to five days out."

"We can launch sorties out of Izmir earlier, refueling them in flight, to attack the GIR forces our satellites are showing massing for their push on Irbil. I believe this is the course we should pursue. We have already weakened their air capability in that area, and this will provide the best chance for us to break through. I recommend that we do this immediately, if we want to have any hope for our plan to support the Kurdistan divisions around Irbil to succeed."

The President considered his options. He had a strong blocking force to the south that he had to maintain in case the GIR also decided to attack Kuwait and/or Saudi. He had to keep the majority of his supporting air forces there on hand and ready to help defend against such an attack. Trying to use part of them to fight through to the north did not seem feasible or practical.

The sorties out of Izmir were clearly the best method of bringing force to bear on the GIR forces in Kurdistan ... and the Kurdistan defenders would be in desperate need of that force early tomorrow.

"OK, Jeremy, make it happen. Have the Reagan stand off further into the Arabian Sea, and have our aircraft out of Izmir conduct operations against the GIR in Kurdistan."

November 3rd, 2005, 05:30 local
Little Zab River, GIR
Outside of Karkuk, Kurdistan

Yesterday had been Abduhl's introduction to battle. It had not gone at all as he had imagined. His unit's advance had been so swift, and so unhindered for most of the day, that they had scarcely been able to stop and get out and stretch their legs, much less engage any enemy units.

At one point however, during one of the rare occasions in which the enemy had stood and fought, Abduhl had seen men die horribly. A BTR-80 in their formation had taken a direct hit from a Kurd anti-tank weapon of some sort. His NCO had called it an American Javelin missile, but Abduhl did not know one enemy missile from another. What he did know was that the armored personnel carrier next to them, with eight soldiers and three crew members just like his, had suddenly become a blazing, hellacious funeral pyre.

They had stopped their own BTR-80 and dismounted while its machine guns provided covering fire. In the distance, Abduhl could see two of their support helicopters circling back to try to locate the attackers. Abduhl and his squad, under the direction of their NCO, had scrambled to the cover of a small levy on the far side of the wash they had been following. The smoke track from the missile that had destroyed the other BTR-80 still hung in the air, and at least two of the men in the fiercely burning BTR-80 were dying horribly, their weakening screams still audible to those who allowed themselves to hear.

"Abduhl, take your sniper rifle and circle over to that rock out cropping to the left. Get as high in those rocks as you can and see if you can spot the enemy who fired that missile."

Abduhl immediately sprang to obey.

"Yes sir!"

In his desire to anxiously obey, for a moment he forgot his training and began to rise. Simultaneous with his feet being kicked out from under him by the NCO, a small "CRACK" sounded just above his now prone body.

"Dear Allah, Abduhl! I didn't ask you to kill yourself. STAY DOWN and get your butt over to that outcropping. This time KEEP LOW!"

Kicking himself mentally, and at the same time grateful to the NCO for saving his life, Abduhl made his way over to the rocks and began climbing.

As he neared the top, he remembered his training and moved off to the side of the "summit" of the rocks so as to not be "profiled" against the skyline. He began to gaze across the scrub brush covered hill that lay in front of him. After no more than five seconds, his peripheral vision caught sight of a group of men, located at a distance of about five hundred yards, who were slowly moving up the hillside towards a small saddle.

"Once they reach that saddle, they'll disappear over into the next drainage" though Abduhl.

Carefully bringing his rifle up to his shoulder, Abduhl took aim at the back of the individual leading the group, adjusting for the range and the slight breeze. He took a deep breath, and as he slowly let it out, he squeezed.

"BANG!"

The leader and the man behind him both fell. The third individual in the group began to scurry towards the summit at a much quicker pace. Again taking aim, this time at the lone survivor, Abduhl pulled the trigger. As the man scrambled for the saddle, Abduhl took three more shots, adjusting for what he anticipated the man would do to avoid getting hit. On the third shot, some twenty feet below the saddle, Abduhl connected again.

Later, it was discovered that Abduhl had severely wounded the leader of the group and killed the second man with his first shot. It had been too low for the first individual and had hit the second man high on the back near his neck, breaking his spine. Fragments of bone and bullet from that shot had severely injured the leading individual.

The NCO had been able to gain some valuable intelligence from the mortally wounded man before mercifully ending his life with a quick shot to the head. "God rest his soul," Abduhl thought, barely keeping fromretching.

This event had initiated Abduhl as a fully functional part of the squad. Despite his age, and despite his origin, such shooting skill was a valued commodity in any combat situation -- one that could make the difference between life and death for any member of their team.

Now here they were, as the darkness yielded to the brightening sky of the next morning, winding up a steep road from the Little Zab River, making their way to the rebel capital, now less than 50 kilometers away.

November 3rd, 2005, 06:55
Kurdistan Blocking Position
One Valley Over, Kurdistan

Jabal surveyed his intelligence once more. The air disaster that had befallen the United States the day before was sobering and had created a serious situation for his forces. Although the US had destroyed larger numbers of GIR aircraft, it was clear that the GIR had gained the advantage by sheer numbers and was advancing rapidly towards him.

His spotters and forward scouts had indicated that the enemy's initial assault division was just over the rise on the far side of the valley, about 6 kilometers away, and that they had the additional benefit of attack helicopters and close air support. There was audible and visual evidence of both. Jabal had heard the rotors already this morning, and he could now make out the contrails in the lightening sky above him.

"Just light enough to see," he thought.

"Will, we are going to be needing that air support soon. The GIR forces are going to come over that ridge any minute and ..."

As Jabal said this, there was a "WHOOOSHHHH" sound followed by a large explosion about fifty meters downhill from them in the vicinity of some concealed bunkers ... followed by yet another "WHOOOSHHHH" and explosion, then a third ... and a fourth. The numbers of impacts and explosions increased to a crescendo where one could hardly discern between one explosion and the next.

In a few moments it was over. Jabal rose from his prone position in the bunker, thankful that none of the multiple rocket impacts had scored a direct hit on his position.

Almost immediately, there was the sound of a low-flying jet aircraft overhead … followed by a thunderous explosion somewhere up the hill from his position. Almost immediately after the initial explosion, several more jets came into view over the top of the rise, from the other side of the valley.

"Hold your fire! Hold your fire! Do not engage any aircraft or helo's until you get my order!"

Jabal turned back to the American special forces commander, turned CIA field team leader.

"Will, we NEED those support aircraft now!"

Will Peterson understood their need. He also understood that, without air superiority, any assets coming into Kurdistan had to fight their way in, and then fight to remain on station.

Just such and effort was in the process of occurring, but it was meeting resistance in the form of many GIR MiG-29, SU-27, MiG-25 and MiG-21 fighter aircraft.

"We're going to have to hold another five minutes, Jabal. We have F-15's and F-14's attempting to sweep the GIR aircraft out of the way so our attack aircraft can get in here and hit those advancing mechanized columns."

"There's a big dogfight, that our boys are about to win, going on right now over the Great Zab River Valley. But until that happens they cannot risk sending the attack aircraft in."

November 3rd, 2005, 07:00
Anvil Flight 42,000 ft
Over the Great Zab River, Kurdistan

"Fox-2, Fox-2. Tracking … scratch another MiG-29!"

"Okay, Anvil flight. Re-form on me. Control indicates the other bandits are punching out of this one. Proceed to point Echo and take up a CAP position at angels forty."

F-16 prepares to attack.

The remaining F-14's of Anvil flight formed up and proceeded to point Echo over the Little Zab River drainage above Jabal's blocking position. They had started the day with three flights of four F-14D aircraft. Now the remaining five aircraft were taking up CAP positions over the battlefield to protect the attack aircraft, F-18's, F-16's and F-15E's that were now approaching and would be used against the advancing GIR armor columns.

Ten miles to the east, a similar condition developed as three F-15 Eagles destroyed the last MiG-29 and took up CAP. These three were from an original group of eight.

"Seven Tomcats lost in one engagement!" thought the Anvil flight leader. "Well, those ragheaded bastards paid dearly for our losses."

In fact, the GIR had lost another eight SU-27's, nine MiG-29's, six MiG-25's and eleven MiG-21's in attempting to hold up the American fighter sweep and trailing attack aircraft formations. Although their efforts had diminished the US Navy and US Air Force ranks by a total of twelve aircraft, they had failed to stop them.

Now, twelve F-15E's, twelve F-16's and eight F-18's were barreling in on the Little Zab drainage and the advancing GIR mechanized Corps.

Even as they approached, the GIR was launching a massive retaliatory raid of its own from GIR bases to the east in the former state of Iran. Within twenty minutes, over one hundred GIR fighters would descend on the attacking American forces.

November 3rd, 2005, 07:07
Kurdistan Forces Blocking Position
Outside Irbil, Kurdistan

The mechanized assault on Jabal's position had gotten very intense in just the last few minutes. He was losing positions too fast to the mortar, artillery and now the direct tank assaults on his bunkers and fortified locations. Clearly the GIR was not surprised that they were here, though perhaps they were still not aware of their full numbers and disposition.

Although the Javelin and LAWS missiles his men employed were having a telling effect on the GIR armor and personnel carriers, there were simply not enough of them. Where was that American air support?

T-80 tanks assault Kurdistan position.

"Red dog, Red dog! There's a platoon of T-80's moving towards your right flank. Say your status."

Jabal knew that the numbers would soon tell on his forces. Without immediate air support, he was going to have to fall back very soon. At least the air assault on his position had finally ceased and he took this as a good sign, particularly with those lazy contrails now weaving and circling overhead. If they weren't firing on him, he figured they must be friends, and if they were friends, perhaps help would soon arrive.

Even as he surveyed the advancing GIR T-80 platoon off to Red-dog's right, he saw a number of missile launches from among the GIR forces. At first he was about to issue orders for his forces to respond, but then he saw that the missiles were traveling up into the air beyond his position. As this occurred, several vehicles that had fired those missiles exploded in bright flashes of light, followed seconds later by the sound waves from those explosions.

Above and behind him there was an explosion in the air as a US F-16 aircraft was hit. This produced fiery wreckage that rained from the sky on his positions. It also produced a parachute as the pilot ejected and came floating down behind his lines.

Within a minute, the leading echelon of GIR tanks and armored personnel carriers began exploding as more US Aircraft streaked in at low altitude and attacked the advancing columns. More and more tanks and armored personnel carriers began exploding and being ripped apart by U.S. air-launched munitions, including AGN-65A and -65C Maverick missiles, GBU-12D Paveway II laser-guided bombs, 30 millimeter cannon fire, M20 Rockeye cluster bombs, IAU rockets and MK82 general purpose bombs.

"Well, Jabal, there's your air support. Look at those fly-boys hammering them! We'd best make the most of it."

Jabal looked at his American "advisor" and nodded his head. The firepower was truly awesome and as more GIR vehicles were destroyed, and the rest veered off to unload their troops and take up defensive positions, Jabal began to have hope that their plan might work after all.

Just as this thought was forming, his radioman indicated he had a call from the government headquarters in Irbil. Jabal listened intently for a moment, put the radio hand set down, and then, with a sober look, he addressed Will Peterson.

"The large GIR forces which took Mosul yesterday are on the move. According to our intelligence, those forces completely destroyed our reserve mechanized division and are now advancing on Irbil and our undefended rear. Can U.S. Air Force attack missions be called in against those forces? It appears to be an entire armored corps."

Will knew that missions could be planned, but he also knew that such planning took time -- a precious commodity of which they were running precariously short. Any aircraft devoted to such a mission (if there were any available) would have to fight their way in, just like the group that was supporting them right now. It was also likely that the GIR would soon be delivering another air attack. It was clear that neither side was able to maintain air superiority at this point in the battle.

"I'll get on the radio right now, Jabal, and try to arrange it. But I do not believe there are many assets close enough to get it done very quickly. We dare not divert any of these aircraft if we want to have a chance to hold this line. My recommendation is to presume that this is all we are going to get, and to make the most of it while we have it."

November 3rd, 2005, 07:25
GIR Assault Forces
Outside Irbil, Kurdistan

Abduhl had never been so scared in all of his life. In the midst of exploding tanks and exploding armored personnel carriers, his unit and several of those around him had somehow been spared. They had dismounted in a rocky gully and had taken up defensive positions as the American attack aircraft pounded the lead elements of the assault division to which he was attached.

Just when he thought they might come away from the air assault untouched, one of the American aircraft found his group and started a steep bank to come around and attack them. His NCO indicated it was an American F-15E Strike Eagle.

"Everyone down! Hit the dirt now!" yelled the Abduhl's NCO.

As the F-15E made its attack run, it used its GPU-5/A Gun pod which housed a GAU-13/A 30 mm cannon, to strafe Abduhl's unit. There was a sound in the air like a large buzz saw, and scores of large "thuds" impacted all around him. The left side of Abduhl's head was severely cut by a chunk of rock that exploded to his right. After the aircraft passed, when Abduhl looked up, he could hardly see anything because of all the dust in the air. As it cleared, he saw that his NCO was ... ruined, destroyed, turned into a bloody mass of meat with no appendages.

"Alright, form up on me! We have orders to mount up and move out."

The Junior NCO took command and they got into their BTR-80, which had been shielded from the attack by two large rock outcroppings between which it had been parked. There were only four of the assault team and two of the crewmembers left to respond. The others had just been killed.

"Five good men gone ... in just a few seconds," thought Abduhl.

As he was stepping into their idling BTR-80, Abduhl noticed a number of flashes in the air to his west and saw two American aircraft fall from the sky. As this occurred, several GIR MiG-29's streaked over their position.

"Our aircraft are back! Sir, look!"

The Junior NCO, demoralized by the extensive losses his squad and division had taken, was heartened as he stuck his head out and watched numerous GIR aircraft fly by.

"Yes, it seems help has arrived. I wish they had been here ten minutes ago. Come on, Abduhl, mount up. This day's work is far from over."

November 3rd, 2005, 18:00
Outside of Irbil, Kurdistan

With the return of large numbers of GIR aircraft, the American aircraft were forced to retire. The five F-14's and three F-15's flying CAP for the ground attack aircraft fought hard, but in the face of overwhelming numbers, and forewarned by their AWACS aircraft, they quickly broke off and retreated after a brief engagement.

Some of the American "ground pounders," who were in the midst of making "last" attack runs, remained on station a little too long against the now disorganized 1st echelon of GIR ground forces. In so doing, they insured their own demise, being caught off guard as scores of GIR aircraft filled the air above the valley, leaving them no place to run.

Even so, the numbers were lopsided as the US forces lost two more F-14's, two F-15's, three F-16's and two F-15E's in this engagement against six MiG-29's, four SU-27's and five MiG-25's. The number of aircraft lost made no difference on the ground once the Americans departed. The GIR had regained air superiority over the battlefield. As the 2nd echelon of GIR mechanized forces pressed the attack, they were able to quickly drive Jabal and his Kurdistan forces from their positions defending Irbil and then begin advancing towards the city.

November 3rd, 2005, 17:00 hrs
GIR Forces
Outskirts of Irbil, Kurdistan

The Junior NCO who was now commanding Abduhl's squad listened intently to his company commander over the radio. After a few seconds he hung up his hand set and turned to what was left of his squad in the BTR-80 that had carried them so far this day.

"By order of the Imam, the assault on Irbil has been unilaterally suspended."

There were a number of audible moans, and a couple of "but why's and: "but we have this scum in the palm of our hands. The NCO continued.

"Imam Hasan Sayeed will make a national statement at 20:00 hours explaining his intent. Apparently, his statement will be broadcast internationally. We will receive it over the command frequency right here in our unit."

"Until then, we have been ordered to take up defensive positions above Irbil in these ridges south and east of the city. Apparently, our sister divisions, which have advanced to within fifteen kilometers of the city from the west, will take up positions there."

"So, let's get our gear in order. We will be able to restock ammunition and provisions at 22:00 hours. Until then, let's set up our camp along the ridgeline, dig into our positions and await further orders. The Imam will address us at 20:00. Let's get finished before then."

November 3rd, 2005, 18:45
Retreating Kurdistan Force
North of Irbil, Kurdistan

Jabal was leading his men overland to a strong defensive position in the mountains between Rayat and Aqrah. From there, if driven off again, they could quickly retreat into Turkey to continue the fight from exile.

Who would have thought that the mighty US forces would be pushed from the air twice in as many days? It was true that they had decimated many of the GIR's aircraft in an awesome and terrible display of firepower, but the GIR was apparently ready and willing to suffer such losses to achieve its goals. Now, the dream of an independent Kurdistan was drifting away like smoke in the wind.

As he pondered the best way to keep up the fight, Will Peterson, who had been talking into his satellite set, hung up and spoke.

"Jabal, US intelligence is reporting that the GIR has stopped its advance on Irbil. Apparently, Hasan Sayeed has made some type of a unilateral decision and intends to deliver an address to the world in about an hour."

Jabal was shocked. Irbil was the GIR's for the taking. Its fall would spell the end of the push for Kurdistan independence. Outside of some harassing forces he had left behind to slow the advance, Jabal knew that the GIR forces could be in Irbil tonight.

"It will be interesting to find out what he has to say. I can think of no military reason for him to stop his advance and take the pressure off of us. Perhaps something has occurred on the diplomatic or economic front ... maybe your people have finally found some threat or lever that has influenced him."

Will did not know, but he doubted the accuracy of Jabal's speculation. The people at the Agency he had been talking to were as mystified as Jabal ... which meant that whatever Hasan Sayeed's reasons were, they were not being forced upon him by the United States. It was more likely that Sayeed saw some advantage to the GIR in taking this action, though what advantage could be gained by "pulling back" when one's forces had the strategic momentum was hard to comprehend. Jabal, Will, and many others, particularly those in US intelligence, were left scratching their heads.

"Well, we'll be able to listen if you want. The entire message is supposed to be only ten to fifteen minutes long, and they are going to pipe it through the satellite so we can hear it here."

November 3rd, 2005, 20:00
Presidential Offices
Tehran, Greater Islamic Republic

"Good evening. I have come before the people of the world this evening, and before my brothers and sisters of faith throughout Islam in particular, to express my deep sorrow for the hostilities gripping the northern regions of the former Iraq, and the attendant loss of life over the last two days. I express my sincerest sorrow to the families, friends, and countrymen of those who have fallen in combat, and those innocents who are inevitably displaced, injured, or killed by the ravages of war."

"It is easy to indicate that such actions were appropriate and necessary due to the actions of a rebellious few. But, despite whatever justifications, despite whatever provocation, the loss of a father, a brother, a husband ... or the tragic death and suffering of a sister, mother, or children, cannot be soothed or reconciled by such talk. Therefore, in an effort to end such tragedy in these regions, I have ordered all GIR forces to unilaterally cease their offensive operations. We will look to diplomacy resolve this issue now."

"In that spirit, I will personally become involved with the negotiations."

"Let me explain to those of my own faith more of the detail of my heartfelt reasons for doing this. It goes beyond the worthy desire which all the world recognizes to soothe the brokenhearted. There is a reference in the Holy Koran to the writings of the ancient prophet, Jasher, wherein Jasher speaks of the days during the rise of the Mahdi. It may interest many listening tonight that the prophet Jasher is also mentioned in the Jewish Talmud and the Christian Bible. Within the Shia faith, our Mullahs, senior clerics and Ayatollahs have had access to these writings for many centuries, and have used them as reference material to the Holy Koran. With respect to the current situation in which followers of Islam are warring against one another, let me quote the following from the words of Jasher:"

"In those days will the Mahdi arise and punish the infidels and the unfaithful with the heavy hand of Allah. But ere he can accomplish this, he shall make peace between his warring brothers and sisters.

"Yea in the midst of battle will he call a halt and himself become as a dove to them, uniting them and restoring them to the house of unity and faith. From thence will he then go forth, gird about with the armor of truth, like a stone breaking forth from the mountains, until it has cleansed and filled the entire earth."

"My brothers and sisters in Irbil, Karkuk, Mosul and all of the regions round about. We must stop warring among ourselves! Can you not see that we are being manipulated by the decadent powers of Europe and America into this quarreling, so that we remain weak and divided before them? It is they who seek to keep us at odds. We must resist their manipulation. We must not fall prey to it."

"Irbil, the capital, lies before the forces of the GIR. It is within our power to destroy it and ruthlessly put down this rebellion. But I shall not do it. No more shall the faithful kill the faithful. I call a halt. We represent the GREATER ISLAMIC REPUBLIC!"

"I will personally make a pilgrimage from Karkuk to Irbil, beginning next week, to resolve this issue through negotiation and diplomacy. I call on all the faithful leaders in the area to meet with me. Together we will resolve this issue peacefully."

"For those who would interfere, I warn you: Though our aim is peace .... though we seek not the invasion or destruction of other lands .... we have proven our ability to resist your interference and to deter you in your vain attempts to divide us. We will not brook interference. We will resolve our issues among ourselves with peace, dignity and honor."

"Good night, and may Allah rest your spirits and soothe your souls."

November 3rd, 2005, 10:16
Broadcast Studios, WNN Headquarters
New York City, New York

As the final touches of makeup were applied in preparation for another Special Report, David Krenshaw reviewed in his mind the events of the past few days.

The many weeks of U.S. and allied buildup in Saudi Arabia and Turkey had culminated in hostilities two days ago. The surprising audacity of the GIR and its willingness to incur casualties as it met its objectives had surprised the world. The videos and reports from Maria at Incirlik Air Base in Turkey, as it was attacked by GIR aircraft, resulting in the destruction of that U.S. Air base .... as well as the live feed of the deaths of Maria and her crew .... were unsettling, and unprecedented.

How could one reconcile the expensive (in terms of human life and materiel) victory as GIR forces bore down on Irbil, followed by the shocking unilateral halt in that offensive, which seemed to be on the verge of accomplishing its costly mission? And now there was the amazing, unprecedented announcement that had just been made by Hasan Sayeed ... Hasan Sayeed who had only been interviewed once by any western media organization ... Hasan Sayeed who had given that exclusive interview to David Krenshaw himself.

In response to an urgent indication from one of the producers, the make up personnel moved away.

"Three, two, one ... On Air!"

"Good morning. This is David Krenshaw with a Special Report from WNN. The leader of the GIR, Hasan Sayeed, has just made a startling announcement indicating a unilateral cessation of hostilities in and around the northern provinces of the former nation of Iraq."

"With the success of the GIR offensive to bring these same provinces into line with the unification election results of two months ago, it was expected that the GIR would only have a mop up operation left after the capture of Irbil, the capital of the breakaway provinces. But, moments ago, Hasan Sayeed called a unilateral halt to that offensive and now indicates that he personally will lead a diplomatic delegation to Irbil."

"In his internationally broadcast announcement, which WNN aired earlier today, Sayeed appealed directly to the Islamic faithful in those provinces to join with him, indicating that this gesture of halting the offensive was tied to obscure and ancient prophesies in the Islamic faith."

"Officials from the Republic of Kurdistan immediately accepted Sayeed's cease fire proposal and his request for negotiations. In truth, given the tactical situation and defeated condition of their armed forces, they had little choice."

"We are still awaiting the official U.S. response. There is no doubt that the GIR has the upper hand, both militarily and diplomatically, as a result of Hasan Sayeed's humanitarian gesture. The real question now is whether he can maintain the advantage he enjoys."

November 3rd, 2005, that same time
Situation Room, The White House
Washington, D.C.

The President sat listening to the WNN report with his closest advisors and cabinet members. Alan Reeves, the Vice President, Fred Resinger, the Secretary of State, Tim Hattering, the Secretary of Defense, John Bowers, the National Security Advisor, General Jeremy Stone, the Chairman of the Joint Chiefs and Mike Rowley, the Director of the CIA, were all listening with the President.

When the broadcast ended and the normal programming resumed, the President broke the quiet and somber mood of the gathering.

"Well, this Hasan Sayeed is a very shrewd operator. He has presented the Kurd leaders with a way out short of abject defeat, and he is effectively forestalling our "knock-out" punch to his air assets within his borders. Jeremy, have we got those airfields targeted?"

Over the last two days, General Jeremy Stone had spent many hours listening to advisors and planners of all types. Personnel at the War College, personnel from the School of Advanced Military Studies (SAMS), national security advisors, advisors from every branch of the armed forces at the Pentagon and, of course, the planners from Central Command themselves had all participated.

After the first day of failing to achieve any of their objectives, the second day had been a partial success. More importantly, the second day had helped pinpoint the location of several of the airfields within the former borders of Iraq and Iran from which the massive numbers of GIR aircraft were originating. Analysis of the last two days had given America and her allies a pretty good idea of when the aircraft were launching each day. This intelligence had led to the planning of massive raids on those airfields for the next morning. Those raids would include cruise missile launches from the Navy and from Air force B1-B Lancers, followed by the launching of strike packages from the USS Carl Vinson in the Mediterranean and from the Izmir Air Base.

"Mr. President, Central Command is prepared to give the launch order for this evening's raid at 3:30 this afternoon. I recommend we give the order in spite of the unilateral cease-fire by the GIR. We need to thin the GIR aircraft numbers out faster. The best time to do that is while they are on the ground. Besides, we need to teach these bastards a hard lesson about messing with the United States of America."

Norm Weisskopf knew his Secretary of State wanted to respond to the General, but he held his hand up to indicate that he, Weisskopf, had the floor, and he was not about to relinquish it.

"Fred, I know what you are going to say, and at this point I have to agree with you ... irrespective of how much I would like to allow the General to carry the fight to those airfields for both of the reasons he gave."

"However, we would be hard pressed to defend such an action in the face of Sayeed's proposal. Particularly since we are not in a declared state of war, and particularly since his forces have stood down."

"Believe me, from my own time over there, I have heard this rhetoric from the more fundamental Muslims over and over. Such cunning strategizing has been going on a long time, and was a major concern before and during Desert Storm. Hasan Sayeed considers the "unfaithful" to be Saudi Arabia, the UAR, Turkey, Egypt and anyone else who is willing to work with the west. In this regard, Sayeed is no different than Sahdam Hussein, except that he is not corrupt, and he is much more dangerous than we ever conceived Hussein of being. In a similar fashion, his desire to unite all of Islam under his fundamental interpretations are no different that Usama bin Laden's were, except Hasan Sayeed is not off trying to do it on his own. He has the full support of the main stream clerics and several Islamic governments behind him. He is going about his goal to unite Islam in a much more strategic manner. Despite the death and destruction Usama bin Laden caused, I believe Hasan Sayeed has the potential of being much more dangerous to this country."

"Mike, what is your intelligence telling you about Sayeed? Where's he taking this thing? What is "punishing" the unfaithful going to amount to?"

Mike Rowley had anticipated this line of discussion. His people had been analyzing the GIR in general, and Sayeed specifically. What the President really was asking was, "How big a threat is Hasan Sayeed himself?"

"Mr. President, as you know, Sayeed has the unparalleled and unprecedented support of both the Shia and Sunni sects of Islam. The people see him as their Mahdi ... in plain English that translates pretty much into "Messiah." An analysis of their writings, prophesies and beliefs, shows us that the majority of Muslims believe that the Mahdi will unite all of the faithful in Islam in a massive Jihad, or Holy War, against the unfaithful and the infidels."

"We at the Agency believe that Hasan Sayeed, on his own, will develop into a very dangerous threat to world stability, world peace and to our own vital national interests. When coupled with his ties to the CAS in general, and to Beijing in particular, the situation has the potential of developing into a bigger threat to the United States than the Axis powers of World War II, or the Soviet Union of the Cold War era."

President Weisskopf had already come to this conclusion, especially the part coupling Jien Zenim and Hasan Sayeed.

"Let's talk about Red China in a moment. Mike, we still have that team on the ground in Kurdistan, right? What is their location and status?"

Mike Rowley thought about the team he had in Iraq.

"Yes, sir. Eight former special forces personnel, most of them former Delta Force. The leader is one of our best field operatives. During the blocking actions they had been divided up between the various divisions as forward air controllers for our aircraft, but are now all reunited with Jabal's headquarters company north of Irbil."

The President mentally envisioned a map of the region.

"Good, Mike. I would like you and John to meet with me after this meeting to discuss the most expedient method of extracting that team. Let's meet right here."

"Beyond that, Fred, I believe that we need to prepare for the eventuality that Kurdistan is going to capitulate, and agree to relinquish its independence and unite with the GIR. I want to know what diplomatic and economic steps we can take to demonstrate our firm disagreement. Clearly the Kurds are being coerced into this. In addition, discreetly arrange an offer for the existing leaders there to have the opportunity to take refuge under our protection and continue their efforts from exile. Please coordinate this."

"Now, a final point I want to make before we adjourn. The Red Chinese are continuing to build their military at a break-neck pace. Their launching of this new "Sea Control Carrier" is indicative of their intentions."

"I know everyone is busy and extremely preoccupied with the situation in the Mid East. That is understandable, particularly given our buildup there, and the current confrontation. At the same time, we cannot afford to take our eyes off of what China is doing. John, make sure the NRO and our other reconnaissance assets don't forget that."

"Specifically, I want to know how quickly they are going to launch theses new carriers, and I want to know how in the world they are going to support them. Somewhere there's a logistics chain built up to maintain these vessels and their carrier wings. I want to know the weak links in that chain."

November 3rd, 2005, 10:37
Situation Room, The White House
Washington, D.C.

"OK, Mike. What is the likelihood that your team can get into position along Sayeed's intended path and observe his "pilgrimage" before we extract them?"

Mike Rowley weighed carefully what his President was asking him.

"Mr. President, I can order them to accomplish such a task very quickly. I have full confidence that they could take up the best possible position for such observation within twenty-four hours. But Mr. President, what is the purpose of such an observation? WNN and every other major media outlet will probably carry Sayeed's "walk" live."

The President understood exactly what he had to order, and he knew these two men were among the most trusted whom he knew.

"Mike and John, I want this perfectly understood. Our duty is to protect and defend the Constitution of the United States and bear true faith and allegiance to the same. We have all served in the uniform of our country in allegiance to that oath. We are to defend said Constitution, and, by extension, the life, liberty and well being of our nation and its citizens against all enemies, foreign and domestic. Do both of you concur? John?"

John already had deduced what was coming. From the moment the President had asked about Sayeed's personal threat, he had guessed where this was leading. When the President asked about that CIA team in Kurdistan, it had removed all doubt.

"Yes, Mr. President. That is exactly how I perceive it."

The President turned back towards Mike.

"Mike?"

Mike knew where this was going as well. He had personally known Tony, whose cover name was Will Peterson, for eight years, and had known of him for long before that. There wasn't a better field operations man to have on the ground over there.

"Mr. President, of course I agree 100% with your assessment."

The President was gratified at the unwavering dedication of these two men. They knew where he was going ... where he HAD to go, and they were steady as a rock in the face of it.

"OK, then, with that understanding, I want your team led by ... is it Tony?"

At Mike Rowley's nod, the President continued.

"Yes ... well, inform Tony, that he has NCA approval to take whatever measures he deems necessary to protect and defend the vital interests of this nation against its enemies while he is observing near Irbil."

Mike Rowley had to be sure of the full implications. He had to voice his need for complete comprehension.

"Mr. President, you understand the likely implications ... the likely consequences for these men?"

Norm Weisskopf was not a stranger to command decisions, or the mortal consequences they could carry. He had agonized over such decisions involving hundreds of thousands of young Americans some sixteen years earlier ... but he had never wavered or faltered in that decision-making capacity. Any man who had ever served under his command, who had any knowledge of him, knew that the "General" would gladly stand in for them in ANY duty he ordered them to fulfill. It was no different now.

"Yes, Mike. I understand all too well the likely consequences. Pass the order along. After making the observations, and executing any measures he deems necessary, have them get out of there and egress to the nearest pick-up point. ... and, Mike, tell Tony directly from me, God's speed."

November 5th, 2005, 15:37
A bluff above the main Highway to Karkuk
Irbil, Kurdistan

There was a LOT of security. Anything within about a thousand meters of the highway was literally blanketed by GIR security forces. Infantry,

APC's, tanks stationed at critical junctures and a lot of helicopters flying up and down the route on both sides. Although the vast majority of GIR troops in the vicinity had not advanced beyond the lines established by Hasan Sayeed's unilateral cease-fire declaration ... he apparently was more than willing to allow a strong contingent to line the road to ensure the security aspect of his intended "pilgrimage" into Irbil.

Will Peterson viewed the scene from just over 1800 meters away. He was clad in a complete desert ghillie suit and had his egress route planned. Jabal had insisted on serving as his security, and they were both in the firing position they had chosen the day before -- a location that overlooked the main road. The rest of Peterson's team, and a number of Jabal's men, were waiting another four hundred meters behind them, further into the hills. They would serve as additional security during their egress, if required.

Very early in the morning on the day before, the orders had come in over the satellite set, direct from Washington. It had not taken Will more than an instant to understand exactly what he was being ordered to do. He contemplated those orders now as he awaited Hasan Sayeed's entourage.

"You will take up a position to observe the advance of GIR military and Command and Control (C&C) assets towards Irbil. You are authorized to act with extreme prejudice in engaging any high-value targets that pose a threat to the national security interests of the United States. After observing the passage of GIR C&C, and taking any action deemed necessary, egress the area and arrange for pick-up at the nearest landing zone (LZ)."

Will's weapon of choice in very long-range situations like this was the "Windrunner" .50 cal. Compact Tactical Sniper Rifle (CTSR). He had arranged for the CIA to purchase one for him some years ago. Will believed this weapon to be far superior to the military's M82A1A .50 cal. sniper rifle. The CTSR was more accurate at longer range than the M82A1A. In tests at the Aberdeen Proving Grounds it had recorded an incredible 1/2-minute of angle (MOA) at over 1000 yards. In addition, the CTSR had a removable barrel with fixed-head spacing, was made of 4140 chromoly heat-treated steel, had an adjustable sliding stock with adjustable cheek rest, and weighed in at less than thirty pounds -- including the rifle, bipod and scope. Will had a standard M14 bipod mounted on the rifle and used a Leupold SN-1/TAR Long Range Precision Sniper Optical System.

"I have them, Will. There are two T80 tanks followed by a BTR-80 command vehicle just coming out from behind that hill to the south. There are BMP-2's on either side of the road and another BTR-80 and two tanks bringing up the rear. They're moving slow, and there is definitely a group of individuals walking on the road in the middle of the formation."

"... yes! There's Sayeed. He's dressed in the lightly colored, robe walking in the middle of a number of Mullahs and a security detachment."

Jabal thought about what he'd just said. A number of Mullah's, probably even Ayatollahs, were with Sayeed ... men of the faith ... Jabal's spiritual leaders. But of course they would be. They had officially recognized him as the Imam for all of Islam.

"OK, Jabal. Great ... I've got him. I make the range just under two miles. We'll let him come to us."

November 5th, 2005, 15:42
On the main Highway to Karkuk
Irbil, Kurdistan

Hasan Sayeed was closer to Irbil and his dream of a united Islam. Thus far, his plans had gone amazingly well. Surely the hand of Allah was with him.

Jien Zenim, the Chinese leader, had called him personally and asked him to reconsider this "pilgrimage." But Jien Zenim did not understand matters of faith. He was a godless infidel ... but he was a very powerful and wise infidel whose influence had opened many doors. Nonetheless, Jien Zenim had not been happy at Hasan's insistence that this pilgrimage, and direct involvement, was necessary if Hasan was going to bring closure to this "rebellion," this fracture with the Kurds.

Of course Hasan's own staff and many of the faithful had also asked him to reconsider, fearing for his life. He understood their concerns, but did not share them. His objective was to see the fulfillment of the burning desire in his breast, the fulfillment of what the internal, eternal voice whispered to him ... Unite Islam! Purge the unfaithful! Excise the infidel! All else, even his own life, or at the least the risks to his life, were secondary.

In Hasan's mind, the choices were simple. If Allah wanted him to complete his calling, he would. If, in Allah's wisdom, he was not to complete it, but was to die in the attempt ... well, what of it? He would not try to defy the will of Allah. He had learned long ago the useless nature of such a fight by seeing others engaged in it.

So, here he was within five kilometers of the outskirts of Irbil. Tonight he would be in the city, preparing for tomorrow's negotiations with the defeated Kurd leaders. He had every confidence those negotiations would go well, and he intended to show great compassion and mercy to the Kurds in general, although a few harsh examples would have to be made.

As these thoughts passed through his mind, he turned to get a better view of his surroundings. This close to Irbil, more and more people were beginning to gather along the security perimeter that had been established by his forces. In addition, a number of western news teams were present.

Viewed from this particular location, to his right there was a long sloping rise to a bluff overlooking the road a little less than two kilometers away. The bluff itself appeared to be outside the direct security area. "Strange," Hasan thought. Looking up there just now he could have sworn he had seen a glint of sunlight reflecting off of something for just an instant.

Hasan Sayeed had been in mortal danger too many times not to give heed to the sinking sensation that suddenly called out for recognition from the pit of his stomach. While he continued to gaze, he spoke to his good friend, the foreign minister.

"Sadiq, have the commander of the security attachment notified. I want him to send a squad of men up to that bluff. I just saw a glint of sunlight up there that is very out of place."

November 5th, 2005, 15:43
The bluff above the main Highway to Karkuk
Irbil, Kurdistan

As Will Peterson saw the upturned face, he took a deep breath and slowly began to release it as he prepared to apply pressure to the trigger. As he did so, Jabal, who was kneeling behind him, thought, "The 12th Imam … he will make peace with his brothers … he will call a halt to the fighting amongst the faithful … he will unite ALL of Islam. Yes, he WILL unite all of Islam!"

As Jabal thought this, Will was just beginning to apply pressure to the trigger as he focused through his scope and became "one" with his rifle. While doing so he thought, "There, just like that, you SOB. Come on now. Hold that pose and I'll…"

"BANG!"

Those were Will Peterson's last living thoughts as a 9mm bullet from Jabal's pistol slammed into the back of his head, destroying his brain stem, killing him instantly.

Jabal knelt over the now-dead body of the CIA operative and former Delta Force commander, as the report of the pistol echoed down the valley and reached the road. The procession abruptly stopped. Security guards jumped on top of Hasan and rode him to the ground, covering and protecting his body with their own. Others, both from the road and from the surrounding security forces, looked towards the firing position, searching for the source of the shot.

"Will, you were a good soldier, but I have finally come to see you for the infidel you were in the service of the Great Satan."

Laying the pistol down, Jabal laid out spread-eagle on the ground as the nearest soldiers, APC's and helicopters converged on his position.

November 5th, 2005, 15:45
Behind the bluff above the main Highway to Karkuk
Irbil, Kurdistan

As soon as the shot rang out, the other members of the CIA team knew something had gone horribly wrong. That was no rifle shot. Their training and instructions kicked in immediately. At a signal from their second in command, Lt. Riley Adams, the team quickly issued orders to their Kurd compatriots and quietly turned away, back towards the scrub-covered hills. Using the cover of the scrub brush along the side of the particular hill on which they were positioned … they successfully moved away while the attention of the security forces was focused on the firing position where Jabal now lay on the ground.

Within two days, the remainder of the team would be picked up by a specially configured CV-22 Osprey tilt-rotor aircraft which had been outfitted for CIA insertions and extractions. In it, they were carried away from the short-lived Republic of Kurdistan, which by the time they landed in Turkey, no longer existed.

November 5th, 2005, 22:55
Special Conference Room, University of Salah al-Din
Irbil, Kurdistan

"My Imam, there is no identification on the body of the shooter. The body itself is that of a male in his late thirties whose exact origins are indeterminate, though his dental work would indicate western origins, probably the United States, perhaps England or Israel. The weapon is an American made .50 cal sniper rifle, but not the type normally carried by U.S. military personnel."

"There is no doubt that this individual was positioned to make an attempt on your life. If the rebel, Jabal, had not killed him, it is likely that the assassin would have succeeded in his attempt."

Hasan Sayeed considered the report from the commander of his security detachment. Someone, probably the Americans, perhaps the Israelis, was getting very concerned about him. Clearly, Allah was watching over him and his call to unite the faithful.

"And what of this Jabal? Is he talking?"

The security commander had spent several hours watching the interrogation of Jabal, who was well known as the military leader of the people they had been sent here to subdue. The interrogation had gone smoothly. Jabal was more than willing to cooperate. There had been no need for extra persuasive measures or threats. Everything Jabal was telling them checked out, in as far as their own security and intelligence apparatus allowed them to verify it on such short notice.

"My Imam, Jabal has indicated that this was a CIA attempt on your life, and that he could not allow it to proceed. He indicated that the name of the dead man is Will Peterson, but we have found no such name in our records, or in any review of the data we have on known American operatives. It is likely that this name was a cover."

"Nonetheless, Jabal pointed out to us where other members of this team had been in hiding and his information has already allowed us to capture a number of the rebels, although any other Americans are still at large. Jabal insists that he would like to speak with the personnel we are capturing. In fact he wants to speak to all of the Kurds, to convince them of the need to take up your cause and join in a united Islam."

Hasan could see that, if this turned out to be true, and Jabal had indeed made a decision based on the true faith, there was a potential political, spiritual and international coup of major proportions to be enjoyed here. Jabal had been an effective leader of the Kurd efforts to gain their independence from Sahdam Hussein. He had led well in this encounter with Hasan's own GIR forces and, if the American plans for air superiority had materialized, he probably would have been successful in preventing the GIR victory. If he was indeed convinced that the call to unite Islam was divine, and of Hasan's own role in that call as Imam ...

"Commander, I would like you to bring Jabal here now so that I can speak with him and interrogate him personally. The Ayatollah Ol Osam Sadiq Shiraziha and I will talk with him here in private, while you and your men wait just outside the door. Leave one of your side arms here with us, but I do not believe we will find use for it."

. Later that night, after much discussion and a lot of pointed and in-depth questioning by Hasan, the plans for the Kurds were complete. With Jabal's unqualified support and urging, the unification of the Kurds with the GIR would be a foregone conclusion. Considering Jabal's knowledge of the Americans, and his leadership and strategy capabilities, the leadership role for GIR forces in this region was also settled.

On the 5th of November, when Hasan made his announcement regarding the whole of Iraq becoming an official part of the GIR, closely followed by Jabal's speech to the world's press, the American's would know. They would know that their plans to thwart the will of Allah were in complete disarray and a total failure. They would also know that Hasan Sayeed knew exactly what they had attempted today on the road to Irbil. Hasan vowed before Allah that those actions would come back to haunt them.

CHAPTER 7

"It is more honorable to repair a wrong than to persist in it." -
Thomas Jefferson

November 6th, 2005, 10:55
CBC, "Face the Press"
New York City, New York

" … this President, like so many other Presidents from his party, has found it necessary to go sticking our nose into the affairs of other nations. The United Nations' General Assembly voted overwhelmingly to allow the elections in Iraq and Pakistan to stand. Many of us in the Senate and in the House opposed the recognition of Kurdistan. If it was so important, why didn't this same President, when he was the General in charge of all armed forces in Desert Storm, demand his President allow the creation of the so called "Republic of Kurdistan" back then?"

"I'll tell you why he didn't … it's because the world community would no more accept it then than it does now. So, instead of allowing a nation of people to vote their conscience and unite with people of like faith and culture, this President too quickly sends in the "Marines" and we get our nose bloodied in the worst air battle disaster since World War II… and for what? The Kurdish people are now willing to unite with the GIR anyway!"

"I'll tell you, it's preposterous. I am calling on my colleagues in the Senate and the House to conduct a full investigation. I believe we have the votes in the Senate to force a vote on censure, and that's exactly what I intend to do."

"The American people I represent are not interested in us forcing our will and our interpretation of the world view on other peoples. They are interested in maintaining low interest rates and high stock values, and in expanding our trade relations with the emerging nations, with organizations like the Coalition of Asian States. This president has taken actions that are damaging to all of these interests."

As the senior Senator from Massachusetts completed his comments, the commentator on the popular Sunday morning news show turned to his other guest, the Secretary of State, Fred Reisinger.

"Well, Mr. Secretary, there you have a fairly stinging rebuke and a threat of censure by one of the leading opposition Senators. How is the Administration reading the apparent disapproval of its actions in the Persian Gulf by many in the Congress, and, according to the polls, a growing percentage of American citizens as well? How does the administration plan to respond?"

Fred Reisinger was a consummate negotiator, but his loyalties were immovable, not only in relation to his friend and boss, the President, but also on principle. This was something he felt sure could not be said for far too many of the career politicians on both sides of the aisle with whom he rubbed shoulders on an almost daily basis. In the Secretary's opinion, the lack of steadfastness to principle was especially true of the inhabitants of the other side of the aisle, and was most particularly apparent in this individual with whom he shared the stage on this morning's show.

"With all due respect to the Senator from Massachusetts, the people of the Kurdish region also voted, and overwhelming I might add, to declare their independence. I find it ironic that the Senator would refer back to the Gulf War, and actions taken during that time by then General Weisskopf. At that time, General Weisskopf was under a Constitutional requirement, as are all of our service personnel, to obey the lawful orders of his civilian leadership. Would the Senator have had him disobey those orders? No ... Norm Weisskopf knows where his duty lies, and I defy anyone, including the good senator, to compare their record with that of the President in this regard."

"Well, we're now fifteen years removed from that conflict and Norm Weisskopf is the civilian leadership, the National Command Authority. He recognizes, along with many leaders in our nation and around the world, the great threat that is building in the Middle East. We have an Islamic union comprised of many states, a number of which have trained and harbored terrorists who have killed innocent Americans in cold blood. An Islamic state with nuclear weapons and rapidly expanding borders. Their influence and rapidly expanding military capabilities are perilously close to interfering with our own vital national interests and those of our friends and allies."

"With respect to the economic conditions, we are at a crossroads and have important choices to make. We can either continue a self-destructive policy of open trade with those nations who show by their actions that they use our generosity against us, or we can take a position to insure that those trade relations are consistent with America's best interests, both now and in the future. I will not attempt to intrude on Secretary Gage's turf, or to speak for him. But I can say that Russell Gage is a recognized scholar of economics. He understands the relation between trade issues and international politics perhaps better than anyone who has ever served as Secretary of the Treasury. It is his contention that the policy of appeasement and "free trade," at the expense of "fair trade," is ultimately destructive to our economy. The NEC to my knowledge has his full confidence and support."

At this point the CBC commentator interjected.

"Yes, but isn't it true, Mr. Secretary, that the European Union, outside of our historically close ties to Great Britain, is very nervous about the current situation in the Mid East? In addition, what of the Senator's contention regarding the announcement from Irbil this morning that they will unite with the GIR? In fact, one of our former staunchest allies in the region, a man your administration has backed, supported and depended upon, has now announced his support of unification. Jabal Talabari was the head of the Patriotic Kurdistan Front, and then, after their declaration of independence, he served as the General in charge of the Republic of Kurdistan armed forces. Let me quote from his announcement yesterday morning:

"I accept the appointment by Imam Hasan Sayeed as the military leader of this region of the GIR. I announce my loyalty to him and to the goal of Islamic unification. I urge all Kurdish people and others living in the region to support our decision to unify with the Greater Islamic Republic and vote "yes" in the referendum vote next week."

"Now, let me say just a word about the drastic change I personally have made. I was raised as a faithful Sunni. I am devout in the faith. I am also of Kurdish descent. I have fought hard for many years for what I believed to be best for the Kurdish people. We fought the tyrant Sahdam Hussein, and we were supported in that fight by other powers, principally the United States. I was led to believe, and indoctrinated by those supporting us, that Hasan Sayeed was just another Hussein. But, to use the western saying, "actions speak louder than words." Hasan Sayeed's actions have spoken louder than all the words Hussein ever uttered, and louder than the foreign voices from the west."

"His unilateral cease fire and his personal involvement with the negotiations ignited a spark within my heart. He had it within his power to rout us, to utterly destroy us, and yet he chose, even as prophesy indicated, to bind up the wounds and make peace with his brothers and sisters. Peace and unity in the faith are the best things for the Kurdish people. Hasan Sayeed offers this. The west offers us only more conflict and division. I came to the conclusion that I must reject what they now offer. I warn them, and their agents, to cease seeking to instigate divisiveness and conflict amongst our people."

"It is our intent to defuse the military situation and deploy the forces of this region of the GIR in a defensive posture. Those forces necessary to secure our borders and rebuild our infrastructure will remain. Other forces will be re-deployed throughout the GIR as indicated by our supreme military council, led by the Imam himself. The movement of troops and equipment and materiel with respect to these goals will begin in the next few days. Thank you."

"Secretary Reisinger, how does the administration respond to this? Here you have a former ally, a key player in this administration's hopes to limit the growth of the GIR, turning one hundred and eighty degrees and now supporting the GIR's expansion?"

The Secretary of State had been up since the early morning hours as news of the agreement in Irbil filtered out. He had spent several hours this morning with the President and his key cabinet members and advisors mapping out their strategy and response. He had, in fact, already voiced that response just a few minutes ago in answer to the liberal Senator from Massachusetts.

"I have already addressed this issue. We are, of course, saddened by this turn of events. Jabal Talabari and his people were staring down the barrel of a loaded GIR gun. I view any of the so-called "agreements" coming out of Irbil as decisions made under duress. Clearly, when not under such duress, the people of Kurdistan voted overwhelmingly to be independent. I believe that is what we should focus on."

"I cannot speak for the Secretary of Defense or the Joint Chiefs. I can say that our own sanctions remain in place. We will watch the diplomatic scene very carefully and will continue to offer any of the duly authorized leaders in the Republic of Kurdistan safe haven and sanctuary with our forces."

With the flashing of the red warning light indicating that there were only two minutes left in the program, the commentator interjected.

"Thank you Mr. Secretary. This ongoing crisis has once again captured the attention of our nation and its people. It has also sharply divided many."

"WNN will continue to carry live updates along with our interviews from both sides of the political aisle. Again, Mr. Secretary of State, Mr. Senator, we thank you both for your time and your comments."

November 14th, 2005, 16:12 local
Off the Coast of India
80 Kilometers west of Cochin

The two fleets sailed in formation a little less than 10 kilometers apart. These joint operations were a first, and many interested eyes were observing. Peering from above were the satellites … American, Russian, Israeli, French and Japanese. On the surface of the ocean, two American Perry class frigates and an improved Los Angeles class attack submarine were shadowing the battle groups, along with several ships and submarines from other nations.

The object of all of this interest was the joint naval exercise between India and the People's Republic of China. This was a major exercise that included the largest and most modern combatants from each nation.

Indian carrier Viraat on station.

The Indians had both of their carriers involved. One was the older jump jet carrier, Viraat, which the British launched as Hermes in 1953 and the Italians purchased in 1986. The Viraat had recently completed a service life extension and been modernized extensively.

Indian Delhi class DDG escort.

The other was the new Indian carrier, Cochin, which the Russians had launched as the Baku and the Indians purchased in 2000. The Indian government had spent three years rebuilding and refitting the former Russian VTOL carrier into a Short Take-off and Landing (STOL) carrier with a ski jump bow. Now, the Cochin was on her sea trials and would ultimately replace the Viraat after a second modern carrier was completed.

The Viraat carried a complement of twelve Sea Harrier VTOL aircraft, while the Cochin carried eighteen MIG-29 attack/fighter aircraft. Escorting the two carriers were eight very capable surface combatants.

These included two of the modern Delhi guided missile destroyers (DDG's), two Rajput class DDG's (which had been upgraded from former Russian Kashin class DDG's), two of the newer Kashmir class guided missile frigates (FFG's) and two of the improved Godavari class FFG's.

Indian Godavari FFG escort.

All of these destroyers and frigates were the most modern classes in the Indian navy and were equipped with the latest radar and sonar, as well as modern anti-aircraft and surface to surface missile systems. In addition, the Indians had the Rajaba and Jyoti replenishment ships taking part in the exercises.

The centerpiece of the Chinese group was the brand new Beijing sea control carrier, which was also conducting her sea trials. The Beijing was carrying a minimal compliment of twelve SU-33's, but was capable of carrying a total of thirty attack and support aircraft. These included the SU-33 derivatives now being license manufactured in China, as well as SU-25 "Frogfoot" attack aircraft and a new STOL early warning (AEW) aircraft the Chinese had recently developed. The Beijing was accompanied by two of the new Haizhou class DDG's, which were upgrades of the most modern Russian Sovremenny designs, two of the indigenous and very capable PRC Luhai class DDG's and four Jiangwei-II class FFG's. With the aircraft carrier and its eight escorts, this was the most powerful Chinese naval group ever assembled.

The exercises were scheduled to last for ten days. During that time, joint air operations, joint anti-submarine warfare (ASW) operations, joint oceangoing maneuvers and joint replenishment exercises would all be conducted. Early on in the exercises, a joint CAP was established over the fleets that consisted of two close-in Indian Sea Harriers and MIG-29's augmented by three SU-33's flying out further from the fleet (40-70 kilometers) along the primary and secondary threat axis. These units were rotated and configured differently depending on the type of exercise being conducted. Scenarios representing cruise missile defense, air defense, war at sea, ground support and forced transit were all exercised.

November 16th, 2005, 16:12 local
COSCO Fabrication Facilities
Port of Macua, PRC

The original fabrication had occurred several months ago in the small city of JingCheng near the confluence of the Yenshi Xi and Xingiao He Rivers in southeastern China. There, in a small fiberglass research and manufacturing facility owned by COSCO, a mold had been developed using rigid polyurethane foam as the primary material. No gelcoat was required, which made the entire process less expensive, in keeping with the planned disposable nature of the finished product.

Once composition and design of the principle product had been decided upon, the engineers in JingCheng began testing various inserts to help strengthen and provide hard points for the addition of various types of equipment ... and weapons. As a result, the product had numerous strengthened areas where various types and sizes of steel plate inserts could be fitted for the desired purposes.

Now, after significant testing and further cost reduction and manufacturing improvements, the master mold was complete and the process was ready to be implemented into mass production at many facilities. That production would occur rapidly in various places along the Chinese coasts and along several rivers that emptied into the South China Sea. Literally scores of production facilities were being prepared to mass-produce these products by the thousands.

There would be four principle production regions, with a principle gathering and outfitting facility for each region. These principle gathering and outfitting facilities were established as follows along the South China Sea Coast of the PRC: One of the facilities was at Shantou, which included twenty feeder facilities along the Han Jiang River. Another facility was at Mawei, which included thirty-seven feeder facilities along the Min Jiang River. A third facility was at Xiamen, which included forty-three facilities along the Jiulong Jieng River. Xiamen also included the research facility at Jingcheng. The final facility was here at Macua which included its thirty-six feeder facilities along the Xi Jiang River.

Now, at long last, the molds and materiel were in place. The senior Director over this project, who was here reviewing its progress, looked at the manufacturing and gathering facilities that had been erected here in Macau.

"So, Tang, when will your production crews be ready? Your facility will kick off the mass production and will generate the initial quality benchmarks and other test results that will serve as a template for the other three principle gathering points. The schedule calls for initial production to start on November 30th, but it appears that you are ahead of schedule."

Tang Xinsheng was indeed ahead of schedule. He was proud of what his workers had accomplished, and he believed that the quality metrics would prove their competence and expertise once production started. He planned to achieve the highest marks possible both for quality and for quantity.

"Minister and Senior Director Qiao. We are in fact ahead of schedule and will commence phased production next Monday, the 21st. We expect to bring twelve facilities on-line each week, reaching full production by December 12th."

In addition to being a Senior Director within the COSCO Group, Qiao Wenzhong was also the Assistant Vice Minister of internal production for the Guangdong Province of the People's Republic of China. He was impressed and satisfied that Tang had this critical portion of the project under control. The other ministers and the Politburo itself would also be gratified and impressed.

"This is very good news, Tang. What rates of production do you foresee when your facility is fully completed and functional?"

Tang had those figures with him. He opened his notebook and pulled out a production folder. After looking at several lines of printout on a number of pages, he answered Qiao.

"Minister Qaio, the addition and testing of the removable turbine engines, the water jets, the navigation and communication controls and equipment, defensive electronics and radar, the living facilities and plumbing, the ramp controls and the weapons will occur in final assembly. As you know this adds several days to the entire process. But once we get the production lines fully operational, I anticipate we will be producing one hundred of these landing craft per week here in the Macau operation."

For Qiao Wenzhong, this was excellent news. If the other three facilities could approach similar production rates, then the People's Republic of China would be turning out between four and five hundred thirty-meter-long landing craft per week by mid December.

Yunana II landing craft in trials.

These landing craft, officially designated as the Project 071, Yunana II class, would be armed with one HQ-7 SAM system containing eight missiles, one multiple 122mm barrage rocket launcher and two 25mm DP (dual purpose) guns. They would be capable of carrying 150 tons of materiel. This could consist of two tanks and two squads of soldiers, two APC's and three squads of soldiers or six squads of soldiers, over a range of 150-250 km for up to ten days of endurance.

The Yunana II class could also be carried on board numerous ships of the PLAN. Four of them would fit in the well deck of the new Amphibious Assault ships that were just beginning to come off their production lines. With the use of large davit systems or cranes, they could also be carried on most cargo and container ships available to the PLAN from COSCO's large fleet.

The design was essentially a lengthened version of the Yunana class, made of fiberglass construction with metal reinforcement and turbine engines. They were designed to be very seaworthy in wind force 6-7 and to be expendable and easy to manufacture in mass quantities.

"Outstanding, Tang. You are doing excellent work here and it will not go unnoticed or un-rewarded. Please, carry on with the tour."

November 19, 2005. 18:35 local
Sea King Boat Company, Mid West Region
St. Louis, Missouri

Sea King forty two foot House Boat.

Marge Basar stared at the monitor of her computer as she read the latest sales figures for the mid west region of the Sea King Boat company. Marge was the regional director of sales for the mid west region, and this year was going to be the best year she had experienced while working at Sea King, as well as one of the best years in the company's thirty-seven year history. Dealers all over the mid-west were selling Sea King boats at a record clip.

Sales of the thirty-two foot cruiser model were up fifteen percent over the previous year, and, on average, the cruisers being ordered were being outfitted with many of the higher-end options. Each of these boats was powered by two Cummins turbo diesel engines and could cruise all day long at over thirty knots, while carrying six passengers and over a ton of gear.

In addition to the sales of the cruisers, in the last three months five of Sea King's very expensive, top of the line houseboats had been ordered. These forty-two foot behemoths were powered by twin Mercury 250 horsepower outboards and were the apex of the luxury boat builders' craft. Each one was capable of sleeping eight passengers and could carry a load of over three thousand pounds, all while maintaining a steady twelve knots.

The orders had come in from dealers all along the Mississippi River. A few phone calls to the owners of those marine dealers had verified additional reasons for Marge to be pleased.

The buyers of these boats had all ordered top-of-the-line communication equipment along with some very sophisticated navigation equipment to go with their "package." All of this would add very nicely to the mid west region's bottom line.

If Marge could manage a sixth houseboat in the region before the end of the year, the mid west region would have sold more of the 42-foot houseboats in the second half of this year than the entire company had sold in any entire preceding year. The bonus money alone would be great, and the credits she accrued towards the company's annual sales trip would insure that she would earn one of those outside cabins on the luxury deck on her way to the Bahamas.

"I'll just have to keep those dealers hopping for another six weeks or so to make this a sure thing," she thought.

Marge picked up the phone to call the CFO of Sea King Boats and give him the good news.

"These sales are just dynamite," she thought to herself as she dialed the correct extension.

Marge Basar had no idea how prophetic that thought would turn out to be.

November 22, 2005, 10:25 local
Marine Recruiting Office, Boise State University
Boise, Idaho

Sergeant Ken Bennett put his hand over the phone and leaned over his desk.

"Leon, this is Charlie Jenkins on the phone. He wants to talk to you."

As Sergeant Bennett handed the phone to Leon, he turned his attention to Billy Simmons.

"Well, Billy, why don't we move over to the conference room and sit down and talk while Leon is on the phone? How's your Dad? It seems like his unit got over to Saudi just in time for them to watch the end of the show and come home. That's too bad, too. We needed to open a can of "whoop" on those folks real bad, and your Dad sounds like just the man to have gotten it done, too. You pretty glad he's coming home?"

Billy had thought a lot about his Dad over the last few weeks. He had been called up and then deployed over to Saudi Arabia so quickly. But that was part of the program. He was glad his Dad hadn't been sent to Turkey where the air battles had been fought … and yes, he was glad his Dad was coming home. Even though America was taking a hit over the inability to preserve Kurdistan independence, Billy was proud that the United States had made the attempt, and that his country was willing to stand forthrightly behind its promises.

"You bet. I'm glad he's coming home and that he's safe. He is currently slated to rotate back to Florida around December 1st, and then will be officially back in reserve status and home by New Year's Day."

As Leon continued to talk with his friend and mentor, Charlie Jenkins, who was calling from Chicago, the Sergeant continued.

"I can sure understand that. I spent several months over there back in Desert Shield and Desert Storm. I'm glad Weisskopf is the President right now, irrespective of those talking heads on the boob tube and cable. I have a sneaky feeling we haven't heard the last of Hasan Sayeed in the Mid East … and I know we are ultimately going to have to face down Red China. Did you hear about that new carrier they surprised us with and are using to conduct exercises with the Indians? Sounds like a tough ship. And I can promise you, they aren't building them as show boats."

Billy had heard about the new carrier. The surprise had been that it even existed because everyone thought the Chinese were working on the larger carriers near Shanghai. Those weren't supposed to be launched for another year or so. The one Sergeant Bennett was referring to had seemed to come out of nowhere.

As a result of all of these surprises, the media and certain elements of Congress were really down on President Weisskopf. That vote in Congress to censure him, even though it had failed, was an embarrassment. Despite the losses in the Mid East, and despite the surprises, Billy agreed with the Sergeant, and he agreed with his Dad ... America was lucky to have President Norm Weisskopf at the helm in these perilous times.

"I have heard about it. Even saw the pictures. It's a pretty radical design with the crossing deck pattern and the island in the back. Makes it clear it's a conversion. If the time to fight comes, though, we'll be putting them down and under. That thing may be good for regional activity against their regional adversaries, but a Nimitz class carrier with its battle group will take it down."

"But lets talk about why Leon and I came over today. We can go into more detail when he gets off the phone, but Sergeant, we've decided. With what all is going on, we're ready to join up ... now, today."

Bennett was surprised. It was the middle of the school year. Football season was still on. Billy was on a full ride scholarship.

"Wait a minute, Billy. This is pretty abrupt. Don't get me wrong. Your country wants your service and will be proud to have you in it. But we can wait until the semester break at least. What about football and your coaches? Have you talked with your parents? "

Fact was, Billy had considered all of these things. With the benefits offered, Billy figured he would finish his education while he worked his career. His coaches were not happy and wanted him to wait at least until the season was over. Billy had worked with his professors and instructors to take tests and finish the semester early. By doing so, he could also accommodate his coaches' wishes. His mom was supportive, but Billy could tell she was worried. She had indicated she would talk to his Dad about it, but Billy knew his Dad would support him. His Dad trusted him. Oh, he might offer some advice, but he had nurtured Billy's independence through high school and had plainly stated that once Billy turned eighteen, he was a man in his Dad's eyes. His Dad had treated him that way, too.

"Sergeant, I appreciate your concerns and your questions. But I have thought it all out. I want to join now and get started. I am going to fly the Super Cobra and make a career out of serving my country. Leon can tell you his own reasons, but he's made the same decision."

In the middle of that exchange, Leon had finished talking with the retired Sergeant Major Jenkins. He had walked into the conference room just as Billy had finished his last comments.

"That's right, Sergeant. We're signing up. I talked to my Mom and she's proud. I figure it will also set the right example for my little brother. I just told Charlie and he's already congratulated me."

"I figure I'm going to ultimately work towards Long Range Reconnaissance Patrol (LRRP). I got a knack for sneaking around and doing it quietly ... I also figure I am going to be a crack shot."

"So, both of us have all our affairs with schooling worked out. We're both ahead in most of our classes and can test out and get the credits for this semester so we can apply those later on down the line. We'll be done with our testing by December 5th, and from then on it's going to be Semper Fidelis!"

Sergeant Ken Bennett had been in the Marines for many years. He had been recruiting all over the country for the last four years. There had been many times when he came away disillusioned with today's American youth. But experiences like this one made up for that, and then some. Whenever he saw young men like Leon and Billy, who were willing to give up their lifestyles and willing to serve their nation, he knew America would always survive and that there would be good hands to which he could pass the torch.

"Well, it seems like you vermin have everything all figured out. Sounds like you got it planned down to the last detail, with all of your I's dotted and all of your T's crossed. You know what? I don't see any holes in your OPLAN either. Let's sit down and map out both of your strategies. One towards aviation and Super Cobras, and the other towards reconnaissance, sniper school and that LRRP spot."

"But before we do that, let me tell you that you boys have made my day. This deserves a real celebration and I'm going to tell you that a Marine takes advantage of such opportunities whenever he can. Yep, I feel a big feed comin' on and this one's on me!"

November 24, 2005, 20:45
National Reconnaissance Office Headquarters
IMINT Directorate
Chantilly, VA

John Bowers looked at the assembled technicians and analysts. "Wow!" he thought. "They really have staffed up over here." It didn't surprise him. With all of the requests coming in from the Middle East, and with the continued demand for information on the Chinese, plus the normal activities, it was little wonder they didn't have more people than they did.

"Tom, let me first offer my congratulations on your promotion. You're going to do a heck of a job managing this operation and I cannot think of a more deserving person. Now, let's see what got you so fired up that you needed to call me over here this evening."

Tom Lawton had been promoted to Manager, Imagery Intelligence Analysts just a couple of weeks ago. His old boss, Bill Hendrickson, had also moved up the food chain and was now a Director of Imagery Intelligence. The promotion had not kept Tom from continuing to work like an analyst, though. He spent several hours each day personally reviewing imagery from the latest hot spots, and, in particular, from Red China -- where his observations and analysis ten months earlier had warned the United States of Red China's extraordinary efforts in the Naval Aviation area. It was his recent discovery of further developments in this area that Tom wanted to show the National Security Advisor.

"John, take a look at this image."

Turning to his computer, Tom typed in a few commands on his keyboard and an overhead view of a Red Chinese Sea Control aircraft carrier was displayed on the screen.

"OK, Tom, that looks like the new Chinese aircraft carrier, the Beijing. It's a good shot of it for sure, but what is so special about this particular image?"

Tom typed in a few more commands. In the upper left-hand corner of the image, some text appeared, identifying the time the image was made, and its location. That text simply read:

11/22/05 03:25.34 Zulu
21:13:45 N 116:26:15 E
South China Sea

"John, notice the date and location."

John Bowers took just an instant before realization dawned on him.

"What! … Wait just a second … Tom, those figures can't be right, can they? The Beijing was supposed to be off the Indian coast … in fact, I know it was off the Indian coast on that date. I remember the briefing. How on earth could that date and location be correct?"

Tom had already gone over this same question in his mind several times. In resolving the dilemma, he had decided that the evidence pointed to the only conclusion possible.

"The picture and time stamp is correct, John. The answer is simple. That's not the Beijing. It's a second Red Chinese Sea Control aircraft carrier."

Taking a seat next to Tom, John's mind went into overdrive.

"But just last week we saw pictures of the second one still in its dry dock in the Tanjin shipyards. How could they have possibly completed, outfitted and rigged that ship in this amount of time?"

Tom displayed another image on his screen. This one showed a similar ship, still in dry dock, but nearing completion. The date stamp on this image was two days after the first picture, and its location was the Tanjin shipyards.

"John, that ship is still building in Tanjin. The first image is an entirely different vessel that the Chinese built and launched without our knowledge at all. What it means is that very soon the Chinese are going to have at least three of these things launched and on trials. "

"… and here's the shocker … at least a possible shocker. We know they were training eight air wings on those temporary landing decks they had installed at several airfields. We know that they are capable of moving these decks and then installing them on these container ships, which they then structurally and electronically modify to produce these sea control carriers. Based on what we are seeing here, we're going to have to presume that the Chinese are building six to eight of these vessels, not just the two."

John absorbed this information, almost reluctantly. It was incredible. But it looked to be exactly what the Chinese were doing. If you added the two larger deck aircraft carriers the Chinese were building in Shanghai to the potential eight … it meant that the Chinese would have ten aircraft carriers operational within the next eighteen to twenty-four months!

"OK, Tom. You don't need to do any further convincing. This is a major development … almost beyond belief, but the images don't lie."

"We're going to have to either divert more of our existing resources, or, more likely, launch more satellite assets to watch this twenty-four/seven. I want to find where these other carriers are being built. We may need some HUMINT help from the Agency. I also want to do a much more thorough analysis of all of the PRC's shipbuilding activities, commercial and military. I'll get Bill into the loop, as well as the NRO Director himself. Use the equipment resources that you have available now, and request whatever overtime or additional personnel you feel you will need, so we can prepare a preliminary briefing for the NCA day after tomorrow."

"I'll set up the meeting with the President, the SecDef, the Joint Chiefs, CIA and State. We'll make the request for more equipment to be launched out of Vandenberg at the earliest window of opportunity. Given what we are seeing here, I expect that particular request will be approved without delay. In addition, we'll discuss the potential for HUMINT operations during the meeting."

November 27, 2005, 22:47
WNN Broadcast Headquarters
New York City, New York

David Krenshaw was ecstatic. Here he was, sitting in the CEO's office being offered the position of which he had always dreamed, and which he had worked so hard to attain.

"David, I can't tell you how excited we are at your acceptance of our offer of a position on the Board of Directors at WNN, as well as your acceptance of the promotion to President and General Manager for our World Wide News Operations. In that role, in addition to our agreement to have you continue as an anchor and producer of Special Reports, your expertise, contacts and historical capabilities will help you in your management responsibilities. You will be responsible for the network's day-to-day news operations for Cable, TV and the net, including all aspects of programming and production. You have a very capable management team made up of Vice Presidents and Directors, most of whom you have known and interacted with for several years."

"Both your position on the Board of Directors and as President and General Manager of World Wide News places you on the WNN Executive Committee. It is an exciting day here at WNN, David, and we congratulate you."

"Finally, although the offer is not affiliated with WNN, my position in this organization allows me to extend to you another offer. On behalf of the Council on International Relations, and as a result of your significant ties with, and involvement in, international affairs, I would like to offer you membership in the Council. As you know, membership is an honor and a very prestigious form of recognition ... it is also by invitation only. At the director level on the CIR, we have discussed you many times, David, and my recommendation on your behalf has been tendered several times. Your work over the last year has caught everyone's attention, and last week the application was approved."

David had desired a position on the CIR for several years. He knew he had to be recommended, and that an offer had to be made, but he had liberally spread the word that he was interested in being a part of the group, dropping the hint, whenever appropriate, to every member he knew. Apparently his behavior had finally "paid off." This new position of influence-wielding responsibility was going to give him the opportunity he desired to not only report the news and help shape it through that reporting ... but to actually help MAKE the news.

"Of course I accept, Phil. As you know it is an opportunity that I have wanted for a long time. I look forward to working with the Council in all its efforts to promote sound world wide foreign relations and to stimulate conditions throughout the world towards those ends."

Philip Rheinholdt was the Chairman and CEO of WNN. He had been helping mentor David for several years. Although, based on David's uncanny ability to break and then produce major news events on the international scene, David's spot on the Board of Directors had become a forgone conclusion, and quite frankly, Philip probably would not have placed him in the management position over World Wide News. Really, it had been a purely political move. David's Asian and Near East allies and mentors were influential and had invested greatly in WNN. Promoting David over the heads of other Vice Presidents and Directors who had better management skills and more seniority would be a management issue he and David would have to deal with. But, all in all, it may not be a bad thing ... keeps the troops honest and a little off balance.

Having David on the CIR would also be a mixed blessing. David was very connected, so much so that sometimes other members were worried about that influence on his loyalty. Phillip shared their concerns. The CIR was interested in people loyal to promoting foreign relations and the network of ties that bound such relations together. In Philip's view such networks transcended ideology and nationalities. This was also the view of many of the senior members of the Council. There was concern that David's commitment to membership in the CIR would be much more a matter of David's desire to promote himself than it was a commitment to promote the goals of the Council.

Philip knew that, to one degree or another, the same was true of all individuals and he was confident that David's other positive and valuable assets could be used to advance the goals of the Council and of WNN, despite the drawbacks. After all, the CIR had been using all types of individuals, from Presidents, to University Chancellors, to Network CEO's, to Senators and military leaders for decades to formulate and build the international community and network as it existed today and as it would exist in the future.

Many of the members of the CIR were very self-centered and ambitious individuals. In a few cases they were downright despicable and sorry excuses for humanity outside of their brilliant abilities in specific areas. The Council used them all, just as it would use David Krenshaw. Just the same, his ambition and loyalties would bear watching, and Philip would relate as much to the Council along with Dave's acceptance.

"Great, David. Congratulations on you acceptance of membership in the CIR and all of your other achievements. I know it is a big day for you. We are going to have a small celebration tomorrow evening on your behalf in the corporate banquet room on the top floor ... just down the corridor from your new office, in fact. Many of our WNN executives will be there along with quite a few members of the Council. Please extend the invitation to your wonderful wife, Jennie, too."

December 2, 2005, 06:20
30th Air Wing Operations, 2nd Space Launch Squadron
Space Launch Complex 4E
Vandenberg Air Force Base, California

The 2nd Space Launch Squadron of the 30th Air Wing of the U.S. Air Force existed to conduct safe, reliable, and timely launch operations in support of Department of Defense and other governmental and commercial launches into space. Its location at Vandenberg Air Force base near Lompoc on

California's central coast allowed the 2nd Space Launch Squadron to be the only squadron in the U.S. Air Force capable of launching payloads directly into low-earth polar and sun-synchronous orbits. Using the Titan IV heavy lift vehicle, the Atlas IIAS medium-heavy lift vehicle, and the Titan II and Delta II medium lift vehicles, the 2nd had the capability for diverse space launch missions unmatched by any other Air Force Squadron.

On this date, the operations personnel were monitoring the impending launch of a KH-12 (formerly known as the KH-11B or KH-11/I) reconnaissance satellite from Space Launch Complex 4E, as ordered by the NCA and carried out through the NRO and the Chief of Staff of the Air Force. The KH-12 weighs over thirty thousand pounds at launch and requires a Titan IV B heavy lift booster to insert it into orbit. That is what today's launch called for, and the 2nd of the 30th was prepared to make it happen.

As to the capabilities of the satellite itself, the sensors of the KH-12 operate in visible and near infrared light, as well as thermal infrared for detection of heat sources. They also incorporate low-light-level image intensifiers to provide for imaging during night operations. The KH-12's have an infrared capability superior to that of the earlier KH-11 satellites, which is used primarily for detection of camouflaged targets and for observing differential thermal inertia in the target area. It is also used for looking at structures or targets buried underground, and for differentiating operating production factories from those that are not.

In addition, the KH-12's sophisticated electronics package provides sharper images than the older KH-11, with a resolution approaching ten centimeters. A periscope-like rotating mirror on the satellite reflects images onto the primary mirror, enabling the KH-12 to take pictures at very high oblique angles. This means that the KH-12 can provide high resolution images of objects hundreds of kilometers away from its flight path to either side.

All of these traits would serve this satellite well as it was launched into orbit to provide much more in-depth coverage of the Chinese coast and Chinese shipbuilding activities. Its mission would be to search for those shipbuilding activities related to the new Sea Control aircraft carriers the PRC was producing. Since noticing the 2nd at-sea carrier, the NRO had discovered yet another, this one conducting trials between the East China Sea and the Yellow Sea.

The information regarding the 3rd Sea Control Carrier had produced rapid results when it was presented to the president and his key advisors by the National Security Advisor, John Bowers, and Tom Lawton of the National

Reconnaissance Office. The concern it evoked at the highest levels of government in the United States was expressed by this expedited launch of a very sophisticated and expensive KH-12.

"We are a go for launch. All systems are checking in good to go. I repeat, we are go. T-minus 15 seconds and counting."

"10, 9, 8, 7, 6, 5, 4, 3, 2, 1 ... Launch!"

Out on the launch pad, the gantry suddenly became visible in the darkness as the Titan IV B's three massive stage "O" solid-rocket motors ignited. Slowly, then with increasing speed, the rocket lifted its payload into the air trailing a massive gout of flame.

KH-12 satellite launched.

"All systems are nominal. Down range tracking is on. Stage "O" separation and Stage 1 ignition coming up on my mark ... mark!"

Approximately two minutes into the flight, the first stage LR87 liquid-propellant rocket ignited as the solid rocket boosters fell away. Then, Stage 2, using a LR91 liquid-propellant engine ignited. Mission parameters used a final Boeing Aerospace inertial upper stage to lift the Kh-12 to the desired orbit.

Within the hour, the Air Force K-12 satellite had achieved its optimal orbit and was completely checked out and pronounced in perfect operating condition for its mission.

December 5, 2005
Along the Kuwait/GIR Border
The Greater Islamic Republic

The entire region surrounding the Persian Gulf was arrayed like a massive chessboard whose the playing pieces were the various Army, Navy, and Air Force groups deployed in the region by the opposing forces. As would occur in any difficult chess match, at times the two opponents observed their adversary's disposition of forces and the intent behind that disposition and then prepared to make countering moves accordingly with their own 'pieces.'

In the Persian Gulf, on December 5, 2005, the movement of forces as a result of the initial clash was underway.

The GIR was maintaining a relatively large force in the vicinity of Irbil, and had established the headquarters for its 2nd Army group in Basra. This army group would be responsible for maintaining order in all of the former Iraq and providing for the defense along the Turkish/Saudi and Kuwaiti frontiers. To that end, this army group was being organized into a force of three hundred thousand troops along with several thousand artillery pieces, over fifteen hundred tanks, three hundred helicopters and seven hundred fighter and attack aircraft. The northern areas were to receive about one third of this force while the southern sector, which faced Kuwait and Saudi Arabia, fielded two thirds of the strength.

The GIR 1st Army group had been reconstituted and pulled out of the former Iraq back deeper into the Greater Islamic Republic, but only as far as Ahvaz, a distance of one hundred miles. This force would consist of close to one hundred and fifty thousand troops, two thousand artillery pieces, five hundred tanks, one hundred and fifty helicopters and six hundred military aircraft. These forces would be tasked with the security and defense of the GIR Persian Gulf coast from Abadan to the Mand River and the security of the internal regions, primarily the Karkeh, Dez and Marun river drainages.

With the reduction in forces in the former Iraq on the GIR's part, and with significant political pressure from opposition political leaders at home who claimed that the reason for the force buildup had vanished, the United States and its allies were also downsizing in the Gulf region. This downsizing would result in the United States and Great Britain maintaining a total reaction force of twenty-five thousand troops (20K U.S. and 5K British) in the Kuwait area who were backed up by the Kuwaiti Army of twenty thousand active duty personnel and a Saudi contingent of ten thousand. It was anticipated that these force numbers would be reduced over the next several months as tensions continued to reduce, but Weisskopf was in no hurry … particularly given the proximity of the GIR 1st Army group.

The U.S. Navy kept a single carrier battle group in the Mediterranean and another in the Arabian Sea. The U.S. Air Force was downsizing its force to one hundred fighter and attack aircraft in Saudi and another one hundred in Turkey, augmented by the Kuwaiti, Saudi and Turkish Air Forces.

Incirlik Air Base in Turkey was in the process of being repaired and rebuilt. U.S. aircraft were already flying CAP missions and surveillance missions from the repaired runways and ground radar installations were operating out of temporary facilities. It would be another two weeks before longer airstrips accommodating E-3, KC-135 or B1-B aircraft were complete.

As these reductions and movements continued, an uneasy calm settled over the entire region. In the chess game, the players eyed each other's movements and tried to divine intentions. They both realized that the brief, violent exchange that had resulted in the termination of the Kurdish independence efforts in all likelihood only represented the opening moves in a longer, more difficult match.

That brief military exchange was being called simply the "Kurd War," or the "Two Day War." It was agreed that, in terms of military measurements, the confrontation had been a virtual draw, with the GIR losing far more equipment and personnel while achieving its goals, while the Americans lost less materiel and personnel, but failed to prevent the pacification of Kurdistan by the GIR.

However, diplomatically and strategically the outcome was viewed as a clear victory for the GIR. Most nations (outside of the United States and its immediate allies) believed that the unification of the Kurdish areas with the GIR was acceptable on the international scene. Still, there was an underlying feeling that business had been left unfinished. This meant that tensions remained high even though force levels continued to reduce.

Some history enthusiasts began to refer to this tense situation and standoff between the GIR and the United States as the "Persian Gulf phony war." This was in reference to the time period during World War II after Germany had defeated Poland, but before hostilities between major powers ensued when France was attacked. Politicians and military analysts on both sides wondered how long this "phony war" might last before erupting into a more major conflict.

December 7, 2005, 10:00 local
Government Conference Center, Beijing
The People's Republic of China

Jien Zenim considered the historic gathering that he had arranged. Here in the secure conference room with him, with no one else but their most trusted advisor in attendance, were:

Imam Hasan Sayeed – The Political, Military and Spiritual leader of the Greater Islamic Republic.

President KP Narayannen – The President of India.

President Jien Zenim - The leader of the most populous and (at least from his own perspective) the most powerful nation in the world.

The three of them made up the executive council of the CAS, or Coalition of Asian States. Through years of discipline and commitment, with unfailing focus and unflinching resolve, he had formed the most powerful economic coalition the world had ever known. Between the People's Republic of China, India, The Greater Islamic Republic and their exclusive rights to Siberia, the Coalition of Asian States was poised to dramatically shift the balance of world economic and political power. One would have to be a fool to think that the military balance would not also be correspondingly shifted.

It was to discuss this eventuality, and their plans for it, that the great leaders had come together here in Beijing at Jien's invitation. Throughout the weekend they had discussed their economic plans and their response to the current American sanctions. They had agreed that between themselves and their own markets, a divided European market and a hungry Russian market they had the demand and the resources to survive, intact, the American economic and international pressure.

Now the time had come to discuss the other matter. The potential for their political and economic activities to produce a corresponding military reaction had been recently displayed to them in a direct way over the Kurd issue. Although Jien had recommended against any premature military adventure by the GIR against the Kurds, correctly predicting the reaction of the Americans ... the more information that had come out regarding it, the better he felt. Particularly now that force levels were reducing.

"Imam, you are correct. The benefits that have resulted from this exchange far outnumber the detriments. I still believe the risks were far greater than what materialized, but that is of no concern now. We have several issues we can make great use of as we build towards our ultimate goals."

1. Through good planning, commitment and attrition, the American military machine can be held at bay and denied their desire to control the battlefield. In the process, if it is forced upon us, we can achieve our goals while so occupying their forces or those of their allies.
2. The Americans can be kept from amassing an overwhelming international or political coalition against any one of us. With our own influence and satellites, we can effectively block the creation of any such coalition by the west against any CAS member state.

3. The Americans have shown their hand in their assassination attempt of Hasan. The evidence provided to us by Hasan is incontrovertible.

"Imam Sayeed, congratulations on your victory. I believe the planning, the tactics and an explanation of the events surrounding your successful attack on the American air base at Incirlik, Turkey and your defense of you own ground forces the next day should be distributed to every military commander within each of our nations. It will be something they can learn from and take heart in. We should derive the basic strategies, how they played on American weakness and then school our own people in these strategies until they know them instinctively."

"Now I believe we can use these three issues to enhance our own plans."

As he said this, Jien motioned and an aide brought in several copies of a leather-bound document and handed one to each person present.

"These plans represent a formal compilation and formulation of what I have discussed with each of you personally over the last several years. We have been successful beyond expectation to date and it is now time to turn these plans into reality. The plan, should it be required ... and I believe from my study of history and my study of the Americans that it will be unavoidably necessary ... is called "Breath of Fire." Please open to the first section and follow along both within the document and on the screen."

At this, Jien Zenim motioned for his advisor, Li Peng, who turned on the multi-media video equipment and prepared to display the various screens and images that would follow along with Jien's presentation. Jien continued.

"Breath of Fire" involves, foremost, our desire to establish the CAS as the dominant economic power in Asia, and an equal competitor in Europe and the Americas. If this goal is interfered with militarily, then it involves leading the Americans and their allies onto fatal terrain. This is a Chinese strategy put forth by the greatest war strategist in history, Sun Tsu. It simply means providing the Americans with the options that they expect where the range of their responses will all lead them into a position where they have no defense and no escape."

President Narayannen carefully considered what Jien said. To date, the CAS had proved a huge economic boom for India. The Indian exploration teams in Siberia were finding and developing tremendous resources. The markets for Indian labor, manufacturing and technology in China, Russia and even in parts of the GIR were growing rapidly, and the European markets were continuing to grow as well.

Thus far, this economic windfall had all been accomplished with minimum risk. As an added benefit, this progress was steadily eating into areas where American firms and markets had long been entrenched. As a result, the Americans had attempted to establish sanctions and policies that would place pressure on India. Although Narayannen was favorably disposed to America's ideological foundation ... he just didn't believe the current crop of American politicians and businessmen were disposed to being truly committed to it themselves. Zenim and Sayeed were committed. Their fundamental ideology might be less appealing, but the results to India were clear, and the unwavering nature of the commitment to the principles that produced these results was something he felt he and his people could count on.

"Let us examine this plan together, Mr. President. We in India will move forward with a determination to avoid conflict if at all possible and establish the CAS as the influence in Asia that we all desire. At the same time, while it pains me, it is only prudent to prepare for the implementation of "Breath of Fire" should it become necessary."

Hasan Sayeed knew that "Breath of Fire," or something like it would be necessary. The Americans were realizing the true nature of the opposition. Hasan knew personally how serious they viewed that opposition and to what lengths they were prepared to go to forestall or eliminate it.

"President Zenim, we were truly blessed to have been successful in our short, but sharply fought efforts to retain the northern regions of the former Iraq. Do not be fooled. We were successful, but it was the type of success any of us could only stand so much of. I am confident that the Islamic people have the heart and the commitment to sustain such losses longer then the Americans, but do not think it will be an easy thing."

"Having said this, I will freely share with you that it is my conviction that "Breath of Fire," as I see it explained here in the overview, will be absolutely necessary. It will be so, not because we desire it, but because it will be forced upon us. I do not believe the Americans, or their allies ... several of which I am sorry to say are unfaithful Islamic states ... will accept a second place status, economically or influence-wise, anywhere on the face of this globe we call earth. They will not accept such a status particularly in areas where they have traditionally been recognized as supreme. So I believe we must study this plan, voice our input, revise it accordingly, and then stand prepared to implement it."

"Finally, I agree wholeheartedly that the tactics and the strategies that proved successful for us in holding off the American air superiority should be shared throughout our command structures. It amounts basically to this ... throw more at them than they imagine. Make them use up all of their expensive weapons and then overwhelm them with what you have left."

"Your people must be absolutely disciplined in such an effort, because they must persevere in the face of horrendous losses. We threw approximately four hundred aircraft at the American base at Incirlik. Initially they had only twelve aircraft airborne. To this they added another eight, and then twelve more. These thirty-two aircraft shot down well over one hundred of ours. Their air defenses shot down another sixty. We lost over one hundred and sixty aircraft to accomplish our goals that day. Do not forget the basic math of this equation."

Jien Zenim was impressed by both of these leaders. As they studied "Breath of Fire" they would find ample economic, political and military challenge and reward for their perspective nations and peoples. Much of it would come down to the discipline and will of which Sayeed spoke. But even more of it would come down to their ability to lead the Americans to the fatal terrain Jien had mentioned earlier.

Jien Zenim was very familiar with, and respectful of, the Americans' capability, and, by extension, the capabilities of their allies. He had no intention, except where absolutely necessary, of directly challenging their strength. Hasan had used brute force and good planning and he had been successful. But as he himself admitted, you could only afford to "win" so many of those kind of battles. No, Jien was not afraid to pay the butcher's bill when required, and though he had the will and the resources to accumulate such bills more so than any other sitting in this room ... he preferred to manipulate circumstances so that the bill was paid by his adversaries instead. This was particularly true for the western allies because they had fewer resources with which to pay such bills, and, every time they did, it would substantially lessen their ability to force such payment terms on Jien and his people.

"Good, let us then review the introduction and overview. I believe you will find the summary to be succinct and to the point. It provides projected time frames, triggering events and goals for initial operations that will hold our adversaries in place, and then outlines how we will draw our adversaries onto the fatal terrain I have spoken of. After reviewing and commenting on the summary, and modifying it where necessary, we can launch into the details of each specific area of the plan."

"It is my hope and goal that we can leave here tomorrow with both our economic plans that we have developed over the last two days, as well as the military options that we develop from these plans, in place."

"Shall we proceed then?"

December 9, 2005, 18:09 local
800 KM Northwest of Krasnoyarck
Siberia, The Russian Federation

Dr. Gavanker was very proud of what his team had accomplished in the five months they had been on site in Siberia. By early August, the test bores had been sunk and they had brought back information beyond expectations. The field would in fact be bigger than the Baku field in the Crimea. He had been immediately informed by first the Indian government, and then the Russians, to expect to be provided with a significant increase in workers and materiel so that he could get initial production underway before winter.

By September the staff on his team had been tripled to almost two thousand workers. A regular "boom" town was developing, and a spur from the main rail lines two hundred kilometers to the east had been built and opened before November. By that time the weather had begun to worsen, but Dr. Gavanker and his team had already sunk six production wells and had also completed pipelines to the railhead so that the initial crude could be transported for refinement. This would have to do until a pipeline could be completed directly to their location. That was scheduled for the end of January, but progress was being slowed due to the weather.

As the increase in workers and materiel and business to support them all mushroomed, the Russians also increased the security forces. Military engineers came in and took the roughed-out airfield and turned it into a dual-use commercial and military air base with the latest military radar and with significant equipment for operations in winter. As a result of his success in helping develop the resource, building the initial airfield and having an unblemished record in securing this resource jewel for mother Russia, Colonel Nosik was promoted to General. In addition to a significantly increased security force, including more men and equipment, some heavy armor, and a number of interceptor and support aircraft, Nosik was given responsibility for the maintaining the security of two other resource projects. One was a new Chinese Cobaltite mine, and the other was a new Indian low-sulfur coking coalmine. The largest operation was here in Gavank, where he established his headquarters.

Over the preceding months, as their fortunes mutually improved, and they assumed more and more responsibility, Dr. Gavanker and General Nosik formed a friendship of sorts. General Nosik held weekly staff meetings and invited Dr. Gavanker to a number of them, to report on the status of the various civilian projects going on at Gavank. In turn, when Dr. Gavanker held his staff meetings, he would reserve a portion of each meeting for the General, or his Chief of Staff, to discuss security issues. Generally, on Fridays, the two men met informally over dinner and discussed the week's events and their thoughts in general. That is what they were doing today.

"Andrei, who could have guessed that things would go so well? Or who would have thought that a crusty old war dog like you would tolerate a theorist and soft foreigner like me to be a part of your operations for so many months?"

The General had to nod. He would not have imagined it himself ... and if someone had told him it would be so a year ago, he would have laughed in their face. Yet it had worked out exactly as Buhpendra described it ... well, almost exactly.

"Buhpendra, you know I would never describe you as a "theorist," my friend. You have shown us all, on countless occasions, your ability to apply those theories to the real world and make this project a success. It could not have been a success without your strong grounding in reality. As to soft ... humph! No one who lives here in the wilds of Siberia as we have done these last months is deserving of the term "soft." I will admit to the crusty old war dog title, though."

Dr. Gavanker also nodded at the General's reply. He had come to enjoy these Friday evening get-togethers. There was so much they could discuss, and hearing and weighing their separate views of world events, politics, ideologies and beliefs had provided many hours of reflection and appreciation over the last several months.

"So, now that forces are reducing, and after some time to reflect, what do you think of the way the Muslims handled the Americans, my friend? I thought it was somewhat surprising."

General Nosik had not been too surprised. He had faced Muslims who were eager to fight, and committed to their faith. Such fighters were fierce, dedicated and willing to take significant losses to achieve their goals.

"I was not overly surprised. All Arabs are not like the Iraqis of Desert Storm. Those poor wretches were forced to be there and had no commitment to their cause. They were a surrender waiting to happen."

"This Hasan Sayeed, though ... he has a commitment, and is gathering a committed people around him. Such a people, driven by their faith ... and believe me, Buhpendra, such fighters are fierce ... would be a very serious adversary. Many will gladly sacrifice their life simply to help attain their collective goals. The Americans, even with their technological advantage, will find it difficult to readily defeat such a people. I believe this is what they experienced in the brief exchange."

"But, I would not count the Americans out. It is true they are soft and have experienced many years where there was no appreciable challenge. It will probably take some fairly bloody noses to get their attention. But, like Yamamoto of Japan remarked in World War II after he pulled off perhaps the greatest defeat of the Americans at Pearl Harbor, I would be careful of waking that giant from its slumber. Better to just let it sleep, if you can, while you tiptoe around it and steal all of its belongings! Ha! Particularly with an old fighting bear like Weisskopf leading them. That's what I think."

Buhpendra was not a military man. He prided himself on being a strategic thinker and on being able to make clear, logical decisions. Those qualities had served him well throughout his career and they were serving him well here in Siberia. Applying them to world affairs was not new to him. His work in the Energy Directorate for his country had required that he factor his ability to strategize into their planning regularly. But the military angle was new to him and he enjoyed discussing it and exploring it with the General.

"I agree about Weisskopf. His political enemies are using the current circumstances against him, but I would not count him out if things flare up again. He is a fighter and a fine leader and has the respect of his armed forces. Thank goodness things appear to have quieted down, even though the Americans' goal for an independent Kurdistan was not realized. Let's hope it remains that way."

December 11, 2005, 22:00
Marine Recruit Training Depot
San Diego, California

"COME ON! COME ON! COME ON! Get off that bus, you maggots! What do you think this is? Where do you think you're going anyhow? To the matinee? Let's go! WHAT ARE YOU WAITING FOR?"

"I am Drill Instructor Sergeant Matthews. At ALL times, you WILL address me as "SIR." If you have a request or a statement to make to me, you WILL formulate it with the words DRILL INSTRUCTOR SERGEANT MATTHEWS, SIR!"

As Drill Instructor Sergeant Matthews continued, Billy and Leon stepped off the bus at the Marine Recruit Training base in San Diego. They had arrived on schedule at ten PM, to be processed in.

"ARTICLE 86 of the Uniform Code of Military Justice PROHIBITS ABSENCE WITHOUT LEAVE. ARTICLE 91 of the Uniform Code of Military Justice PROHIBITS DISOBEDIENCE TO A LAWFUL ORDER. ARTICLE 93 of the Uniform Code of Military Justice PROHIBITS DISRESPECT TO A SENIOR OFFICER ... these are ABSOLUTE, NON-BREAKABLE laws you WILL LIVE BY for the next 13 weeks ... and throughout your military career."

Other armed services give their recruits a slight break during the in-processing phase of basic training. But not the Marine Corps. Discipline starts the instant the recruits step off the bus. Leon and Billy had been informed by Sergeant Bennett how things were going to be. They were finding out that he had been absolutely correct. Marine Corps drill instructors must be addressed loudly as "Sir." They hadn't even gotten off the bus before being taught that first lesson.

As they entered the building, Drill Instructor Sergeant Matthews continued to instruct them in clear, loud tones about what it was they needed to do, and about many of the other regulations they would have to live by for the next 13 weeks of their basic training.

The other services do a quick in-processing and allow recruits to get some sleep for the remainder of the first night. But in the Marine Corps new recruits are up the entire first night and all of the next day. During this time, they complete paperwork, get their hair cut off ... all of it ... turn in every bit of civilian clothing and articles they own, are issued their initial uniforms and field gear, and receive personal hygiene items from the PX, the cost of which is deducted from their pay.

Leon and Billy would spend the next three to five days in Receiving. During that time, they might be tempted to believe they were already in boot camp with Drill Instructors yelling at them, drilling them, marching them, showing them how to wear their uniforms, showing them how to make their "rack" presentable for inspection, feeding them, etc. ... all "by the numbers."

While in Receiving, Leon and Billy would also be given their Initial Strength Test (IST). To pass (and avoid being assigned to a Physical Conditioning Platoon), they would be required to do two pull-ups, thirty-five sit-ups in two minutes, and a one and one half mile run in thirteen and a half minutes or less. Leon and Billy would have no problem with the IST.

As Leon and Billy would learn, after Receiving the fun really begins when they are transported to their squad bay and introduced to their Senior Drill Instructor and his two assistants. These three would be the constant instructors, prodders, transformers, mentors, examples, trainers, indoctrinators and daddies of the sixty to eighty recruits who made up Leon and Billy's platoon in Company B of the 1st Battalion at the San Diego Recruit Training Depot.

The hard core definition of the Marine Drill Instructor (DI) indicates that he is a short-tempered, impatient, deep-voiced, screaming, seemingly-psychotic, un-patronizing, but deeply-devoted and fully-dedicated Marine NCO who works his magic on new Marine recruits. That magic teaches them to "surrender body and spirit to harsh instruction so as to receive a soul." It instills into them the makings of disciplined Marines who will stand and fight for duty, honor, country and their comrades when every other inborn instinct tells them to run.

The DI is an individual whom the new recruits hate ... but whom the new Marines revere. The DI magic would work especially well on Leon and Billy, as future events would indisputably reveal.

December 16, 2005, 16:30
Oval Office, The White House
Washington, D.C.

The President had once again gathered his principle foreign relations team in the Oval Office. This team included the National Security Advisor, the Secretary of Defense, the Chairman of the Joint Chiefs, the Secretary of State, the Director of the Central Intelligence Agency and the Vice President. They had been discussing the continued issues associated with the growing Coalition of Asian States and the influence it was having in Asia through the People's Republic of China and India, and its influence in the Middle East in the form of the Greater Islamic Republic.

"Summarizing, then, from diplomatic and relations standpoint: with the addition of Vietnam, North Korea, Cambodia, Mongolia, Laos, Nepal and Bangladesh, the CAS continues to grow as a world economic and ideological power. The Siberian resources are beginning to flow into China and India from the new oil fields, natural gas fields, gold mines and other mineral mines that are being rapidly brought into production. We estimate that there are one hundred and seventy-five to two hundred thousand Indian workers in Siberia now, and that there are in excess of two hundred thousand Chinese workers there. Russia is benefiting from their own percentage of each find, as well as from their royalties on the portions delivered to India and Red China."

"Russia is also reaping rich profits and boosts to their economy by the arms sales going on to China, India and the GIR. Their arms and munitions plants, their armor factories, their naval yards and their aircraft factories are operating at levels in excess of the highest production rates during the cold war."

"Mr. President, all of this adds up to significant economic and political pressure on many of our allies. Japan, South Korea and much of Europe are much more dependent on Mid East oil than we are. For our allies in the Fareast, all of that oil flows through waters in which the CAS is showing a greater and greater presence. With their naval build up, the military installations they have established on so many critical islands and their tremendous influence on OPEC pricing and production, our friends are getting very nervous."

As the Vice President paused, Norm Weisskopf assessed the strategic situation in his own mind. Someone on the other side was one heck of a chess player. As far as he was concerned, that someone had to be Jien Zemin. But where was he going with it? What was his end game? Better yet, how long before the confrontation?

Norm Weisskopf was absolutely sure the confrontation was coming. He couldn't see any way to avoid it if the United States wanted to maintain any high degree of influence in the Western pacific, or in the Mid East.

"John, let's put this in perspective. Please summarize what we're seeing in terms of intelligence and surveillance on the military side."

John Bowers had been playing point on this for the President for some time now. Although he had gotten over his discomfort in speaking to matters that he was sure Defense and the CIA felt were their own areas of influence, he was still somewhat ill at ease speaking for them. Nonetheless, he had learned to work well with the various teams those two organizations could provide and spent countless hours in briefings and planning sessions with them.

"Mr. President. The greatest immediate threat remains in the Middle East. The GIR has pulled back an entire Army group, but they are still largely intact in the vicinity of the former Iraq/Iran border. They have not dispersed nearly as much as would be expected if they were going to garrison all of the bases and facilities located throughout that area of the GIR for peacetime deployment. We feel they are still poised to threaten Kuwait and Saudi Arabia."

"The forces in the former Iraq are deployed in strength along or near the Kuwait and Saudi border in the south, and the Turkish border in the north. They outnumber our forces considerably in both areas, particularly as a result of our force reductions since Desert Sentinel ended."

"Of significant note is the announcement of joint training exercises by Syria along the GIR border in Late January and early February. That is a situation we will have to watch."

At this point, General Stone, the Chairman of the Joint Chiefs added,

"Sir, if I might add a thing or two here. First, Incirlik Air Base is fully functional again. We have increased our normal contingent of F-15's by a factor of two there. In Saudi, our first operational wing of F-22 Raptros has been deployed and is adding significantly to our defensive capabilities for the Kingdom."

"One other thing, if I may. Our Israeli friends are very nervous about the GIR, as you can imagine. They have increased their force readiness and alert across the board by one step. They are also significantly increasing their forces along their borders, particularly on the Golan Heights."

As the General finished, John continued.

"One more item of concern in the Middle East: Our old friend, Quadafi, in Libya is mobilizing his forces and putting them in a state of readiness that we haven't seen since Reagan thumped him real hard in the 1980's. He is also assisting Chad with men and materiel in the final phases of their suppression of rebel forces there. There is a significant concern that he will soon announce his allegiance to Hasan Sayeed and his desire to become an official part of the GIR."

"As you are all aware, there are also approximately two hundred thousand Chinese in Chad. To begin with, they were involved in relief work, but lately we have word that many of them are working in arms factories, and are participating in the training of new Chad recruits. This is another area that bears watching. Mike, do your people on the ground have anything newer than my meeting at Langley last week?"

The Director of the CIA had gotten a report the evening before. As a result of John Bowers' meeting and the discussion of this very issue, Mike had instructed the Deputy Director of Operations to contact the embassy there in Chad and their operatives. The results of that inquiry had come in late last night.

"As a matter of fact, John, I do. Late last night we received a situation report (SitRep) from our people in Chad. It is clear that the Chinese there are assuming a more and more active role in armament manufacture, and in training and instruction of military forces. Many more Libyan advisors have also arrived in just the last week to ten days."

"Mr. President, given the numbers involved, and given the apparent militarization of the Chinese relief workers, I believe we should view these developments gravely. Particularly when you consider the close ties Sudan has with Libya and its recent positive behavior towards the GIR. Our friends in Egypt are concerned about an encirclement of fundamentalism that could threaten their interests."

The Secretary of State chimed in on this particular topic.

"Mr. President, we should immediately lodge a protest with the United Nations. Red China was operating under very specific guidelines in its appeal to provide assistance to Chad. That assistance is limited to humanitarian relief alone. If they are in any way involved with military assistance, we must lodge a protest and seek a vote condemning their actions and revoking the UN resolution that sent them there in the first place."

The President understood Secretary Riesinger's concern and the reason for his protest.

"Fred, I understand your frustration and your diplomatic ire. I agree we should make the protest. But I do not believe we will succeed in getting things turned around. Red China will simply veto any security council initiative, and we have seen that there is little prospect for a vote in the general assembly."

"Just the same, I believe it is necessary to make the effort. Please have our ambassador to the UN make the necessary arrangements and see who we can get to support it. Alan, please work with our allies and coordinate with Fred and the ambassador. Now, John, please continue."

John Bowers wasted no time in doing so.

"OK. Finally, we have several issues in the Fareast that are equally distressing, if not as immediate. This involves the Red Chinese and the CAS."

"Of immediate concern is the buildup of North Korean forces along the demilitarized zone for their winter exercises. This is always a tense time of the year, and we are paying particular attention to their movements this year as our commitments in the Middle East have us spread fairly thin."

"We believe that conditions in the North are still extremely desperate in terms of food, but Red China, as a result of its continued economic growth and as a result of North Korea joining the CAS, has announced a food relief program of large proportions. They are getting millions of metric tons of wheat from Russia, Brazil, Venezuela and Canada and shipping it to North Korea. Along with the wheat, thousands of Chinese relief workers and newer farming equipment are being "loaned" to the North to improve their farming techniques. The first of the materiel has already arrived there."

"Finally, turning to the continued buildup of the PLAN: They continue with the very rapid manufacture and deployment of their newest generation of destroyers and frigates. Also, as you all know, in addition to their two large aircraft carriers being built in the Shanghai area, we have discovered that the Chinese have also embarked on a very rapid development and build of these smaller sea control aircraft carriers. The first of these, the Beijing, was launched in September and almost immediately took part in joint naval exercises with India. Since that time, they have launched two more and are building five others. We have utilized our best surveillance equipment coupled with Mike's HUMINT assets to discover the four shipyards where these conversions are taking place."

"Apparently, the Red Chinese purposely allowed us to find one of these facilities operating in the open some months ago in the hopes that our attention would be diverted. They were successful. In the meantime, they developed three other yards with completely enclosed dry dock spaces for the clandestine manufacture of more vessels. The result is that they will have eight of these very capable aircraft carriers in the Western Pacific in the next four to six months, followed by two larger deck carriers by next summer. This will represent a significant shift in power and one we cannot ignore or take lightly."

The picture that was developing was not pretty economically, diplomatically or militarily. While there was always the chance that diplomatic and economic conditions in the world could shift, rise, fall and equivocate either to the nation's good or ill, there was no excuse for being in the military position they were now in. That is, no good excuse. Apathy, comfort, technological prowess and sheer arrogance all had grown to the point of extreme overconfidence. All of that had resulted in spending plans, building plans, force dispositions and strategies that reflected the same ... and had done so for several years. The situation couldn't be turned around overnight.

That arrogant overconfidence had gotten the wind knocked out of it a few weeks ago in Kurdistan, the President thought. It reminded him of Desert Storm and his first weeks there, when he knew that if Sahdam Hussein had chosen to come at Saudi, there was nothing that he could have done to stop it. Back then the enemy, for reasons of his own, had chosen not to come. A few weeks ago, the enemy had come and had come in overwhelming numbers. ... twelve F-15's against four hundred enemy aircraft. What do you do when your missiles are expended and your guns are empty? Answer ... you either run or die.

"Ok, let's talk about what we can do about this. I want diplomatic, economic and military options on the table by the end of this meeting. Let's go in the order I just outlined. Alan, first you, and then Fred, outline your thoughts on diplomatic efforts that might be employed to stabilize this situation."

December 17, 2005, 16:30
Sea Worthy Marina, Along the Fox River
On Highway 31, North of Batavia, Illinois

Ahmed Haddad emigrated to America from Lebanon in the early 1990s. He came to attend school at Northwestern University in Chicago, majoring in medicine. His visa had indicated that he was a student of Dentistry. Indeed, he went on to earn a degree from Northwestern and opened a dental practice that served the burgeoning immigrant population in that city. Allah was kind, and his business flourished, making Ahmed a wealthy man and leading to his becoming a naturalized American citizen.

And, to all outside appearances, Ahmed Haddad became the model American citizen. He worked hard, owned a business, and was a leader in his local community. What none of his American friends knew about him was that his parents had been killed in an Israeli bombing raid just before he left his home country.

The Israeli government had called it an attack on a terrorist base, but there had been civilian casualties and Ahmed's parents were unfortunate enough to be in the wrong place at the wrong time. Shortly after their deaths, Ahmed joined the Hezbolla.

Soon thereafter, through the Hezbolla leaders, Allah had decided in his infinite wisdom that Ahmed would come to America. There, he was to bide his time until he was in a position to strike at those who had paid for the bombs which had taken the lives of his parents and so many others. Until then, his instructions were to simply work hard, stay out of trouble, fit into the society and wait patiently for instructions. Last month, those instructions had finally come.

Ahmed Haddad smiled as he signed the paperwork that completed the purchase of his forty-two- foot Sea King houseboat. As he was doing so, the salesman commented.

"Mr. Haddad, you and your family are really going to enjoy yourselves on this boat. It will make a wonderful Christmas present for the family."

"I am sure we will have many unforgettable experiences on her. She is indeed a beautiful boat." Ahmed said.

As he said this, he also thought, "Are all American so ignorant? A Christmas gift indeed. Can't this fool see that I am Arabic?" No matter, after the last few years and the general underlying distrust of anyone who had Arabic features, it would be best to not let any irritation whatsoever show.

The salesman continued.

"She is absolutely top of the line, sir. We've outfitted her exactly as you requested. The GPS gear and the radios you ordered have been installed and checked out. The radar equipment has also been installed and tested, just as you asked, and her name has been painted on the rear of the boat."

Ahmed smiled to himself as he signed the check to complete the transaction. What the salesman didn't know was that Ahmed was just getting started customizing his new boat. Once the houseboat left the dealer, it would be transported to a large warehouse that Ahmed and several of his close friends owned on the outskirts of Chicago near Schaumburg. There, further and more extensive modifications would be made to the boat, none of which had ever been anticipated by its designers. Just like the modifications that would be made to the other more than half a dozen cruisers and house boats that Ahmed was involved with having purchased.

"Thank you so much for your service to me." Ahmed said as he shook the salesman's hand and rose to leave. "A truck will arrive later this afternoon to transport the boat to my slip."

As he shook Haddad's hand, the salesman had one last question.

"You're very welcome, Mr. Haddad. You know, that's quite the name you have for her. We've never had a boat named the "Dhul Fiqar" before. Excuse me if I pronounce it wrong. What does it mean anyway?"

Ahmed had arrived at the name for this particular boat long ago.

"No matter. It is not uncommon to mispronounce it in English. It's pronounced D'-hul Fi'car and it's an old Arabic expression of faith. Again, it has been a pleasure doing business with you."

Seeing the salesman nod, Ahmed turned and left. What he hadn't told the salesman was the complete meaning of the name. In Arabic, "Dhul Fiqar" translates into "The Prophet's Sword."

CHAPTER 8

"See first with your mind, then with your eyes, and finally with your body"
- Yagyu Munenori

Christmas 2005

Throughout Christendom, the festive, joyful atmosphere was in full swing. All across Europe and North America, record purchase volumes had been set as shoppers visited the malls and their favorite stores and shops to purchase gifts for their relatives and friends. Christmas day dawned bright and cool across the better portion of North America and Europe, although in the northern sections a lingering snow cover from snowfall several days earlier made for a white Christmas nonetheless.

The President of the United States and the Prime Minister of Britain made a joint, Christmas Day appearance to troops in the Mid East who were still stationed there as a result of the hostilities that had occurred in early November. Both men made a morning appearance on the ground in Kuwait to their Army and forward deployed Air Force personnel. Then, later in the afternoon they made appearances on board two ships in the Persian Gulf. President Weisskopf visited the USS Shiloh (CG 68), an Aegis class guided missile cruiser (CG) of the US 7th Fleet. The British Prime Minister visited the HMS Argyll (F 231), a Duke class, Type 23 FFG and flagship of the United Kingdom's 6th Frigate Squadron.

Both ships were deployed, along with several others, in the Persian Gulf to supply radar warning, additional anti-air defenses and fire support to allied ground and air forces should it be required. No major capital ships such as American or British aircraft carriers or large amphibious assault ships were being allowed into the Gulf. With the GIR's proven willingness to launch massive air assaults and take tremendous casualties, the confines of the Persian Gulf made the prospect of these large ships and their embarked air wings and expeditionary ground forces too risky.

Security for these visits was extremely pronounced. No fewer than fifty interceptor aircraft were in the air at all times in conjunction with the Presidential and Prime Minister's visit. Although there had been some threats from specific terrorists groups which created a corresponding higher alert status at each of the bases. No untoward incidents occurred.

Meanwhile, a potential inter-Arab crisis and condition was developing along the border of Syria and the GIR, at the former Iraqi border. The Syrian Army and Air Force were conducting exercises south of Turkey along that border. Syria indicated through diplomatic channels that these exercises were needed for its armed forces and were also meant to send a strong message to the GIR to respect Syria's borders. Syria had participated in Desert Storm on the side of the allies and many western analysts viewed this as a much needed and strong signal to the GIR and Hasan Sayeed. They presumed it indicated that Sayeed's influence did not extend to all of Islam, including some of those states viewed as very fundamental and faithful to the Islamic faith.

The exercises themselves involved upwards of one hundred thousand personnel as three full divisions practiced armored assault, mechanized advance and air assault operations. Syria's logistical supply operations were also exercised in support of these operations. In addition, close air support and combat air patrol operations were held in support of the armored and mechanized exercises.

The GIR communicated many warnings to the Syrians regarding these exercises throughout the week between Christmas and the New Year. Hasan Sayeed personally warned King Asad to insure that no encroachment occurred by the one thousand tanks, twelve hundred armored personnel carriers and four hundred military aircraft involved in the exercises. Most of this equipment was newer and perceived as a significant threat. T-72 and T-80 tanks, BTR-80 and BMP-2 armored personnel carriers, Mig-29, Mig-27 and SU-22 aircraft and HIND-E attack helicopters were all employed.

Mediation by various members of the Arab League was attempted as the GIR beefed up its own forces in the areas along their northern border with Syria. This involved transferring some of the forces that had been deployed around Irbil and Karkuk after the defeat of the Kurds. As part of the GIR 1st Army group that had been pulled back deeper into the GIR began mobilizing for movement, negotiations and calls for caution were issued by the European Union, the Security Council of the United Nations and by the United States.

On December 30th, Jien Zenim announced that the People's Republic of China would lead a delegation of several of the Coalition of Asian States to the region during the first week of January in an attempt to negotiate and defuse the crisis. Jien's close confidant and ally, Li Peng, would head the delegation on behalf of the PRC and the CAS.

New Year 2006

As the people all around the globe rang in the New Year with celebration and festivities, the world also anxiously awaited the resolution of the crisis brewing between the GIR and Syria. While the delegations were preparing for the Chinese brokered summit, and while Syrian and GIR troops by the hundreds of thousands faced each other over what appeared to be a very tense frontier, other disturbing developments were coming to light on the international scene.

North Korea's annual military exercises were the largest in its history. Over three hundred thousand North Korean combat troops and their equipment were gathered along the DMZ conducting exercises meant to simulate the North's capability to invade the South. These exercises and the numbers of troops participating meant that the US forces and South Korean forces were placed on their highest state of alert. Recognizing that an outbreak of hostilities on the Korean peninsula would almost certainly end up involving them, Japan and Taiwan also placed their forces on their highest state of readiness.

All of this added substantially to the overall unease felt around the world, particularly in the west and in those nations of Asia that had not become a part of the CAS. Markets were down sharply, particularly the high tech and petroleum markets that depended on these regions for their production.

Growth of the Coalition of Asian States

While this was occurring, the CAS continued experiencing growth and prosperity. This prosperity was enjoyed by all of its member states, but particularly China, India and the GIR. Russia was also benefiting immensely from her relationship to the CAS through the exclusive exploitation of Siberia, and through its blossoming arms sales to members of the CAS and the GIR. By January 1st, 2006 the number of nations that had officially joined the CAS included:

China	Cambodia
India	Mongolia
The Greater Islamic Republic	Laos
Vietnam	Nepal
North Korea	Bangladesh

The GIR was itself growing and engulfing many Arab states and reaching ever further towards the Imam Hasan Sayeed's goal for a unified Islam. By January 1st, 2006, the GIR included all of the former states of:

Iran	Tajikistan
Afghanistan	Kyrgyzstan
Turkmenistan	Pakistan
Uzbekistan	Iraq

This amounted to a Islamic population of over two hundred and seventy million citizens who looked to the Imam Hasan Sayeed as their political, military and spiritual leader. The developing Islamic Republic, like its predecessor Iran, was a fundamental Islamic state where freedom of religion was not recognized and freedom of speech and the press was severely suppressed. The fact that most of these people were choosing to live in such conditions was mystifying to the west, but alluring to other Islamic nations that leaned towards fundamentalism.

January 5, 2006. 16:00
Foreign Ministry Press Room
Damascus, Syria

"All I can tell you is that we have reached a very delicate stage of the negotiations. The Syrian and GIR military and diplomatic representatives have requested to continue meeting and negotiating behind closed doors. Thus far we have made tremendous progress which the various news services have witnessed in open meetings of the last three days. Now, the time has come for more delicate issues to be discussed which will be pivotal in having the two armed forces back away from their high levels of alert and move away from their borders. I have every confidence that within the next few days we will be successful in those aims."

"I will take a question or two. ... Yes, the young lady on the second row."

As Li Ping motioned to the ABS reporter who had raised her hand, he briefly thought about the status of the meetings to date. Things were going just a Jien Zemin and Hasan Sayeed had planned. This very news conference had been a part of that elaborate planning, and here were all of the major news services of the world, particularly of the western world, hungry for the story. That hunger was represented in all of their eyes and their clamoring to ask their questions. The ABS reporter he had chosen first, Linda McPherson, was a well known journalist whose dislike and disdain for the current US President was well documented.

"Mr. Li, you indicated that great progress had been made thus far at this summit. Can you outline for us what that progress consists of?"

Excellent question, thought Li.

"I would be happy to, though you will understand if I do not delve deeply into specifics at the moment. Syria is clearly reacting to the presence of so many troops near its borders as a result of the unfortunate hostilities in the area last November. Although the GIR stated in plain language that it had no intent to violate any other nation's sovereignty or borders, nonetheless, one can understand Syria's prudence when there is someone with a big stick standing outside your unlocked and largely undefended back door. This is particularly true when the individual carrying the stick is confused for a bully who has been known to wield the stick at weaker neighbors in the past."

"This prudence has invoked a similar reaction from the GIR, whose new borders also need to be secure. When they see large forces on their doorstep, they naturally move a countering force nearby … just in case."

"The most important progress to date has been our ability, as respected mediators and friends of both nations, to point out that the old bully on the street is no longer there. That both neighbors need to cautiously realize that miscommunication, presumptions and historical fears have led to the current situation … in essence, that the two nations and forces really need not fear each other. To realize that the most likely situation that would lead to hostilities in this particular situation is the proximity of the forces and their high degree of alert … not a pre-determined desire or plan to violate the border of one or the other. I believe we have arrived at that understanding, which places us in a position to move forward."

"Next question. There, in the third row on the left, the young man with the brown blazer."

The leading Middle East correspondent for WNN stood up.

"Yes. Without going into any specifics of the "delicate" portions of the current negotiations, can you tell us what your preferred time table would be, and what general steps could lead towards a stand down by both forces?"

Li decided that this would be an opportune time to release some leading information. Information the "free press" would surely take up and spread abroad. Information that would be used to pressure politicians and military planning in a manner congruent with the long term plans of the CAS.

"Well, the short answer on the time table portion is ... as soon as possible, or as you Americans say ASAP."

Li paused for the laughter that rippled through the press room. When it had died down, he continued.

"But, more seriously, I expect we can arrive at a detailed plan for bringing the border regions into a normal mode within three to four days. Once we achieve that understanding, and develop non threatening logistical plans towards that end, we can then proceed to lower threat and alert levels, reduce combat air patrols and move forces back away from the border itself. I hope this gives you a general feel for where we hope to take these negotiations. One last question ... yes, you here on the back row."

JT Samson could not believe his good fortune. His Internet news site, SierraLines, had been in operation almost eight years. Up until last year, it had operated on a shoe-string budget, barely earning enough to keep his few employees paid, and have enough left over for living expenses. In fact, had it not been for his wife's medical practice, which was really what was putting bread on the table, SierraLines would have gone under long ago.

But all of that had changed during the last presidential elections. At a fund raising dinner in Denver, it had been JT's microphone which had caught now President Norm Weisskopf's unguarded and now famous remark about "wrestling" with the husband of his opponent, a former President himself, who had commented on Weisskopf's age.

That brief recording and its subsequent publication on his site, had brought him all of the notoriety and advertising and news contracts he needed to turn SierraLines into what was now considered the pre-eminent conservative news site on the internet. It had given him the time and the money to travel and chase after major news events all over the world ... and JT had proven quite good at it. The fact was, he had always been good at it, he just needed the opportunity.

So here he was, chasing his instincts. He remembered seeing the video of the event he had in mind, the muffled crack of a single gunshot and then the security forces riding Hasan Sayeed to the ground. He had seen it only once on the networks … and then no more. Yes, he had a question for Li Peng, an individual JT recognized as an "insider" in the PRC political machine … and that question wasn't related to the current Syrian "crisis" at all.

"Mr. Li, is it true that you and the PRC leadership are privy to substantial evidence that during Hasan Sayeed's recent pilgrimage to Irbil, before he successfully negotiated the permanent inclusion of the Kurds into the GIR, that he was the victim of an assassination attempt? Do you, or do you not have clear evidence that the assassination attempt was conducted by the United States CIA and was foiled by none other than Jabal Talabari, the former leader of the Kurd military and the current leader of the GIR military in this crisis?"

As the question had been formulated, the pleasant smile on Li Peng's face had slowly given way to a guarded incredulous look. The room had gone deathly silent, a silence that lingered for a few pregnant heartbeats as Li prepared to answer.

Then … bedlam as the room erupted into a deafening chorus of shouts, questions and attempts to get Li's attention. All hands were raised, most reporters were on their feet. Li looked around, wondering how the mood and the focus of the meeting could have turned so drastically. Finally, he raised his voice loud enough to be heard over the din.

"I cannot comment on any such report. The security forces of the GIR and their investigative agencies are in the best position to answer such allegations. Thank you all. This concludes the press conference."

January 10, 2006. 14:00 local
General People's Congress
Tripoli, Libya

Premier Mubarik al-Shamik stood and walked to the podium and the microphones. The People's Congress had voted and the voting had been unanimous, just as their leader, Muamar Abu al-Qahdafe had predicted it would be. Now, it was left to him, Premier Mubarik Shamik to make the historic announcement.

"My brothers, citizens of Libya, today we are becoming part of history … part of a divine destiny. It is with great pleasure and pride that I present you with the results of the historic vote. Let it be recorded that today, Monday,

January 10, 2006, the General People's Congress has voted unanimously to unite ourselves with the Greater Islamic Republic and to proclaim the Imam Hasan Sayeed as our Mahdi.".

"The recent revelations regarding the Great Satan's, America's, role in the attempted assassination of the Imam have hastened this decision. We, as the faithful in Islam, must unite to stave off these insidious influences and attacks by the west."

"In addition, I am further pleased to say that as I speak, concurrently in Algiers, Algeria; N'Djamena, Chad; Khartoum, Sudan; Sanaa, Yemen; and Muscat, Oman similar announcements are being made."

"It has become an irresistible force as sure as the pull of gravity and it is sweeping all of Islam. Our people and faith are being united into a greater whole and the Imam Sayeed is God's instrument in making it happen. I urge all Islamic people's to join with us. Our revolutionary leader, Muamar Qahdafe was the first to sign this document and he has authorized me, on his behalf, to endorse our unification in the holy name of Allah."

As a roar of approval erupted from the congress, Premier Shamik returned to his seat. He sat down and contemplated the coming struggles. With today's announcement, enough members of OPEC (four out of eleven) were now a part of the GIR to be able to hold up almost any measure they desired. The west would understand the meaning of this. In addition, almost one third of the Arab League (seven out of twenty-two) was now a part of the GIR. If things worked as the Imam had planned, soon a much higher percentage of both organizations would be a part of the GIR.

Shamik was relatively cynical. He had been involved as a politician and a leader under one of the most ruthless Muslim dictators in the world and had therefore seen his share of purges and elimination, faithful follower of Allah or not. Yet, despite this, he was himself a man of faith and it took his breath away to contemplate the coming together of so much of the Muslim world.

More of Islam joins the GIR.

Iran	Tajikistan	Yemen
Afghanistan	Kyrgyzstan	Chad
Turkmenistan	Pakistan	Algeria
Uzbekistan	Iraq	
Oman	Libya	

All of these were now one nation! Could it be true? Would it hold and allow Allah's will to be manifest through them? Shamik felt that much of that depended on the Arab states that were resisting. Saudi Arabia, Egypt, Morocco, Turkey, The United Arab Emirate, Syria, Jordan and Lebanon had still not made any definitive move. In fact, some of them were openly hostile. Those states and how they reacted to coming events would be the key for the realization of the long awaited dream, Shamik was sure of this.

January 12, 2006, 15:25 MST
Salt Lake City International Airport
Salt Lake City, UT

"Ladies and Gentlemen, Delta Airlines welcomes you to Salt Lake City where the local time is 3:25 PM Mountain Standard Time. ..."

The landing was smooth and Hector Ortiz was awakened from his nap only by the roar of the engines operating in reverse thrust and the customary arrival announcement by the flight attendant. Ortiz looked out the window and saw the mountains to the east of the airport in the valley of the Great Salt Lake. His flight had begun in Monterey and having already cleared customs at Dallas-Ft Worth, he anticipated a quick stop at the Avis counter and a short drive to his hotel. Tomorrow, he had a number of appointments to keep in both the Salt Lake and the further south, Utah valleys.

While Hector Ortiz enjoyed his frequent trips to the United States, the home of his customers and the source of his income, he had no love for the American people or their system of government. He hoped, and worked for the day, that the map of the American continent would be very different. Secretly, he had rejoiced when the bin Laden organization had successfully attacked America some years ago. He had not let it show then, or at any time since. He was far too shrewd for that ... but he had secretly hoped at the time that those events would have toppled the American eagle off of its perch. When it hadn't, he had filed and stored the experience, understanding that without supporting actions such attacks, even as large as those that occurred in September of 2001, had little hope of doing more than momentarily stunning a nation as large and capable as the United States.

Ortiz was engaged in the business of international trade. In its visible activities, his trucking company was one of several which facilitated the burgeoning flow of goods from Mexico to the United States as a result of the North American Free Trade Agreement. The freight manifests of his company showed finished goods of all kinds, including home appliances, hardware, automotive parts and industrial electrical devices which were assembled in the maquiladora towns for export to "El Norte." This above-board enterprise provided him with knowledge of traps and hazards to be avoided in conducting his shadowy and even more profitable operations - conveying contraband cargo across the long and porous border between the two nations.

Ortiz saw the United States as a land of contradictions. A nation whose economic vitality was born in its traditions of liberty and free enterprise, now America ironically provided profit opportunities to smugglers like himself through its prohibition policies, just as the ban of alcohol had given rise to the gangland entrepreneurs of the early 20th century. A land both powerful and yet so very vulnerable, dependent upon its webs of technology and energy. That vulnerability had been very aptly demonstrated back in 2001, and the Americans had attempted to respond, while maintaining their open society. The President at that time had created a new cabinet level position, the "Office of Homeland Security" and many procedures and plans had been established to protect the more obvious targets within America. Plans and procedures had been in place for the last five years, but they had never been really tested. Soon now, perhaps they would be.

Despite his personal financial success resulting from his businesses, Ortiz, who was borne in Ciudad Juarez, was a student of history. He held that the lands of the US southwest were stolen by conquest in the wars of 1836 through 1846 or coerced purchases, and that they rightfully belonged to the Hispanic people. For more than thirty years, Hispanic nationalists within the US had been promoting the idea of Aztlan, a new nation which would be comprised of these lands. Certainly, demographic trends that might be conducive to such a development were already developing in the United States. In addition, the events of the past year involving the Greater Islamic Republic had proven, to an even greater degree than the breakup of the old Soviet Union, that such monumental changes were possible, and perhaps even inevitable.

To that end, Ortiz had been contacted recently by an old friend, an aging head of state, who asked for his assistance in bringing about similar changes to North America. Hector would use his own resources to study the current state of the infrastructure networks - the pipelines, irrigation systems, power lines and their nodes throughout the wide open and sparsely populated spaces of the American West. Then, based on further instructions from his friend and compatriot, he would put together a number of "projects" related to that infrastructure.

Hector recalled a conversation with Miguel Santos, one of his drivers from the early days when his business was small, but who had risen to be a trusted senior member of Hector's inner circle. Miguel had told him of working in the United States in the mid to late 1990s as a range land fire fighter. Once, over two thousand fire fighters were brought in to fight a brushfire in an isolated area of the state of Utah where brushfires are usually left to burn out behind a fire line. Miguel mentioned that an electric power substation some fifteen miles from the town of Fontaine was the junction point for transmission of 10% of the electric power required for southern California. The men had been brought in to insure that this transmission point was not damaged and they had been ordered to keep the fire from it at all costs.

That had been a number of years ago, and the firefighters, who had camped in the Fontaine, Utah, City Park, had in fact saved the transmission station. Now, in conjunction with the assignment from his employer, Ortiz had already done substantial research on this facility, along with many others, and the Bonneville Power Administration Company that maintained and administered it. He had used on-line resources principally, but since his friend funded this effort so well, he had also purchased SPOT satellite images of the station. This had revealed much to him about the substation and how it had been designed and placed generally.

However, as he had learned from his underground business, there was no substitute for first hand, close up observations. Ortiz was committed to making those observations over the next two days between and after his legitimate business appointments. Those observations would also include an assessment of how America's "Office of Homeland Defense" may have instituted policies that would prevent or inhibit his plans out in these rural areas, over the next two days.

January 16, 2006. 19:38 local
White House Situation Room
Washington, D.C.

The mood was tense. They had been meeting here for over four hours, and for the President of the United States, four hours was huge block of time. Conditions warranted it.

"OK, then all of SIGINT data and all of our NRO images are indicating then that the GIR and Syria are moving away from one another, but NOT standing down?"

Jeremy Stone paused before answering the President's question.

"Mr. President, that is essentially correct, but I believe that the flavor John Bowers is putting on this is much closer to what the real picture could shape up to be. We have two very large forces, whom we believed, up until a few days ago, were potentially belligerent towards one another. But, the positions they are moving towards along the Turkish border, and the disposition of their logistics trains are causing our War College and think tankers a lot of concern. I guess I can best sum it up by quoting what one of junior analysts quipped the other day before the direction and disposition became clear. I believe his exact words were, "Boy, if those two forces were on the same side ... now that would be one hell of a pincer about to employ into Turkey". This quote opened a lot of eyes and led to our current concerns Mr. President."

As the President digested the magnitude of what General Stone had just said, John Bowers, the National Security Advisor to the President contemplated the ramifications.

Simply put, they had been suckered and led around like an animal with a ring in its nose. The Syrians had over one hundred thousand combat troops moving west along their border with Turkey. The Greater Islamic Republic had over one hundred and twenty thousand troops moving east along their border with Turkey. Between them, they had over twenty three hundred main battle tanks and almost thirty five hundred armored personnel carriers in those two army groups, not to mention some eight hundred and fifty combat aircraft. If they somehow could coordinate their activities and move, pincer-like into Turkey ... well Turkey's total military strength comprised about 390,000 of which 340,000 were draftees. Turkey had almost 4,000 tanks, but only 1,000 of them were modern. The entire Turkish Air Force consisted of only 350-400 modern aircraft. This could get very dangerous, very quickly.

"Jeremy, Tim and John ... how quickly can we, or the Turks have forces in place to counter a move should the Syrians and/or the GIR invade Turkey?"

The Chairman of the Joint Chiefs fielded the question.

"Mr. President, we have staffed down significantly in terms of ground troops. Incirlik has a strong air wing and we could start ferrying troops in there fairly quickly … but we are many weeks away from having a large enough blocking force in place with the equipment to effectively block such an operations. The Turks are certainly watching this, but their total Army is barely larger than these two forces combined. They could block maybe one of these thrusts if they started today and the GIR and Syrians held off for at least a couple of weeks … otherwise, there would be serious loss of ground before a defense could be set up."

It didn't take very long for the President to make up his mind.

"OK, let's get the 82nd Airborne headed for Turkey. I want the orders cut and the initial people in the air by tomorrow. Tim, work with General Stone and follow that up with planning to place a force in depth there to assist Turkey as soon as possible."

"Fred, we need to immediately set up a conference call between myself and the President of Turkey. We need to apprise him of our concerns and suspicions and coordinate a meeting ASAP between our military people and Turkey's. Make sure we include NATO in this as we are looking at a potential NATO response should there be any hostilities. Tim, please insure that all of our military people are hooked tight into this very quickly."

"Fred, also get me a conference call with Hasan Sayeed, we need to make our intentions and commitment with respect to Turkey very plain".

"Finally, Tim and Jeremy, please have the basic ingredients of your plan for the defense of Turkey prepared to discuss with the Turkish government and any NATO personnel during the meeting that Fred will be setting up."

"Let's meet back here tomorrow morning at seven o'clock AM to work out the details of the schedule for all of this. Ladies and gentlemen, with these developments in Turkey, the developments along the DMZ in Korea, the continued build up of Red China and the political and military encirclement of Egypt, we face a developing crisis as large as that preceding World War II. We must face it with the same level of gravity and commitment."

January 17, 2006 07:30 AM Local
Pope Air Force Base Flight Line
Ft. Bragg, North Carolina

On the flight line of Pope Air Force Base, the first group of C-17 Globe Master III Heavy Lift Transports were spooling up and preparing for departure. The C-17 military airlift aircraft could carry payloads up to 169,000 pounds anywhere in the world to land on small, unimproved airfields. In this case, they were going to be carrying their payload to the recently repaired airfield at Incirlik, Turkey. The payloads could include these troops and their equipment, up to and including HUMMV's, Bradley Fighting Vehicles, Sheridan Tanks and M1A1 main battle tanks. In this case, the initial flights would be heavily laden with troops and some of their supporting equipment, principally HUMMV's and some of their APC's.

This early winter morning, long lines of soldiers carrying their personal equipment and effects were strung out next to each aircraft as elements of the 1st Brigade of the 82nd boarded. Their collective breath could be seen rising in small clouds as the temperature outside was hovering at twenty-five degrees Fahrenheit. These troops would be arriving in Turkey in eighteen to twenty hours as the initial phase of the United States response to the looming threat of the Syrian and GIR forces massing on the Turkish border.

Away from the flight line, crews were in the final stages of preparing attack helicopters from the 1st Battalion of the 82nd Aviation Regiment for transport to Turkey. The 82nd Aviation Regiment was the only Army attack and support helicopter unit prepared to deploy anywhere in the world within eighteen hours notice. Right now, they were feverishly preparing their OH-58D and newly delivered RH-66 Comanche helicopters, and their UH-60 (from the 2nd Battalion) helicopters for transport and combat.

As the first C-17 Globemaster lifted into the air and crossed the outer barrier of the base, a small Fiat sedan parked just off the base in an area frequented by military enthusiasts, started its engine and drove away. Inside, Jabeel Suma, a twenty-three year old Arabic student at the local community college in Fayetteville, North Carolina, closed his notepad and set it on the seat next

to him. He drove into Fayetteville, in an area fairly far removed from his apartment, near downtown where he stopped and got out of his car. He walked into the city park.

Five minutes later, from a bench in the middle of the city park, Jabeel used his cell phone to send a coded message. The message gave the details of the

A C-17 departing for Turkey

deployment of the 82nd Airborne Division to his primary contact, an attaché to the Greater Islamic Republic ambassador to the United Nations in New York City, New York. From there, the information was transmitted to Tehran and Damascus and then routed to the Syrian and GIR headquarters along the Turkish border. That message, detailing the time and initial quantities of C-17's involved in the take off arrived within four hours, fully fifteen hours before those same C-17's were due to arrive in Incirlik.

Over the next two days, seven similar messages would be sent as more and more elements of the 82nd Airborne Division departed Ft. Bragg and flew to Turkey. But, it was that first message that had the most telling effect.

January 18, 2006 9:30 PM
Presidential Press Room
Tehran, Greater Islamic Republic

"… therefore, as of 8:00 PM tonight, a state of war exists between the Greater Islamic Republic and those Islamic Nations which have broken the faith, embracing the infidel western societies and whored our collective resources to them, who are destroying our faith, the very foundation of our culture and society. These nations include Turkey, Kazikstan, Egypt, Saudi Arabia, the United Arab Emirate and Morocco. The sword of Allah hangs over them and they shall be brought into line with the faith."

"Concurrent announcements are being made in the capitols of the following member nations as I speak."

Iran	Tajikistan	Yemen
Afghanistan	Kyrgyzstan	Chad
Turkmenistan	Pakistan	Algeria
Uzbekistan	Iraq	Syria
Oman	Libya	Jordan
Sudan	Ethiopia	

"Today's announcement includes four new names, who themselves are announcing a solidarity and unification with the Greater Islamic Republic, Syria, Sudan, Ethiopia and Jordan."

"To the western nations, particularly the United States, NATO and Israel, we say, do not interfere and you will not be

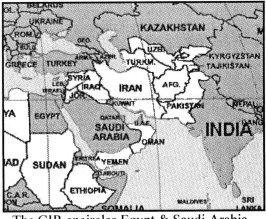

The GIR encircles Egypt & Saudi Arabia.

interfered with. We seek to live at peace with the rest of the world and will allow you your faith, your commerce and your culture, as faithless and as corrupt as much of it is."

"But, make no mistake, we will answer the beck and call of our brothers and sisters in Islamic states who are being disenfranchised, corrupted and destroyed by governments that have a solemn duty to uphold and defend their faith. The nations I have spoken of all fall into this category and it is to their governments that we solemnly proclaim … cease your whoring, cease your desecration, cease your persecutions of the faithful for we will humble you if you do not do so at once. To the faithful in those countries we say, rise up and join with us. Our armies, your faithful brethren will soon be amongst you and will bring you all into the fold."

"This concludes my remarks."

January 18, 2006 8:00 PM (That same time)
Approaching Turkish Air Space
Off the Coast of Turkey over the Mediterranean

Colonel Newhouse glanced at his Multi-Functional Display (MFD). He was in navigation mode while his co-pilot monitored various other aspects of the aircraft and their surroundings. The aircraft, carrying the command element of the 1st Brigade of the 82nd Airborne Division and its security detachment, was about fifty miles off the coast of Turkey and still some three hundred miles from Incirlik Air Base.

Colonel Newhouse's C-17 Globemaster was the lead element of a flight of fifteen Globemasters strung out over one hundred and fifty miles. There was approximately ten miles distance between each aircraft in this first flight of fifteen.

Additional flights of C17's and C-141's, carrying the entire 101st Airborne were strung out all the way back to North Carolina. All of the flights represented a veritable river of men and materiel flowing towards Turkey. They had last refueled over the middle of the Mediterranean and had plenty of fuel for their approach ad landing at Incirlik.

The Colonel was contemplating the rapid turn around he was scheduled to make at Incirlik when he was contacted by the AWACS aircraft, code named Skyman, controlling this final leg of the trip. Skyman also controlled the four F-22 Raptor fighter aircraft that were escorting the Colonel's flight of C-17's into this potentially hostile air space.

"Greyhound one, come to bearing 135 degrees angels 10. Many unidentified aircraft approaching from the southeast, range 225 miles. Bogies are going supersonic. Incirlik had declared an air emergency and is under heavy ballistic missile attack at the current moment"

Immediately Colonel Newhouse and his co-pilot snapped to. Warning lights were flashed to the loadmaster and the passengers in the cargo and carrying area. The "passengers" immediately took their seats and strapped themselves in. The co-pilot switched to the defensive system option on his MFD while Colonel Newhouse maneuvered the aircraft.

"Roger that Skyman, 135 degrees, angels 10."

Switching to his aircraft command frequency, Colonel Newhouse continued

"Dave, contact the entire flight and have all aircraft immediately wave off from Incirlik and divert to Izmir, then get me on the command frequency to Izmir … we may only have a few minutes."

As Colonel Newhouse's co-pilot complied, all four F-22 Raptor aircraft vectored off to the east-southeast to intercept. They went to "super cruise" mode to reach supersonic speed without engaging their afterburners, thus saving significant fuel.

The F-22 was the crown jewel of America's (and everyone else's) fighter aircraft industry. It was capable of carrying as much ordinance as the F-15, but further, faster, with vectored thrust, and it employed the latest stealth technology.

F-22's are vectored to intercept GIR aircraft.

There were simply no other aircraft in that could engage it head to head. But the GIR had no intention of engaging America's superior technology one on one.

Each of these carried six AMRAAM missiles and two Sidewinder missiles and would be in missile range in four and a half minutes.

January 18, 2006 8:05 PM
Over the Turkish Coast, outside Turkish airspace
West of Adana, Turkey

Once again, GIR Air Force General Mahdavi Ardakani, surveyed the aircraft that were accompanying him as he prepared to attack American interests.

On this day, an even larger attack into Turkey was occurring than what had occurred in November, a little over two-and-a-half months earlier. Many of the same elements of the GIR Air Force in this theater, which had been reinforced to make up for earlier losses, were being joined today by a large portion of the Syrian Air Force in this assault on Turkey. Incirlik airbase was again targeted and was even now being attacked by well over 200 ballistic missiles carrying conventional munitions preparatory to an attack by well over two hundred aircraft.

Every major airfield and military base in southern and eastern Turkey was going to be hit this evening and throughout tomorrow as the Syrian and GIR armies crossed the border in a two pronged drive into central Turkey along the Tigris River, and along the coast towards Adana. All in all, between the GIR and Syria (which itself had just announced its own unification with the GIR), over eight hundred military aircraft were involved here in what they were calling simply "Operation Turkey".

The General's flight of forty-eight fighter aircraft was specifically targeted on the incoming C-17 aircraft carrying the advance elements of the 101st Airborne Division. Thwarting a strengthened American presence in front of the invading armies was critical. Thirty-two of the aircraft were SU-27's, but the General's aircraft and another eleven were the more modern SU-35's which were flying in three flights of four in the middle rear of the overall formation. The General also had along four of the tandem seat SU-34's which were being used as electronics warfare aircraft. All of the General's

SU-34 in General Mahdavi's 2nd attack on Incirlik.

forty-eight aircraft were now within a few minutes of catching the large aircraft, which his radar was showing scattering "Like a small herd of sheep before a pack of wolves", thought the General.

He was surprised he had not picked up any escorting American fighters.

No matter, given the range and their fuel status, he calculated that his aircraft should be able to down four or five of the advanced, and very expensive cargo planes before he had to turn back.

Just as he was preparing to order the various flight leaders to vector towards their corresponding targets, missile launch warning tones began erupting in the cockpits of all of the aircraft in the lead flights.

Cries of "Missile launch" and orders for evasive maneuvering were heard over the command frequency as the various flights being targeted sought to evade the oncoming missiles which appeared to have materialized out of nowhere. Very quickly, two of the General's SU-34 EW aircraft had backtracked the oncoming missiles and re-calibrated their instrumentation.

"Hawk Leader, we have marginal identification on four enemy aircraft, bearing fifteen degrees, altitude approximately ten thousand meters, range forty-five kilometers.. We are identifying these as US F-22 Raptor aircraft. Very little electronic, radar or thermal signature."

"Raptors, finally a head to head combat confrontation with the latest American fighters. From the looks of it, they are everything they have been advertised as being", the General thought.

There had been no warning, just the missiles themselves in the air ... AMRAAMS from the looks of it. Well, he hoped that his SU-35 and SU-34 combination he had included in this attack would allow him to not only complete his mission, but to defeat several of the F-22's as well.

January 18, 2006 The next five minutes
Over the Turkish Coast, outside Turkish airspace
West of Adana, Turkey

Over the next few minutes, four more launches of AMRAAMS by the US aircraft were accomplished before the range closed and the GIR aircraft got close enough to make IR contact and lock with the Americans. In that time, of the twenty missiles launched, fourteen of them found their mark and brought down SU-27's.

In the ensuing fight, General Ardakani committed four of his SU-35's and twelve of his remaining SU-27's against the four F-22's. With his remaining eight SU-35's, eight SU-27's and all four SU-34's, the General accelerated through the melee and continued on towards the C-17 aircraft which were now low to the deck and making an evasive egress towards Izmir.

Three F-22's were destroyed, two by R-27T1 infrared homing missiles and one by gunfire as the combat closed to "knife fight" range. The fourth F-22 was able to escape. This had cost the GIR another four SU-27's and two of the four SU-35's that had engaged the Americans. The total GIR cost to break through to the C-17 cargo aircraft had been twelve SU-27's and two SU-35's versus three F-22's. Although the numbers were again very lopsided, the data recorded of the battle with the F-22's would later prove very advantageous to the GIR and her allies. It was also heralded as a great "victory" as the GIR not only accomplished its mission, but also overcame the vaunted, supposedly undefeatable American technology in doing so, despite horrendous losses that would not be so heralded.

General Ardakani's flight of aircraft caught up to and shot down three of the C-17's. Colonel Newhouse's aircraft was not one of these. In the action, pursued by no less than four SU-35's, including General Ardakani's aircraft, Colonel Newhouse's C-17 evaded six R-27 GIR missiles before being severely damaged by a R-27T1 infrared homing missile, which took out one of the C-17's engines, and another impact from a R-27R1 radar homing missile above and behind the cockpit. The explosion killed the co-pilot and severely injured the Colonel. Despite severe damage to aircraft hydraulics and attitude control, the Colonel was able to make an emergency landing along a dirt roadway fifteen miles inland in Turkey. His heroic actions in landing the aircraft under these circumstances saved the lives of the command staff for the 1st Brigade of the 82nd Airborne and would earn the Colonel a Medal of Honor.

January 18, 2006 4:35 PM
Situation Room, The White House
Washington, D.C.

As the reports came in, everyone in the room was silent for the time being.

Not two hours ago the world had been shocked at the announcements from the GIR. War had been declared by the GIR against America's staunchest Arab allies, including Turkey, Saudi Arabia and Egypt. Several new nations had announced their unification with the GIR, including Syria, which only confirmed the worst fears of those in the United States. The President had immediately called his closest advisors into session in the situation room to monitor events. This included the Secretary of Defense, the Secretary of State, the National Security Advisor, the Chairman of the Joint Chiefs of

Staff and the Vice President. Immediately following the announcement by Hasan Sayeed of the declaration of war, had come another attack on Incirlik, equally devastating to the one of a two months earlier and the ambush of the lead elements of the 82nd Airborne division off the Turkish coast. In that ambush, three F-22's and four C-17's were destroyed (this included the emergency landing of the C-17 by Colonel Newhouse where the decision had been made to destroy the aircraft on the ground after landing and evacuating it). This resulted in several hundred members of the 1st Briggade being killed along with the destruction of their equipment.

Now, from around the region, more bad news was pouring in. After the end of the latest report coming in from secure satellite link in Saudi Arabia, Jeremy Stone, the Chairman of the Joint Chiefs addressed those assembled.

"So, lets summarize what we know so far. We have a two-pronged invasion of Turkey, one consisting of a large GIR army group moving along the Tigris River with an apparent initial goal of Diyarbakir. The other is led by the Syrian Army Group, now also a GIR group, and is pointed along the coast with an apparent initial goal of Adana. Logistical support is already in place for both of these Army groups and men, equipment, materiel and supplies are flowing behind them. Our resources in the area are severely hampered by the destruction of Incirlik and the apparent airborne landing occurring in the vicinity now. Izmir is receiving the 82nd, but we are clearly on a defensive posture there and are working with the Turkish armed forces to establish a cohesive line of defense extending from Mersin on the Mediterranean coast to Samsun on the Black Sea."

"Latest reports from Saudi indicate that the large GIR army group in the vicinity of Kuwait is also on the move. We expect a crossing of the Kuwait border sometime early tomorrow. We are experiencing heavy ballistic missile attack throughout the region as we speak and expect heavy air attacks to follow. Our air forces in the Saudi Kingdom are strong, but we frankly do not have enough men and materiel to fight anything short of a holding action in the Kuwait area. Given their announced intention to punish Saudi Arabia and their declaration of war, we believe that the GIR will proceed directly through Kuwait into the oil rich areas along the Persian Gulf Coast of Saudi Arabia and The United Arab Emirate. Mr. President, our initial recommendation will be to fall back and inflict as much attrition on the advancing GIR forces as possible. Again, their logistic lines are in place and set up to feed this invasion force as well. This map of the region should make clear what the GIR's intentions with respect to Saudi Arabia are."

"Finally, Egypt is in no better condition. With Chad, Libya, the Sudan and Ethiopia all joining with the Greater Islamic Republic, Egypt's position is as encompassed about as Saudi Arabia's and just as grave. With the declaration of war on Egypt, the disposition of forces to the East and South of Egypt bring the strategic picture into clear focus. We expect that those Libyan and Sudanese forces that have been mobilizing are in a position to attack Egypt within the week. If for any reason the Chinese in Chad join in this, the prospects for Egypt are very grave."

President Weisskopf soberly took this in. There was little doubt that Hasan Sayeed was eliminating western influence, and particularly U.S influence in the Mid East. But in attacking Turkey, the stakes had been increased significantly. Would the NATO nations honor their commitments?

"Fred and Tim, can we expect full support and involvement by all of NATO in protecting Turkey?"

Tim Hattering considered this. Militarily it would require a full NATO mobilization to repel the GIR forces that were currently assaulting her, and those mobilizing to support that assault. But, whether or not all the NATO nations would do so was the question. Those nations were much more dependent on the oil from the Middle East than the United States.

"Mr. President, if all of NATO honors their treaty obligations, we can repel this invasion. My concern is the oil issue and the influence it is sure to have on many of these nations. Fred, what is your read? I believe we can really only count on Canada, Great Britain and Germany."

Fred Reissinger had been talking to his counterparts in Europe over the last week since it had become clear that a potential for an attack on Turkey existed. The results had not been good.

"Mr. President, I believe we can count 100% on Great Britain and Canada. I believe Germany is 90% there, but we are going to have to help them find alternate sources for petroleum. Outside of this, I believe the Danes, the Poles and the Czechoslovakians may also join, but they are very iffy."

The President again soberly considered this.

"Well, let's get the House and Senate leadership of both parties over here. In the mean time, Fred, get the Prime Ministers Great Britain and Canada and the Chancellor of Germany on the line in that order. It is my intention to request declaration of war between the United States and the GIR as of this evening. I want the vote in Congress done quickly so I can announce the same in a nation wide broadcast."

January 18, 2006 10:30 PM EST
The Oval Office, The White House
Washington, D.C.

"My fellow Americans. It with heavy heart but with crystal clear intent that I must speak with you tonight."

"Most of you have heard of the declaration of war announced by the leader of the Greater Islamic Republic earlier today on the nations of Egypt, Saudi Arabia, Turkey, Kuwait and the United Arab Emirate. These are some of America's most trusted and loyal allies in the Middle East."

"The GIR has followed up that announcement with immediate attacks on Turkish and Saudi Arabian installations and cities. With great regret I must announce that these attacks included attacks on American installations in Turkey, Saudi Arabia and Kuwait. There has been significant loss of life. Incirlik airbase has once again been devastated by an unprovoked and overwhelming attack. GIR airborne forces have landed there and there is fierce fighting going on there as I speak to you tonight."

"My fellow citizens, we have strict obligations to our allies in this region. Turkey is a member of the North Atlantic Treaty Organization (NATO) to which we also belong. In the fifth article of that treaty, we are bound to treat any attack on any member as an attack on ourselves. We intend to comply with and fulfill our treaty obligations."

"In addition, our own forces have been attacked in an unprovoked and malicious way. It is clear that Hasan Sayeed and his leadership intend to coerce all Islamic nations to join with them. Those that will not are to be forced into their totalitarian and dogmatic society, a society where the most basic and fundamental of rights to religion and free speech are not only denied, but brutally suppressed. The United States of America WILL NOT STAND BY and watch our friends and allies be coerced into such an environment in any way, and particularly not at force of arms."

"This is not like the attack we suffered a few years ago that we all remember. In that attack, a rogue network of terrorist organizations supported by one or two governments assaulted our homeland. In this instance, we have dedicated and large armies invading our allies. Where the "War on Terrorism" was against fiercely dedicated but small cells of terrorists and the relatively minor governments that supported them, this conflict will be waged against large nations and their armies. These nations have demonstrated their intent on conquering other nations and will, if not stopped, ultimately threaten our shores with similar attempts at conquest.

Therefore, I have consulted with the congressional leadership and a vote by your representatives has already taken place. As of 10:00 PM this evening, January 18, 2006, a State of War officially exists between the Greater Islamic Republic and the United States of America."

"I must urge calm upon all of our citizens. This war will not be easy or quick. The GIR and its allies represent a population greater than our own, and production capacity almost equal to our own. The GIR sit astride some of the largest oil deposits in the world. They are in the process of attempting to take, at force of arms, oil deposits for which we and our allies have contracted with friendly nations to make use of. The hardships that this situation has the potential of inflicting on our citizens are enormous."

"I am calling up 300,000 reservists today, to bolster our Army, Air and Naval forces so that we can contain and then kill this naked aggression.."

"As tyrants, warmongers and despots have discovered ... when aroused, the American people are capable of not only suffering through great hardship, but are capable of rising to levels of production and commitment unseen throughout the rest of the world. This is because we are free and because our freedom is founded upon absolutely firm moral principles."

"I urge all Americans to make tomorrow, January 19th a national day of prayer and reflection. Let us consider the roots of our liberty and what it is all based on. Then let us ask the hand of Providence to support us as we go forth once again as a people to defeat tyranny that would crush ourselves and our friends under its unrelenting heel."

"In conjunction with this announcement, I am informed that the Canadian and British parliaments are in session considering similar articles of war which will place them in this war at our side. We expect to hear of the positive results of these votes within the hour."

"Announcements regarding mobilization of all reserve units, of emergency actions regarding production and usage of strategic materiel and of war time policies will be forth coming beginning tomorrow."

"My fellow citizens, let us rise to the occasion and as a people answer these atrocities and these incursions with fierce resolution and with the American ingenuity and attitude that has been the hallmark of American history. God bless you all, Good night."

January 19, 2006 7:00 AM EST
News Stands
New York City, New York

"Extra, Extra! Read all about it ... War Declared in Mid East. US declares WAR on the Greater Islamic Republic! President calls for national day of prayer and reflection ... read all about it!"

The newsboys were shouting it all over the city, waving the latest, hot off the press editions of the New York Herald Post. Similar scenes were being played out across America's major cities and throughout the world..

Herald Post   **Special**

Edition

WAR DECLARED !!

Washington, D.C., January 19, 2006 - An indignant Hasan Sayeed announced to the world yesterday that his nation, or group of nations making up the Greater Islamic Republic, had declared war on the nations of Turkey, Saudi Arabia, Kuwait, the United Arab Emirate and Egypt. Coincident with this announcement was the announcement that Syria, Jordan, Sudan and Ethiopia would be joining the GIR.

Within eight hours, and after attacks on U.S. military installations and personnel in the area, the President of the United States, Norm Weisskopf, announced that the U.S. Congress had met and declared war on the Greater Islamic Republic. This announcement was followed shortly thereafter by similar announcements from Great Britain and Canada, which are now added to the earlier announcements by Egypt, Saudi Arabia, Turkey, Kuwait and the United Arab Emirate.

As of 5 AM, EST, GIR armies had already penetrated into Turkey on two fronts and were closing on the Kuwait border. Heavy fighting is reported in both areas, as well as at the U.S. Air Force base at Incirlik, Turkey, where GIR air borne forces landed in strength after a massive ballistic missile and air attack rendered the air base inoperable.

In addition, two GIR Army groups are massing near Egypt, one to the west of Egypt near the Libyan border and another to the south along the border with Sudan. Both of these groups are expected to invade Egypt within the next few days.

The news rocketed around the globe.

January 19 became known as another "Dark Thursday" as both the DOW and NASDAQ plummeted. By the end of the day, both indexes were down record amounts on the day, despite safe guards that halted trading and then restarted it several times. Total losses for the day amounted to in excess of 10%,. Trillions of dollars of wealth had evaporated against the fear of negative impact on energy and against an anticipated expanding war.

German politicians continued a very hot debate regarding their treaty obligations under NATO. By the end of the day, Germany voted in favor of honoring article five of their NATO treaty commitment, but it was a very narrow victory.

In Italy and Spain, the vote never occurred. Those against those nations entry into the war held enough power for the moment to thwart the vote coming to the floor of their respective legislative bodies.

In the far east, Japan, Korea, The Republic of China and other far eastern nations took "wait and see" attitude about the conflict, although Australia immediately voted to logistically support the United States and her allies in any way possible short of declaring war themselves.

The CAS released a harshly worded communiqué on behalf of Red China and India, denouncing what it called "the hasty decision" by NATO countries to declare war on a member state of the CAS. That same communiqué praised other NATO countries for showing restraint in what it viewed as a regional issue centered around religious persecution and intolerance by those states upon whom the GIR had declared war. Both the Russian Federation and Red China offered to mediate and called for an immediate meeting of the UN Security Council to work out a meeting of the parties at the negotiating table.

January 22, 2006 9:30 PM Local
CP, 39th Security Forces Squadron
Incirlik Air Force Base, Turkey

Captain Hanson surveyed what he had left as a fighting force. He was down to about one third strength for his security forces, but had augmented that with various grades of enlisted and officer rank personnel left over from the 39th Support, Transportation, Logistics and Medical groups and a few from the Air Wing Group. A few members of the 628th Air Mobility Support Squadron and US Army Corps of Engineers were also with him.

He had been fighting a rear guard action since the major evacuation fo the base after the devastating ballistic missile and air attacks of the 18th. His original job had been to insure that all critical equipment and materiel left behind in the evacuation was destroyed and that any stragglers were gathered up for the final evacuation which was supposed to have occurred late yesterday afternoon. But that was before the GIR had landed in battalion strength in airdrops to the south and east of the base the afternoon of the 20th, soon after the major evacuation was completed. They had been lucky that the transport, support and escort aircraft had made it out, and that the ground convoy had escaped.

The GIR had been reinforced and now controlled roughly two thirds of the base. He had destroyed a lot of classified materiel and equipment, but useful equipment had still fallen into the hands of their attackers.

Captain Hanson did not expect any further re-supply. The first evening, the U.S. Air Force had returned in strength and supported him, accomplishing close air support and dropping ammunition, medical supplies and other materiel to the beleaguered defenders. But last night the sky belonged to the GIR, and it was looking like they had established air superiority in the region. His radio communications were being effectively jammed, and the last message had given him the initiative to continue the fight for as long as practicable, or retreat at his discretion. Reports indicated that an entire GIR

Army group, numbering in excess of one hundred and twenty thousand men, had broken through Turkish defenses near Osmaniye, fifty miles to the east. This meant that advance elements would be arriving very soon, possible this evening, and certainly by tomorrow morning.

Two of Captain Hansom's Avenger-2's.

Hanson had decided to withdraw this evening. He had six deuce-and-a-half trucks for transportation, his last three Avenger-2 Missile systems (mounted on HUMMV chassis) for anti-air coverage, his last three V-150 APC's, six

Peacekeeper APC's and six HUMMV's (two of which were outfitted with TOW missiles). Altogether, he had two hundred personnel to transport, with twenty-seven of these being severely wounded and unable to assist in any defense.

In order to accomplish the withdrawal, the Captain had requested a volunteer force of twenty security personnel, which he would lead as a diversion. He planned to use one Avenger, one V-150 and one of the Peacekeepers with this force to punch through the GIR lines and attack a logistics depot on the opposite side of the base near the northern perimeter. Two of his scouts had discovered this logistics point last evening as they were reconnoitering behind enemy lines. The depot appeared to be fairly well defended.

This "diversion" would be Captain Hanson's answer to the GIR brokered cease-fire for him to consider terms for surrender. A part of the diversion included an escape route north into the hills for any who could manage it.

An hour ago there was still an open corridor back through Adana to a small security detachment, also under his command, with the 39th Wing A 39 Supply Squadron in Yumurtalik, thirty kilometers away. Once his XO joined up with them, they would retreat to the east and join U.S. or Turkish forces north of Mersin along the defenses being created there.

January 22, 2006 10:23 PM Local
GIR Logistics Point
Incirlik Air Force Base, Turkey

The firefight was over. It had been short and incredibly intense. Colonel Ahmass could hardly believe the audacity of it. Twenty minutes ago when he had been informed that the Americans had made a breakthrough and were proceeding towards his position with several APC and an unknown number of personnel, the Colonel had prepared accordingly.

Colonel Ahmass' ZSU-23 air defense.

Colonel Ahmass' unit was a lead element of the large GIR/Syrian Army that was invading Turkey along the Mediterranean coast. The Colonel had arrived yesterday and was the one who set up the logistics depot and its defenses.

Those defenses consisted of a detachment of one hundred and fifty soldiers with two ZSU-23-4 AAW vehicles, four BMP-2 tracked APC's, four BTR-152 wheeled APC's and several 7.62 MM PK machine guns.

As the Americans approached, the Colonel called in air support in the form of two Mi-28N Havoc attack helicopters from locations just behind the advancing GIR army group. When they arrived, the lead unit immediately attacked one of the American APC's, the Peacekeeper, with an Ataka anti-tank missile and completely destroyed it.

To the Colonel's shock, the small U.S. attacking force included a very capable AAW platform, the U.S. Avenger, which immediately engaged both Havoc helicopters and shot both out of the air with Stinger missiles.

The American V-150 laid down a deadly fire with its 20 mm cannon, immediately engaging one BMP-2 and destroying it. As the other GIR BMP-2's came into play, American soldiers on foot employed their man-portable M47 Dragon anti-tank missiles and destroyed two of them.

Finally, the last BMP-2 scored a direct hit on the rear of the V-150 with an AT-4 Spigot missile, and then finished the vehicle off with its 30 mm cannon using twenty to thirty AP-T (armor piercing – tracer) rounds. That BMP-2 then quickly dispatched the American Avenger unit as it tried to escape to the north. This was accomplished with a second AT-4 Spigot missile which quickly traveled the 1500 meters that separated the two vehicles, completely destroying the lightly armed Avenger in a spectacular explosion as its remaining Stinger missiles cooked off in the conflagration. After this, a brief firefight ensued which ended up driving off the last four or five American soldiers who retreated to the north.

The GIR logistics depot had been defended, but it had cost Colonel Ahmass the two Mi-28N attack helicopters, three of his BMP-2's, one of his BTR-152's and about forty personnel. For this carnage, he could count two American APC's, the Avenger and what appeared to be the bodies of about fifteen American soldiers.

Captain Hanson was among the five survivors who escaped into the hills to the north where he ultimately joined up with Turkish partisans in what would prove to be a very long and bitter fight against the GIR forces which were sweeping across Turkey.

January 22, 2006 10:35 PM Local
Outside Adana International Airport
Adana, Turkey

As the firefight at the logistics depot ended, the retreating American column sped along the four-lane highway on the outskirts of Adana near the International Airport. The Americans were unaware that just two hours earlier a number of transports had landed GIR special forces at the airport. These forces, supported by attack helicopters, took control of the airport in a brief firefight with elements of the local Turkish defense forces. Thereafter, twenty-five transport aircraft landed a full armored reconnaissance company at the airport as an advance contingent of the armored division that was currently en route along the coast.

As the retreating Americans passed the airport entrance, four Type-63 light tanks had just taken up position there along with four BMP-2's and four BTR-80 APC's. Both sides were completely surprised to encounter one another. The ensuing fight was brief and deadly as the Americans attempted to force their way past.

In the fight, the Americans lost four of their six deuce-and-a-half trucks and most of the personnel riding in them. In addition, they lost both V-150 APC's, four of their six Peacekeeper APC's and three HUMMV's. Most of these vehicles were destroyed by cannon fire from the Typre-63 tanks and anti-tank munitions from the BMP-2 and BTR-80 APC's. Both Avenger AAW units were able to speed past the airport entrance in the fighting and confusion.

Of the nearly two hundred personnel retreating in the American convoy, only sixty five personnel made it past the airport and ultimately joined up with the smaller security detachment for the A 39 Supply Squadron that was anxiously waiting for them in Yumurtalik. One hundred and three Americans were killed, most in the loaded and unprotected deuce-and-a-half trucks, and another forty-three were wounded and captured along with twenty other personnel who had not been injured in the fighting. Of these sixty-three captured personnel, the GIR spared fifteen officers and senior enlisted men for questioning while mercilessly executing the rest where they stood or lay to the horror of the fifteen survivors.

In the fight, the American V-150's and the TOW equipped HUMMV's exacted a heavy toll from the GIR forces. Two of the Type-63 tanks, three of the BMP-2's and three of the BTR-80's were destroyed. Most of the soldiers in the GIR APC's were killed as the units had just arrived and the troops had not unloaded from them when the fighting began. In all, eighty-three GIR personnel were killed and fifteen wounded. An armed scout helicopter that was sent to attack the fleeing Americans was shot down by one of the escorting Avenger AAW vehicles, and thereafter the American retreat was not interfered with.

With this battle, the fall of the U.S. airbase at Incirlik, Turkey was complete and the GIR had established a strong foothold along the coast of Turkey.

January 24, 2006 16:35 CST
Lazy H Ranch
Outside Montague, Texas

Jess took off his over boots as he stepped onto the back porch.

"Boy, that north wind is howling," he thought as he took off his insulated coveralls and placed them on a peg.

"At least those are still easily found, Made in America," he thought as he went through the back door. Jess took great satisfaction in only buying "Made in America" goods for his own personal clothing and implements. The rest of the family had never been quite as serious about it, though they did make the effort, for which Jess was grateful. But, Jess had been to many of those "foreign" places and saw how the people lived, how their governments treated them. He did not want that for America and figured, in his own small way, he could help avoid it by "buying American"..

"Hey sweetheart," he called, "what's to eat?"

Cindy not only heard Jess come in, what with that north wind blowing, she also "felt" him come in by the blast of cold air that accompanied his entry.

"We've got some Chili Beans and cornbread honey, made just the way you like it and piping hot."

"How cold is it out there anyway. Wind's been blowing all day and I know I've seen some flakes of snow blowing past the windows here."

Actually, the snow was coming down harder now and Jess thought they were in for at least several inches by morning. Temperature had been dropping since yesterday when that norther came through and it had fallen through the twenties today and was sitting at eighteen degrees right now. Despite impressions to the contrary, here in north central Texas, especially up here near the Red River, snow, ice and cold were a typical part of winter, even if the winter was relatively short.

But Jess knew that this small talk about weather was just that. He knew Cindy was concerned about the declaration of war and the notice he had already received. This was not going to be any short duration TDY type of thing. He was being called to active duty for the duration ... and his intuition told him that it could be a long time.

He couldn't tell Cindy where he was going. The verbal orders, delivered over secure lines, posting him to Israel to deliver a secretly purchased squadron of Comanches and to train the Israeli military in their use was all very much top secret ... and it was indicative of the view of leadership just where this fighting was going to ultimately lead. But, he knew he could be completely open with her about the gravity of the situation and its likely duration, and he knew he would have to do that tonight.

"Boy that smells good honey! Can't wait to get a bowl full into me. Even with the welder going in the barn, it was awful cold out there this afternoon."

After the prayer, and after Jess got started, Cindy broached the topic.

"... so, I got your things together and they are packed and ready. Saturday morning is going to come quick. Do you think this will blow over as quick as that last set-to did?"

Jess could only be as honest as his oaths and sworn duty would allow ... but he owed it to this, his best friend and closest confidant in the world.

"Honey, I am afraid this is "the big one". The GIR has a lot of resources and is buying up a lot of modern equipment. From everything I have read, they have developed a phenomenal training program and they are committed. Who would have thought they could pull off those attacks on Incirlik, and now the invasions of Turkey, Kuwait and Saudi."

"It's going to be a tough, long fight in pushing them back ... and that's if some of these other tinhorns that have an axe to grind with us don't jump in somewhere else around the world. No ... I believe you'll see me now and again on leave when that can be arranged, but I'm afraid we're in this for the long haul. Probably end up being a lot of austere war-time provisions, maybe a lot like our parents experienced in World War II."

Cindy had feared as much, but she was grateful that Jess always served it up to her straight. They discussed preparations and they discussed Billy and his likely role ... particularly his timing as he finished his training and went on to the various schools. Then as they finished cleaning up the dishes, Cindy took Jess's hand and said.

"Babe, given what we are facing, we're just going to have to work real hard to get as prepared as we can. We'll also have to work extra hard at giving you the kind of send off my man deserves and one you can keep close to your heart through whatever you may be called to face."

January 26, 2006, 22:00
Marine Recruit Training Depot
San Diego, California

Company B of the 1st Battalion at the San Diego Recruit Training Depot was ready to enter its live fire training. For the next two weeks, they would become versed in the operation and firing of the standard issue M-16A2 assault rifle.

"OK girls, listen up! Over the next two weeks you are going to be dedicated to extensive weapons training and all-out live-fire training with your M-16 rifles. You'll fire on a variety of targets, still, moving and pop-up and you will fire on both normal straight ranges and combat ranges."

"All of you WILL qualify as a "marksman" before this two week period is complete."

'Each of you has already spent many hours taking this rifle apart, cleaning it thoroughly, and putting it back together, familiarizing yourselves with every piece of it. But now, before we actually let you children fire one of these fine weapons, you will practice aiming and dry-firing your rifle until you can't stand it anymore. By the time you fire that first actual shot, you'll have dry-fired your rifle in every conceivable position many hundreds of times."

"In addition to rifle training, during these two weeks, you'll receive basic training on grenades and other types of weapons."

"I expect each of you to pay close attention. As has already been drilled into you, this is your most basic implement as a Marine. We are teaching you to kill and destroy our nation's enemies, and as recent events are proving, we have plenty of them that would like nothing better than to bring the eagle down. So, of necessity, we are training you to be very good at it. While all of your training is paramount to your survival, coming to know and respect your weapon in intimate detail will make the difference in your life or death. The weapon must become an extension of you, and we'll make it just that."

"Remember this, every Marine, from the lowliest private to a fighter jock, to medics and doctors is an infantryman first and foremost. You take and hold ground with people… plain and simple. It's the way it has always been, and it is no different now, regardless of how much high tech they create and introduce. Don't ever forget it Marines, and at some point, that knowledge and your understanding of it will be your friend and save you butt."

Billy on the firing range.

Both Billy Simmons and Leon Campbell listened intently. They were both natural leaders and other recruits were already following their lead. Jess had a lot of experience with rifles, having shot many thousands of rounds through his Mini-14 on the ranch back home. He had also been well versed in its operation, maintenance and assembly by his Dad. Leo had learned quickly and had benefited from his close friendship with Billy. To anyone noticing, it was clear that Leon had every intention of taking his DI's words to heart and applying them with extreme prejudice … the rifle was becoming a part of him, and he a part of it. It was the path he had chosen, recon … sniper.

They had both come into boot camp in relatively good shape, but the last six weeks had honed each of them down to the epitome of lean, mean fighting machines. Drill evaluations, 3- 4- and 5-mile hikes with fully loaded packs, the Confidence Course, Combat Water Survival and Martial Arts training had all contributed.

Both were also excelling in their academic classes. Core values, first

Leon during training exercises.

aide, Marine customs, survival and many other topics were adding to the well rounded nature of the training all of the recruits were receiving, where excellence was demanded. Already, in their own private discussions, the

DI's from various platoons and even the other companies were talking about the "magnificent duo" that existed in Billy and Leon.

In private, more than a few bets were being placed on how these two, in the same platoon, would impact the overall platoon competition that was a part of the tradition. Of course, none of this was ever alluded to in front of any of the recruits. There, the equality of the discipline and "strong encouragement" to excellence, to achievement and to learning and maintaining the high standard of the Marine Corps reigned supreme. It could be no other way.

February 2, 2006, 06:00 AM
Situation Room, The White House
Daily War Briefing
Washington, D.C.

Jeremy Stone had taken on the daily task of briefing the President and his key cabinet members. His briefings were attended by the other Joint Chiefs of Staff and key Congressional leaders whenever possible.

"Let's begin. Mr. President, we will start with the current, on-the-ground situation in Turkey, followed by the same in Saudi Arabia. We will then briefly touch on developments in and around Egypt."

"In Turkey, we have established a defensive line from Samsun to the north, down to Kayseri in the center and it is holding. The GIR Army Group out of the former Iran has only probed our defenses there, and it's a good thing since the defense is not yet established in depth. But that is improving as those lines are augmented by elements of the 82nd Airborne, just arriving British forces and of course, in the main by the Turkish army. We expect the first heavy armor out of Germany and infantry out of Canada to arrive in the next seven to ten days, but this will then take several days to get moved to the front lines. In the mean time, the GIR is consolidating its holdings and is being helped by the more hard line Islamic citizens who are welcoming them as heroes, especially in the cities of Erzurum and Malatya.. Nonetheless there is significant partisan and guerilla activity behind their lines, particularly in the mountains. We are in contact with the remnants of part of the Incirlik security forces, in fact the commanding officer of those security forces has linked up with some Turkish partisans there."

"To the south in Turkey the news is not as good. Our original plan to try and establish an anchor on the coast at Mersin has failed. We were unable to get enough forces in place after the rapid fall of Incirlik and Adana. A full battalion of the 82nd Airborne was flown in and worked well with the local

Turkish forces, but it was a case of too little too late. Heavy losses were inflicted on the advancing Syrian Army Group, but that close to the GIR, with their massive numbers of aircraft, air superiority was not achieved and we were left with no choice but to withdraw. It was orderly, but we suffered moderate losses amongst elements of the 1st Brigade of the 82nd Airborne that were engaged there. We also suffered significant attrition in the air wing of the U.S.S. Eisenhower as it flew support operations along with our aircraft out of Izmir."

"We are now working at establishing an interim defense point at Ulukisia in the canyons there exiting the Taurus Mountains, but it is likely that our firm defense will have to be set up where the central plain there narrows between Lake Golu and Konya."

"Speaking of the GIR air forces, satellite imagery indicates that they are close to having the airbase at Incirlik repaired and operational. We expect a fairly massive influx of aircraft there as they seek to establish forward air bases to support their ongoing offensive in Turkey. We are waiting for those aircraft and intend to spring a surprise of our own. Admiral Crowler and General Livingston will hold a briefing on this operation at 4 PM today."

"Finally, in Saudi Arabia. Our Marine Expeditionary Unit has made an orderly retreat with elements of the Kuwait army in front of the advancing GIR 1st Army Group. We estimate that nearly two hundred thousand effective combat troops with twelve hundred tanks and the same number of APC's are moving across the Kuwait border as we speak. We intend to fight a holding action from the Saudi border at Al Khafji on the Persian Gulf to KK Military City. If the GIR forces are serious about advancing, we will conduct a fighting withdrawal from those points back to firmer defenses we are now establishing stretching from Abu Hadriyah to Az Zilfi to Medina."

"Mr. President, knowing the Kingdom as you do, I believe now is the time for the Summit you proposed so that the King can prepare the people for this invasion. As in Turkey, there are factions within Saudi Arabia that will welcome Hasan Sayeed and proclaim him their Imam."

The President asked a few pertinent questions regarding the disposition of forces and defensive plans as well as offensive capabilities and how long it would take to gather enough forces to blunt the enemies offenses and then mount a credible offense of their own. Having had experience in Desert Storm, he knew it would be a long wait. The "nightmare scenario" from Desert Storm, an invasion of Saudi Arabia before their defenses were prepared, was playing out in front of him. Not only that, another serious invasion was already in process in Turkey and a third appeared to be imminent in Egypt.

"Fred, are we ready for the summit? We are talking about Egypt, Turkey, Saudi, Great Britain, Canada and Germany. I expect to talk frankly about these events and regarding what I view as the very real possibility of conflict in Asia while this is occurring."

Fred Reissinger was on top of this. He had made all of the contacts and he had done it discreetly. The plans were already in place for a discreet, really a secretive, meeting early next week.

"Mr. President, the meetings are set up for next week, February 6th and 7th in Iceland. You will be flying out on Air Force One Sunday morning the 5th, and returning to Andrews on the morning of the 8th."

Norm Weisskopf nodded his approval.

"Good, it can't be soon enough. I have a feeling we are looking at a long hard road in front of us gentlemen … of major world war proportions. We must discreetly prepare and plan accordingly. After lunch, we will be meeting with Curt to put FEMA preparations into motion for our Federal War Time footing, which we then hope to roll out to each of the states. General Stone, please continue, what is the situation in Egypt?"

February 2, 2006, 11:10 local
Lot 8, Building 14, Woodfield Industrial Park
Schaumburg, Illinois

The industrial park consisted of over one hundred buildings, each with either a private, or semi-private entry drive that could accommodate semi tractor-trailers off of Woodfield Road, near its intersection with National Parkway in Schaumburg. Each industrial building had elevated docks for shipping and receiving and many of them had entry bays, which could accommodate equipment or vehicles up to thirty feet wide and twenty-five feet tall.

Ahmed Haddad entered the small door that was inset into the large bay door. His presence had been noted and accepted by the security staff that manned the security console twenty-four hours a day. That staff was small, but well trained. Like Ahmed, most had been in America for many years, some had been born here. They had all worked in the security profession for most of their careers, some having included local law enforcement work.

Ahmed's presence had been noted when his vehicle turned into the lot, his license had been matched via digital video recording, character recognition and comparison. Once Ahmed exited his vehicle and began approaching the building, he was watched closely by the duty officer. Finally, before entering the building, a personal identification card, which was digitally encoded with Ahmed's entry code, was read at the door. The bay door and the inset door within it, were both made of solid steel, three inches thick.

But, to outward appearances, other than the reader on the inset door, the entire facility looked like the other bland warehouse and industrial buildings in the complex. The only identification was a small sign on the front door that said, "Haddad and Jones Enterprises". Any checking into the name would show that the firm specialized in the repair and rework of medical equipment, specializing in dental equipment. Nonetheless, with the enhanced security in America since September of 2001, one could never be too careful.

The bay that Ahmed entered was a self-contained portion of the building. It had the single outside entry and a single, similarly secure inside entry to the rest of the facility. Within the thirty foot wide, by sixty foot long, by twenty-five foot high bay, there were numerous work, equipment, machinery and storage facilities ... and sitting in the middle of the bay was the, "Dhul Fiqar", the "The Prophet's Sword".

As he looked over the lines of this forty-two foot houseboat, he noted the visible progress on the modifications. The strengthened and protected attachment points along the railings, the mountings along the aft quarter deck and the numerous antennae and electronic fairings along the top of the wheel house, which was really looking more and more like the control room it would be. As he noticed this, he called out.

"My brothers, how is our work progressing today?"

Almost immediately, a dark headed and bearded man of approximately thirty years of age stuck his head out of the wheel house and responded.

"Ahmed, GREAT to see you my friend. Progress is proceeding ahead of schedule. All of the electronics are in, all of the attachment points are completed ... we have only to test the circuitry and then apply a thorough quality test for reliability and functioning under shock conditions. I anticipate we will be ready to load the boat for transportation to our berth within a four to five days if you so desire."

Ahmed considered this response. It was really quite good news, but they weren't scheduled to be complete until the 10th of March, with actual travel occurring almost anytime thereafter. But, having a few extra weeks would be good as long as security held. The other boats were not ahead of schedule and Ahmed wanted to make sure that the timing of all of the missions was as perfectly synchronized as possible.

"Outstanding Jahmil. I was just at the other Schaumburg location off of Golf Road and Esau is on schedule. Two of our other locations, Aurora and Joliet are actually two days behind, so early completion here will allow us to shift the proven expertise of your group to assist in those locations. Loading and transportation will stay on the current schedule. We'll just use the extra time to insure everyone is ready. Now, show me how the special equipment is going to attach to the hardened and protected points you've created."

February 3, 2006, 13:23 local
Gavank, 800 KM Northwest of Krasnoyarck
Siberia, The Russian Federation

The insulation sleeve had been fitted around the last joint and the welders had finished their task. This was the last section of the pipeline that would now carry the fruits of their labors to India and to the Russian Federation. From his control vehicle, Dr. Buhpendra Gavanker observed the final construction sequences with satisfaction.

These last few miles had been accomplished in conditions that Dr. Gavanker would have thought impossible. Winds howling at over 80 km/hour, actual temperature at minus forty centigrade, snow coming down horizontally and drifting well over two meters. No, Dr. Gavanker had been briefed, he had seen films, he had heard the stories, but to experience it was something else all together. Thank goodness the Russians had sent in their team of specialists … men who were versed in applying Gavanker's instructions in these harsh conditions. The results,? well, very soon now, perhaps as early as tomorrow, full time, year round crude oil production would commence.

The railhead would still be used for transportation of materiel, supplies and personnel. The year round airfield the General had built was also capable of transferring in personnel and supplies … but the crude, in the quantities that these fields would produce … that required the large pipelines like the one that had just been completed. By spring, another one just like it would be in place. Given the escalating war in the Middle East, it was going to be very timely. His nation would be able to significantly reduce its dependence on Middle East oil … even if the GIR was officially part of the CAS.

"Always best to be self sufficient in critical resources," thought the Doctor.

As he contemplated this, his assistant, who was monitoring outside communications from the front portion of the cabin, turned in his seat and addressed him.

"Dr., I have a relayed call to you from General Nosik. Would you like to take it back there at your seat sir?"

The Doctor nodded his assent, and when the red light on his handset blinked, he picked up the phone and spoke.

"Andrei, how are you? Very good to hear from you. I imagine you are interested in the progress on the pipeline?"

Listening for a brief moment to the General's reply, the Doctor continued.

"Yes, we have just finished with the final assembly and fabrication. We are finalizing the test of the welds and the integrity of this last section and expect oil to be flowing as soon as tomorrow morning, perhaps by tomorrow evening. . How are the mining operations progressing? The Chinese Cobaltite and our low-sulfur coking coal mine."

The Doctor's eyes lit up at the short response.

"Now, now, Andrei. You know I am not intending to breach your security. For mercy's sake, those mines and their locations have been written up in several trade publications with readership on three continents. And your own nation announced to the world your promotion to General and your responsibilities over the security for those very mines. Or do you fear your own internal security my friend?"

Buhpendra laughed at the reply.

"Fine, I will be more careful on these "un-secure" lines. Are we still on for that schedule review day after tomorrow? I have been requested to make a personal report back in New Delhi at the end of the month and we will need to work that into our mutual operational plans."

After another short pause, Gavanker finished the conversation.

"Great, we will see you then. Goodbye."

February 4, 2006, 17:28 Local Time
COSTIND Headquarters
Beijing, PRC

General Hunbaio was excited about this meeting. It was a preliminary culmination of many years of work. COSTIND's weapons and systems development efforts (over which the General presided) were proving successful beyond their most aggressive projections. To see many years of work come together in success was always rewarding and gratifying, particularly when it had such a strong impact on his nation's strategic goals.

As anticipated, several of these new systems were coming on line now, ahead of schedule, and were already well into their trial periods. New aircraft, new missiles systems, new Ship classes of all types, new weapons systems ... all coming together at the appointed time.

The new conversion ships were astounding in their ease of manufacture and their capabilities. Four of the Sea Control carriers, eight of the tactical assault ships and six of the Amphibious Assault ships were already at sea. The latter two classes of vessel were still unknown to the west, because until used for their appointed purposes, they could pass for the container ships from which they had been converted. This was exactly the intent, as several more of each would be ready before commencement of "Breath of Fire".

The Project 071, Yunana II class landing craft that would be so critical for the full implementation of "Breath of Fire" were now being produced by the score. The new LRASD Super Cavitating weapons and the ship borne strategic missile derivatives had been fully tested and excelled in all of their operating parameters. Production efforts for these two weapons systems had ramped up to where dozens of each were being produced each week.

In attendance at this meeting were Admiral Lu Pham, Sr. Vice President, Sung Hsu, Assistant Vice Minister Qiao Wenzhong and the commanding Admiral of the PLAN, Li Huang and their aides. All of these individuals would be briefing not only General Hunbaio, but more importantly, they would be briefing their special guests, President Jien Zenim and Chairman Chin Zhongbaio and their top aides regarding the operational status of each of these systems and their availability for the upcoming operations.

After an introduction to this effect, Chin Zhongbaio, the Chairman of COSCO and a high ranking Politburo member, addressed the gathering.

"Comrades, I need not go into great detail regarding the importance of these meetings and the briefings they will encompass. The work your various organizations have accomplished are of the utmost importance to the future and viability of our People's Republic and our continuing People's Revolution as couched in the work of the Three Wisdoms that our leader has introduced to the world. The change and improvement to social equity and justice that this revolution will now bring to the world as a whole, and to the developing nations and their people will be as momentous and as long lasting as any change witnessed throughout recorded history. Your efforts represent the very foundational insurance for that change."

"I want to reiterate to each of you, our foremost desire is for these changes to occur as the peaceful, natural consequence of social evolution that they represent. However, in order to overcome the less equitable capitalistic and class-dividing western systems that currently pollute our regions, it is likely that we will have to make use of the insurance your developments represent. As you know, we anticipate this to be the case and have prudently made plans accordingly. We look forward to now hearing of your preparations and status with respect to those plans."

Lu Pham sat through these opening remarks reflecting on the amazing developments in the last few years. Not only for him personally, but for the nation and social system that he was involved with. Oh, he knew as well as the Chairman here, as well as Jien Zenim himself in fact, that the system they were talking about would still have its inequities. Such a system would always need those with the strength and vision to implement the necessary changes. He was marveling that somehow he had become one of those directly involved with the vision.

"It has always been thus," thought Lu … Marx, Lenin, Stalin, Mao, Ho Chi Minh … and now Jien Zenim. The Americans had developed their own … Washington, Jefferson, Adams, Lincoln, Roosevelt, Reagan and now Weisskopf. But Lu was convinced that this developing system would truly eclipse all others in terms of its ability to provide for fuller social justice and equity for the teaming masses of Asia and any other developing nations. The American model pitted people against one another as individuals, always striving to improve themselves over others around them. Lu felt this had provided for marvelous innovation and the ability for a relative few to fulfill their potential. But, he felt it was limited by its nature in its ability to bring such achievement and fulfillment to the entire society. The model Jien Zenim espoused called for the group, the collective to willing work together and improve all … and it was molded for once in a fashion that Lu truly felt would allow for it to be accomplished, far superior to the corruption plagued Stalinist systems of prior times.

Of course, what Lu failed to take into account in this optimistic analysis was that his enthusiasm for the new system was directly related to his own personal involvement in the upper levels of the decision-making. His relative new status as one of the inner circle allowed him to enjoy the types of latitude and personal decision making freedom that he eschewed the rival "western" system for. It would only be after significant trial, hardship and eye opening experience acquired over years of actually attempting to implement the "Three Wisdoms" dream that this would dawn on Lu.

CHAPTER 9

"The beginning of strife is as when one letteth out water" - Solomon

February 6, 2006, 03:23 Local
USS Michigan SSGN-727
300 nautical miles South of Adana, Turkey
Mediterranean Sea

All along the length of the boat, behind the sail, the coverings for fifteen of the Multiple All-up-round Canisters (MAC's) were hinging back to reveal the lethal cargo they protected. Underneath each covering, fitted into each of the former tubes for Trident missiles, the MAC's housed seven Tomahawk SLCM's (Sub Launched Cruise Missiles).

The Michigan was one of four conversions that had been made to former Trident SSBM submarines between the years of 2001 and 2004, enabling them to carry up to 154 SLCM's each, along with a significant contingent of Navy SEAL personnel for special operations. Two served in the Pacific and two in the Atlantic. Since the outbreak of hostilities last November, one of the two Atlantic boats had been on patrol in the Mediterranean for just such a contingency as this current mission.

"We have the mark. Conn, steady as she goes, bearing one two zero degrees. Missile Control, you may commence your firing sequence when ready."

SLCM launched toward Incirlik.

In the missile control center, the fire control officer responded.

"Aye, aye sir, all systems are GO and ready for launch. Ripple firing sequence commencing on my mark. Three, two, one ... Mark!"

The MK 98 digital computer fire control system, which had been modified for the SSGN conversion to integrate the tactical Tomahawk weapon control systems, took over from that point. Target coordinates and flight profiles had already been downloaded into the missiles.

Within four minutes, over one hundred SLCM's had been launched and were out of the water and on their way. Flying at a very low level for most of the trip, each missiles would arrive at their destination precisely thirty-three minutes after launch, where they would perform a pop-up maneuver over their targets and announce their deadly presence.

February 6, 2006, that same time
Thruster Flight, B1-B Lancer Bombers
357 miles West of Adana, Turkey

The four stealthy wraiths were flying nape of the earth, just under Mach one over south central Turkey. Over Egridir Lake, Thruster flight reached its launch point.

"Weapons release in on my mark in three ... two ... one ... Mark!"

At the eight attachment points along the under side of each B1-B Lancer bomber (commonly called "Bones"), a total of fourteen ALCM's (Air Launched Cruise Missiles) began their pre-programmed release from each aircraft. These were followed by six ALCM's from each aircraft's rotary launcher in the internal bomb bay, making a total of twenty ALCM.s that were launched from each aircraft.

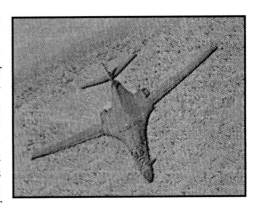

B-1B Lancer "Bones" over Turkey.

High above Thruster flight, two flights of F-22 fighters patrolled, but they were not interfered with. The large diversion attack along the front lines to the north and east near the hotly contested city of Keyseri was attracting the attention of most of the GIR's air assets. One large contingent of aircraft that the GIR did not have involved in the fighting along the front lines was the large number of attack aircraft, fighter aircraft and even two flights of TU-22M Bombers that had landed within the last two hours at Incirlik airbase near Adana. These aircraft, almost two hundred of them, were now being refueled and rearmed for use by the GIR commanders in this theater.

Those very GIR assets were the focus of Thruster flight and USS Michigan. Having been notified of the landing of those GIR aircraft at Incirlik by satellite observation, the orders had gone out to the USS Michigan and B1-B's at Izmir. Within the next few minutes, the results would be apparent.

February 6, 2006, 04:02 local
GIR Incirlik Air Base
Near Adana, Turkey

The aircraft were crowding every portion of open space on the service apron, along the taxiways, the newly constructed revetments and the few hangars that had been reconstructed since GIR forces had taken the airfield. They were a mixture of SU-25 "Frogfoot" attack aircraft,, MIG-27 "Flogger" attack aircraft,, SU-24 "Fencer" attack aircraft, SU-22 "Fitter" fighter aircraft, SU-27 "Flanker" fighter aircraft and the two flights of TU-22M "Backfire" bombers. These one hundred and eighty aircraft had arrived over the last few hours. Their presence here, when added to the two dozen fighter and attack aircraft already present at the base, represented the GIR's "front line" air craft commitment to the southern sector of their Turkey operation.

A flight of four SU-27 fighters was up providing combat air patrol (CAP) for the base at all times, controlled by a GIR Ilyushin Il-76 "Mainstay" AEW aircraft that was loitering above the base.

Numerous ZSU-23, vehicles had been stationed around the airfield in revetments especially built for them. These rapid-fire 23 mm anti-aircraft weapons were very effective against low flying aircraft. It was hoped that the SA-11 and SA-13 missile batteries stationed around the base would be effective against many of the American and Turkish aircraft and those of their allies, and force them to fly low and in range of the ZSU-23-4's.

The incoming U.S. cruise missiles were targeted for every revetment, radar emplacement, command and control facility and anti-aircraft emplacement that had been located by satellite. Each had been assigned multiple missiles. The first missiles were targeted at the anti-air defenses themselves.

The missiles were flying very low, and were designed to be difficult to acquire on radar. But with the GIR Mainstay AEW aircraft aloft, its doppler radar spotted the first missiles in the stream from the USS Michigan when they were fifteen miles away. Traveling at 500 knots, this meant that the defenses had a little over one-and-a-half minutes to prepare.

"We have many inbound missile tracks to the east southeast, counting twenty tracks and growing ... altitude 100-200 meters. Have all missile batteries hold their fire, while we vector Wolf Flight to intercept. Have close in anti-air defenses prepared for cruise missile attack."

The controller on the Mainstay vectored the four SU-27 aircraft to an intercept course. Wolf flight, with four SU-27's that had their own effective doppler radar, picked up the American SLCM's and engaged them.

"Engaging with radar guided missiles, and then cannons!"

Radar lock was difficult to obtain and the SU-27's found themselves having to engage, circle and re-engage. In the process, many missiles "leaked" through before Wolf Flight had expended its ordinance. In so doing though, twenty-two of the first one hundred and five cruise missiles were destroyed.

The GIR had a system of revetments for it ZSU-23's all around the base where they rotated from one revetment to another. As the first missiles leaked past Wolf Flight's intercept, they were engaged by the ZSU-23's. Many of these first missiles were targeted on the ZSU-23 revetments themselves. With its excellent low level radar, its wide engagement angles (elevation of -4 to +85 degrees; 360 degrees azimuth) and its high rate of fire - 800 to 1000 rounds per minute for each of its four barrels - the ZSU-23 was a very effective close-in AAW platform. The eight units on that eastern side of the base were able to knock down another eighteen SLCM's before succumbing themselves to the multiple missiles targeted on each revetment.

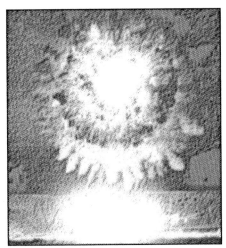
US SLCM destroys GIR aircraft.

At this point, forty missiles had been downed and another thirty-two expended on the ZSU-23 and missile defenses. This left thirty-three missiles from the initial stream launched by the USS Michigan still targeted on the airfield and its structures. Of these, another fourteen were downed by portable, shoulder fired SA-14 "Gremlin" missiles. With an all aspect targeting capability similar to the US Stinger missile, the "Gremlin" was a potent tool in defending against low level aircraft attacks of all types.

The twenty missiles that impacted the service aprons, revetments and hangars caused heavy damage to the aircraft being refueled and rearmed there. Many secondary explosions occurred as ordinance and fuel exploded with the aircraft. Many highly trained pilots and other personnel were killed..

Even as the last missiles in the stream from the USS Michigan were noted inbound by the GIR AEW aircraft, controllers on that same aircraft picked up the second stream of eighty ALCM's coming from the BI-B flight. These eighty missiles were engaged by the SA-11 and SA-13 batteries as the SU-27 CAP had expended its munitions. Those batteries were far less effective against low-level cruise missile attacks and had themselves been subjected to losses from the first group of SLCM's from the USS Michigan. Although scores AAW missiles were fired at the incoming stream of ALCM's, only thirteen missiles were downed by the missile batteries.

Once over the base, the remaining sixty-six missiles were again engaged by SA-14 "Gremlins" fired by personnel on the base itself. Another nine ALCM's were destroyed as a result of this last defensive flurry. The net result were that another fifty-eight cruise missiles impacted all over the airfield amongst already burning aircraft, amongst aircraft that personnel were desperately trying to move out of the way and amongst the support facilities that the GIR had hastily repaired and built on the base. More aircraft were destroyed or damaged, more personnel were killed and injured and more facilities were wrecked or damaged.

When the all clear signal at Incirlik was given at 05:00 hours, over one hundred and twenty aircraft on the ground were either destroyed or heavily damaged. In addition, several hundred personnel had been killed or injured and the airfield itself was closed. Because of its proximity to the Sea and the exposure to quick SLCM attack, Incirlik would not open again as a major airfield, the GIR preferring smaller fields further inland where they would have more warning and where they could develop more layered defenses.

February 7, 2006, 14:00 local
Secure Conference Center, U.S. Embassy
Reykjavik, Iceland

The meetings were wrapping up. For these last two days, the principle western allies in the two-week old war in the Middle East had been in summit. The United States, Canada, Great Britain, Germany, Turkey, Saudi Arabia and Egypt were all represented. They had met the entire time in the secure conference center in the U.S. embassy under very tight secrecy and security. Top aides had accompanied each of the leaders. The best "war college" scenarios that each respective nation could produce had been analyzed.

Military operations were ongoing during the summit. Airlifts into Turkey, Saudi Arabia, Egypt and the UAE were proceeding. Pre-positioned materiel and equipment all around the region was activated and transported to logistic areas well in advance of the on coming GIR forces. These efforts were focused on building up adequate defenses, in an attempt to stem the tide of the GIR onslaught.

In the field, the allies were back on their heels and some difficult strategic decisions were necessary. Kuwait had fallen, Saudi Arabia had been invaded and the GIR forces were advancing along the Persian Gulf Coast toward the UAE and inland towards the Saudi capital. Defensive lines kept shifting further south and west in hopes of slowing the GIR advance.

Despite a highly successful tactical attack on Incirlik, Turkey was in desperate circumstances as the GIR armies had literally divided the country and were pressing their advantage. A significant GIR buildup in the center of the line gave every indication of producing a break through soon, which would mean the defensive lines in Turkey would also shift to the west.

Additionally, two large GIR armies were moving towards the Egyptian border from Libya and the Sudan. Deploying sufficient allied strength in front of them to slow any advance across the Egyptian desert was going to be difficult at best, particularly given the pressures and requirements for allied deployments to protect the Arabian oil fields and Turkey.

In light of all of this, the leaders had discussed overall strategy and come to some initial, path setting decisions. President Weisskopf was summarizing as the meetings wound up.

"We have agreed that the United States and its forces would provide over-all strategic control and that the theater commanders will be American, supported by allied commanders in their various roles and in specific operational areas. I understand that this will produce some political difficulties, but in light of the desperate and monumental task before us, and in light of the vast majority of equipment and materiel coming out of America in each operational area, we will proceed as we have agreed."

"We have discussed a number of likely reactions to and consequences of the current conflict and we have agreed that escalation is likely, particularly in the Far East. As a result of this, we have agreed that the Middle East and the Mediterranean Theater will be our first order of focus. As with World

War II, should war break out in the Far East, we will focus on securing and winning the war in the west first. While pursuing this primary objective, in so much as it is practicable, we will fight a holding action in the Far East Theater until we can turn the full weight of our production and capability to that part of the world. Each of us must take these decisions back to our military and civil command structures and implement them accordingly, coordinating through the command structures we have discussed here. I expect that summits like this will be held regularly, perhaps every four to six months."

As President Weisskopf paused, the Prime Minister of Great Britain spoke.

"Mr. President, should the Far East Theater escalate into war with the CAS, we can expect Japan, Korea, Australia and other European nations to become a part of this summit. In that event, there will be great pressure exerted on our priorities and strategic decisions. I just want to insure that we all understand our commitment here and the decisions we are making today."

President Weisskopf had contemplated this exact issue at great length.

"Mr. Prime Minister, I understand your point. Although I myself have concerns about the Far East, and particularly any participation by the CAS as an ally of the GIR, I cannot see that we have any choice in that eventuality."

"I will close my remarks with this ... we are facing a challenge and a danger of unprecedented proportions. Should the CAS and the GIR unite in conflict against the west, as we consider likely ... in my estimation we will be facing a threat far greater than that of the combined Nazi and Imperial Japanese capability of sixty-five years ago. This should sober us, it should galvanize us and it should spur us on to the necessary decisions and actions as allies and on each of our home fronts. I believe this summit is a good start at that, but I believe we must not for an instant let our guard down or forget the nature of the threat we face. Thank you, and may God bless our united efforts."

As he returned to his seat, Norm Weisskopf again contemplated his remarks and the decisions they had made. The Far East escalation was a projection, the war in the Middle East was real and it was a desperate fight. World wide oil production was at stake. Whole economies were going to be ruined.

Nonetheless, President Weisskopf still wondered about that over-riding strategic decision they had made regarding the Far East conflict, should it come. Really, at the current time, just as he had indicated to the Prime Minister, they had no choice ... but putting that decision into motion in the deployments, in the production schedules that would result, in the build-up ... it would be difficult if not impossible to change later.

Still, he just couldn't shake the feeling that the primary menace was that big red dragon that had yet to project its influence and real intent onto these events. Norm felt an overpowering conviction in his soul regarding that dragon's fury. Should it be unleashed and not quickly contained, it would be more difficult to suppress and overpower than they could possibly imagine.

As the meeting ended, President Weisskopf began working with his staff on his national address slated for the next evening. He intended to review the basics of this meeting with the allied leaders and then "lay it out" for the American people, many of whom had not yet had the reality of the true nature of this conflict hit home for them. What the President did not yet appreciate himself was how remarkably accurate his convictions regarding the threat in the Far East would prove, or how much he would regret not pushing harder to establish a strategy accordingly when he had the chance.

February 9, 2006, 10:02 local
U.S. Army Recruiting Station
NW 53rd Terrace
Miami, Florida

Hernando Rodriguez waited patiently in line. It really wasn't too terribly long a line at all, in fact not nearly as long as he'd expected. After last night's speech to the nation by President Weisskopf, which Hernando would always remember as the most patriotic and inspiring speech of his life, he'd expected the recruiting center to be literally packed with people signing up. The speech had surely affected him that way and he naturally expected it to have effected others in the same way.

And to some degree it had. The recruiting station here at The Augusta Building on NW 53rd Terrace had been doing a fairly brisk business all morning. Never more than eight or ten people waiting, but there had also not been an open counter all morning as young men and women came in and joined the Army.

The recruiting officers had been noticing a gradual pick up in recruitment ever since the declaration of war in the Middle East three weeks ago. This was occurring here in Miami and at other major recruiting stations around the country. There had been a few very brisk days right after the declaration, but it had leveled off somewhat as people watched events unfold and as the buildup proceeded. But the continued rapid decline in the stock market and the anxiety over fuel costs and rumored fuel allocations were driving home to people that this was a "real" war, and one that would not be soon in ending.

Today's surge in activity was associated directly with the President's speech last night. In that speech he directly and succinctly outlined the gravity of the situation facing America and its allies. Even with the reserve units he was calling up, there would not be enough men at arms to stop and then roll back the Greater Islamic Republic and its naked aggression in the Middle East.

The President had made it clear that now was one of those times in history when America's cream must rise to the top. The President had shown by way of graphs, multi-media displays and heart-felt explanation that the situation was dire. America could "expect worse news before better" ... that in all probability our friendly oil supplies would be taken or destroyed in the conflict and that America was facing energy shortages in the near future.

Then the President had outlined the emergency provisions he was directing all federal agencies to adopt. Many of these agencies interfaced with the public and many of them regulated activities that the public was involved with, like the transportation department's involvement with gas pricing and distribution, and the defense department's interface with the defense industry. It was clear that millions of Americans would be impacted. The President then asked for the governors and legislators from each of the fifty states to adopt similar measure to conserve strategic resources and to more fully organize the public sector for what lay ahead. The President had ended by announcing a call up of 500,000 more reservists, an appeal for more enlistment and finally an inspired statement of confidence in the nation, it's strength, depth and basic goodness. Hernando had "felt" those words and with that feeling had come the clear knowledge of what he must do.

Early this morning he had called into the maintenance department at Florida State University where he worked. He had told his boss Stan that he would not be in today, that in fact he would not be coming back at all. When questioned, he had simply told Stan that he was joining the Army.

Stan had thought him crazy.

"What? Come on Hernando, you have to be kidding me, right?"

When Hernando had made it clear that he was not kidding, Stan had continued.

"Look man, there's no draft. They have an 'all volunteer Army" for this, you don't have to do it. We'll end up kicking this Sayeed guy the same way we did bin Laden."

The reply had been immediate, "I don't think so Stan, didn't you hear what the President was saying last night?"

But Stan would not listen, or consider. He just knew he was losing a very good worker, and someone he considered his friend.

"What about your future, Hernando? You are in a position here to get your education paid for and you have a very good job that will provide for the future you keep taking about with Maria."

All Hernando could think to say was, "I am doing it for our future Stan, Maria's, our kids ... that's what this is all about. Look, I'm sorry you don't agree, and I am sorry this is so abrupt. God bless you man, you've been a good boss. Pray for me ... I gotta go."

How could Hernando explain it to someone like Stan. Stan had never experienced, or heard first hand about what life was like without the basic liberties and freedoms he and so many other Americas took for granted. Despite the unbelievable death toll America had sustained as a result of the terror attack in 2001, once the terrorists and the governments supporting them had been defeated, many Americans felt that chapter in history had been put behind them. Once again now, only a few years later, the apathy and the attitude of entitlement was setting in.

After talking to Stan, the call to his mom and dad had been a little harder to initiate, but much more gratifying in its reaction. They were concerned ... but they were PROUD of him.

"God bless you son, you are a true American," his father had simply said. But with those simple words, his heart had soared.

"God WILL bless you Hernando. We have raised you well and will pray for you every night. Have you told Maria? Don't worry, we will help take care of her while you are gone. My heart fears for your safety, even as is bursts with pride over your goodness and commitment"

Hernando had told Maria. They had been at his place watching TV when the speech had been given last night. He had immediately shared with her what his convictions were. They had done the only thing two devout Catholics, who were intended for one another in their hearts could do ... they had sought out their Priest after the speech, explained their circumstance and then been wed late last night in a simple ceremony with just themselves and the Priest present. They had then spent last evening together, their first ever, and last for a long time.

"Mom, Dad, Maria is now your daughter in-law. Please forgive me, but we were married last night by Father Chapman. Maria has let her folks know and she will be living in my apartment."

"Mother of God! Why ... this is ... this is ... oh Hernando, this is WONDERFUL news. We will treat her as our own. She will need to save her money! We will work with her parents and insure that she is watched over and taken good care of ... you need not worry over it."

Hernando loved his parents. They were good, solid people. They worked hard. They had an abiding faith and they practiced it devoutly and freely. He had every confidence that between Maria's parents (who were similar in all ways to his own) and his own parents, that Maria would be well watched over until he returned. Besides, Hernando knew that Maria was his equal in faith, commitment, drive and energy and would be watching out for herself.

Beyond this, as first generation Cuban Americans, people who had escaped relatively recently from the continuing hell hole that Cuba was, Hernando's parents only wished that the fight would be carried to what they called the "old scoundrel" in Havana.

Well, Hernando didn't know about that, he had been too young when his parents had escaped by boat, really just a small child of six years ... he just KNEW that he had to do this. At twenty-two years of age, Hernando knew he had to stand up now and fight for liberty so that he and his Maria could enjoy it and pass it on to their children after them.

February 12, 2006, 14:30 CST
FTA Trucking, U.S. Headquarters
Dallas, TX

Miguel Santos leaned back in his leather chair. As he waited for his boss and close friend, he gazed out of the window of his office. His office was a corner suite on the fourteenth floor of a fifteen-story office building at the intersection of Central Expressway and the LBJ on the north side of Dallas.

"What a view," he thought to himself as he looked to the south and saw the majestic skyline of downtown Dallas. The Americans certainly did love their material wealth, their glamour. It was written not only all over many of their faces, it was etched into their very skylines. Yes, Miguel admitted it was entrancing, and it was almost intoxicating. Look at how many other entire nations sought to emulate them. It was at such times that Miguel had only to think back on his childhood, the poverty and want he had experienced in Cuba, to break the spell in which it often held him. All that misery at the hands of these Americans who were living in such opulence, who had cut his nation from the trade and aid that could have benefited so many!

He had seen it as a youth and a young adult in Mexico, the place he called home now. The same poverty, the same hunger, while just across an imaginary line so many enjoyed so much.

Well, Miguel had risen above it himself, and he was thankful to be a part of something that he felt certain was going to help uncounted others too. In fact, it never ceased to amaze him that he, a former poultry truck driver, once living in Chihuahua, could have risen to such a position. Here he was, senior VP of U.S. Operations. He had Hector to thank for it all. Hector who had taken a liking to him early on, who appreciated not only Miguel's willingness to work very hard, but who also recognized the organizational and management potential in Miguel. Hector had nurtured those talents and both men had prospered greatly, now both owning substantial Haciendas back in central Mexico where their wives and children were safe from the darker and more dangerous aspects of their businesses, and away from the alluring material influence of America.

They had profited enormously through the opportunities afforded by America's openness, particularly through the expansion of their international trucking business resulting from provisions of the NAFTA agreement. They profited even more by dealing very carefully in the illicit trades that were so desired by many Americans, mixing in a healthy dose of trafficking in the items they required for their future political aspirations ... weapons and the people who knew how to use them.

As he mused on this, his secretary rang to let him know his guest had arrived and was on his way in.

"Hector, my dear friend, how good to see you!"

The two men met half way across the floor and hugged one another while slapping one another's backs.

"Miguel, my friend, as always, it is my pleasure to visit with you as well. I can't tell you how pleased I am with your success, and my certainty that the performance of your operations will end up exceeding our goals and projections. Let's get right to the review and the plans for the future."

All of this was genuine, but it was also couched in key words. Miguel's operations were indeed out pacing the expectations set for them, but the review they would be conducting today had nothing to do with trucking. The two men were so adept at discussing one thing while meaning another, that they had even built entire presentations around the art. Pictures, charts and verbiage appearing to mean one thing, while conveying something entirely different.

Miguel moved to his desk and activated the automatic curtains for his office windows. The multi-media presentation required that the sunlight be blocked, but the curtains coming down blocked much more than sunlight. Even though the room was "scrubbed" daily for listening devices, by pressing another button, Miguel activated some soft background music, which was especially digitally encoded and projected more than simply audible melodies. The final element of their security was then activated, a projector that created an ionic shield which helped foil any electronic eavesdropping not effected by the other security measures.

After implementing all of this, Miguel joined Hector at the small conference table and keyed the remote audio-video equipment. Hector's digitally encoded RWDVD was placed in the machinery and the presentation began.

The presentation centered on the various trucking "corridors" on which FTA Trucking concentrated to transport goods back and forth from Mexico as well as other central and south American countries into the United States. Originally they had focused on the "I-35" north-south corridor, which ran from southern Texas up into Minnesota. They had been so successful along that line, with their ability to haul freight at reduced rates using their equipment and personnel from Mexico that they had soon expanded. By using US Highway 287 and the I-40 corridor, and by using the I-20 and I-10 corridors, they had tapped next into the I-25 corridor running from El Paso all the way up into Montana. Finally, they had expanded further west along the I-10 corridor and were now mounting very profitable operations from southern California up the I-15 corridor into Utah and Idaho and up the I-5 corridor into northern California, Oregon and Washington.

As they discussed each of these corridors, operations and their profitability, what would not be apparent to anyone overhearing the presentation, was that the two were reviewing in detail the status of six other "projects" associated with each corridor. Projects related to the planning and execution of the mission given to Hector Ortiz by his friend, the aging head of state.

"So, Hector, it appears we are in fact ahead of schedule in all six corridors. What is the company's current target date for reaching the final profitability figures in each?"

Without the slightest pause or hesitation, Hector answered both questions that had been posed by the single interrogatory.

"We must reach these figures by early March. The exact timing is something we can float a couple of weeks, but no sooner than March 5th and probably no later than the 20th. As we get closer to our year end financial reviews back at the corporate offices in Mexico City, I will communicate a more exact date to you."

"As you know, I intend to personally come and meet with the employees in the three western corridors to congratulate them on a job well done, while you personally handle the appreciation here in Texas and in Colorado."

Miguel was pleased that Hector was following through with his commitment to get in the field and personally coordinate three of these "projects".

"Yes, my friend, I know. I am confident that our employees there will give you every reason to congratulate them. They are looking forward to your time with them. It means a lot to them Hector, and it is one of the things about FTA that our employees like the most, the willingness of upper management to be involved right there in the trenches with them."

February 17, 2006, 19:30 local
Presidential Office Suite
Tehran, GIR

"Continue with the briefing General."

Hasan Sayeed waited anxiously for the details of what he already knew generally. GIR forces were advancing on all fronts. It was true that the advance was not as quick as he would like, and it was true that their losses were extensive. Despite this he respected and followed both General Jabal Talabari's and his foreign minister's, and trusted ally, Ayatollah Sadiq Shiraziha's, advice to pace their advance so as to insure that occupied areas were properly consolidated and capable of supporting logistics activities for his advancing forces.

Nonetheless, in the space of just a few weeks, half of Turkey had fallen and Kuwait had been inducted into the GIR. Additionally, the rich oil fields along the Saudi Arabian coast had been taken as far south as Al Jubayl and significant progress had been made into interior portions of the Arabian Peninsula toward Medina. Now, another offensive was about to begin in the western deserts of Egypt and from the south moving north along the Nile.

Against this, the Turkish, Saudi, UAR and of course the American forces were making a determined defense with there as yet inferior numbers. More NATO troops, including British and German were coming into both Turkey and Egypt. But the numbers were not with them yet, and Hasan had no intention of allowing them to build up forces while he sat behind berms and in trenches as the fool Hussein had done over ten years earlier.

"Please begin with your estimates of the American buildup in eastern Turkey, Egypt and Saudi Arabia. What can we expect to be up against as our forces continue to advance?"

General Jabal Talabari was prepared to answer his Imam's questions. He had risen rapidly in the ranks and had become the Theater Commander by Hasan's personal order. The overall Defense Minister and Generals who were in Tehran were his nominal direct line commanders, but he enjoyed and respected that Hasan himself sat in on these briefings.

"My Imam, we are progressing nicely in both Saudi Arabia and in Turkey. We have broken through the initial defensive lines in both areas, but have suffered significant attrition in moving up to their second lines of defense."

GIR T-90 advances in Saudi Arabia.

"We fought our first pitched armored battle in the coastal deserts just north of Abu Hadriyah two days ago. In that battle over seventy-five American Abrams tanks were destroyed while we lost over one hundred and sixty of our own. The Americans had set up a defensive position along the coast, extending out into the desert towards the Ad Dah Na. Their defense was in-depth with significant air cover. By making a feint in force towards Riyadh, we were able to draw enough of their strength away to commit our reserve right along the coast and punch through all the way to Al Jubayl and the oilfields there. The Americans were quick to recover and we suffered significant losses, but we achieved our objectives."

"It will be of interest to you, and should be passed on to our allies that we have developed a tactic with our T-80's and T-90's where we can defeat the M1A1 Abrams. It requires a two-to-one superiority and it requires enough air cover to keep the A-10's and Apaches off of our columns. by working

M1A1 Abrams counters GIR armor.

two of our T-80's as a team focusing on a single M1A1, we are finding that in 70% of the engagements at least one of our T-80's moves on, leaving a smoking M1A1 hulk in the desert."

"In addition,, we have devised another tactic regarding the very capable U.S. MLRS system. These tracked Multiple Launch Rocket Systems are deadly against massed armor of any type, or massed infantry. Our armor and infantry face so many lethal threats, the Apache helicopters, the A-10 aircraft and the MLRS, before we are even able to engage the American armor directly. MLRS systems have punished us terribly during the entire campaign in Saudi to date.

Over fifty of the tanks we lost in the battle I just described were due to an MLRS battery the Americans employed. I am happy to inform you that we were able to completely destroy this battery. We kept a full squadron of SU-25's in reserve

MLRS engaging GIR armor.

for just this purpose, escorted by a squadron of SU-33's. Since our counter battery fire has been ineffective against the highly mobile MLRS, once we had determined the location of the MLRS attack by radar, we immediately dispatched the SU-25's. Our aircraft caught the MLRS battery in transit away from the positions they had fired from and destroyed them. Our SU-33's engaged several American and Saudi aircraft, but only three of the SU-

25's were lost. This is another tactic that should be passed along and used against the American technology."

"Still, once we are able to engage the American armor directly, we require the numeric advantage. This brings me to my major point before speaking to the American buildup. I would plead with my respected superiors ... our logistics lines MUST remain open and the 4th and 7th Army groups must quickly move up to reinforce and strengthen the 1st and 2nd groups respectively. The Americans are employing their B1-B's and their cruise missiles to great effect in hampering our supply lines. I plead with you to either find a way to prevent this, or send enough support to insure that the requisite amount of men, equipment and munitions reach our staging areas."

And so the meeting went. Hasan Sayeed was very satisfied with Jabal's performance. He had chosen correctly when he named Jabal theater commander over the objections of his Defense Minister and leading military commanders. To their credit, they were now exploiting Jabal's understanding of how the Americans would employ their forces and react.

Nonetheless, the American and NATO buildup was progressing at a faster than expected rate. At the current rate, it would allow them to field enough of their technology to blunt the GIR advance in the next eight to ten weeks. Hasan could not go into the details in this meeting, but he was expecting that rate to dramatically diminish in the next three to four weeks. He would take Jabal aside after the meeting, sometime later this evening while they were at dinner, and quietly let him know what to expect from "Breath of Fire" so he could have contingency plans prepared accordingly.

February 20, 2006, 18:55 Local
GIR Forward Position
East of Cicekdag, Turkey

Sergeant Abduhl Selim watched the highway below, running through the valley. His position on the hill overlooking the main highway to Ankara was the furthest position forward on the current GIR line, and from his point of view, clearly the most exposed. But that was nothing new to the Sergeant.

GIR forces had broken through the Turkish and British lines at Kayseri on the 17th, just as reports of advancing German armor and Canadian reinforcements were being received. As a result of the breakthrough, they had caught the German and Canadian forces in transit and forced them to retreat. The last three days had brought them to this position. Reconnaissance flights and patrols indicated that the German armor and

Canadian infantry had withdrawn and heavily reinforced the U.S. 82nd Airborne Division which was already dug in at the next line of defense just three kilometers up the road, around the hills off to the west.

Abduhl was promoted to the senior NCO for his platoon three weeks ago after the former NCO had been killed. In fact, Abduhl and two other men were the only surviving members of the original squad that he had entered the former Iran with in September. So here he was, a crack shot eighteen-year-old who had become battle hardened in the space of six months.

Abduhl's men prepare to dig in.

"Okay, okay! I want each of you men dug in along this line on each side of the ridge towards the east here, five-meter separation. We may be up here all night. In fact, we probably will be up here all night and nothing is coming up that valley or over that ridge without us knowing about it and reporting back to the company. Let's go, be quick about it!"

Turning to several sets of two man teams that had just arrived at his position, Abduhl began issuing them orders too.

"Set up both of those anti-tank positions on each side of the ridge, near the military crest in positions fifteen meters back form the forward end of the line, and those anti-aircraft teams in the middle on each side of the ridge."

"Any aircraft or armor they send this way scouting are going to pay a heavy price. Dig in deep, once they find we're here they will barrage us quickly."

In fact, the men didn't know it yet, but the young sergeant was going to have them dig a secondary position two hundred meters to their rear as soon as they had completed this one. He figured he had just enough time to get those second positions prepared, and then get his men into their forward position with their low light night vision headsets on before it got too dark.

His two AT-4 Spigot anti-tank missile teams would be fine for engaging scout or recon APC's or IFV's, but they would be of questionable use against frontal armor of the American and German main battle tanks (MBT's). To date, he had fought against the older variety if MBT's the Turkish employed, the M-60's. Since the Spigot had a tough time penetrating those tanks frontal armor, he knew that against the newer tanks his missiles would even be more questionable. In that event, he would alert his command of their presence and attempt to wait and let them begin to get past him, allowing their side and rear armor to be targeted, before engaging them.

The SA-14 Gremlin missiles his two, two-man teams carried were effective against helicopters or low flying attack aircraft. They were the Russian built equivalent of the American "Stinger" missile. Perhaps not as capable, but capable enough. Abduhl knew that when his teams launched them, the targeted aircraft immediately attempted to evade and egress … but he also knew that his entire position would then be targeted in return.

As Abduhl sent out the first of his reconnaissance /security patrols that would cover the surrounding area to their front and flanks through the night, he thought about the coming ground confrontation with the Americans.

"The American 82nd Airborne," he thought. He had heard his former NCO's, talk a lot about the American 101st and 82nd Airborne Divisions, hoping they would have a chance to fight them. Even though they wanted a chance to confront them, Abduhl knew they had a very healthy respect for them. Abduhl had seen what American air power could do … most of those NCO's he was remembering were now dead because of it, the rest due to what resistance had been offered by the Turks. He knew that the American ground forces were going to be just as effective as their air forces had been and he was going to just have to do his best to prepare for that.

"Perhaps we will find out tonight … it'll be getting dark within the hour … and everyone has told me that the Americans like the night."

February 20, 2006, same time
82nd Airborne Scout
East of Cicekdag, Turkey

Sixteen hundred and seventy-five yards to the north and east of Sergeant Selim, along the next ridgeline over and running tangential to the front, Master Sergeant Michael O'Malley was watching the GIR forward position through his 10X dual purpose day/night vision monocular/range finder. The

Sgt. O'Malley observes GIR position.

Sergeant and his three-man security/communications team was a forward observer for the very 82nd Airborne Division that Selim was worrying about.

"Okay, these guys are real smart. It looks like they are preparing a secondary fall back position. They have anti-tank, anti-air and some forward observation in an oversized platoon. They're sending out a patrol right now, you got them Johannsen? "

Private Johannsen was one of two soldiers providing security for O'Malley. He was quick to respond to his sergeant.

"I got 'em, six guys, heading north along this side of the ridge. I'll keep an eye on them and let you know if they start our way."

"Great Private, you make sure you do. Corporal, pass these two coordinates that I'm about to give you back to battalion. Go ahead and get them on the horn ... this'll take just a couple of seconds."

The Master Sergeant checked his optics and then compared it to the representation that he called up on the ruggedized tablet computer he carried. He used a stylus to scroll to the correct position on the 3-D digital map of the surrounding area that was loaded into the computer. As he did, the coordinates he desired appeared on the display.

He had an option to upload the information via wireless communication directly to a JOINT STAR aircraft if one was available and had been programmed into the system, or he could store the coordinates locally and then use standard radio communication to call them into his battalion headquarters. Since total air superiority had not been achieved, and the loss of one of the very expensive JOINT STAR aircraft late last year over eastern Turkey was still fresh in everyone's mind, no JOINT STAR aircraft would be risked this close to the front. That left the radio.

"OK, here's the first coordinate ... let's see if we can't arrange a little surprise for these folks around 0430 when the counterattack kicks off. That is, if they stay put that long"

February 24, 2006, 16:50 MST
Simplot Corporate Offices
Boise, ID

Geneva glanced at the clock. Ten minutes until five on a Friday afternoon. She was probably going to have to work a few minutes late in order to finish up the word processing that was needed for Monday morning. She might even come in on Saturday if necessary.

Geneva had gotten the job several months ago. She had taken a local class on computers and then on word processing and surprised herself and Alan too when she had literally excelled at it. The school had a placement program and Simplot had taken her on as a temp in their word processing pool. After three months as a temp, they had brought her on full time and she really enjoyed the work.

The one caveat had been she needed a week's vacation in March to drive down to San Diego. Simplot had very strict rules about vacation and sick leave and when one could qualify for it. However, in Geneva's case, when they had heard what the vacation was for ... her supervisor had talked with management and they had arranged for her to take the time as a paid leave, not impacting future vacation she might accrue.

Simplot had a reputation as a very strict, no-nonsense company that was somewhat of a corporate piranha. It showed in their earnings, even in the hard times. Simplot was also a VERY patriotic company. Few people knew that the company had tragically lost a number of civilian employees in World War II when the Japanese invaded and took over Wake Island. Several Simplot employees had been captured along with the Marines defending the Island and they had been, almost to the man, executed by the Japanese. So when it came to a Marine Boot Camp graduation, Simplot was not only understanding, they were extremely accommodating.

"Let's see," Geneva thought for a moment, "February 20th, this will mark the end of his eleventh week, only two more weeks to go! I'll bet that boy is cutting quite the figure after all that training!"

As she thought about him and continued her work, she saw the other employees leaving as the five o'clock hour came and passed.

"RINNNNGGG!"

"Oh! I wonder who that could be this late on a Friday afternoon?" Geneva thought as she picked up her extension and answered it.

"Simplot, this is Geneva Campbell in Word Processing."

On the other end of the phone the familiar voice of Alan spoke up.

"Hi mom, what's happenin' girl?"

Geneva had to smile, Alan was always checking up on his mom. Sometimes it made her wonder just who the parent was.

"Alan, what's going on? You better have a good reason for calling, 'cause you know you're not supposed to call me at work. This is a company line."

Alan loved his mom. He knew she took her work and her work ethic seriously, and he was sure it was rubbing off on him just as it had on Leon.

"Mom, that's why I waited until after five. I knew you'd be slavin' away doin' the "perfect" job and all, and I just wanted to see when you thought you'd be home. I'm going to fix YOU dinner tonight."

Geneva smiled. That Alan, he sure was a sweet talker … and it was genuine. It was hard for anyone to remain out of sorts with Alan.

"Okay, okay. I figure I'll be leaving in the next fifteen minutes or so … that should get me home between five-thirty and six.."

Alan paused for a moment on the phone ... And then he set the hook.

"Well, okay. I just wanted you to know that Leon called. He said he'd call back at five-thirty. He wants to finalize the schedule and plans for our trip down to his graduation in two weeks."

Geneva took back everything she'd just thought. That rascal Alan!

"Alan, I swear boy you are going to drive me crazy ... Why didn't you just tell me that to begin with. No, I know, I know, you just wanted to lead me along … I'll be home at five-thirty … you make sure Leon waits for me … and you stop playin' with my emotions so!"

Alan laughed out loud … not in a bad way, but in the good natured, loving way that always disarmed his mom, even if she was put out with him.

"Okay Mom, but I'll have that dinner ready when you get here. Love ya."

February 28th, 2006, 22:30 local
2nd Infantry Division Headquarters
Camp Red Cloud, Uijongbu, South Korea

The 2nd Infantry Division was the United States principle ground combat unit within the US Forces Korea (USFK). Over twenty thousand soldiers were continuously standing in the breach between the free world and totalitarianism. Along with their South Korean allies and comrades in arms, who numbered a half million in the active armed forces, they faced off against a standing army of over twice their size, with ready reserves that could turn the ratio to eight to one in a matter of days.

Particularly on the occasions, like now, when North Korea conducted massive military exercises along the DMZ, the alert levels were high and the tension was palpable.

In the intelligence section, Colonel Martinez, who was in charge, was pacing the floor. He was a constant, almost twenty-four hour per day presence around the intelligence offices while the North Korean exercises were going on. He literally slept and ate here. He felt he had good cause. He wanted to be available personally to make the decisions necessary if the North ever decided to "come". He didn't want any confusion or indecision in those critical first few moments that an attack was either discovered, or launched.

Just as he was walking past the analyst section, a young Lt. noticed him and waved him over.

"Holy cow Colonel, take a look at this."

The protocol may not have been the best, but the Colonel focused on results. This young man may look the "nerd" to a lot of the "gung-ho" soldiers … and in fact he was a nerd … but he was a committed to his job. He was also as good at analyzing photographic and SIGINT data and tying the two together as anyone the Colonel had ever known.

"Okay, Lt. Finley, what's got you so excited you forgot to say, Sir?"

The Lt. blushed in embarrassment as he answered.

"Oh! Sorry, Sir! I have correlated our latest reconnaissance photos from an over flight along the DMZ two hours ago with the latest NRO data. In fact, the folks back in NRO in northern Virginia were so anxious that they ftp'd me their data just a few minutes ago. I've got both sets of data and the graphics up on the screen right now. Please sir, take a look while I brief you on it … though I believe the graphics tell the story pretty straight forwardly."

As Martinez studied the screen, the hair on the back of his neck literally stood up. There it was … laid out for them. The reconnaissance photos showed several suspected forward deployment positions for North Korean artillery occupied with stacks of munitions being piled up next to them. You could actually see the workers stacking the shells. In several images, the positions revealed North Korean 127mm mobile rocket launchers, again with stacks of reloads piled near the launchers.

In addition, the National Reconnaissance Office satellite photos showed a steady stream of supplies moving towards the front from depots in the rear. Those satellite photos confirmed that a lot more ammo, troops, equipment and heavy armor were moving towards the DMZ. If more shells for those howitzers and rocket launchers was moving up in those numbers, then ...

"Okay, great job Lt. Captain, get CINCCFC on the line immediately, I MEAN RIGHT NOW!"

He didn't know how long he had ... let's see ... two hours. Looking at those photos it could go anytime now. Which would mean ... my God, their special forces ... the sappers!

"Lt. Finley, you get the Base Commander on the line NOW! I want to speak with the commander of the Security Forces here on the base as well. Then line up the same at Camp Humphreys, Camp Henry, Husan Air Base and Osan Air Base ... in fact, the more you can conference on the line, the better."

February 28th, 2006, that same time
Forward Observation Post (FOP)
West of Chorwon, Along the DMZ, Korea

There was a lot of activity out there tonight. You could hear the Korean voices drifting across the DMZ along with a lot of equipment moving. But, no one had ventured out into the forbidden area between the two nations, so the small contingent of American soldiers who were on duty here tonight kept their eyes and ears open, but did not display overt concern.

Except for Private Teasedale. He was out at the observation post right now along with the Corporal while the other six men of their squad rested back in the FOP bunker or monitored the listening, infrared or electronic devices that were also watching their section of the DMZ. Three, who were not on watch duty at the time, played games, read books or slept, waiting their watch.

But, Private Teasedale was new to Korea, having been "in country" for only six weeks now. As a part of his "in processing" he had heard several lectures, read some operations manuals and listened to the required audio tapes. One tape he could not get out of his mind was the excellent report that the Commanding General of all USFK had given to the United States Congress a few years earlier. It had been so succinct, so well delivered, that the 2nd Division had made it a standard part of their "in processing" for new arrivals. The one phrase from that tape that had been riveted into Private Teasedale's mind that day had been this:

"The North Korean Army would be able to sustain a rate of artillery fire of five hundred thousand shell per hour for prolonged periods."

As he sat there this evening, watching the DMZ with his night vision scope, hearing all of the Korean talk, movement and equipment across the zone ... that statement kept coming back to his mind again and again.

" ... a rate of artillery fire of five hundred thousand shell per hour for prolonged periods."

Now, from across the way, the Private heard several whistles being blown. Sounded like dozens of them, no ... scores, maybe hundreds. He turned to the Corporal, who had also perked up and was listening.

"Corporal, do you hear that? What does it mean? Why are they blowing those ...."

As he asked this question, from down the tunnel in the bunker he heard the land-line begin to ring.

"Rinnnggg, Rinnnggg, Rinnnggg"

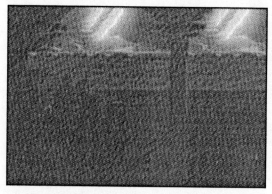

North Korea launches missile barrage.

... and then the entire sky, from horizon to horizon along, the DMZ in front of him lit up brightly. But it was a flash that did not die. It kept being repeated time and again, giving the appearance of a huge, bright strobe light, just below the horizon over there and stretching for miles in either direction. In addition, thousands of streaks of light reached rapidly across the sky in what must have appeared to be the grandest and mightiest fireworks display of all time … except that these streaks and that whistling sound, were all coming towards the young private.

Then the 127mm rockets and the 122mm, 152mm and 180mm high explosive (HE) rounds began to land and nothing else mattered.

March 1, 2006, 05:30 local
Politburo
Beijing, China

"Kim Jong-Il's forces are moving forward faster than expected Mr. President. Since the initiation of hostilities last evening, the entire DMZ has been over run and the attack is proceeding ahead of schedule."

"Democratic People's Republic forces are advancing along a broad front and are entering Pyokche and Uijongbu on the outskirts of Seoul. The civilian population is in complete pandemonium and the chaos is hampering ROK and US forces. This morning's missile strikes in Seoul have included strikes on their financial and governmental centers that have hit several of the high rise buildings. Subsequently, many of these buildings have collapsed into piles of rubble adding to the chaos."

"This missile and artillery barrage is being coupled with massive air strikes in advance of the three pronged assault on Seoul. One leg of that assault is a thrust at Inchon along the coast, which is hitting the outskirts of Seoul to the west. This is the army group now entering Pyokche. A second thrust is coming from the north through Uijongbu. The third thrust is splitting off several divisions from the attack down the middle of the country through Ch'unch'on, approaching Seoul from the north and east."

"Along the coast DPRK forces have advanced as far as YangYang. Right now, the penetration, except for small pockets of resistance, is along a line running from YangYang, eastward to Ch'ung'on, over to Uijongbu and then to the eastern coast at Pyokche. We expect DPRK forces to enter Seoul this afternoon, either tonight or tomorrow morning at the latest. Given the current rate of advance, I would be surprised if it wasn't today."

"We can attribute much of this success to the DPRK special forces who were extremely successful in sabotaging many ROK and US aircraft before they could take off, which were followed up by massive ballistic missile strikes on all airports and airfields. Those strikes are continuing to this moment. Unfortunately, those same forces were not successful in eliminating the U.S. 2nd Infantry Division leadership at Camp Red Cloud, although they did penetrate the perimeter briefly where they attacked a number of housing units. This added significantly to the confusion."

Jien Zenim sat back in his custom-made Natuzzi chair and considered the developing world situation. The GIR was continuing to advance in the Middle East, albeit their rate of advance was slowing. The Americans and NATO had been pouring men and equipment into that region for many weeks now and would be in a position to start seriously challenging GIR forces within a few short weeks. Now, they would have this to deal with.

He tried to picture the "situation room" in the White House. Surely they were concerned, perhaps even panicking, worrying about China's response.

"Li, make sure that we open up a direct line call to President Weisskopf. I want to … try and calm the situation … offer to mediate … and make sure word of that is passed onto David Krenshaw at WNN."

Jien doubted that the conversation with Weisskopf would even take place, although the American State Department (and probably their Defense Department too) would be urging the President to avoid any confrontation with China at this point, given the over all world situation.

Jien was well aware of that situation. He and his comrades had been manipulating it towards this for years. After all, the cold war was over, America was the world's only superpower and that had warranted those deep cuts. It just made such perfect sense, particularly when China was catching the capitalism fever and wanted to "open" its markets, particularly when so many American politicians were so easily bought off with money or vice.

No, Jien knew exactly what situation America's military was in, and what situation his own was in. The irony of it was, that America had funded both for their own cut backs and China's build-up with their own money!

Now, the Americans were in a situation where a single major theater engagement was a stretch for them … and now they were facing three major theater engagements in Turkey, Saudi/Egypt and now Korea. Soon, the beleaguered Americans would be facing a fourth theater scale confrontation, and Jien had insured that the fourth one, his own, would be the largest and costliest from the outset. China's role in "Breath of Fire" would be, "the straw that broke the camel's back", as the Americans would say … or as Sun Tsu taught, the application of overwhelming force when your enemy was distracted in another direction.

In the mean time, Jien would cause as much political and moral damage as he could by continuing to manipulate the American public through their press up until the very 11th hour. The more dissension, the more discord, the more confusion and loss of confidence he could instill in them, the better.

February 28, 2006, 13:17 AM EST
Situation Room, White House
Washington, D.C.

"This is an unmitigated disaster! Akin to what happened in the Philippines after Pearl Harbor. "

"You are telling me we are down to 50% operational strength for the 7th Air Force over there ... in just one day? How in the hell did that happen, Jeremy? ... and we're down to 65% in terms of combat effectiveness for the 2nd Infantry Division."

"Gentlemen, we were supposed to be on heightened security alert and measures at all bases! The North was conducting exercises that emulated this very attack!"

Jeremy Stone understood his President's frustration. Jeremy was frustrated too, and knowing that the President himself had been one the most successful military general's in the last half century, he could just imagine the old general wanting to come out in him. But, while being frustrated, he could also understand why the disaster in Korea was occurring.

"Mr. President, I have to be honest with you. It may not help at the moment, in fact the only thing that will help those boys over there at the moment is their grit and determination and that of our allies, the South Koreans ... and us getting them some relief as quickly as possible. They are going to have to conduct a fighting withdrawal while forces to the south establish a strong defense line. It'll mean abandoning Seoul and Inchon. If we wait though, our forces there are going to be surrounded and we'll be looking at a surrender of those forces in a matter of weeks, if not days."

"But, in terms of the current disaster, Mr. President, we were just too thin. When our enemy can lob ballistic missiles and rockets at us by the thousands per hour, sir, there just are not enough Patriot, Improved Hawk or any other defensive missiles to get them all. ... and we've been watching them build up like this for years, while we staffed down and tried to "talk". No disrespect meant, Secretary Reissinger, but we should have backed up all of that talk with a credible force."

"The results were predictable. Our defenses were overwhelmed, despite our hi-tech advantage. In addition, despite the increased security measures of the last few years, it turns out the North Koreans had dozens of sleepers working at each of our bases. People we had known and reviewed for years, in some cases decades. That contributed to the sabotage of our aircraft, equipment and storage as they let the DPRK special forces units onto the base in most cases, and conducted some of the sabotage themselves in others."

"Had it not been for one quick thinking Intelligence Officer in the 2nd Infantry Division, a Colonel Martinez I believe, we very well could have been decapitated as well. As it was, his quick analysis of recon photos and NRO satellite photos from guess who? ... that's right, from Tom Lawton's people ... and Martinez' quick witted decisions, probably saved the command echelon of many of our prime units there. The 2nd Infantry Division, the 19th Theater Army Area Command, the 8th and 51st Fighter wings of the 7th Air Force, the 6th Calvary Brigade and the CINC of all USFK were each warned in time. Those warnings allowed those commanders and most of their staffs to be surrounded by security troops very quickly and escorted to secure areas while the attacks were being made. Unfortunately we still lost some of their staff, and the commanders of the 1st Signal Brigade and the 8th Military Police Brigade were lost due to enemy action last night."

"Since then, as you know, the situation has been chaotic, and there's been a lot of ground loss ... and we're going to lose more. But our forces are beginning to come together along with the ROK forces who were equally targeted. I believe they are capable of a fighting withdrawal while we establish a firm line further to the south."

The President knew Jeremy was right. America had been downsizing the military for years after the end of the cold war with the Soviet Union. Even the horrific terrorist attacks of 2001 had not altogether halted that trend ... but it had slowed or abated it in some critical areas.

"Well, thank God for small miracles," thought the President. He would hate to have to respond to these crises had the headlong trends continued completely unabated. Nonetheless, America had continued to bank on and count on the "silver bullets" of high tech. That was good as long as you had plenty of it to shoot, and keep shooting at the enemy. It generally worked GREAT for small or single theater confrontations. But now, the whole world was erupting around them and there just weren't enough. Not enough forces overall, and certainly not enough hi-tech inventory. They were going to have to implement a full-scale war time production effort. He'd have to address that in his speech to the nation tonight.

"Mr. President, how do you want to respond to this request by Jien Zenim for a conference? He wants to try and mediate."

The President knew exactly how he wanted to respond.

"Fred, I firmly believe that Jien Zenim is up to his eyeballs in all of this. I think it is only a matter of time before his hammer falls, and I believe we MUST respond decisively in Korea to have any hope of forestalling that. Tell President Zenim that I appreciate his offer, but regrettably, given the circumstances, we will have to talk later. Perhaps in a few weeks, after we get some help to South Korea and start pushing these tyrants back, then we can hold a summit. Tell him three to four weeks and arrange it. ... and just for the sake of everyone sitting here, my message at such a summit is going to be VERY direct to the Chinese. DO NOT interfere. I will also make sure that they understand that North Korea is not going to exist as a nation state after the fighting is over and President Jien Zenim can take that to the bank!"

"Now, Tim and Jeremy, we are going to have to call up significant numbers of reserves, I'm talking a million men to add to our current forces. We are going to also have to push very hard for much more enlistment. I want a package from the Congress, committed to today after their formal declaration of war on North Korea that gives great incentive for folks to join. Something like the old GI bill used to be, with just as many perks. We will have to make those perks retroactive for everyone who is already serving. It's going to cost a lot ... but not nearly as much as the other measures we are going to have to take if we expect the light of liberty to continue burning brightly in the world. As much as those costs may add up to, they will be NOTHING compared to what it will cost should we fail, because I believe THAT cost will end up being our national survival."

"Okay, Tim and Jeremy, here's what I would like to do in broad strokes. I want to establish two Marine Air Ground Task Forces (MAGTF's) for Korea, each made up of two augmented MEU's. Can we do that?"

The Secretary of Defense, Tim Hattering, deferred to General Stone.

"I believe we can Mr. President. We have two of our east coast MEU's already on the ground in the Mid-East, but the Army had built up enough force there now that they can bring one of them home. If we take the other East Coast MEU, the 24th, and have it do a rapid transit to the west coast for temporary basing there, we could move all three west coast MEU's towards Korea to form up with the 31st in Okinawa. I would want to have them escorted by two Carrier Battle groups that would join up with the Kitty Hawk out of Japan."

The President considered this, and then looked at Tim.

"Well, Tim, what do you think?"

Tim was thinking about the strain on the numbers of amphibious assault ships and Carriers. Four carriers already in the Mid East, and now three in the Far East ... that's seven of twelve, and three were in service life upgrades. Similar numbers existed for their twelve large amphibious assault ships.

"Mr. President, we are going to have to either halt or expedite some of the Service Life Programs that are going on if we want to have any Carriers and Amphibious Assault ships in reserve. Also, we are going to have to have the Marines begin to form up more MEU's. If we do that to backfill, I would feel very comfortable expediting this."

The President was in high gear. He was beginning to see what types of things he had to get done to stabilize an extremely dire and unstable condition. He felt he had the team here with him who could make it happen.

"Great, I will sign off on the requisite orders. I want each MAGTF to comprise ten thousand fighting men and I want them in Korea yesterday. You guys make it happen, the carriers will stay on in support."

"In addition, since we already have the 82nd Air Borne in Turkey and the 101st in Egypt, Jeremy, we're going to have to look at flying more men into Korea. I want another ten thousand men already there when these MAGTF's arrive. The materiel is already pre-positioned for this."

At this, Tim Hattering spoke.

"Pardon the interruption Mr. President, but our military transport and our civilian air carriers are maximized right now trying to build up our forces in the Middle East and still maintain their commercial operations. We're going to have to get significant additional buy-in from the commercial sector to make what you just stated possible, and we will have to subsidize them if they are to remain financially viable."

Norm's mind was already out in front of his Secretary of Defense. When he thought full-scale war mobilization, he meant it. America already had a model for such efforts and he had lived through it as a young boy.

"I understand Tim. You have done a GREAT job working with the airlines to date, and now we are going to have to depend on you to even do more. I will make this a part of the speech tonight, we're going to have to get more lift out of the commercial carriers. Please have the FAA Administrator and the appropriate Congressional representatives meet with us this afternoon."

February 28, 2006, 19:12 PM, EST
WNN Broadcasting Studios
New York City, New York

As the commercial was running, David thought how much he continued to enjoy his job, a job he felt he did extraordinarily well. Here he was, continuing in his plum anchor roll, while being on the Board of Directors and the President of World Wide News for WNN, involved in the principle management decisions for the entire network. When you add to that his bird's eye view of emerging events through his membership in the prestigious Council on International Relations, well life just didn't get much better. Perhaps in a few years, he'll allow these roles to propel him into politics. But now, the thirty-second light had come on and he needed to get back to today's dramatic events.

"This is David Krenshaw, back with WNN. Continuing the status of fighting in Korea. WNN has learned that the Combined Command structure of both the Republic of Korea and the United States have decided to withdraw from Seoul and Inchon rather than fight what they consider to be a losing battle and risk having what forces remain being cut off. Those commands indicate to WNN reporters on the scene, that fighting is heavy, that there have been significant losses inflicted upon the North's forces, but that significant losses have been experienced amongst allied forces as well."

"The dramatic pictures you just saw on WNN earlier were of actual fighting in the outskirts of Seoul. As missiles were launched into the heart of Seoul, apparently targeting governmental offices there, you saw the collapse of many high rise buildings within the city itself due to missile impacts that weakened the buildings and the fires which caused those weakened structures to ultimately collapse. The death toll amongst the civilian population in Seoul is thought to number in the many thousands."

"The result has been a further Declaration of War by the U.S. Congress and by the Republic of Korea on North Korea. Almost immediately, the GIR also declared war on South Korea and announced solidarity with North Korea in the name of their CAS economic agreement. By invoking the CAS economic agreements as a reason to enter this conflict, when they are already embroiled in a conflict thousands of mile away with America, the GIR has raised a question that interests the entire world. Where is China in this conflict? What will China's response be?"

"WNN can announce that through an exclusive phone interview, we are in a position to provide some answers and insight into that question."

"Earlier today, I spoke with Li Peng, the head of the Chinese Parliament and a close friend and confident of President Jien Zenim. Li asked me to convey his respect to the American people and indicated that his government was not involving itself in the fight between North and South Korea. He indicated that China viewed it as an internal matter and would not become involved unless it spilled over and began threatening either China or other surrounding nations. He went on to speak of his efforts to communicate with and provide immediate mediation in the conflict … here are the words he spoke during that interview, as recorded earlier this afternoon:"

"The People's Republic of China stands ready to immediately step in and provide mediation of this conflict. We have a vested interest in peace in this part of the world since we are the largest trading partner of the Democratic People's Republic of Korea, and one of America's largest trading partners as well."

"Unfortunately, the current administration in America has indicated that they cannot meet with us on this critical matter for several weeks. This is most unfortunate. We urge the United States to utilize every tool at their disposal to stop the death in Korea, where brother is fighting against brother. We urge them, as we have now for many years, to extract themselves from that conflict so these brothers can most effectively solve their differences without any undue, outside influence or military forces. We urge the American people to prevail upon your elected officials to allow this mediation summit to occur. We have already talked to the Kin Sung-II's foreign minister and there is a willingness to call a halt in place to allow for it."

"That was an exclusive WNN taping of Li Peng, the leader of the Chinese parliament. He has made an extraordinary appeal to mediate and we will keep you informed of those efforts as well as the Weisskopf administration's response to them. Now, onto other news while we wait for the President's national address at 8 PM."

February 28, 2006, 20:00 EST
The Oval Office
Washington, D.C.

"My fellow Americans, I come before you tonight with news that is not pleasant, with news that is in fact distressing. As you are all aware, massive forces of the Democratic People's Republic of Korea, whom we call North Korea, ruthlessly attacked their neighbor to the south and our ally, the Republic of Korea. This attack was unprovoked and was carried out while North Korean forces were conducting what they called, "training exercise".

"I wish I could tell you that the attack has been foiled and thrown back. I cannot. The harsh reality is that we are rapidly being pushed back on the Korean peninsula. Seoul has been invaded and there is heavy fighting going on there as we speak. Many of you saw the horrific photos of high-rise buildings in Seoul collapsing after being shelled and struck by North Korean missiles. The civilian death count is unimaginable."

"Our forces have fought well, but have also suffered significant casualties."

"As a result, at 5:56 this afternoon, our Congress voted to declare war on the Democratic People's Republic of Korea."

"My fellow citizens, I must be blunt and direct. What we have witnessed in the last few months, the tremendous struggle taking place in the Mid East, and now this dastardly and major attack in the Far East, is rapidly turning into a Third World War. We are ill prepared for it. As a people, we love peace, and I am afraid that our love for peace, which in and of itself is a very good and desirable thing, and our fixation on our material pursuits, has resulted in tremendous complacency and apathy about the dangers that surround us. About the true nature of the world we live in."

"Any individual who has spent any appreciable time outside of the borders of this great Republic has a notion of what that nature is. While conditions vary, particularly in Western Europe, the harsh reality is that most areas of the world are terribly poor, and they are very ignorant and they are easily taken advantage of. This gives rise to despots and tyrants who seek to control those people and others in their quest for power, riches and vice."

"In short, it is a dangerous world, dangerous for truth, dangerous for the open study of knowledge ... in short, dangerous for liberty.'

"But, we are "the land of the free" and we must face these dangers directly and with squared shoulders, or we will forever sacrifice and surrender those liberties to those who would take them by force and destroy them.""

"We have come awfully close to doing just that my fellow Americans. We convinced ourselves that the world was a safer place to live in with the demise of the former Soviet Union, and then we began to act like it actually was. We cut our armed forces, we reduced our numbers and our research into future programs and procurement. We cut training and we glossed it over with a relatively few high technology weapons we convinced ourselves would keep us safe. We were wrong.""

"I led the military campaign in the Persian Gulf a number of years ago where we utilized many of those high technology weapons to win a war and to make it look much easier than it was. We were lucky my fellow Americans. We were lucky that the tyrant of the day wavered and did not push on into Saudi Arabia at the time. We were lucky that his conscripts were more afraid of him than they were of us and were thus willing to surrender in droves when the actual fighting started. Finally, we were lucky we were still basking in the appropriate build-up of arms and materiel that had occurred under the prior President, one of the greatest President's in my opinion.""

"As a result, we squandered away the very numbers needed to confront any truly dangerous tyrant, one who uses charisma and the strength of their personality to convince an entire people to follow a misguided cause. We have slashed our defenses, we have been too proud, and we have placed ourselves in positions of dependency when we ought not to have done so.""

"All the while, conditions in the world as a whole have not changed. Evil still exists in great abundance. Ignorance still exists in large measure, poverty still exists in most places. All of these remain a seed ground for evil and conspiring forces. Unfortunately, as we have found by spending trillions, it is a condition that we cannot fix. The peoples of these nations have to fix it, they have to want to fix it. We can only assist those who really do, otherwise, we are planting the seeds and funding the very forces that would destroy us, who hate our liberty and way of life. This is the harsh, cruel reality of the world in which we live. It has always been so.""

"We saw a natural evolution of this in 2001 when one such tyrant attacked our nation and killed many innocent people. It was a misguided, evil effort to lash out at and destroy our morale, our financial capabilities and thereby our influence. We responded and brought that individual and his organization to justice, along with the few governments who were willing to support him."

"Now, the evolution of despair, ignorance and hate has stepped up. Now we find, once again on the world scene, ruthless dictators and despots who have convinced entire people's to follow them and support them in their tyranny. We can no more allow this to stand than we could allow the acts of September 11, 2001. In fact, even more so, we must come together as a people and like, "the greatest generation", we must astound the world with our ability to produce, to unite and to successfully confront tyranny."

"Let there be no mistake, it is going to take just such an effort. We face a situation every bit as immediate and as dangerous as our fathers and grandfathers faced in the early nineteen forties. Perhaps even more so."

"So, to the questions of how do we respond? And how do we avoid this in the future? I intend to give some answers tonight. I intend, with the support of the congress and the support of the people, to place us on a path to win this war. We WILL win it decisively and will win it in a manner that will cause us to never forget, to never allow ourselves to become so complacent again. Here is the formula. It is not a new formula my fellow Americans. It is the same formula our founders used to win our independence and vouchsafe those unalienable rights that have been endowed to each of us by, as our founders labeled Him, "the Creator".

"First, we must immediately embark on a full war time mobilization. A mobilization of fighting forces and a mobilization of industry to give those forces what they need to wage and win this struggle."

"In that regard, I am calling up one million reserves. Details of this call up will be announced by the Secretary of Defense starting tomorrow. In addition, I have spoken with the leaders in Congress and gotten their support in calling for a significant increase in what used to be called the GI Bill. We will elevate it to what it used to be in terms of providing for education, health care, homesteading and job opportunity for those who serve."

"I expect this to be a long and costly war. We may yet suffer attacks on this land. We are going to need every able-bodied man between the ages of 18 and 45 to be prepared to serve their country, at home and abroad. We do not want and have no plans to institute a "draft", we want volunteers and we are going to make it worth the while of those who do so. It will take the agreement and the willingness to do so of those who are not in a position to serve to make this possible. I ask you tonight my fellow Americans for that commitment, for that willingness."

"But that is not all I ask of you."

"For those not able or willing to sign up directly with the military, our Director of Homeland Security will be announcing in the next few weeks a program for "Home Guard" units who will work with their local Sheriffs to help maintain security here on our shores. These units will be volunteer units, they will be armed, they will be trained and they will have communications devices to get them immediately in touch with their local sheriff's and through them with their state's National Guard. The training, the weapons and the communications will be provided by the government and will become the property of those who volunteer."

"With respect to mobilization of fighting forces, we are going to have to come to the aide of our allies and friends, and our own forces in Korea. I have ordered up immediate relief in terms of several Marine units and the ships and aircraft to support them. I am ordering significant ground forces to be ferried over by aircraft, both military and commercial. "

"Now this is going to place a significant burden on our airline travel, our commercial travel. But the need is urgent and the situation is critical. We need to move ten thousand men to Korea, and escort them safely there, in the next two weeks. These men will then be supported by several times their number arriving with the Marine Task Forces. In order to do this, restrictions on commercial flying will be announced tomorrow by all of the major airlines. These restrictions are voluntary ... but once volunteered, I have made it plain that they will be in existence through the duration of the emergency. I have requested and received the agreement from the CEO's of all of the major airlines ... I am proud of these patriot leaders in our business community."

"In that vein, let me turn to the second requirement for our mobilization. That is our tremendous industrial capacity. Sadly, we have squandered much of it away over the last few years in the name of building a so called "service economy". Well, in my mind a "service economy" is an economy of servants, and it has placed us in this very dangerous situation. In the name of so called "free trade", we have shipped much of our capacity off shore, in some cases to the very nations that now either threaten us, or are being destroyed by those who do. In order for trade to really be "free", it must also be fair, and we have neglected that side of the equation, particularly for our own industries. We cannot afford to allow this to continue. Not for energy, not for manufacturing, not for food, and not for any other strategic and critical industry. "

"Therefore, today, I am announcing all of the following:

1. There will be an immediate cessation of all restrictions on the search for, and production from, oil reserves that are local to the United States and its territories. This includes the Alaskan north-slope fields and the fields just off of our west coast. We were already moving in this regard, but were being severely hampered by provisions of several Acts of Congress, some of which had expired but were still funded. All acts that have expired will, as of this date, no longer be funded or recognized by this administration or any of its agencies. Other acts hindering our ability to remain energy free in either the petroleum, nuclear, coal or alternate fuel areas will be rescinded by Congress. I have requested this of the leadership in Congress and both sides of the aisle have assured me, in the interest of national security and survival that it will be done. I have instructed all of the Directors and Secretaries of Executive Branch agencies accordingly through executive order.

2. I have requested and expect to get agreement from Congress and from all state governors, agreement regarding the establishment of priorities for the use of strategic materiel required for the war effort, or the re-institution of industries critical to that effort. This will result in some rationing by the state governments for private citizens and non-essential industries. I want to thank the governors who have already responded and those I expect will respond, along with the congressional leadership for their approval of these measures. Again, once implemented, they will be in effect for the duration of the emergency. I expect that over the next few weeks, executive branch agency heads and state officials will announce the specific allocation plans.

3. I have instructed the Secretary of Commerce to draw up import and export guidelines, similar to those we recently implemented with the CAS that will now apply generally. We intend to allow free trade, my fellow Americans, but never again will our free trade be unfair to our own. Any nation seeking to do business with America will have to do it on our terms, or not at all. They will have to comply with our standards, or not at all. If their governments subsidizes their efforts and they comply with our standards, then our producers will either get an amount equal to what that government if providing, and it will come from THAT government, or they can take their business elsewhere.

    The playing field will either be level, or they will not be allowed on it in America. In this way, we will keep our industries competitive right here in America if they are willing to apply that Yankee ingenuity we have always been famous for. It will also allow us to slowly remove the artificial supports that have been put in place in some industries that never should have been there in the first place. They were efforts that tried to address playing fields that was so lopsided that they could not hope to be addressed. We will remove the burden from the American taxpayer and put it where it belongs, on those nations and those companies wanting to do business here."

"Other measures may become necessary as time goes on and depending on circumstances with the war effort. As they do, I will speak with your representatives, your state leaders and with you as I have done here tonight."

"In closing, my fellow Americans, this is a time for three things:"

"First, it is once again a time for national prayer. We must unite our collective faith so we are equal to the challenges that lie before us. We have a long road, it is a road that may get worse before it gets better. It will require our collective faith to walk that road. Therefore, I am calling for March 1st to be established as an annual National Day of Prayer and Reflection. All federal government offices will release their workers tomorrow at 11:30 AM and allow them to gather in their churches, their synagogues, their assembly halls, their mosques and their own quiet places for the remainder of the day. In future years, this will be a full day holiday."

"Second, it is a time for unity. Let us put aside all of the hyphenated Americans. Let us put aside our differences, so that we might remain free to have them. Let us work together as compatriots, as brother and sister Americans to walk this path, to climb this hill, to put down this dark tyranny. It is a tyranny that would force on our friends, and ultimately on us, the denial of individual rights in the name of some collective, a collective invariably controlled and ruled by a select few. We have seen this ideology in our world my fellow Americans, history is littered with the skeletons and debris of the peoples who mistakenly embraced it, and with those peoples who were not resolute or strong enough to stand up against it. We shall not be such debris … we shall stand!"

"Finally, it is a time for sacrifice. The collective effort to produce the materiel, the arms, the personnel and the equipment to allow our eventual triumph is going to require that we step outside our comfort zone. It is going to require that we willingly, voluntarily give up some of our creature comforts through the duration of this crisis, so that we can retain them in perpetuity for our children and grandchildren."

"I urge each of you, to voluntarily find the ways you can give, to find the ways you can help, to work with your relatives, friends and neighbors, to follow your elected representatives."

"... and I commit to you, that I, and each member of my staff, and every member of any agency working for me will sacrifice similarly and accordingly. I commit that under our constitution, whatever measures we take will be in strict accordance with that constitution. It is the banner we look to, after we look to our faith. It is the instrument all of your public representatives and officials swear an oath to bear true faith and allegiance to. I commit to each of you, that throughout this crisis, I will insure that I am always true to that oath, and that everyone working for me is true to it, or be removed from office, so help me God!"

"God bless you each. May He be with us all as we go forward. May God bless America this night and in the future to be strong, to be brave, to be committed and to be true ... whatever the cost. Good night."

CHAPTER 10

"When China awakens, the world will tremble." - Napoleon Bonaparte

March 7, 2006, 06:30 Local
15 Kilometers east of Shanghai
Flag Observation, PLAN 1001 Beijing
China Sea

As Admiral Yao Hsu stood on the flag officer's observation post outside of Air Operations, he turned and looked back over the wake of his flagship as she glided through the mild seas and away from land. Even after all of these years, this was a time he cherished greatly, a time of anticipation and expectation. Every time he made out to sea, he experienced these feelings, and the years and circumstances never seemed to dim them.

Trials for the PLAN's new Sea Control Carrier had gone better than expected and now circumstance dictated that he take her out for a different type of trial, a trial by fire. The apprehension associated with that, with wondering if the tactics, the weapons systems and the experiences so new to the PLAN would be sufficient to the task at hand, understandably dampened the Admiral's normal feelings as they made to sea. But the anticipation and excitement associated with making out to sea, and with testing himself and his nation against their most formidable adversary, overshadowed any apprehension or other concern.

To starboard and perhaps two or three kilometers off his bow, the lead ship of the Haizhou class guided missile destroyer had accelerated to thirty knots to take up its position as the close-in escort for the carrier. As he watched her, his thoughts focused on the undeniable beauty of what he was seeing.

"What a beautiful ship she is ... sleek, low to the water and a match for any surface combatant on earth, even the so called "war God" Aegis cruisers that the U.S. Navy employed."

Thinking of the Americans caused him some reflection. Funny, for many years he felt awed by their navy, their ship handling, the balance of the various ship classes, their carriers, their battle groups ... and particularly the technology they employed. In fact, a lot of that technology had gone into the development of the ship he was standing on. Through so-called "exchange" programs, Admiral Hsu himself had been aboard U.S. Carriers and U.S. Aegis warships in the late 1990's and seen how they functioned. The information and knowledge had been invaluable. In addition, through acquisition of "dual use" technologies, some by bribery, some by clandestine methods and others as simple gifts from the Americans, many of the electronics, sensors and automated controls had been refined far beyond what the PLAN would have been capable of just a few years ago.

But now, all of that had all been improved upon and refined to produce newer classes of ships, newer tactics and newer weapons systems that were, in the Admiral's view, a match for any thing the Americans could offer.

The Beijing task force was centered around the carrier, and included two Haizhou class DDG's, two of the very capable Luhai class DDG's, and four Jiangwei-II class FFG's. All of the Luhai and Jiangwei-II vessels, in addition to their other formidable armaments, had been armed with four of the new LRASD weapons and the targeting and fire control computers and other equipment to control them.

The Beijing itself had a full combat load of twelve SU-30 fighter aircraft, six SU-35 EW/attack aircraft and twelve SU-25 attack aircraft. In addition, she carried four of the new Biao STOL AEW aircraft and four Ka-28 ASW helicopters. All of these were being built in China, and at a rapid production rate to outfit the new carriers being produced.

Beijing's VLS SSM battery.

In addition, the Beijing carried vertical Launch Missiles (VLS) which included forty tubes for anti-aircraft missiles and ten tubes of anti-surface missiles. Unlike the American system, these could all be automatically reloaded within minutes and the Beijing class of carrier carried five reloads for each. The anti-air missiles were the new ship board KS-2 missile which had a range of 45 kilometers and an effective altitude ceiling of 25,000 meters … very effective indeed. The anti-surface missile were the SS-N-26 Yakhont missile (also now license produced within China), which had a range of 300 kilometers and were mach 2.5 sea skimming missiles.

Still, one had to have great respect for the experience, knowledge, tactics, weapons and technology that the Americans employed. They had the operational experience, and they still had the numbers in terms of ships, ship classes and aircraft. One could never underestimate them.

As he thought this, the rising sound of jet turbines pulled his attention to the port launching position. A quick glance to port confirmed that an SU-30 was spooling up, preparing to launch. He glanced at his

An SU-30 prepares to take off from the Beijing.

watch. It read 0635 local. He nodded his head almost imperceptibly. This aircraft was due on station at 0640 for the morning Combat Air Patrol (CAP). Another SU-30, behind and to the side of the first one, also began to spool up. Within forty-five seconds, both aircraft had launched right after one another. As they circled to gain altitude, the Admiral turned and went back inside and made his way through Air Operations towards his cabin.

· "Admiral, a moment if you please."

Captain Tuan Hongwen had waited for the commanding officer of Task Force Beijing to come in before addressing him. Having served for several years with the Admiral in other capacities, he knew of the Admiral's love for taking a moment alone while making out to sea and he had not disturbed him while he took those few moments. The matter was not urgent, but the Admiral did need to hear of it. As Admiral Yao stopped and turned towards him, Captain Tuan continued.

"Admiral, all units report under way towards point SUN. Recent intelligence indicates that a massive American fleet has put to sea and will be rendezvousing with the USS Kitty Hawk near Okinawa within seven days. They are not taking any great pains to hide their intentions."

The Admiral considered this information for a moment and then replied as he continued towards his cabin.

"Thank you Captain. I would not expect the Americans to do anything other than charge forward at this point, particularly given their deteriorating position in South Korea. Keep me appraised ... by the way Tuan, the ship and crew are very fit, my compliments to you and your staff. Until my staff briefing at 0800, I will be in my cabin."

As the Admiral entered his cabin moments later, his eyes were drawn to his locked security safe. He opened it and withdrew his orders. As he took them in hand, he sat down and reviewed them once again.

```
XXXXXXXXXXXXX/////  170003MAR06  \\\\ XXXXXXXXXXXXX
FR: COMEAST                              TO: COMBEIJING
XXXXXXXXXXXXX/////              \\\\ XXXXXXXXXXXXX
SJ: EXECUTE OP SENTINEL
```

1. SITREP: US, UK and CAN naval forces forming for approach Korean peninsula. US CBG's Stennis, Constellation & Kitty Hawk with many Amphib groups. UK two (2) CHV, one (1) LPH. CAN SAG.
2. Sub threat high
3. ORDERS: Utilize rendezvous point SUN. Coordinate movement and operations of TFs Gansu, Yunman, Fuijan, Hunan, Jilin and Hennan according to op Sentinel. <u>Warning</u>: Prepare execute op DragonsBreath between 14MAR & 16MAR.
4. ROE: weapons status white until execution order.

XOXOXOXOXOXOXOXOXOXOXOXOXOXOXOXOXOXOXO XOXOXOXO

The Admiral reflected on the import of these orders. The moment he, Admiral Li Huang Chin Zhongbaio, General Hunbaio and so many others had worked and planned for so many years was soon to be upon them. The Tactical Attack Ships (TAS) that would be under his command were already under way, with their escorts to their respective operational areas. Others, the first several out of production, were long since under way to their positions off the east and west coasts of America. Those were the most vulnerable, they had no escort and would have to fend for themselves.

If Dragon's Breath were executed, and with these orders it appeared almost a certainty, his life, and the life of all his countrymen would change dramatically. If successful, it would place China and the Coalition of Asian States in the forefront of economic and political development for the entire western Pacific and Asian areas for the foreseeable future. If it failed, they would have a much more difficult time attaining that goal.

But, he did not expect it would fail. The Americans were so predictable, and they felt themselves unassailable. Despite their bruises and losses in the Mid East, they felt that these had occurred principally in the air and against overwhelming number where they had inflicted severe losses on those numbers. They simply could not conceive that they could also be assailed on the open seas ... or that a true military strike was possible on their own shores.   Well, Dragon's Breath would either prove the planning, commitment and strategy of the leaders in the People's Republic to be accurate and successful, or it would prove that the American arrogance was well founded. It was now time to find out which it would be.

He looked again at his watch, 0655. Time to plan his staff meeting for 0800.   In that meeting, after his intelligence people spoke, after the commanders of the various ships in his Task Force had the opportunity to speak, he would brief them all on the true nature and import of their orders.

March 7, 2006, 04:25Local
250 nautical miles West of San Diego
Rendezvous Point Designated Point Conception
Eastern Pacific

The orders that the President had issued had been reviewed and the details developed for the support of South Korea. Those detailed orders for troops embarking on air carriers, and for Marines embarking on naval vessels had been passed down the line and were now being carried out. As airliners flew over the Pacific from various points in the country, ships of the U.S. Navy set sail from all along the western coast of the United States.

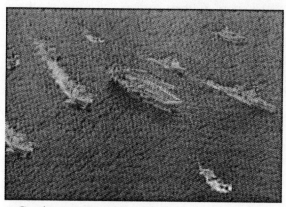

Now, the many ships that would be transiting the Pacific to Korea were gathering at their initial rendezvous point, point Conception   The gathering force would be the largest task force of U.S. Navy warships in the Pacific since the World War II.

Carrier group seven nears point Conception.   The Task Force would use   the   designated number for the Combined Task Force (CTF) in the Western Pacific, CBT 77, which would be under the overall command of Admiral Reginald Patterson.

To prepare for that transit across the Pacific, large portions of CBT 77 were gathering off the California coast. That transit group would consist of two CTF's, CTF 77.2 and CTF 77.3

CTF 77.2 would be centered on Carrier Group 7 comprised of the USS John Stennis (CVN 74) and its escort and support vessels. CTF 77.2 would also include two augmented Amphibious Squadrons (PHIBRONs). The first would be PHIBRON 3, centered on the USS Bonhomme Richard (LHD 6) Amphibious Ready Group (ARG) embarking the 11th MEU. The second would be PHIBRON 1, centered on the USS Peleliu (LHA 5) ARG, embarking the 15th MEU.

CTF 77.3 would be centered on Carrier Group 2 comprised of the USS Constellation (CV 64) and its escort and support vessels. CTF 77.3 would also include the augmented PHIBRON 7, centered on the USS Wasp (LHD 1) ARG, embarking the 13th MEU.

Once the transit groups reached the Okinawa area, they would be joined by CBT 77.1, which would include Carrier Group 5, centered on the USS Kitty Hawk (CV 63) and its escort and support vessels. CBT 77.1 would also include PHIBRON 11, centered on the USS Essex (LHD 2) ARG, embarking the 31st MEU. Carrier Group 5 and PHIBRON 11 were permanently deployed in Japan and at Okinawa respectively.

Altogether, three Carrier Groups and four Amphibious Squadrons would be included in the task force. Each of the Carrier Groups would be comprised of the following:

One (1)	Aircraft Carrier (CV or CVN)
Two (2)	Aegis Cruisers (CG)
One (1)	Burke Class Guided Missile Destroyers (DDG)
One (1)	Spruance Class Destroyer (DD)
One (1)	Oliver Hazard Perry Guided Missile Frigate (FFG)
Two (2)	Improved Los Angeles Attack Submarines (SSN)
One (1)	Fast Combat Support Ship (AOR)

Each augmented Amphibious Squadron would consist of the following:

One (1)	Amphibious Assault Ship (LHD or LHA)
Two (2)	Amphibious Transport Docks (LPD)
Two (2)	Dock Landing Ships (LSD)
One (1)	Burke Class Guided Missile Destroyers (DDG)
One (1)	Spruance Class Destroyer (DD)
One (1)	Oliver Hazard Perry Guided Missile Frigate (FFG)
One (1)	Replenishment Oiler (T-AO)

In addition, attached to each of the CTFs in transit, sailing with one of the augmented PHIBRONs, the following ships were included:

One (1)	Amphibious Cargo Ship (LTKA)
One (1)	Ammunition Ship (T-AE)
One (1)	Combat Stores Ship (T-AFS)
One (1)	Oliver Hazard Perry Guided Missile Frigate (FFG)

This amounted to eighty U.S. Navy warships, fully one fifth of the entire U.S. Navy war fleet. Onboard these ships would be over twenty-five thousand sailors. In addition, there were over twenty thousand U.S. Marines embarked on the ships of the various PHIBRONs.

Off the southern coast of Japan the plan called for CTF 77 to be joined by two allied Task Forces. One was a British task force centered on two of their Invincible Class jump jet carriers (CVH) and two of their newest amphibious ships, the HMS Ocean (LPH) and the HMS Albion (LPD), along with several escorts and support vessels. The second was a Canadian Task Force consisting of two Iroquois guided missile destroyers (DDG's), two Halifax guided missile frigates (FFG's) and two new Canadian sealift ships. These two task forces were transporting another three thousand troops to assist the United States and the Republic of Korea in their fight on the peninsula.

March 7, 2006, that same time
250 nautical miles West of San Diego
Task Force Commander's Cabin, USS Lake Chaplain (CG 57)
Eastern Pacific

JT Samson was enjoying himself immensely, despite the gravity of the situation. The very fact that he was a part of a very limited press pool on this mission to South Korea had to be one of the high points of his career as a journalist ... an admittedly "conservative" journalist.

As the owner and Chief Editor of SierraLines, JT's reputation for ferreting out stories and then reporting on them from a VERY pro-American standpoint ("pro" in the sense that JT ALWAYS insisted on coming at his reporting and editorials from a Constitutional perspective) preceded him. That reputation had caught the administration's eye when JT had thoroughly derailed a press conference by Li Peng, the head of the Chinese Parliament, in Damascus back in January. The pointed question he had asked, had gotten him an invite to the White House. There, the President's chief of staff, at the direction of the President, had personally briefed him on the situation and indicated how the President "hoped" at least some in the media would handle that particular story once they had all of the "facts". The

President had even given his permission to use the Chief of Staff specifically as the source.

The ensuing story had vaulted SierraLines into the spotlight and finally established once and for all that an Internet News outlet could compete head-to-head with the major networks. It had also earned JT a "point" position on any story associated with the war just by requesting it. He had selected to be "point" on this operation. Tens of millions of Americans were anxiously awaiting his daily reports, subject to military screening, regarding the progress of the largest U.S. naval combat operation since World War II.

USS Bohnomme Richard.

JT was now waiting to board a Sea Hawk helicopter to return to the USS Bonhomme Richard, the ship on which he was embarked. The USS Lake Chaplain, an Aegis guided missile cruiser, was Admiral Patterson's flagship for the entire combined task force.

JT had just completed his initial interview with the Admiral. Calling it an interview was really a stretch. Actually the Admiral had invited JT over to introduce himself and to make sure that he was being treated according to the guidelines that had been established.

It was clear that the Admiral was very interested in getting a clear, concise, accurate and positive report back to the American people regarding this operation. JT was committed to all of those things, but would allow the "positive" portion of it to be decided by the people, and he made sure that the Admiral understood it.

The Admiral had understood and indicated he was convinced that if the report were simply clear, concise and accurate, that the positive portion would take care of itself. He had ended their time together with a hearty handshake, sincere thanks, and a statement to his Chief of Staff, Commander Lewis, to see to JT's needs and schedule a more thorough interview within the next few days.

JT would include this, and his impressions of it, in his evening "update".

March 11, 2006, 16:42 WST
Marine Recruit Training Depot
San Diego, California

Alan could not believe how strong his brother had gotten. He had just given him a hug, and had squeezed as hard as he could to try and impress Leon. But the squeeze back had nearly cracked Alan's ribs! Leon must have known it, because he lightened up at about the moment Alan thought he couldn't take any more. Neither brother had said anything, they had just looked at one another with that "knowing" look.

Alan was so proud of Leon … he looked so good in his Marine uniform. It was clear that Leon could not be any prouder than he had been when he showed Alan and their mother the Eagle, Globe and Anchor emblem of the U.S. Marine Corps that he had earned. The emblem had been given to him by his DI after he had completed the Crucible, two weeks ago. The Crucible was the supreme test for Marine Corps recruits. It was where they either made it or broke it. A 54 hour physical, mental and moral test which included food and sleep deprivation while marching over forty miles to obstacles ranging from the long march, to combat assault courses, to problem solving and reaction course, to the team building stations spread out along the way. Once a recruit successfully completes that test, from thereafter they are one of the few and the proud. Leon had completed it, and he was proud. He was proud of himself, proud of Billy, proud of his new friends, and proud of his country for giving him the opportunity.

Alan moved out of the way for his Mom to get a hug. As Leon hugged his Mom, and held on tight for several seconds, Geneva Campbell said,

"Boy, I am so proud of you! Just look at yourself. I wish your daddy could see you now."

Leon considered this for a moment, and then, bowing his head so no one would notice the tears, he said,

"Mom, I believe he does see it … I really believe he knows."

Right then, Billy Simmons walked up, with his Mom, Cindy.

"Leon … bro! How does it feel? We actually did it man, can you believe it, we are now officially U.S. Marines !" After Billy and Leon exchanged congratulatory bear hugs, Geneva embraced Billy, giving him a big kiss and asked "What's next for you boys ?" Billy replied : "Now, Mrs. Campbell we're off to Camp Lejeune over in North Carolina to get into our Infantry training and then some specific Military Occupational Specialties (MOS) that we're both going after."

As Leon and Billy were talking, Geneva noticed Cindy holding on to her son's arm like she didn't ever want to let go. She didn't see Billy's Dad, Jess.

"Cindy, where's Jess?"

Cindy turned to Geneva, and smiling, responded,

"Oh, Geneva, he's off doing what these boys are learning. He got his orders several weeks ago, and off he went. He's over in the Mid East somewhere. I got a letter from him just last week. He's involved with something all hush, hush because he can't say a thing about where he is. But, I've gotten use to it. The good Lord will take care of Jess and me too, until we are reunited."

"Well, why don't we all go and get us some dinner? I'll tell you what, I'll treat the whole bunch of you!"

March 12, 2006, 19:55 EST
Situation Room, White House
Washington, D.C.

"Ladies and gentlemen, I have to warn you, what you are about to see is EXTREMELY disturbing and EXTREMELY graphic. We have all heard rumors and talk about the atrocities being committed b North Korean forces in the South, and particularly in Seoul. What you are about to witness is documented proof of that. Anyone who either does not want to witness the following, or who feels their stomach may rebel, please step out into the waiting area and we will invite you back in after the film."

Despite the warning from the President's Chief of Staff, no one left. They were all leaders of their nation. None of them got any pleasure or approved of graphic violence or sex, but they would not step back from the reality of the situation in Korea either. They knew that if such a culture and society were allowed free reign in America the same thing would happen. They knew that if they did not stand up to it while it was afflicting their friends and allies, they opened the door to the possibility that it could come to these shores. So, despite the Chief of Staff's warning they all watched with misgivings as the film was started.

As the film was played, on a number of occasion exclamations of "My God," "Dear God, no," "sweet Jesus," "those sorry bastards," and many other such comments were made by those in attendance.

What the film showed was the literal rape of Seoul. A U.S. Army cameraman, who had gotten separated from his unit, had been trapped behind lines in Seoul and had been able to record scenes of abject horror. In one particularly graphic incident, lines of North Korean soldiers could be seen coming down either side of a main thoroughfare, with armored vehicles, tanks and IFV's advancing down the center of the street. Smoke was rising from several modern buildings in the background, and rubble from large building collapses could be seen everywhere. There were bodies strewn in the street, the smoking hulks of many cars and a few South Korean APCs.

As this group advanced, they came to the entrance to a building. Apparently, one of the soldiers heard something. He lifted his hand and the line stopped on that side of the street. Crouching down, the lead soldier and seven others rushed into the building. Seconds later, they exited the building, leading a group of four American GI's and a family of six Koreans. The GI's were not armed, had their hands raised, and were forced to lay down spread eagled on the street with two North Korean soldiers holding each down, one with his boot on the neck of each GI. The Korean family was a man in his forties, his wife, what looked to be two teenage daughters and a son about ten years old. They were all being handled roughly by the soldiers.

An officer was called to the front. When he got there he separated the three women. As he was doing so, the father rushed after his wife and daughters and the officer ruthlessly and coldly shot him in the face with his service pistol. He then walked to the ten year old boy, who was standing there sobbing and wetting his pants and shot him in the head. All of the American soldiers were struggling to get up. The officer barked out an order and all four of the Americans were executed where they lay.

All three women were separated. The entire column was now halted, and other soldiers, drivers and vehicle commanders were milling around. The officer barked out several orders in Korean and many of the men began lining up around each of the three women. Then, to the horror of those watching, those poor women were literally raped to death. The cameraman could be heard reciting Mother Mary's and quietly sobbing as he filmed. Long after the women had either lost consciousness or died, the horror continued. Finally, their limp bodies were dragged out into the street and the same officer delivered a final shot to the head of each. Then, the soldiers got back into their vehicles, reformed their lines and continued down the street.

After it was over, the President himself spoke to those gathered.

"Let us spend a moment in silent prayer for these poor souls whom were so brutally sent on to the next life …."

After another moment's pause, the President continued on soberly.

"I showed this to you today so there would be no doubt in your minds what types of horror we are up against over in Korea. Our suspicions of similar things going on in Turkey and parts of Saudi Arabia, were recently confirmed by a young Lieutenant who escaped after being held prisoner after the taking of Incirlik air base. He provided detailed accounts of summary execution of our soldiers by GIR forces. Please listen to his statement"

Turning to his Chief of Staff, he indicated that the audiotape of the Lieutenant's statement should be played. What it recounted, in grim, brutal detail, was the execution of the wounded, and those not deemed having any useful information after the battle at the Adana International Airport. Sixty-three Americans had been captured, of these forty-eight had been executed, by their captors. The young Lieutenant broke down as he recounted the sudden violent death of his friends and comrades. He then told of the brutal death and torture of others as a means of extracting information from those whom the GIR retained. He had escaped several weeks later and had ultimately made it to friendly lines.

"Ladies and gentlemen, this is the nature of those whom we fight. According to this Lieutenant, and we have no reason to doubt him, even senior officers participated in the atrocities he both saw and experienced. Regarding the film out of Korea, our analysts have enhanced parts of that film and found that the North Korean officer during the one scene is a full Colonel."

"Let the reality of these atrocities burn into your memories. We are not a vengeful, or a fanatical people. But, we will have justice and there will be a reckoning and a lasting retribution. As you can see, these incidents were not isolated, or committed by a single unit. They are widespread. Wherever the cameraman went he filmed similar atrocities. We must never forget this."

"This film and the audio tape will be made available to our commanders and to our allies so they can understand the abject brutality and inhumanity of these attackers. We expect in South Korea, it will spur the people as a whole to resist with every thing they have, and they need to. I will spend some time deciding how we can best present the knowledge of this to our own people."

"Now, General Stone, please proceed with the overall military briefing."

General Stone gave a thorough briefing. The military situation was not good. After brief success with a counter attack by the 82nd Airborne Division in the center of the defensive line in Turkey, the GIR funneled more troops and aircraft into the area. Within three days all of the ground made up had been lost. Now, the GIR was closing in on the Turkish capital.

In Saudi Arabia, the situation was similar. GIR forces there had reached the United Arab Emirate (UAE) and had expanded their coastal operations towards the Saudi capital of Riyadh. American armor in all areas was still terribly outnumbered and was falling back. Though they were being forced back, they were exacting a heavy toll on the GIR forces arrayed against them. It was generally considered that once sufficient forces built up in staging areas over along the Red Sea and on the Mediterranean, that US, NATO and other allied forces would push the GIR back from all of their gains.

In Egypt, the General reported that the Libyans and the Sudanese had begun their offensive. Egyptian and US defensive lines were set up well to the east and north of these attacks. Allied forces were doing little more than harassing the advance, hoping that the advancing GIR columns would break themselves on allied defenses and on allied air power, which in that portion of the theater were well established. Israel had offered to help Egypt and the offer was being seriously considered.

As the film had indicated, the situation in Korea continued to be very grim. Seoul had been lost along with Inchon. The remainder of the 2nd Infantry Division and the 6th Cavalry brigade had narrowly avoided encirclement. They were barely able to maintain an orderly fighting withdrawal back along the western side of the peninsula to defenses that were being set up along a line running from Ulchin on the east coast, through Ch'ongju, to P'yongt'aek on the west coast.

U.S. soldiers were arriving by airlift in Pusan and being moved towards the front as rapidly as possible. Even though there were plenty of small arms and ammunition, the heavy armor and artillery available was not sufficient to guarantee that the defensive line could hold. The Marines and their equipment were needed there desperately. They were expected to arrive at Pusan within the next three to four days.

March 14, 2006, 16:20 local
Israeli Defense Force (IDF) positions
Golan Heights

Colonel Abraham Eshkol warmly shook the hand of the American Major who would be working with them for the next few months.

"Major Simmons, it is a real pleasure to meet you, and I don't mind saying, it is even a greater pleasure to meet your aircraft!"

Jess Simmons returned the vigorous handshake.

"Colonel, the feeling is mutual. You sure have a wonderful view up here ... and I might add an extremely defensible one."

The Colonel turned and gazed in the direction the Major was looking. The direction where any attack out of Syria was likely to come from.

"Any military person who comes here immediately grasps the import of this position. It is why we refuse to give it up. We would be foolish to do so."

"The ground was taken from an aggressor nation, the same one that sits out there below us now. I believe should another war come, and it is looking more and more likely, that we will simply annex the area and officially call it a part of Israel and be done with it. That is of course presuming that we are victorious ... and that is the only presumption I will allow on these heights."

Jess could tell that he was going to like this Colonel.

"Colonel, I'll you what, in as much as I am sitting up here with you ... that's the only presumption I will make as well. We are absolutely united on that point ... back home in Texas we would say ... "we're closer than two peas in a pod on that." I hope you understand my meaning.

"Now, let me show you and your people you a thing or two about these twelve birds your country has purchased from mine. After that, either late today, or early tomorrow, we'll take them up and show you a thing or two about what they can do in the air, and you can see for yourself on your equipment how difficult they are to acquire and track"

The Colonel enjoyed this Texas Major's manner of speech, and the way he thought. Beyond that, he was looking forward to having the Comanche helicopters here. Their specifications and reputation preceded them. In addition, despite it being relatively quiet here now, and despite that no Arab country had yet attacked Israel in Hasan Sayeed's war, there was no doubt in the Colonel's mind that they would desperately need these helicopters in the future. In Colonel Eshkol's estimation, that eventuality would be all too soon in coming. He planned, with the U.S. Major's help, to be as prepared as humanly possible when it did.

March 14, 2006, 22:45 EST
North Side of Little Havana
Miami, FL

Isabelle Rodriguez read through the letter from her son, for the sixth time. Her husband Oscar had read it earlier in the afternoon, and had already written a reply and gotten it to the post office that afternoon.

But Isabelle needed more time to gather her feelings, to formulate her thoughts and then to respond to her son as only a mother could.

Dear Mom and Dad,

Basic training is very hard. I mean, I have never worked so hard in all my life! I have never been so sore in my life. I have never been so tired in my life. And I thought I was in pretty good shape.

Dad, the drill instructors are tough, mean and on us all the time. But you know what? I'm grateful for it. After a while you get used to it, and if you respond and don't fight it ... you can almost hear in their next insults and demands ... well, a respect, like they can see you're getting it. Anyway, I know we're going to have to react quickly and be mentally alert and tough to handle what we are being trained for and that's what their job is ... to get us there.

Everyone here talks about it all the time at night when we are in the barracks before bed. We read the letters from our loved ones ... we hear the news. It's pretty plain that our country needs more of us, a lot more. Most here are anxious to get out there and help stop what's going on ... particularly before it can ever get to our shores.

Anyway, I emailed Maria today. You guys should really get a computer and getting set up so you can get email. It makes the communication quicker, cheaper and ... well just more effective.

She seems to be doing very well ... and guess what? We're going to be parents! You and Dad are going to be grandparents! Maybe Maria already told you, but if she hasn't ... let her.

Well, I have to go now, pretty soon it's lights out, and I am dead anyway. I'll write more when I can. Only eight weeks to go!

Your son,

Hernando

Isabelle had to wipe the tears away ... again.

She was so proud of her son ... so happy for him and Maria and the coming baby ... and so scared for him. It was becoming obvious, with the President's remarks, the restrictions on air travel and gasoline ... this was a serious, serious situation and would probably last a long time to come.

As she began to write a reply to her son, she voiced a silent prayer.

"Dear God, please bless Hernando. Help him to be brave, help him to do well. Help him to learn ... and please, please, keep him safe."

March 15, 2006, 01:12 EST
220 Kilometers East of Norfolk, VA
Bridge of PLAN 2004 Guizhou TAS
Atlantic Ocean

Captain Bin Lin had his crew navigate their container vessel turned Tactical Attack Ship into the assigned position he had amongst other cargo and container vessels awaiting transit into U.S. territorial waters. Based on past experience, he calculated that he had about a twenty-four hour wait. That was fine. He expected his execute order to come in the next twelve to

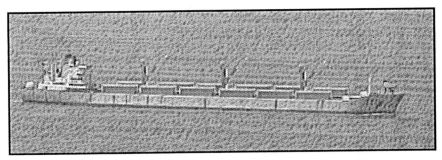

The PLAN Tactical Attack Ship Guizhou, loaded with LRASD's.

eighteen hours, and if it was longer, he was prepared to execute his orders from wherever he stood at the time.

To anyone looking, the ship appeared to be a standard COSCO container vessel. Only by boarding and actually opening the crates that surrounded the LRASD box launchers, or moving the pallets covering the tactical missile hatches, could anyone determine that his vessel was anything more that what it appeared while he operated in a passive mode like he was now.

Captain Bin had at first wished that he had been assigned to the forces that would be confronting the U.S. Navy directly in the western Pacific. He wanted to pit his skills against his American counterparts. Besides, each of those vessels had two escorting Luhu or Luda class destroyers with them, each of which carried four more LRASD weapons along with their other anti-air, anti-submarine and anti-surface weapons. But, as he thought about it more, he felt honored to be one of those who had been selected to be involved with the American mainland directly, even if he was working alone and therefore more vulnerable to counter attack.

If attacked, he had no intention of being boarded. He had a contingent of one hundred well-armed Chinese Marines aboard to prevent that. He had his LRASD weapons to defend against surface or submarine attack, and he had the very capable KS-2 VLS battery, each tube with five reloads, to defend against air attack.

Of course, if the Americans identified him and tasted of any of these measures, they would quickly enough come at him with standoff weapons and overwhelm his defenses. He hoped all of that could be avoided. He would prefer of course, to just fire his missiles, and then turn to the south as planned and make for the COSCO facility in Bermuda.

There were fourteen other such vessels taking up positions along the entire coast of the United States. From Maine to Georgia, from Pensacola to Corpus Christi, and from San Diego to Seattle, PLAN Tactical Attack Ships loaded with over five hundred conventional ballistic missiles were preparing for a surprise attack on the continental United States.

Most would get the execute order while well out to sea like himself. Others would be closer in, and a few might even be in port when the order came. This last condition was, of course to be avoided if at all possible. The new "Homeland Security" rules for vessels desiring to dock at U.S. ports called for a thorough examination of all ship's cargo before they were allowed to enter U.S. waters. This had been implemented not too many months after the attacks of 2001 when American defense analysts began worrying what a terrorist with a large cargo ship could do if it were full of any potent explosive … or just full of the right type of fertilizer for that matter.

All ships had explicit orders to not allow any boarding to occur if at all possible. They were to time their approach to be buffered by other vessels desiring entry. Failing this, they were to stay well out to sea, feigning mechanical problems. If avoidance was impossible and they were boarded, and nothing was found, then they would have to enter port.

Of course, if they were boarded and something was found, the U.S. Coast Guard and U.S. Customs agents would be eliminated along with their vessel. In such an event, that particular vessel would then run for the open sea like a rogue ship … which is exactly what they would be labeled as by their own government … and they would be expected to scuttle their ship in the deepest water available. This was the circumstance to be avoided at all costs.

"Officer of the deck. All stop, all stop. Drop anchor, and maintain position. I'll be in the Combat Information Center (CIC). Maintain an EMCONN status of passive except for our normal, commercial surface and air radar."

March 15, 2006, 02:57
National Reconnaissance Office Headquarters
IMINT Directorate
Chantilly, VA

"Okay, Diane, let's review this … it's late, but we need to understand it and decide what priority it takes."

Tom hung up the phone and waited for his new, junior analyst, Diane Smiley to come in. Diane had joined the group recently as a result of more funding, and was all of four years out of college. When Diane arrived, Tom had her sit down and then swung his dual screen monitor around so she could see it.

"Earlier today, while reviewing some pictures of newer Luhu class destroyers, you noticed some railing missing behind one of the life boat davits of that ship. Thinking it odd, you zoomed in on that portion if the ship and noticed, in the shadows of an overhang from the next higher deck, what appeared to be some additional, or new structure. Enhancing the photo, you were able to produce this."

Tom called up the image of a rectangular object on the right hand screen of the dual screen display.

"Then, as a result of heightened interest, you began looking at all new, or recently refitted Luhu's to see if there were more of these structures, and came up with this really clear picture."

Tom called up a clear picture of one of the structure in full light on a Luhu class destroyer. At this point you brought it to my attention, right?"

Diane meekly looked down and nodded her head while saying,

"Yes sir."

Tom continued.

"Okay … at that point I asked you to look at other large PLAN class destroyers to see if you could find more, while I followed some of my hunches. As a result of your efforts, around 10 PM you came back and told me you had in fact found more of these structures on Luhai, Luhu and Luda class destroyers. Is that correct?"

Again, feeling even more uncertain of herself, Diane nodded and repeated,

"Yes sir."

Tom was getting perplexed with the effect he was having on Diane.

"Look Diane, you're not in trouble here or anything, OK? I am asking all of these questions because as analysts, that's what we have to do to make absolutely sure we understand what we are talking about. So, don't be so worried or concerned. I happen to think that what you've found here is of critical importance. I'm just trying to get my arms around it."

"Anyhow, after discovering more of these structures, I asked you to broaden your search while I continued to follow up on my ideas. Were you able to find more?"

Having heard Tom indicate that the data could be critical and that he wasn't giving her the third degree because of any problem, Diane perked right up.

"Well, no, I didn't find these "boxes" on any other ship classes, but I did find something else. Why don't you call up this file."

Diane gave Tom the network location of a file that he quickly called up on the screen. It was a picture of some kind of swivel joint.

"Tom, this is the attach point of one of those "boxes" on the deck of a Luhai destroyer. This joint appears to allow for both traverse and elevation movement. When I take that knowledge and factor it in to the locations on the decks of the ships, it is clear that these "boxes" will swing out from the side of the ship through a fairly broad angle."

Tom took this information and factored it into the things that he had discovered. It was beginning to paint a picture that he didn't like one bit.

"Okay Diane, I believe that is important information regarding the function of these things. Let me tell you what I have discovered."

"As you know, we have been concerned about the PLAN's recently demonstrated capability to convert some its container ships into very effective sea control Aircraft Carriers in a relatively short space of time. We have been scouring Chinese port and repair facilities to locate all of the places they are doing this. In looking at all of those facilities, we have found three potential sites, two of which we are sure of."

"There are many other sites where COSCO refits and repairs its container ships, or other places in the PRC where this could occur. We have been checking them all. One of the things I noticed coming out of other locations, not involved with the carrier conversions, were container ships that left their dry dock or repair dock looking like this."

Tom called up a container ship just leaving a dry dock facility. Zooming in on the deck, there six of large rectangular containers along each side. Tom zoomed in on one and highlighted the container and brought it up on his left-hand screen.

"Now look what happens when we compare your "boxes" to these containers."

Tom called up one of Diane's "boxes" on the right screen, highlighted it and dragged it over to the left hand screen and superimposed it over the container. The "box" fit right inside.

"Those "boxes" from the destroyers fit right inside these containers from the container ships with about six inches to spare all around."

Diane thought about this for no more than a second and then jumped right on the implication that came to her mind.

"Okay, perhaps the Chinese are using the pretext of the refit or repair of their container ships to transport these "boxes" to where the destroyers can get at them. Now I want to know what they use them for on those destroyers."

Tom appreciated Diane's focus, but she was still young and not used to looking for a bigger picture in case it was there.

"Good idea, that was my first thought too. So, I went and looked for container ships that have been refitted at these same places over the last three months are more. I figured I would find some photos of ships that had the containers at one point, and then later "lost" them."

"But that's not what I found. What I found was that in all cases the container ships still had the containers on them that the boxes fit into. In all cases, once these ships put to sea doing their container hauling, the other cargo and containers were stacked around them. Then, when the other containers are off loaded, these remain."

"You want to know what I think now that you've shown me how they are attached?"

Actually, Diane was anxious to hear. Her boss Tom was sharp and she wanted to learn a lot from him. His reputation as an analyst himself was legend around here and she was excited that her first major "find" had caught his attention.

"Absolutely, shoot."

Tom did.

"I think these are weapons of some sort, and that we now have armed container ships plowing the seas. Ask yourself why the Red Chinese would do this. Who are they afraid of? Who do they feel these ships, particularly the container ships, are going to have to fight?"

"Now, this is a preliminary assessment and we're going to have to do even more research to verify or disprove this … but I believe it is critical that we do so."

"Look, it's very late. Why don't you head home and get a few hours sleep. After I work out some plans and assignments for this, I will do the same. Meet me back here at 9 AM and we'll get right back on this."

Diane was glad for the opportunity to go home and get some sleep. She'd been here since 7:30 AM and now it was after 3 AM ... almost twenty hours!

"Okay boss, thanks for the help and thanks for the encouragement. I'll see you here at 9 AM."

As she left his office, Tom did draw up plans and assignments for Diane to address the next morning. When he was done with that, he stayed on and continued to do the research, analysis and contemplation necessary to either firm up, or dispel his theory. By 9 AM when Diane arrived, he had arrived at the conclusion that the PLAN was deploying an unknown new weapon system on all of its Luhai, Luhu and Luda class destroyers and on many of its container ships. After meeting again with Diane at 11:30 AM and confirming his apprehensions, he sent a report at 12:30 PM to his NRO command chain, CINCPAC and the NSA.

It would take this report a good five hours to be read, analyzed and forwarded to bases and units around the world, including CBT 77. By then, it would be too late to make any difference in the events that would play themselves out that early evening of March 15th, 2006 in America, and at the same time in the early morning of March 16th in the Western Pacific.

March 16, 2006, 05:35 Local
420 nautical miles ENE of Okinawa
Flag Briefing Room, USS Lake Chaplain (CG 57)
Western Pacific Ocean

The briefing had just ended. Admiral Reginald Patterson was pleased. He had served in many positions in his twenty-eight year tenure with the United States Navy. He had served on many staffs, and had quite a few staffs serve under him. He honestly believed that the staff serving with him now in CBT 77 was the best, and in the Admiral's way of thinking, that's exactly the way things were meant to be.

USS Lake Chaplain.

The decision had been made several days ago to send the CBT 77.1 with the USS Kitty Hawk CBG and the USS Essex ARG further north, to transit into the Sea of Japan north of the southern most main island of Japan. This was occurring this morning. In the mean time, CBT 77.2 and CBT 77.3, transited into the China Sea north of Okinawa.

The rendezvous of all elements would occur off of Pusan day after tomorrow, which would allow the Kitty Hawk to provide needed air support to the US and Korean forces for two full days before the landings off Pusan would begin.

"Commander Lewis, you gave a very good overview of the exclusion zones and the current status of allied and neutral shipping with respect to them. It seems pretty crowded out there."

Lewis, in addition to being the Admiral's chief of staff, was also an excellent tactician and intelligence analyst.

"Admiral, as you know, this is one of the highest traffic seal lanes in the world. There are always a lot of ships in here. I suppose short of all out maritime warfare directed against Japan and its shipping, there's not much that will slow it down."

"The bit about the Chinese "escorting" their container ships bothers me though. As a supposedly neutral power, I suppose it may be understandable … but we both know how much military, tactical, logistic and supply support they have given the North Koreans before the outbreak of hostilities. There's not a one of us who believes that the North Koreans would ever have undertaken this invasion without the tacit approval of Beijing. There neutrality is dubious and therefore their warships are potential belligerents."

Admiral Patterson understood. The fact was, most of the chain of command believed the same thing, including, as he understood it, the NCA himself.

"Well, they are not violating any of the zones we've established, but we'd best keep an eye on them. I am not overly concerned about any two, or any ten of their Luhai and Luhu class destroyers. It would be suicide for them to consider trying to get close enough to inflict damage on this task force. Just the same, draw up instructions for each task force commander to develop operational plans to keep each of those those particular Chinese groups under close observation."

"I'm more concerned about their two Chinese carrier task forces, the one centered on the Beijing south and west of Okinawa in the China Sea, and the one centered on the Shanghai in the South China Sea. We need to keep those groups under constant surveillance, whether by satellite or by aircraft out of Okinawa or from this task force. I know those are already standing orders, let's just make sure they are emphasized."

Unknown to Admiral Patterson and Commander Lewis, those "not to be overly concerned about" Chinese groups centered on the "container ships" had already launched long range weapons at them. The results would make history, and they would establish the parameters that would govern maritime warfare throughout the remainder of World War III.

March 16, 2006, 06:00 Local
250 km WSW of Okinawa
Combat Information Center, PLAN 1001 Beijing
China Sea

Admiral Yao Hsu would remain in the CIC throughout the engagement. Captain Tuan Hongwen was working with his people to insure that the Beijing was prepared to execute her portion of the attack at the appointed hour. That would amount to a launch of four rounds of his SS-N-26 missiles at Okinawa's airbase and command and control facilities. Forty-eight missiles arriving in four waves of twelve, each wave would be less than five minutes apart. Arriving with the fourth wave would be an air attack of six SU-30's, three SU-35's and ten Su-25's, supported by one AEW aircraft.

It would be critical that air cover from the mainland arrive over the carrier to augment the six remaining SU-30's'and four SU-35's' at the proper time. Everyone expected some sort of air attack from Okinawa or American airfields in Korea and Japan. At the appointed time, ships would conduct ballistic missile attacks on American airfields in Japan, while Chinese missiles from across the Yellow Sea would be hitting bases in Korea.

Finally, the Shanghai, PLAN 1002, would lead a strike on the HMS Ark Royal Task Force that was approaching from the South China Sea. With the carrier's air group, with the carrier launched surface to surface missiles (SSM) and with assistance from PLAN aircraft from the mainland, it was expected that the HMS task force would be quickly and totally overwhelmed.

As it stood now, one hundred and twenty-five LRASD devices were rapidly approaching the American Task Forces. When they commenced their destructive work, the moment of truth was upon them all.

PLAN attack submarines were passively listening well off of the American task forces. As soon as any one of them reported that the engagement had begun, an order would go out to all of the waiting Chinese forces. Tactical Attack Ships both here and off America, the Chinese missile bases and the various other task forces, including this one, would launch their attacks.

"Perhaps America is a sleeping giant," thought the Admiral. "Well, we will not make the mistakes of the Japanese sixty-five years ago. We will not deal in half measures. Our "surprise" will knock the American's unconscious. By the time they awaken and try and respond, the new order of things here in the Pacific and Asia will be too far advanced for them to counter."

At least, that was the plan.

March 16, 2006, 06:22 Local
371 nautical miles ENE of Okinawa
Control Room, USS Jefferson City (SSN 759)
Western Pacific Ocean

SSN-759 surfaced on the 15th.

"Captain, we have multiple contacts well off our port bow."

Captain Wellington looked up from the plotting board as his executive officer made this statement. He had just been reviewing their patrol course out in front of Carrier Group Seven.

"What do they have?"

The executive officer, responded.

"Sir, they say they'd like you to come over and listen. They're not sure."

The Captain considered this, almost made a sarcastic remark, but then said,

"Okay, Steve, you have the Conn."

The Captain quickly made his way over to sonar.

"Okay guys, what do you have down here that requires me to listen?"

Looking up form his station, the duty officer, a Lieutenant, at sonar responded as he handed the Captain a pair of earphones.

"Sir, I've got the sound of many propellers, faint, but closing. Range about 20,000 yards. They are definitely mechanical, no known acoustic match."

The Captain put on the earphones and was silent for a moment. Sure enough, he could faintly hear the sound of propellers against the background.

"How many, at what approximate depth, and what's the closure rate?"

Looking at the readout on the screen at his duty station, the Lieutenant quickly pressed a few keys on the keyboard there and then answered.

"Captain, the count keeps increasing, now twenty-one targets. Range to closest is now 19,100 yards and closing on a tangent of 223 degrees. Depth estimated at 600 feet. Speed is 48 knots."

Digesting this, the Captain quickly calculated and then said.

"That course is taking them in towards the Task Force."

Picking up a communications phone, the Captain got his XO on the line.

"Steve, sound general quarters. This is no drill. Set course to interdict these incoming targets, go to 20 knots and arm tubes one through four."

March 16, 2006, that same time
386 nautical miles ENE of Okinawa
PLAN 2012 Gansu LRASD Strike
Western Pacific

The twenty-five LRASD strike that had been launched by the Gansu group were one of three strikes that were now inbound toward CBT 77.2 and CBT 77.3. The LRASD devices were programmable by both acoustic signature and sonar image. They were also programmable by depth, course, distance, loiter time and loiter pattern. The devices had been set up to have several different primary and secondary targets. The lead units of each strike were programmed to look for U.S. attack submarines … predominantly LA Class submarines that were typically escorting carrier battle groups.

At 18,000 yards, both lead LRASDs acquired the faint acoustic signature of the Jefferson City which was now approaching them. The two lead units plotted an intercept course at their current 48 knot speed and continued until the range had closed to 10,000 yards. At this point, both units broadcast a tight sonar pulse down the bearing of the acoustic match. The resulting sonar signature confirmed their acoustic data.

What followed was the culmination of Lu Pham's engineering efforts. In the space of three seconds, the two devices lined themselves up on an interception course for the Jefferson City, set their proximity destruction to preprogrammed parameters and ignited their jet engines. Within two seconds, the devices began supercavitating as they were designed to do and reached their maximum speed of 600 knots within five seconds. By this time the range had closed to 8,000 yards, less than twenty-five seconds from impact.

March 16, 2006, 06:34 Local
Sonar, USS Jefferson City (SSN 759)
369 nautical miles ENE of Okinawa
Western Pacific Ocean

Captain Wellington had remained in sonar with the Lieutenant, relaying his commands to the Executive Officer in the control room.

"Okay, Lieutenant, what have we got? "

The Lieutenant now believed that the Captain's nerves were made of steel. Since the two closest targets had briefly gone active, they had continued their approach. At the captain's order, the Jefferson City had also gone briefly active and had much more data regarding the approaching threat.

They knew that these entities were approximately fifty feet long and a good six to eight feet in diameter. Traveling underwater at forty-eight knots, the Captain had concluded they were some type of small miniature submarine.

"Captain, they are continuing on their current course towards us at forty-eight knots. Range now ... just under 10,000 yards .... WAIT!, there's a change in aspect ratio. WOW! Something new here ... new propulsion ... very loud! Speed increasing ... Captain! These two targets are now approaching at 600 knots!"

The Captain was stunned for an instant ... 600 knots! Unbelievable ... no, it couldn't be! There was no time. He didn't ask the Lieutenant if he was sure, he knew full well the import of that speed and what had happened.

Grabbing the phone set, he called to his executive officer.

"Steve, EMERGENCY STOP! BLOW ALL BALLASTS!"

Since the Lieutenant had voiced the warning that the incoming targets were approaching at 600 knots, the Captain had reacted quickly. He had issued his orders to his executive officer in just under ten seconds. The executive officer had issued those same orders within another five seconds, now fifteen seconds after the Lieutenant's warning. The ship actually began to slow and rise at the nineteen second mark, six seconds before impact.

Given the nature of the information they were presented with, it was quite remarkable that the captain and crew had reacted so quickly. It was a testament to their training. But nothing they had been trained for as a crew prepared them for this, and it wasn't fast enough.

AT 06:35 AM on March 16, 2006 in the Western Pacific, as the Jefferson City rose through a 400 foot depth, the pair of LRASD weapons arrived almost simultaneously. One hit just under of the sail, the other low struck amidships. Each LRASD carried a 2000 kilogram (4400 pound) high explosive warhead. The resulting, almost simultaneous explosions tore the Jefferson City into three pieces. The center section was pushed another 100 feet higher in the water before joining the fore and aft sections in sinking.

Captain Wellington, his executive officer, the Lieutenant in the sonar spaces and the entire crew only had enough time to briefly stare one another in the eye in the closing seconds as they heard the onrushing sound of their doom. They had to accept their deaths in whatever means that were left available to them in those brief seconds. Then they, and their boat, were committed to the deep. A few moments later a small emergency buoy rose to the surface to announce the news to listening satellites, while the explosion itself announced the deed to closer ears.

The one hundred and forty-two officers and crew of the USS Jefferson City (SSN 759) thus became the first casualties of a war with Red China that would prove to be the longest and most costly conflict in American history.

March 16, 2006, 06:38 Local Time
385 Miles ENE of Okinawa
Bridge, USS Jarrett (FFG 33)
Western Pacific

"Whoa! … Sir, sonar reports a very large underwater explosion, could have been two almost simultaneous explosions of some type, bearing 31 degrees. Must be twenty to twenty-five miles out."

Commander Carleson considered the report from the bridge duty officer.

"That would be in the Jefferson City's patrol zone. Are we getting anything else?"

The duty officer consulted momentarily over the phone and then responded.

"No sir, just that large explosion. Had to be very large to come across the way it did."

Carleson considered the information. He was sonar and missile picket, about twenty miles in advance of the main body of Carrier Group Two of CBT 77.2. The Jefferson City was the vanguard, doing ASW work along the primary threat axis.

"Okay, have our Sea Hawk immediately investigate and pass the report back to the battle group commander. As soon as the Sea Hawk is within ten miles of the area, get them on the line for me. I want to personally talk to them as they approach."

March 16, 2006, 06:44 Local Time
402 Miles ENE of Okinawa
Admiral's Cabin, USS Lake Chaplain (CG 57)
Western Pacific

After his morning walk up on the bridge, and breakfast, Admiral Patterson had just finished a quick shower and was almost done dressing when the knock at his door came. As he took a couple of quick steps to the door and opened it, he answered.

"Yes, what is it?"

The young ensign quickly saluted and reported.

"Begging the Admiral's pardon sir, Commander Lewis requests your urgent presence in the CIC sir regarding reports from the Jarrett concerning explosions in the Jefferson City patrol area, sir!"

The Admiral listened attentively.

"Okay Ensign, I'm coming with you right now. Let's get down to CIC."

As they quickly made their way, the Admiral finished buttoning his shirt. He also thought about the import of the information he'd just received. It must be serious or Lewis would have waited. Lewis was an "on the ball" officer and had the knack of knowing precisely when something needed to be passed up the line, and when more information was warranted before doing so. That is precisely what made him such an excellent Chief of Staff.

As they walked into the CIC, things were extremely hectic. It was clear something serious was developing. On entering the CIC, he acknowledged Lewis, and then approached the Captain of the Lake Chaplain, Captain Merrill, who was in an animated conversation with the CO of Carrier Group Seven, Admiral Flynn.

"Admiral! The Jarrett has reported multiple inbound submerged targets approaching this task force from his position! He is now reporting explosions from both the Jefferson City and the Salt Lake City patrol areas!"

After a pause, the Captain continued.

"I know that Sir, but I believe we are …."

The Captain turned and consulted briefly with another of his officers who handed him a note.

"Excuse me sir, we have just received word from the Jarrett. He is reporting he is under attack, I repeat, he is under attack. Submerged contact has turned towards him on a collision course and is approaching at … my God, approaching at 600 knots!"

Admiral Patterson digested the information. As the CINC of the entire CBT 77, he could wait no longer.

"Captain, please give me the phone."

The Captain informed Admiral Flynn that CINC CBT 77 was going to speak to him and handed the phone to Admiral Patterson.

"Jim, yea, this is Reg. Look, we are clearly under attack. Get on the horn with your PHIBRON and then patch me through to Ben over at CBT 77.3 and then to the Kitty Hawk."

"I want you all to immediately execute a turn back to the southeast on an axis directly away from the reports of these contacts … that should be a heading of about 220 degrees. Make sure your S3's lay out patterns between this task force and the oncoming threat … yes, I know that it will take some time, but we have to put more space between us and what's coming. Also, launch your ready alert birds and augment both your anti-air and anti-surface birds."

"I'm not sure who it is yet, but there can only be a couple of possibilities. Clearly someone has developed and fielded a supercavitating weapon and is using it against this task force. Please patch Troy and the Kitty Hawk through to me right here."

After giving the commanders of Task Force 77.3 and 77.1 the same orders, the Admiral got the attention of Captain Merrill.

"Captain, how many contacts were there reported by the Jarrett and what speed were they approaching at?"

The Captain cupped his hand over the phone for a moment.

"Admiral I am on the line with the Commander of the Jarrett right now. He's in trouble sir. He indicated in excess of twenty in bounds moving at 50 knots initially, but they have now increased their speed to 75 knots. Just one moment sir."

The Captain uncovered the phone and then spoke briefly. In the middle of a sentence he stopped, called urgently and loudly for Commander Carleson several times, and then, turning to the Admiral, he spoke in a now surprisingly quiet CIC.

"Sir, Commander Carleson was cut off in mid sentence. This ... threat was approaching and then, right in the middle of describing the unbelievable speed of the approaching track ... nothing. We lost radio contact with the Jarrett."

Turning to one of his officers in CIC, the Captain asked,

"Radar, what do you have on Jarrett."

The radar officer, gazing closely at the display answered.

"Sir, rapidly weakening signal at Jarrett's last reported position."

Admiral Patterson reacted quickly in the stunned silence.

"Okay, Commander Lewis, get the following SITREP off to CINCPAC and to Washington ...CBT 77 under attack. Multiple inbound threats detected, probably supercavitating devices of some type. USS Jarrett lost, USS Jefferson City and USS Salt Lake City presumed lost. Taking evasive action ... Send it NOW!"

The Admiral had already done the math, it would be ten minutes before all of the ships in the task force could turn in an orderly fashion. At 75 knots these weapons would be amongst them in those same ten minutes. That would be too late.

"Captain, on my authority, you are to turn this vessel around to the southeast IMMEDIATELY while continuing to cover for the John Stennis. Patch me through to the Task Force commanders, and the Captains of the John Stennis, the Constellation and the Kitty Hawk. I intend to order all vessels in all task forces, meaning all ships in the Carrier Groups and PHIBRONS to immediately turn and egress at maximum speed away from these threats."

March 16, 2006, 12:45 Local
Naval Headquarters, CINCPAC
Honolulu, Hawaii

"Sir, we are now picking up emergency distress signals from four LA Class attacks submarines in the western Pacific. We have the USS Jefferson City and the USS Salt Lake City with Carrier Group Seven attached to CBT 77.2, we have the USS Santa Fe with Carrier Group Two attached to CBT 77.3 and we have the USS Pasadena with Carrier group Five attached to CBT 77.1. All within the last ten minutes."

Commander Banks digested this sobering information. Distress signals from attack submarines on station meant one thing ... that the boat had gone down and the buoy had been released after the hull passed crush depth. But to have four at once ... and from a task force standing into combat.

"Okay, Lieutenant, work on exact fixes for each of those and continue trying to contact CBT 77 for a situation report. I have to contact the CINC."

Before Commander Banks could finish entering the emergency number for the CINC of Pacific Naval Operations, the SITREP from CBT 77 came in.

"...CBT 77 under attack. Multiple inbound threats detected, probably supercavitating devices of some type. USS Jarrett lost, USS Jefferson City and USS Salt Lake City presumed lost. Taking evasive action."

The Commander finished keying in the number. Almost immediately, Admiral Sullivan, CINCPAC, picked up.

"Admiral sir, sorry to disturb you sir, but this is Commander Banks in operations. Between 23:37 and 23:45 we picked up four, that is four, emergency distress beacons from attack submarines attached to CBT 77. At 23:49, we received a SITREP from Admiral Patterson NE of Okinawa indicating that the Task Force is under attack, that several vessels were lost, and that he was taking evasive action."

The Admiral listened in stunned silence … but just for an instant.

"Okay commander. I will be in operations within ten minutes right about midnight. I would like to speak directly with Admiral Patterson at 00:10 if at all possible."

"Please immediately contact Admiral Crowley and arrange to conference him into to that call. Sullivan out."

March 16, 2006, 06:55 Local Time
Approximately 400 nautical miles ENE of Okinawa
Western Pacific

Admiral Patterson's orders were prudent given the information he had at the time. They would have more effective except that two other LSRAD strikes were approaching his task force as well. A total of seventy-five LRASDs had been launched at the sixty-two ships in CBT's 77.2 and 77.3. One group of these was approaching from the southwest, which diminished the effectiveness of the retreat to the southeast.

As the ships of the two Carrier Groups and three augmented PHIBRONS, now having lost the semblance of an orderly formation, completed their turns, the LRASD devices, moving at 75 knots, entered the target area. As they did so, they slowed and surveyed their surroundings.

The lead LRASD units, upon detecting and identifying targets that fit their programmed profiles, aligned themselves on those targets and activated their jet engines. From distances ranging from 6,000 yards to 12,000 yards, 2000 kilogram high explosive underwater missiles began attacking their targets at 600 knots, a closure rate equal to approximately one mile (1700 yards) every five seconds.

March 16, 2006, 06:56 local time
404 nautical miles ENE of Okinawa
Bridge, USS Lake Chaplain (CG 57)
Western Pacific

Admiral Patterson had decided to join Captain Merrill who had gone to the bridge to observe the action. Commander Lewis had accompanied the Admiral there.

Seconds after their arrival on the bridge, there was a tremendous flash off to the north, just over the horizon, but producing flames that must have reached hundreds of feet into the air to be seen at this distance. The Admiral, still looking to the distant explosion, asked,

"What was that?"

Captain Merrill, who had been monitoring the attack while the Admiral made his way to the bridge from CIC, took the phone from his ear and answered.

"That was the Elliot. One of those submerged devices had just lit up and was bearing down on her as you came in Admiral."

After listening to his phone for just a few seconds, a look of disillusionment passed over his face and he said,

"Dear God, the Decatur is reporting that the Elliot has broken in half and is sinking rapidly ... few, if any survivors."

A sober moment passed, then closer in, Commander Lewis got their attention and pointed to the south,

"Sir, there in the PHIBRON group!"

As the Admiral and the Captain turned to the south, they could see that Carrier Group Seven and PHIBRON One, one of the two PHIBRONs that they were escorting, were beginning to mix. Off to the south, perhaps four miles out, the LHA Peleliu, a Tarawa class amphibious assault ship, had completed its turn to the southeast.

As they watched, the large, carrier-like ship began to lean into a hard turn to starboard. While this was occurring, two faint streaks in the water approached at unbelievable speed and struck the Peleliu. Two tremendous geysers of water accompanied by two tremendous explosions obscured and then hid the entire ship. When the water fell and the smoke began to clear a few seconds later, the great ship had completely capsized, revealing two horrendous gashes in her side, the lower ends of which were already below the water line. Clearly, the ship was sinking rapidly and would be gone in just a few more moments.

Admiral Patterson could only exclaim,

"Dear God in Heaven, there were over three thousand sailors and marines on that ship!"

The horrors were far from over. As they were absorbing the shock of the loss of the Peleliu, two S3B's flew over them at very low altitude and continued not far above the waves for approximately a mile before turning to and lining up on two more streaks approaching from that quarter. Admiral Patterson immediately assessed the threat.

"Those two are headed for the John Stennis."

As they watched, each S3B released a Mk-50 torpedo in front of the rapidly approaching streaks. One was clearly too late and hit the water hundreds of feet behind and to the left of its intended target/streak. But the second S3B managed to lay its Mk-50 a good quarter mile on front of its streaking target. Almost immediately, the streak converged with the place where the torpedo had entered the water and there was an explosion. That streak did not continue past the point of impact.

Captain Merrill was exuberant.

"Yes! Did you see that? That S3 driver NAILED that SOB!"

But the remaining streak covered the mile-and-a-half to the John Stennis in just under eight seconds, far too quickly for the big carrier to avoid it. As the three men on the Lake Chaplain watched in shock, another huge geyser erupted, followed by a tremendous explosion and what appeared to be a literal "lurch" in the ship's aft section where the hit occurred. The big ship immediately lost headway as tremendous amounts of smoke and fire poured out of her aft, port elevator where a jagged gash, extending down below the water line had appeared above the point of impact.

For several seconds, the three men sat in disbelief, stunned into silence, as they watched one of the very symbols, the essence of American military projection slow in the water and then begin to stop. Fires and large secondary explosions attested to the damage inflicted upon the John Stennis.

Commander Lewis spoke first.

"She's hit bad Admiral, real bad."

As they watched the drama play out, within a few moments, a crack extended above the gash, right though the elevator and onto the flight deck. Presently, the entire aft end of the great ship tore away from the fore section.

That aft end began to sink quickly. The forward three-fifths of the ship began to settle in the water by the new aft end. Although it would be longer in suffering, it was clear that the fore section of the USS John Stennis, nuclear powered super carrier, would share the fate of the smaller aft section.

The silence was broken by more reports coming in to Captain Merrill. As he reported on the status of CBT 77.2 and CBT 77.3, Admiral Patterson ordered Commander Lewis to send a FLASH SITREP to CINCPAC and Washington.

"FLASH: From CINC CBT 77. Continuing to evade large numbers of supercavitating weapons. USS Elliot sunk, feared lost with all hands, USS Peleliu capsized and sinking rapidly with heavy loss, USS John Stennis broken in two and sinking. No recent contact with the Constellation."

The Lake Chaplain turns to avoid an LRASD.

As Commander Lewis returned to the bridge after sending the flash message, the Lake Chaplain, began to turn extremely hard to port. All three men had to hold to railing to remain upright. Captain Merrill continued to issue orders while the Admiral and Commander looked on. They then noticed and followed the horrified gaze of the Captain well off to the starboard side of the ship.

There, coming directly at them with astonishing speed, was a streak like the others they had seen over the last few minutes. It appeared that Captain Merrill's violent maneuver was going to cause the weapon to miss. Then, at its closest approach, a mere twenty feet from their hull, the 4400 pounds of high explosive detonated according to its proximity programming.

The force of the explosion caused the Lake Chaplain to lean over drastically. Right at the moment when the men on the bridge who were still capable of sensing it, having been thrown violently to the floor and injured, felt that the ship must capsize, she righted herself.

Captain Merrill was the first up and he immediately helped Admiral Patterson up. The Admiral had broken a shoulder in the fall and was in great pain. Nonetheless, they went over to the fallen form of Commander Lewis to help him up … but he was beyond help. The fall had violently thrown him into a bulkhead and he had broken his neck.

Captain Merrill attempted to get damage control on his phone, but communications were out. He and the Admiral walked over to the starboard side and looked over the side of the ship. Smoke was pouring out of a rent to their aft. Clearly, the hull had been compromised by the explosion.

"We'd best get you to sick bay Admiral, that shoulder look broke to hell."

Turning to one of the uninjured officer, the Captain gave some orders.

"Ensign, get the Admiral here below to sick bay. I will be here on the bridge coordinating damage control as we establish communications."

The admiral, in great pain and holding his arm close to his body to keep it immobile, could only nod in assent.

As the Ensign led the way into the ship, the Lake Chaplain began to list to the starboard. It began relatively slowly, but the further they went, the worse it became. By the time they had arrived at sick bay, it had gotten so bad, that again, they began to feel they would surely capsize.

They were right. At 07:08, the USS Lake Chaplain, an Aegis guided missile cruiser, rolled over and sank. Along with 90% of her crew, Admiral Patterson and Captain Merrill went down with the ship.

March 16, 2006, 07:00 Local Time
Western Pacific

The LRASD attacks were not just centered on CBT 77.2 and CBT 77.3, nor were the LRASD attacks the only portion of the attack on American forces and her allies conducted by the Chinese in the Western Pacific that day. But, they were an important part, because neutralizing American carrier power in the western Pacific was critical to the overall success of the operation.

With the initial attack on the Jefferson City, two Han class Chinese attack submarines, that had been sitting quietly and passively, and would not actively participate in the fighting, monitored the explosions well out in front of CBT 77.2 and CBT 77.3. They had been told to expect it, and they had very specific orders regarding it. As soon as the explosion was detected, a single communications buoy was released by both subs. The buoy rose to the surface and transmitted a single code word in Mandarin, "Breath".

Units throughout eastern China, on the high seas in the South China Sea, in the China Sea, in the Yellow Sea and in the Sea of Japan had been awaiting this transmission. When received, they all began countdown to attack sequences.

It had been planned that within twenty-five minutes of any LRASD attack on any escorting American attack submarine, the other LRASD units would arrive and begin decimating the American fleets. Therefore, twenty-five minutes after that attack on the USS Jefferson City, at 07:00 hours, other Chinese forces began unleashing their attacks as well.

From Taiwan to Okinawa to the islands of Japan to the Korean peninsula, massive ballistic missile barrages began raining down on US installations and the installations of its allies. These continued throughout the day and were interspersed, or followed up, by attacks from Chinese land based, or carrier based aircraft. The attacks included strikes against the British Task Force approaching from the south, and against Japanese Maritime Defense Force (JMDF) ships in the Sea of Japan.

Surprise was total.

Within days, the surprise Chinese air attacks on Korea and Taiwan, would be followed by large numbers of Chinese ground troops. These would be carried to their destinations by the new Yunana II landing craft, by the new Amphibious Assault ships and by many other craft.

The invasion forces would be escorted by Beijing class carrier groups that would protect them attack by Korean, Japanese and ROC (Taiwan) forces. If today's operation went as planned, no American intervention was expected.

… and this was not all. The transmission for the successful beginning of China's part of Dragon's Breath was also transmitted to the Tactical Attack Ships waiting off the coasts of the United States and to operatives whose teams within the United States were staged and ready. These unleashed, their attacks on American soil with a savagery and effectiveness that surprised even the Chinese planners.

March 15, 2006, 19:04 EST
Presidential Quarters Entry Way
White House
Washington, D.C.

As the first couple exited their armored, specially outfitted limousine, Linda Weisskopf thought fondly on the dinner they had just shared.

"Now wasn't that the wonderful dinner?"

She thought. Norm had been such a gentlemen, and had take such pains to have everything appear normal, though she knew that events and their potential impact were weighing heavily on his mind. In fact, a National Security meeting was waiting for him in the situation room right now.

As they stepped up to the entry, flanked by their Secret Service detail, she thought she would mention her gratitude and appreciation to him.

"Norm?"

She said, as she tugged on the sleeve of his coat. He turned to look at her.

"Yes sweetheart."

As they briefly paused, she continued.

"I just wanted you to know how much I appreci ..."

That was as far as she got. Before she could finish that word, the agent in charge of their detail came bursting back through the entry and yelled.

"Turn around. Get the President and first lady to Marine One and away from the White House NOW!"

He had his hand to his ear, listening as he said this. Norm, turned and took Linda by the arm and they literally ran around the building to the landing area where Marine One, was already spooling up its engines.

The pilot immediately prepared for take off, waiting for the President, First Lady and their immediate Secret Service detail to board. A Marine was standing just outside, waving them emphatically on.

As the aircraft lifted off, the President, gaining his wits quickly asked.

"Alright Burt, what on earth is going on?"

He turned to the President with a very desperate look on his face.

"Mr. President, NORAD and local tracking just picked up multiple ballistic missile launches within the last three minutes. All are between one and three hundred miles off the coast. Multiple tracks targeting Washington, D.C. sir."

The President grimly took this in. Ballistic launches only a few hundred miles away. My God, he thought. If they are nuclear … looking directly at Burt while holding Linda's hand, The President could see in Burt's and the other agents' eyes the grim conclusions that they had drawn.

"If they launched that close in, that means their flight time would be …"

The answers to the timing and the composition came right then.

BLAM!!!!

Marine One was scarcely two hundred feet in the air and only a few hundred yards away from the White House when the first of four conventional missiles targeted on the White House impacted. Luckily, though the turbulence was severe, the pilot was very experienced and had seen worse in other situations he had flown through. He brought them out of a roll to the left, steadied the aircraft and kept gaining altitude and distance.

As the President and first lady watched out their windows in horror, three more missiles impacted on and around the White House, then more missiles began impacting on and around the Capitol building, and the Pentagon. Very quickly large pillars of smoke and tremendous flames began to rise from all three of these places.

The U.S. Capital is hit by missiles.

As the flew on the President asked, "Has Andrews been attacked?"

The agent in charge went forward to the pilot's compartment and returned in a few seconds.

"No sir, Andrews appears to be intact at the moment. We are receiving reports of significant attacks at Newport News and Hampton Roads, others coming in from elsewhere in the country."

The President didn't hesitate. Calling to the pilot.

"Okay, Captain!"

The response from the flight deck was immediate.

"Yes Sir!"

"Get me over to Andrews. Contact them and tell them it is my direct order to have Air Force One standing by when I arrive, ready for immediate take off."

Though the agent in charge tried to protest and suggest that they fly to a site that was not so high profile a target, the President would have none of it.

"Burt, I appreciate your concerns ... but this is a direct order from your commander in chief. Now get me to Andrews and get me on Air Force One. I MUST establish communications with military and political leaders, I can't do that any better than from Air Force One!"

As Marine one banked towards Andrews and communicated with flight control and the command chain there, Norm Weisskopf sat back and consoled his wife, while watching the landscape pass underneath him.

March 15, 2006, that same time ˙
Construction Yard, CVN-77
Newport News Shipbuilding
Newport News, VA

In many ways, except for an "odd" look to her island, she looked just like the super carrier that was in dry dock next to her undergoing its Service Life Extension Program (SLEP). But looks can be deceiving.

CVN-77 was the first of the "new" generation of U.S. aircraft carriers. Billions of dollars had been invested in the construction, the new technology, the practices and the configurations that would make her more operationally effective, over 20% less costly and would require over five hundred less crew. This would make way for more improvements in her follow on sister ships, one of which was already under construction further down the "line".

Several of the improvements and innovations that the "CVX" class would incorporate over the current "Nimitz" class would include:

- A open system architecture for all computers and combat systems,
- A fully integrated information system,
- A composite construction island,
- Multifunctional embedded antennas,
- Redundant fiber optic cabling for all communications,
- Zonal electrical distribution systems,
- The SPY-1F AEGIS radar system,
- Improved close-in defenses adding the Mk-31 (RAM) missile system,
- Provisions for upgrading to linear electromagnetic-motor catapults.

In addition, these would be the first carriers to be built with the new air wing composition in mind. That air wing would consist of twenty-four F/A-18E single-seat air-superiority fighters, twelve F/A-18F two-seat attack/fighters, twelve JSF V/STOL attack/fighters, and 14-16 Common Support Aircraft (CSA). The CSA would likely be comprised of four E-2C AEW aircraft, four Electronic Warfare aircraft (EA-6B or new EF-18G aircraft) and ten S3B ASW aircraft.

But, plans for the early fall launch of this formidable new carrier, the CVN-77, and her sister ship, as well as for the re-launch of the SLEP carrier were now being put on long term hold.

Over ninety ballistic missiles were now falling on the carriers and the construction yards that were building or refitting them. Each missile carried a one thousand-pound warhead guided unfailingly by GPS coordinates that had been programmed into them resulting from the many Chinese military "exchange" guests who had visited the facilities. In fact, in attacks on fixed American installations in the United States and the Far East that were occurring this day, and would occur in future attacks, the unerring accuracy resulted from this same "guest exchange program". Like at the White House, the Pentagon and the Capitol, there was very little warning time, only three to five minutes.

Machinery and equipment critical to the construction was exploding all around. Huge, gaping holes were appearing in the carrier decks, followed immediately by bone rattling detonations that further ripped the carrier decks apart and gutted the interior spaces. The islands were hammered into a smoking pile of twisted metal and equipment. Skilled laborers were killed and injured by the hundreds at each location.

When it was over just a few minutes later, the construction yards and docks were left in a burning, smoking and twisted ruin. The ships themselves were wrecked hulks burning out of control. On this day, America really lost five of its super carriers. Two operational carriers in the Western Pacific, and three here at Newport News.

March 15, 2006, 18:12, CST
Construction Yard, DD-21
Ingalls Shipbuilding
Pascagoula, MS

The sleek, new ship was scheduled to be launched in July. Built low to the water and gliding through the waves on new electric drive propulsion, planners had been hoping for a July 4th christening and launch to punctuate the patriotic nature of this next Naval "defender" of America.

The lead ship in the DD-21 program was being built to revolutionize sea warfare. A fully modular design, this class would initially be delivered as a Maritime Fire Support Ship with two new, one hundred mile rang 155mm guns, two sixty-four cell VLS block holding many Land Attack and anti-surface Tomahawk missiles, and evolved Sea Sparrow missiles for self defense against air attack.

Later versions of the design would incorporate full anti-submarine capabilities and then, still later, theater wide anti-ballistic, anti-air capabilities.

The technology being used to construct the ship was state of the art and specially designed for the many innovations in propulsion, fire support, radar and automation being incorporated. Ingalls Shipbuilding was one of two primary shipyards building destroyers for the United States Navy. The other was Bath Iron Works in Maine.

At 6:12 PM, sixty tactical missiles fired from less that two hundred miles away began raining down on these shipyards as well. The primary targets were the construction yards for the DD-21 and the construction yards for the continuing construction of the Block II A version of the Arleigh Burke class of guided missile destroyers, another of which was under construction.

As large explosions racked the yards from secondary explosions of fuels and other combustibles stored there, workers ran in a frenzied panic to seek shelter. Within a few short minutes, both ships and the equipment and facilities for their construction were either very badly damaged, or destroyed in the attack. In addition, hundreds more very skilled ship builders were killed, some with skills honed over thirty years of building modern destroyers for the U.S. Navy.

The same scene was played out at Bath Iron Works in Maine, where the second DD-21 ship was under construction and where another Arleigh Burke class destroyer were being built. There, the ships themselves were completely destroyed and again, hundreds of skilled workers killed.

March 15, 2006, 18:09 CST
Propane Storage Facility
Missouri Shore of the Mississippi River
Just North of St. Louis, MO

The propane storage facilities here were massive, close to two million gallons of propane were stored at this single site. Fully 12% of U.S. available resource was stored here for transmission across the country. In addition to trucks and pipelines that carried the gas away from the facility, large propane storage barges were used to transport the fuel up and down the Mississippi River to alternate distribution sites.

Ahmed Haddad, Jahmil and his six subordinates on this particular mission had selected this target well. They had studied the schedules, they had documented the security, both ashore and on the water. Traveling in their refitted Sea King houseboat, the Dhul Fiqar, they had just made the turn toward the facility, traveling at their maximum speed of twelve knots.

Below, surrounded by a special protective shielding of Kevlar armor and hardened stainless steel, were two thousand pounds of C4 explosive. The shielding would protect it during transit to the target, and then project its force in the desired manner upon detonation. Ahead now, about two miles directly in front of them, was the target, a huge propane barge moored next to a large storage tank taking on propane.

"Keep her steady Jahmil, Aim directly for the middle of the barge. We will soon be in paradise together my brother."

Jahmil knew that what his friend of many years said was true, and he looked forward to it.

"Allah Mak, Ahmed, God is truly great, and hopefully we will send many of these infidels to hell when we step into paradise this day my friend."

As they continued their approach towards the facility, finally … as they knew it ultimately must, came the sound of a large horn off to their left. From behind a group of several other craft that had shielded the Dhul Fiqar's turn towards the facility, a forty-one foot U.S. Coast Guard Ports and Waterways patrol boat turned directly towards them and picked up speed.

This craft, and two others like it, worked three shifts and were the principal waterway security for the propane facility. Powered by two Cummins diesel engines, the patrol boat was capable of sustaining twenty-eight knots, far faster than the Dhul Fiqar. It was armed with a bow mounted M2 HB fifty-caliber machine gun and two M-60 thirty-caliber machine guns. It was also armed with a very powerful loud speaker.

"Sea King houseboat, heave to. You are approaching a restricted area and are ordered by the U.S. Coast Guard to heave to."

Ahmed looked at Jahmil briefly then ordered him to continue. They only had a little over a mile to go now, and they could be there in about four minutes.

The pilothouse of the Dhul Fiqar, where Jahmil was stationed, had been reinforced and was also coated in Kevlar armor for just this contingency. In addition, the Dhul Fiqar was well armed for any encounter with the U.S. Coast Guard. They had installed mounts for one twenty-millimeter cannon and one M-60, thirty-caliber machinegun. Ahmed now had five of the other team members taking out this weaponry and preparing to mount it. Two of his men would man the twenty-millimeter cannon, while another manned the M-60 machine gun. Two other team members would be armed with M16A1 assault rifles mounting 40mm M202 grenade launchers. The last member of Ahmed's team would maintain the engine, and serve as a reserve for the firing positions, wherever needed.

When the U.S. Coast Guard officer saw that the Dhul Fiqar had no intention of stopping, he tried one last broadcast.

"Dhul Fiqar, you are ordered to heave to. If you do not comply immediately, we will be forced to fire upon you."

Several Coast Guard crewmembers were now out on the forward deck uncovering the fifty-caliber machinegun mounted there. Two other members were already manning smaller M-60 thirty-caliber machineguns on mounts towards the aft potion of the boat.

To indicate they meant business, the Coast Guard officer commanding the craft ordered his crew to fire several rounds across the bow of the Dhul Fiqar.

BAP BAP BAP ... BAP BAP BAP

The rounds kicked up impressive geysers in front of the Dhul Fiqar.

When the Dhul Fiqar began taking evasive maneuvers by turning slightly in a weaving pattern towards the propane facility, the Coast Guard boat increased speed to their maximum 28 knots. From several hundred yards to the side and behind, the patrol craft began overtaking the Dhul Fiqar rapidly, firing as they came.

1200 yards to go.

Ahmed and his men took cover behind specially prepared Kevlar coated positions at their firing stations as many rounds hit the boat, tearing off materiel and punching holes in the hull. When the Coast Guard patrol boat had closed to within 200 yards, Ahmed ordered his men to man their firing stations and open fire. As they rose up and began firing back at the Coast Guard vessel, the Coast Guard crew began targeting them. Almost immediately, two of Ahmed's six men were cut down, but the other four began returning a murderous fire on the unarmored Coast Guard boat.

The twenty-millimeter cannon began scoring direct hits on the Coast Guard pilothouse and the boat veered off as those piloting the U.S. craft were killed or injured. The twenty millimeter-cannon then began concentrating on the Coast Guard patrol boat's hull, punching many large holes in it and damaging other vital equipment. Upon seeing this heavy weapon and its impact on their vessel, the Coast Guard crew manning the fifty-caliber machinegun raked the twenty-millimeter position and killed both men there.

800 yards to go.

As this was occurring, the remaining grenade launcher found his range and dropped one forty millimeter grenade in the aft section of the Coast Guard boat, killing both of the Coast Guard M-60 machine gunners and destroying the two Cummins diesel engines used to power the craft. As the Coast Guard patrol boat went dead in the water and began to burn, the fifty-caliber machinegun crew again raked the Dhul Fiqar, seriously wounding Ahmed's man who held the grenade launcher, knocking him overboard.

300 yards to go.

Ahmed made his way towards the pilothouse. Now only he and Jahmil were left on the Dhul Fiqar. Just as he was opening the door to the pilothouse, a fifty-caliber round hit him in the shoulder and threw him violently into the pilothouse and onto the floor. Jahmil quickly closed the door. The Kevlar protection, three inches thick around the pilothouse, was not a guarantee of safety, but it had worked thus far. Looking down at his friend, Jahmil saw that he was terribly wounded and bleeding profusely. The fifty-caliber round had taken off Ahmed's entire right arm and part of the shoulder. Although he was still conscious, and trying to stand, there was no doubt that Ahmed would soon die from shock and loss of blood.

100 yards to go.

Now, with only about fifteen seconds before impact, Ahmed's condition did not matter. Jahmil locked the rudder into position and then helped his friend, Ahmed, stand up so he could see their fate.

Workers were running for their lives. Many were diving into the river trying to swim away and others were running down planks onto shore. Some of the brave security personnel were firing on the Dhul Fiqar, but their small arms and rifle fire was ineffectual. Jahmil knew that any escape and any resistance was truly futile at this point. He and Ahmed had wrapped the fate of all of these, and many more, together with their own.

Impact.

The Dhul Fiqar plowed into the middle of the propane barge and the last thing Jahmil and Ahmed perceived was a brilliantly bright flash of light, as the pressure sensors on the bow of the craft worked as they had been designed and set off the C4 explosives. Those two thousand pounds of very high explosive created a brilliant, elongated fireball that expanded to over 75 yards in diameter and 150 yards long in milliseconds. The elongated fireball was due to the casing of Kevlar and hardened steel surrounding the C4, directing its energy forward into the barge, although as it turned out, with the Dhul Fiqar so close to the barge, it was wholly unnecessary

Within milliseconds, the propane stored on the barge, almost a full load of one hundred thousand gallons, ignited in a much larger explosion. The fireball from that detonation was a full two hundred yards in diameter and immediately incinerated anything within its reach. That reach included the nearest storage tank, which was being used to load the barge and where over one quarter of a million gallons of propane were stored. The fireball from that conflagration was fully one-third of a mile in diameter and set off a domino effect of similarly massive explosions as every storage tank in the facility, six of them, detonated one after another.

The blast and shock waves resulting from the massive explosions of the propane storage tanks leveled every building within a one half-mile radius of the facility, and set fire to most structures within a mile. Over twenty thousand people worked or lived within a mile radius of the facility ... the mortality rate to those individuals was just under thirty percent, with double that number injured, many of them seriously.

March 15, 2006, 18:27 MST
Bonneville Power Administration Substation
15 Miles Northwest of Fontaine, UT

Hector Ortiz and his five comrades looked down on the substation.

There was no one around.

Hector turned to his men and simply said.

"Okay, let's go."

They drove their four wheelers down the slope to the gravel road that ran next to the substation. Three of the men went down the road a quarter of a mile to provide security, but as it turned out none was needed. Apart from some small motion detectors that Hector recognized inside the fence, and what appeared to be a video camera, there appeared to be no security. The camera and the motion detectors were quickly dispensed of with a silenced pistol Hector carried.

No matter, they were all well disguised just the same, and the VINs for all of these units had been ground off. The units themselves were built of so many spare parts, that no trace on their ownership or origin would be possible.

Hector and his men had camped out in a popular four wheeling area for the last two days several miles west of the substation. At night they rested and planned, and during the day they did the minimum amount of four wheeling necessary to keep up appearances that they were learning to use these new vehicles they had purchased from friends. Outside of friendly advice from passers by, no one asked anything other than passing questions.

Then, last evening the warning for the execution of their operation came in code over Hector's radio. Immediately after receiving the message, they all retired and rested very well for the rest of the night. This afternoon, the actual execute order had come and they had gathered their "equipment" and drove over the intervening hills to the substation.

Now, explosives had been set to completely destroy the substation and several of the high voltage lines leading into and away from it. They were all wired together to a single timer, and the timer had been set. All of them had then moved back into the hills where Hector brought out his remote detonation device in case it was needed.

It was not.

From a distance of two miles, they watched the explosions as the substation was destroyed and as the towers came down. As they crashed to the earth, 10% of the power supply to Southern California was also cut off.

This had a rippling and cascading effect throughout the western electric grid, particularly considering the success of some of Hector's other teams that day. It all amounted to complete power outage that lasted three days to over ten million Americans in the western United States, at a time when fear and chaos gripped the entire country.

But not all of Hector's teams enjoyed such success that day.

March 15, 2006, 18:42 MST
Above the Dam
12 miles northwest of Boise, ID

Brent was watching the hills and ravines across the canyon from their hilltop. David was watching the near side, down and to the right and to the left of their position on the hill. Both men had normal and thermal night vision scopes for their M-14 rifles, and both men had been well trained in their use.

Brent and David carried Motorola, frequency hopping, hand-held military radios with which they communicated with the Ada County response team located below them, near the dam. Brent and David were volunteers in a State of Idaho program providing local security to local infrastructure.

The program was called, "Homeland Defenders", and it had been started four years earlier in nearby Gem County. Basically, it called for volunteers from the local population to stand watch over major infrastructure, and augment local law enforcement in protecting them from terrorists. It had been the brainchild of a local citizen in Gem County in the wake of the terrorist attacks on New York City and Washington, D.C. in September of 2001. The program simply called for the local Sheriff's office to recruit and train volunteers who would stand watch twenty-four hours a day. Eight, three hour shifts of two-man teams at each critical infrastructure were called for. The positions were completely volunteer, meaning there was no pay, but the team members did get the training and they got issued fine thirty-caliber rifles and with day and night scopes, which they got to keep.

There had been more volunteers than there were places to guard.

The idea had caught on in Idaho. From several county Sheriffs who adopted it, to the State Governor who officially endorsed it in 2004 and implemented it statewide. The next year, the governors of Montana and Nevada did the same thing. This was the program the Director of National Homeland Security wanted to implement nation wide.

Now, this early evening in Ada County, Brent and David were above their local dam taking their watch. That watch would end at 9 PM.

"Holy crap, Ada County Three-Seven, this is Sentinel, I've got something!"

David listened for a moment. He had been coming up here three times a week for the last year with Brent, and though they'd seen a few teenagers hiking around and perhaps an occasional local misdemeanor, he'd never heard Brent use this tone.

"Go ahead Sentinel, this is Ada County Three-Seven. State your observations."

Brent continued speaking into the microphone clipped to his lapel.

"Six … no eight guys. Coming down the slope three hundred yards to the east of the gate at the top of the dam. They're using the military crest on the opposite side away from view of the dam to descend. Four appear to be carrying large duffel bags over their backs, the other four are armed with what appears to be assault rifles … I'll call them AR-15's."

David scanned his area again, and seeing nothing, he looked over to where Brent was indicating. Sure enough, with the aid of the scope, he could clearly see several men stealthily descending in a manner that would allow them to approach the entrance gate to the facility at the top of the dam unobserved. Right now they were stopped and two of their number were using thermal scopes of their own to check out the facility.

"We copy that Sentinel. Be advised. Ada Air One-One is en route. Ada County Three-Seven will interdict as they cross the road. Please advise when they are crossing and provide covering fire if necessary. You are authorized to fire upon any Tango who raises a weapon once the order to stop and surrender is given."

Brent looked at David, knowing that he had heard.

"Okay David, we'll target the shooters. You take any shooter on the left, and I'll take the right. I'll pass the word to Ada County just before they reach the road, and we'll go from there."

Over the next half hour, and as dusk set in, the eight man team slowly made their way to a position about one hundred yards up the canyon from the gate, holding back in the brush about ten yards from the road. When they had held that position for another twenty minutes, assuring themselves that they were ready and that no vehicles were approaching, and allowing it to get completely dark, they began to approach the road.

As they reached the road, a spotlight was turned on from Ada County Three-Seven, an armored, four-wheel-drive Swat Team carrier.

"You next to the road, this is the Ada County Sheriff's office, you are surrounded and covered. Throw down your weapons and put your hand in the air NOW."

The response was immediate, three of the shooters raised their rifles. Brent and David fired simultaneously and one of the shooters went down. The others opened fire and took out the SWAT Team light.

What followed was a classic nighttime firefight. The SWAT team and the terrorists had tracer ammo, so a deadly light show showed positions and aim. Both sides had thermal and starlight equipment to assist them, so the shots were not entirely wild, though a few wild rounds were directed at the hilltop upon which Brent and David sat. But, with Brent and David on the opposite hill commanding the high ground with their M-14 sniper rifles, and with the arrival of Ada Air One-One, the terrorists never had a chance.

In the end, after two Sheriff's deputies were killed, and another two wounded, all eight terrorists had to either be killed or seriously wounded before they would stop fighting. Once this occurred, the Sheriff's deputies began to warily approach the area, while Ada Air One-One spotlighted the location. Before the deputies could get to them, and as Brent and David looked on, the least wounded of the three wounded terrorists quickly used a small hand gun to kill the other two ... and then himself.

Later, as Brent and David were debriefed, it became clear what the purpose of the assault on the dam was intended to do. The duffel bags were filled with 100 pounds of C4 each, and with all the necessary implements to set up shaped contact charges, wire them, and blow out the dam.

Below the dam, in the Boise River valley, over fifty thousand people, the Capitol and the Governor's mansion would have all been at mortal risk from any breach of that dam. Brent and David were justifiably hailed as heroes in Idaho, and across the nation. The "Homeland Defenders" program would now easily be established nation-wide after news of its successful implementation in Idaho spread around the country.

March 16, 2006, 07:27 Local Time
Flight Leader, "Spider" Flight, SU-35
320 Kilometers south east of Taiwan
South China Sea

Commander Ni Hsu reflected on the past fifteen minutes of combat as his flight returned to his carrier, PLAN 1002 Shanghai. So much had happened so quickly.

With twelve SU-30's, eight SU-25's and two SU-35's supported by twelve B6-D bombers and twelve A-5 Fantan strike aircraft, Commander Ni had expected the British task force to be a push over. He had been wrong.

First of all, the Shanghai carrier group had not been able to get in position to launch a strike with its SS-N-26 Yakhont missiles. Had those missiles arrived just prior to his attack, he was certain that the entire British Task Force would have been destroyed. As it was, they were forced to rely on air-launched missiles alone, which required them to get much closer and forced them to contend with the Harrier air cover over the two British carriers.

His eight air superiority SU-30's should have been more than a match for the Harriers, except he had not counted on the numbers of Harriers that quickly got into the air, or the effectiveness of the AMRAAM missiles they carried. Reflecting back, the ability of the new AEW.7 Sea King helicopter to detect them at two hundred and eighty kilometers as opposed to the one hundred and eighty they had anticipated made a significant difference.

What had been a CAP of four aircraft had quickly turned into eight and they were immediately vectored toward his flight. Another eight Harriers quickly replaced the first eight over the two Carriers.

The ensuing dogfight required Ni to employ his other four SU-30's, which were supposed to have been reserved for surface strike missions. The long range AMRAAM's from the Harriers destroyed six SU-30's before they had a chance to engage. Once the remaining SU-30's became involved at close range they downed six of the Harriers and sent the remaining two into a headlong retreat while losing another two SU-30's.

While this had been taking place, the second group of eight Harriers had been vectored towards the twenty-four HY-4 anti-shipping missiles launched by the B6-D bombers. These twenty-four missiles heavily damaged one British Type 42C escort, the York, and sank a Type 23 escort, the Duke. In addition, they necessitated the expenditure of large numbers of Sea Dart & Sea Wolf AAW missiles by the British task force while drawing off the Harriers. This left the path open for Ni's strike force to launch its missiles.

An SU-25 from the PLAN Shanghai.

Each SU-35 carried four AS-11 Kilter anti-radar missiles. All eight of these were launched. At a speed in excess of Mach 2, they attacked the British radar systems, particularly on the two Type 42 air defense AAW destroyers.

Simultaneously, the SU-25's came into range and launched their AS-17 anti-ship missiles. These had been specially configured by the Chinese to operate from their naval SU-25's. Each Su-25 carried four AS-17's. Very quickly, thirty-two mach-two missiles were inbound on the British task force. The effect of these missiles was the most devastating.

Twelve of the AS-17's were targeted on the Invincible. Sea Dart AAW missiles accounted for one of these, Sea Wolf AAW missiles accounted for another two, and then the CIWS on the Invincible downed three. But six of the AS-17's scored on the carrier. As she slowed and then stopped in the water, fires burned out of control all along the flight deck and secondary explosions racked the ship. Another eight AS-17's targeted the HMS Ocean, the new helicopter carrier. Only one of these was destroyed before the Ocean's CIWS accounted for another two. Five missiles impacted the Ocean and left her moving slow in the water and burning.

The last twelve AS-17's were split evenly between the carrier Illustrious and the assault ship Albion. Having to choose between protecting the carrier or the LPD, most of the defenses were directed at knocking down the missiles targeted on Illustrious. Between the escorts and the Illustrious' CIWS, this effort was successful and no impacts were scored on the second carrier. But four of the six missiles targeted on the Albion scored direct hits, setting her ablaze from stem to stern. Thirty seconds after these impacts a tremendous secondary explosion broke her back and sent her beneath the waves.

The HMS Invincible and the HMS Ocean in the China Sea

During this attack, another six Harriers from the Illustrious ravaged Ni's attack group destroying two SU-30's, one of his SU-35's and six SU-25's.

The A-5 Fanton attack followed all of this action. Its missiles sank the burning Invincible and the damaged Type 42 escort, damaged another Type 42, and sank a second Type 23 escort. In the process this group lost nine of their aircraft to Harriers returning from their attack on the HY-4 missiles.

Now, as Ni was returning to the Shanghai, he counted the costs. From a total of twenty-two attacking aircraft with his group, he was returning with seven. The land based air group lost nine aircraft. That's a total of twenty-four high performance attack aircraft for three destroyers, a carrier and an amphibious assault ship. It certainly had not been a push over, but it was a great victory nonetheless.

The decimated British task force turned away, trailing dark smoke from the HMS Ocean. Ultimately, it would make good its escape. The Illustrious, a

Type 42 escort, two Type 22 escorts and the heavily damaged Ocean were all that returned to England. No British help would arrive in Korea.

March 16, 2006, 07:45 Local Time
Fantail of USS Bonhomme Richard
415 Nautical Miles ENE of Okinawa
Western Pacific

JT was not a deeply religious man. Oh, he believed in God, and he knew that God was the source of rights and true morality, he just wasn't one to very often articulate such things. Today was an exception. No, today, He thanked God openly and vocally that he was alive.

All around him, similar sentiments were being expressed. Feelings of humility, sadness, shock, bewilderment, anger and all of the emotions one would expect in such circumstances were running wild amongst those who were not on duty. Many of them, like JT, were on the fantail of the vessel taking a smoke to relieve the tension as the ship put more distance between itself and the horrendous ambush that had been staged against the U.S. Navy.

Some of the toughest, deadliest Marines in America's compliment were unashamedly crying. Some of the crustiest, most foul mouthed sailors on the face of the earth were weeping uncontrollably and uttering whispered prayers. All of them were still shaken from their near death.

"Seeing almost six thousand men and women die right before your very eyes has a way of doing that to a person," thought JT.

The USS Constellation's destruction had been just like that. No more than three miles off their starboard side, JT had watched the ungodly speed of those streaks in the water, leaving their surreal wakes, as they sped towards the Constellation. And there was not a solitary thing anyone could do to stop them. Two of them had hit the Constellation within about one hundred feet of one another directly amidships.

To see a structure that massive, that housed that many people just split apart and fold in two like that, and do it so quickly was beyond words to describe. Even now he could hear the God forsaken sound of that rending, see all the aircraft ... the F/A-18F's, the S3B'a, the EA-6B's and the Hawkeyes ... sliding together like so many toys into that maelstrom in the middle. He could almost believe that all those specs sliding down the deck, flying through the air, were men and women... in fact he knew they had been.

It was an image that would stay with him the rest of his life, and with every living soul who had witnessed it ... it was an image he had to share, share with America so that they could understand what had happened here. It was also an image of a sudden death that JT had almost shared.

Had it not been for the USS Thach, that marvelously quick and nimble frigate, whose commander had unflinchingly run in between the Bonhomme Richard and a similar approaching death, it was a fate JT knew he would be experiencing right now. What an act of selflessness and what an act of heroism that saving action had been. JT hoped that the Captain of the Thach was awarded the Medal of Honor ... JT knew he deserved it.

"God bless them and rest them ... God bless them all!"

JT voiced out loud with great emotion and tears streaming down his face as he thought on it. Surrounding sailors and Marines could only nod, or voice an "amen" in response ... they knew exactly what he was talking about.

No, America MUST hear this tale and see the images he had digitally recorded. So that they could understand what the awful ambush had produced in the way of death and anguish, and in the way of heroism. So that they would never forget ... and so that America would produce the righteous indignation and absolute commitment to a just retribution that this act MUST produce for an ultimately victorious America.

But right now, that victory looked to be a long, long ways away.

March 16, 2006, 08:04 Local Time
Flag Conference Room, USS Kitty Hawk
Exiting Bungo Strait
Between Kyushu and Shikoku, Japan

Admiral Ben Ryan reflected on the grim reality of this day, a day that had barely started on the clock, but that had already lasted for an eternity. He was the soul surviving task force commander of CBT 77. So many good men, so many close friends, so many future plans ... all gone.

He looked at the shocked faces of those gathered with him for this briefing.

"Folks, I know you are shocked, I know we have all lost a lot of good friends and compatriots today. But, I need you to pull together now. We have been trained to defend our nation in just these circumstances, and our nation has been savaged today ... and not just here in the Western Pacific."

At the mention of this, several faces looked up, an alertness returning to their eyes. This is exactly what the Admiral had hoped for.

"That's right, there have been other attacks. The principle of which ladies and gentlemen occurred on the Continental United States!"

Audible intakes of breath could be heard as the Admiral paused for just a moment and then continued.

"Apparently, hundreds of ballistic missiles were used, all of them conventional thank God. Just like those we saw an hour or so ago descending on airfield and shipyards in Japan. The White House has been destroyed, but I can say that the President is safe, having narrowly escaped. The Vice President and several members of the cabinet were killed. The Pentagon, the Capitol, Newport News Shipyards, Ingalls Shipyards, Bath Iron Works, San Diego, Bremerton and many other sites have been hit. There are reports of terrorist attacks on all types of infrastructure in inland areas. There are many, many civilian and military casualties."

After allowing this to sink in for a few seconds, he continued.

"We have been trained to do something about this, and we are going to try and do so. Just after the attacks began, we received a communique from the National Reconnaissance Office (NRO). It indicated that the Chinese had fielded a new weapon of some sort on many of their container ships and on Luhai, Luhu and Luda class destroyers. We now know what these weapons are and what they are capable of."

"We also know the location of five to seven "groups" of Red Chinese ships that launched these weapons on us. They are made up of a single container ship escorted by two destroyers from those classes I just mentioned."

"Due to the nature of the risk and due to the need for force protection for the gators that have survived, we have been ordered to retire to Hawaii with all due haste. We are to gather the remainder of CBT 77, from the other Joint Task Forces as we go."

"As we depart, I have ordered the aircraft from the John Stennis and the Constellation, which were airborne when the attack came, to form up and make a strike on one of these groups. They will attack in conjunction with a Tomahawk strike that has already been launched from our task force. Based on the outcome of that attack, we may plan additional air strikes on the other groups while we are still in range to do so. We will launch as many

Tomahawk missiles as we can. The Japanese Air Force and Navy have assured me that they will continue to do likewise after our departure."

Regarding the Japanese Navy, they will be augmenting our escort as we depart by providing additional ASW and AAW support. You will see two of their new Takanami class guided missile destroyers and one of their Kongo class Aegis destroyers, the Myoko, form up with us in the next hour or so. They will travel with us for fifteen hundred miles, until we are clear of imminent danger. They are doing this at great risk to themselves, at a time when they are sorely needed. We should remember this, they are going to need our help over here as soon as we can possibly return."

March 16, 2006, 08:21 Local Time
Raptor Strike
280 nautical miles SE of Okinawa
Western Pacific

They had named themselves "Raptor Strike". Although they were a mixed group from two carriers that no longer existed, they still carried a lot of sting.

Each carrier had already sent an E2-C Hawkeye AEW aircraft aloft that morning before the attack. In addition they each had two F-14D's aloft for CAP and two, F/A-18F's aloft for anti-surface duties. When Admiral Patterson had ordered the ready birds to be launched around 06:45, both carriers had launched two more F/A-18F's, two more F-14D's, a KS-3A tanker and an EA-6B EW aircraft. Now, from this, a strike package was

An F/A-18F of Gator Strike.

assembled to go after one of the Red Chinese container ship groups, the one off to their southwest that had attacked them this morning.

Four F/A-18F's carrying four AGM-94 Joint Air to Surface Standoff Missiles (JASSM), two EA-6B's carrying four AGM-88 High Speed Anti-radiation Missiles (HARM), four F-14D's flying escort and one E2-C Hawkeye providing radar and early warning coverage were approaching their launch coordinates.

"Raptor flight leader, this is Frisbee two-three, be advised that Tomahawk strike is now seventy miles from target and closing. You have reached your launch window and may launch at any time."

The flight leader knew that timing was everything, he felt that they were behind schedule and therefore, rather than launch at the maximum distance, decided to close another twenty miles on the target.

"Frisbee two-three, this is Raptor lead. We roger your last. We will ingress further to maximize strike effectiveness. Will advise, out."

This would have the dual advantage of getting his JASSM's, which were slower than the Tomahawks, in much close before launch. This would give them a better chance of a hit and would have them arriving soon after the Tomahawks. It would also allow his anti-radar missiles, which were very fast and which would surge ahead of the Tomahawks to optimize the spread between themselves and the trailing Tomahawks. Launch too soon, and the HARM's get there too far in advance of the slower Tomahawks. In that event, the enemy simply turns off their radar until the HARM's expend themselves, and then turns it back on to engage the Tomahawks. Launch too late, and the enemy has engaged all of your slow Tomahawks before your HARM's can do anything about it.

When Raptor flight closed to within fifty miles of their target, but still twelve to fifteen miles outside of the range of the KS-2 missiles that the targeted ships carried, the flight leader had all aircraft launch their missiles. Eight HARM's and sixteen JASSM's were launched. As this took place, twenty-four Tomahawks from the Kitty Hawk battle group were just entering the effective range of the KS-2.

Except for two F/A-18F's left to observe, Raptor flight then turned towards the Kitty Hawk. En route, they would refuel from the KS-3A's and then proceed to land on the carrier's overloaded deck.

As the inbound Tomahawk strike closed on the Chinese group of three ships, the first

F/A-18F landing on the Kitty Hawk.

layer of defenses encountered was the KS-2 anti-air missile. The KS-2 was a very effective missile, but the Tomahawk was also effective, coming in low, just above the waves, and having many electronic counter measures built in. The result was that the stream of twenty-four Tomahawks was reduced to twelve by the long-range KS-2 defenses of the three Chinese ships. The most effective of these was the Tactical Strike ship itself, the PLAN 2019 Hunan. With its forty VLS cells filled with KS-2 missiles, and its reload capability, it simply kept pumping out the missiles until the oncoming threat was too close. Then, the close-in defenses of each ship came into play.

The escorting Luda class destroyer was the weakest anti-air platform of the three, so therefore to it fell the dire task of illuminating all of its radar so as to draw missiles away from the other two ships. As a result, it took the brunt of the HARM missiles attack, soaking up six of the eight missiles. These hits severely disabled the ship and may have sunk it, but that was rendered moot a few moments later as three of the surviving Tomahawk missiles also struck the craft. With the penetrating design of the Tomahawk warhead, and its one thousand pound payload of high explosive, the Luda class destroyer was completely obliterated and she sank with all hands in just under two minutes.

The Luhai class destroyer escorting the Hunan was a much more modern and capable design. Her close-in defenses were layered and effective, consisting of both short range Crotale missiles and eight thirty-seven millimeter close in weapon systems (CIWS). As a result, four of the five Tomahawks targeted on her were downed by her defenses, but the last two HARM missiles and one of the Tomahawks impacted. This slowed her to twelve knots and knocked out her close in missiles and four of her CIWS.

The Hunan also had effective close-in defenses. This consisted of eight, thirty millimeter, fifty-four caliber, AK-630M gatling guns that operated much like the twenty millimeter Phalanx systems on U.S. ships, but shooting a larger projectile. This system knocked down all of the Tomahawk missiles targeted on the Hunan, the last being destroyed a mere four hundred yards from the port side of the ship. This near miss damaged the ship as exploding fuel and debris, continuing to move forward with their failing inertia, impacted the ship, killing a number of crewmen, setting a moderate fire on deck and disabling two of the LRASD mounts on that side.

While the Hunan and her Luhai escort were engaged in defending themselves against the HARM and Tomahawk threat, the JASSM strike launched by the F/A-18F's was bearing down on the two vessels.

Of the sixteen JASSM's launched, only four were destroyed by the distracted and therefore much less effective KS-2 defenses. Of the remaining twelve missiles, eight were targeted for the Hunan and four for the remaining Luhai class escort. Four of the eight JASSM's impacted on the Hunan, resulting in many serious secondary explosions, and slowing her to six knots with a significant list to her port side. Two of the four JASSM's targeted on the Luhai impacted with catastrophic results as she went dead in the water, took on a terrible list and then capsized and sank a few minutes later taking most of her crew with her.

All of this was observed by the pair of F/A-18F's that remained in the area to observe results of the attack. They were able to do this with impunity, remaining just outside of KS-2 range, since there was no Chinese air activity this far south of Okinawa on this day. Based on their reports a follow-on strike of eight Tomahawks found the Hunan ninety minutes later as she tried to limp away, and sent her to the bottom of the Pacific.

It was a very hollow and poor victory on this day of abject defeat.

15 March, 2006, 20:29 EST
150 Miles NE of Cape Hatteras, North Carolina
Bridge, USCGS Gallatin (WHEC 721)
Atlantic, Ocean

Captain Thames listened as the reports continued to come in. Death, destruction, terror and chaos were gripping areas all over the country.

Apparently the President was alive, but he was still not in a position to address the nation. A nation that was not sure how many of its other political and military leaders were alive.

USCG Gallatin searching for Guizhou.

The Pentagon had been hit hard, much worse than the September 2001 attacks. Three of the five sides took hits and many portions collapsed. The Capitol building was attacked ... and apparently the dome had completely collapsed with much of the structure under the weight of several direct hits. Many representatives and senators had not escaped.

News of the military disaster in the Far East had not yet reached them.

"Well," the Captain thought, "we're out in the water now trying to track down one of the perpetrators."

The message had been broadcast to all units now, Chinese container ships may have weapons aboard, including long range ballistic missiles.

He felt his High Endurance Cutter (WHEC) was up to and capable of tracking down and prosecuting such a target if he got the chance. With his seventy-six millimeter dual-purpose deck gun, his twenty millimeter Phalanx (CIWS) and particularly his eight Harpoon missiles, he was ready to catch up with any vessel that had attacked his nation and either take it down, or put it down.

Right now, he was prosecuting one such lead. A single Chinese container ship had been waiting for clearance into the Chesapeake when the attacks occurred and several other ships that were also waiting had named this ship, the Guizhou, as the shooter. He had a track on it now, about seventy miles in front of him.

"Jake, get Lieutenant Ross on the horn for me."

Less than thirty seconds later, the Captain was handed the hand set. Lieutenant Ross was the pilot of the HH-35 Dauphin helicopter that was embarked on the Gallatin. The Dauphin was a good design, perfect qualities for the multiple roles required of the Coast Guard of search and rescue, interdiction, and potential combat. The Captain keyed his hand set.

"Mallet, this is Cut-base, how do you copy? State your situation"

A clear signal came immediately back.

"Cut-base, I read you loud and clear. I am about thirty miles from the tango-01 and have him on radar. You should be getting the feed. A single ship, looks like a container ship from here, but I am going in for a closer look."

The Captain talked briefly with his Combat Information Center, they did indeed have the radar track and already had four Harpoons targeted on the vessel.

"Ross, we have the digital feed and all targeting is already programmed. Try and get a positive ID, then get back to me. Be careful, Cut-base out."

The line was silent for a several seconds, then

"I roger that Cut-base ... we are closing to twenty-five miles now and reducing altitude ... WAIT ONE, we are being illuminated, I say again, vessel has lit us up. MISSILE launch, I have a missile launch ... two, three launches. Evading."

Dauph-1 approaches the Guizhou.

The abrupt nature of the change stunned the Captain and everyone on the bridge momentarily ... but only for a second or two.

"Ross, get down on the deck and get the hell out of their range!"

"CIC, fire! I say again, FIRE! Engage the target with Harpoon missiles!"

"Ross? …. Mallet? … Radar, what do you have on Mallet?"

The radar officer looked at his scope and then at his screen.

"Captain, he's off radar and we have lost the data feed."

Just then, from forward of the bridge, massive gouts of flame kicked out of launch canisters as one after another, four RGM-84A Harpoon missiles were launched. They accelerated to near 600 knots and after an initial climb, they arched over and descended to about fifty feet above the water, continuing on their track towards the target.

Eight minutes later, when it was clear that at least three of the missiles had been shot down before they could reach the target, the Captain ordered another four missiles launched. He also ordered max speed of thirty knots and continued on towards the Guizhou.

This time, only two of his missiles were definitely shot down, but the radar image of the Guizhou was still on the screen and moving, although now the speed had slowed from twenty to eight knots. Smoke could be seen over the horizon as the Gallatin continued to close.

At a range of twenty miles, the masts and upper super structure of the Guizhou could just be seen over the horizon, with smoke still billowing up from forward of the super structure, but still below the horizon. The Captain ordered the Gallatin to close to within firing range of their seventy-six millimeter dual-purpose gun, another twelve miles. They were never going to make it.

At a range of eighteen miles, the sonar operator shouted a warning of an object in the water coming at them at unbelievable speed from off the starboard bow. The Captain ran to the starboard side of the bridge and was just in time to see an unbelievably fast underwater streak, trailing a fearsome wake close on his ship and explode almost directly beneath where he was standing. It was the last thing he saw on this earth.

The USCGS Gallatin (WHEC 721) stopped dead in the water as the sea flowed into the gaping rent. Very quickly, she settled and then sank four minutes and twenty-eight seconds later at 22:07. Only thirty-three members of the crew, out of total of one hundred and seventy-seven, escaped alive.

The Guizhou, damaged by two Harpoon missile hits from the Gallatin, continued to limp further south, where she was located at 23:25 hours by a flight of four P3-C Orion's out of Oceana Naval Air Station. Each Orion employed very powerful surface search radar and carried four Harpoon missiles. Twelve of these missiles were launched at the Guizhou from well

outside of anti-aircraft missile range. Of the twelve, five got through her KS-2 and CIWS defenses and scored hits on her. One of the hits produced a massive secondary explosion in the forward section of the ship as reloads for the VLS missile system detonated. This explosion literally blew off the Guizhou's bow and at 23:52, she too sank beneath the waves.

The position of the Guizhou's sinking was painstakingly noted by circling US aircraft as rescue ships were dispatched. American intelligence agencies, shocked and stinging from the days events, were already very anxious to gather as much information regarding the new Chinese technologies and weapons systems as possible. They intended to accomplish this in whatever manner they could, from surviving crew, from wreckage floating on the

A P3-C from Oceana.

ocean surface or from a deep-sea salvage operation if necessary. As far as they were concerned, and given the gravity of the situation, the sooner that information was recovered, the better.

EPILOGUE

March 16, 2006, 10:00 Local
Government Conference Center
Beijing, The People's Republic of China

Jien Zenim stood resolute before the cameras. In a few seconds he would deliver a historically momentous statement to the people of China and to the world. That statement would be direct. It would announce in fact what the original CAS announcement had said in principle almost one year ago.

In the end, Mao had been right about politics and where that power derives.

As he waited, he thought of the events of this morning. Initial reports were beyond belief in terms of their success. "Breath of Fire" was exceeding expectations, both in Asia and America. He was certain that the hold that America had on eastern Asia had been broken, and he was convinced that China's leadership in the CAS would keep it that way.

As the light flashed to green, he began his prepared statement.

"People of China, it is with sorrow that I announce to you that a state of war exists between The People's Republic of China and the United States of America. This is not what the peace loving people of China desired."

"However, as a result of unequivocal information that we have received and evidence that proves it beyond a doubt, it has become clear that the United States government has embarked on a systematic program to thwart the will of free peoples around the world. They have done this by plundering the resources of other nations, by undermining the social order of other nations, by ignoring the confirmed vote of other nations, and by seeking to murder the heads of state of other nations whenever it suits their presumed needs."

"We have seen this recently in the former state of Iraq, where the people voted to align themselves with the Greater Islamic Republic after the death of their head of state. Evidence indicated then that the United States might have been complicit in the death of that head of state. America then tried to thwart the will of the people by raising up and supporting a puppet, break away government in northern Iraq. They resorted to military force to force the issue. When GIR forces liberated those areas, and when the leader of the GIR unilaterally offered an end to the fighting, America resorted to an attempted assassination to thwart this leader's attempt to bring peace."

"Now, here in Asia, we see an internal dispute among the Korean peoples. Again, the United States is seeking to exert its will. They were sending a vast armada with tens of thousands of soldiers to accomplish this."

"The People of China are a patient people. We are a peace loving people. But we are also a just people who can only stand back so long while such a bully ravages others ... particularly others who have entered into peaceful and profitable economic and friendship agreements with the People's Republic of China. Today, the Chinese people reached their limit. This morning at 06:00, I ordered elements of the People's Liberation Army to engage and interdict American forces. I must tell you that our forces have succeeded beyond our projections. You can be proud of your heroes, they have made all of China proud, and they will continue to make us proud as we push this alien mentality back across the ocean from where it came. "

"In that regard, as I am sure most of you have heard, I also ordered our forces to strike America in its homeland, the same way they have done to so many other nations. The targets were all military in nature, from their command and control, up to and including their commander in chief, to their shipbuilding, air force and other bases. We have heard reports of terror attacks on American citizens and we unequivocally disavow such attacks. We have no knowledge of, and will provide no support to, such attacks."

"To the people of America I say. We are your friends. We seek peace. Use the tools and institutions you have to remove those in your own government who use your resources in such terrible ways. Elect new leaders, who are truly interested in peace, and there will be peace."

"To America's allies I say, cease your support for such a monstrous government. We invite you to adopt the Three Wisdoms of which you have heard us speak. Adapt it to your particular culture and economic principles. If you do not desire this, that is fine.. But, if you persist in your support of the monstrous policies of the current American administration, then we will wage war on you until you can no longer export such a base value system."

"To all the people of China, and to all the peoples of our Coalition of Asian States I say, let us unite and keep interlopers and intruders and those who would destroy our cultures and our peace away. Let's push them and their corporations of greed and death and vice far from our shores, and let us not stop until they are not capable of exporting them here again. Good night."

March 16, 2006, 01:20 EST
Aspen Lodge , Presidential Bedroom
Camp David, Maryland

Norm Weisskopf could not sleep. He was thankful for his wife's deep, even breathing, for her life. He was also thankful that he finally got aboard Air Force One. For about half an hour they had been very close to a full nuclear exchange with China. But when it was clear than none of the missiles were nuclear, biological or chemical, that crisis had passed.

"Well, we all failed our nation this day," thought the President, and boy had they. The list of estimates kept appearing again and again in his mind.

EYES ONLY – TOP SECRET --- ESTIMATED LOSSES – 03/16/06

Ship Class	Ship Name	Damage	Killed	Injured
CVN-74	John Stennis	SUNK	4,758	1,108
CV-64	Constellation	SUNK	5,965	48
LHA-5	Peleliu	SUNK	2,760	235
LHD-3	Kearsage	SUNK	1,850	653
LPD-15	Ponce	SUNK	885	575
LPD-10	Juneau	SUNK	774	250
LPD-8	Dubuque	SUNK	1,212	38
LSD-52	Pearl Harbor	SUNK	921	208
LSD-50	Carter Hill	SUNK	450	376
LSD-45	Comstock	SUNK	621	256
LSD-42	Germantown	SUNK	345	173
CG-65	Chosin	SUNK	421	85
CG-75	Lake Chaplain	SUNK	389	118
DDG-73	Decatur	SUNK	231	78
DD-967	Elliot	SUNK	277	114
FFG-43	Thach	SUNK	198	79
FFG-33	Jarrett	SUNK	149	94
AOE-7	Rainer	SUNK	321	123
AOE-10	Bridge	SUNK	298	175
SSN 763	Santa Fe	SUNK	142	0
SSN 759	Jefferson City	SUNK	142	0
SSN 752	Pasadena	SUNK	142	0
SSN 716	Salt Lake City	SUNK	142	0
USCG-721	Gallatin	SUNK	144	18
LHD-2	Essex	25%	124	221
LPD-17	San Antonio	35%	155	289
LPD-49	Harper's Ferry	30%	106	189
LSD-47	Rushmore	35%	154	202
LSD-43	Fort McHenry	40%	195	102
CG-73	Port Royal	20%	89	47
DDG-65	Benford	60%	108	105
DD-965	Kinkaid	50%	67	124

TOTALS	SUNK-25 DAMAGED-8	24,535	6,091

That was just the losses at sea. When you add to that the losses on Okinawa, the losses on Japan, the losses in Korea ... and then the horrific losses here in the continental United States itself; Bath Iron Works, Norfolk Shipyards, Newport News Shipbuilding, Ingalls Shipbuilding, San Diego, Los Angeles, Bremerton, the Pentagon, the Capitol, the White House ... the unspeakable toll in St. Louis ... the numbers were too much to take in ... too much to contemplate. America may well have lost more people in this one day than in all of the Vietnam War!

... and it was just the beginning. Reports while on Air Force One and since indicated large Chinese invasion forces, with hundreds and hundreds of small landing craft gathering along the coasts of China. They looked to be preparing for incursions into Korea across the Yellow Sea, the invasion of Taiwan and another force that could well be targeting the Philippines.

"My dear God ... where art Thou?" thought the President. It should bring tears to his eyes just to think on all of this and what it would mean ... but he had no more tears to shed.

Tomorrow morning, here at Camp David at 06:00 in the Laurel Lodge, he would hold his cabinet meeting. Dear God, some good people and close friends were gone! Alan, Timothy and Mike were all dead. Great Americans killed in the fulfilling of their duties. Apparently the three of them had been attending to other business upstairs while they waited on him to return from lunch to start the National Security meeting. The rest had already been seated down in the situation room and had been spared, albeit Jeremy and Fred had both been injured. The Vice President, the Secretary of Defense and the Director of the CIA were all dead and it was all he could do to contain his emotions.

Then at 8 AM he would have a joint session of Congress ... at least those who were alive and healthy enough to come. They would hold it in the Chapel here at Camp David and tend to the business of declaring war on the Chinese. Congress ... also decimated by this attack. Over one hundred Congressmen and thirty-seven Senators were dead in the collapsed Capitol. More good, cream of the crop Americans ... gone.

At 10 AM he would address the nation, and he prayed that God in Heaven would give him the strength and the wisdom to know what to say, to know how to lead his nation out of these horrific circumstances and return peace and stability to the world. It would take strength, it would take steel.

His mind wandered to the Pentagon ... over two thousand five hundred missing. Lots of good, loyal and hard working Americans who had made a life time out of serving their country. What about Admiral Patterson? There was an honest to God, modern John Wayne American if there ever was one ... now gone ... died fighting for his country.

All of those loyal, gifted craftsmen at the shipbuilding companies. So many of them gone this day too.

The DD-21 and the CVX ... destroyed before they could even be completed.

My God! The John Stennis and the Constellation! Both gone? Too much to absorb ... too much to take in.

... and then that lying, smug bastard Zenim. The very idea of his audacity! How dare he make such statements over the blood he shed this day! Well, he certainly left no doubt as to who the enemy is.

"Dear God in Heaven, let it be his undoing. Fashion us as an instrument to bring about the just retribution for the Jien Zenim's and Hasan Sayeed's of this world, a retribution they so richly deserve."

As the President thought this, he finally, mercifully, drifted off to sleep.

March 16, 2006, 09:57 EST
Presidential Office, Laurel House
Camp David, Maryland

Just a few minutes from now and a nation in shock, a world on the precipice, would receive America's answer, an answer as voiced by Norm Weisskopf.

He had slept deeply for the few hours available to him. Then, this morning he had held his meetings ... there would be many, many more.

His cabinet meetings had gone well, considering the familiar faces and good friends who were not there, who would never be there again. The agency heads were receiving a lot of information and the picture of what had been done to America was becoming horrifically clear.

It was becoming more and more clear to the President that China was the principle enemy, the probable mastermind behind most of what was going on. China had waited until America was fully engaged in the Middle East, and then lured significant American reserves into the Far East through its proxy, North Korea, before attacking. It was deadly serious, as China had made clear with the very nature of its attack. The fact that the terror attacks across the nation had occurred at virtually the same time made clear that they were part and parcel of the same attack, doing things that even China didn't want to "officially" muddy its hands with.

Thousands and thousands of American civilians were dead. Millions were without electricity. Propane heating fuel was going to be short for the rest of the spring.

The nation was going to have to take some significant time and effort to secure its borders, to secure its coastlines. All efforts would be poured into mobilizing America for war, her military, her industry, her financial dealings ... her people.

The congressional session had also been heartening, considering the circumstances and the many who would never be there again. But, other Americans would step in. Special elections would be held soon. The Declaration of War had been unanimous. The President has then shared with the representatives, and the cabinet who were present in the room, what his intentions were. He was heartened by their support. The nature of the threat was clear, and exactly who the enemy was, was also clear. Other political or partisan issues would be placed aside, defeating the common enemy would take precedence over all else.

On the allied front, the British, who were also savaged with the loss of the majority of their task force, were squarely in the war beside the United States. Canada and Australia had made their own declarations of war against China. The major European nations were taking up the matter. The United States was demanding that all NATO countries honor article five of that agreement.

As the cameras turned on, the President could be seen sitting in the Presidential office of the Laurel house at Camp David, with the Presidential Seal behind him and an American flag to his side.

"My fellow Americans. I spoke to you on February twenty-eighth about the true nature of the conflict we find ourselves embroiled in. I spoke of sacrifice, of faith, of self-sufficiency, and of unity. The absolute need for all of these was brought home to us yesterday in a dastardly, sneak attack without provocation or precedent on this nation."

"We have suffered a terrible ambush and a tremendous loss. Our White House is destroyed, along with many loyal Americans who worked there including several of the cabinet, and including, regrettably, the Vice President of the United States."

"Our Capitol building has been destroyed along with close to one hundred and fifty of our representatives and senators, all of whom were going about their sworn duty to this nation."

"Our Pentagon was again attacked, and damaged terribly, much more so than the attack in September of 2001. We have lost many, many good and loyal Americans who have devoted much of their lives to the protection of our nation, of our liberties. Now they have offered their very lives."

"Our military forces in the Far East were decimated and savaged in sneak attacks by ships posing as commercial and by a nation professing its neutrality. This is the same nation that carried out the attacks against our homeland here that I have just described to you. It is certain that the total death toll from these attacks will be close to 50,000 Americans. A number that may exceed our total combat losses in all of the Vietnam War."

"Yesterday, we heard the brazen words of a tyrant, a tyrant who tried to couch acts of terror and reprehensible acts of treachery into flowery phrases. We reject his phrases as the blatant lies that they are. We in America have seen and fought and defeated his kind before, and we shall do so now. The time for flowery words is past. We will bury our dead, we will approach or God in our grief, and then we will fight."

"As of 9:30 AM EST today, March 16, 2006, a state of war exists between the United States of America and the People's Republic of China. It will be a long war, it will be a costly war, but it will be a war fought for liberty and freedom and against the most blatant and abject tyranny the world has seen since Hitler, Stalin and Mao."

"I will not propose to speak to the citizens of other nations, but I will speak directly to Jien Zenim. I want you to listen to me Zenim, from this date forward I will never attach any title to your name, you are not deserving of any. So, listen well. You have made the same fatal mistake that Admiral Yamamoto made when he attacked America at Pearl Harbor in 1941. On that occasion, sixty-five years ago, Admiral Yamamoto indicated that he "feared they had awakened a sleeping giant and filled him with a terrible resolve." You have done just that Zenim. Read your history and find out what we Americans did with Admiral Yamamoto. We discovered where he was flying and then sent our aircraft in overwhelming numbers and killed him. Then we defeated their armies and their navies, and when they would not surrender unconditionally, we firebombed and then nuclear bombed their cities until they did. We did essentially the same to Nazi Germany and the world has been better for it. You have filled us with a resolve that is many times greater than that from Pearl Harbor, and you and any peoples who stand with you, shall suffer the consequences."

"This is not a threat … it is a promise. It is a personal promise from myself, and from any one who follows me in this office, to you, and to those who support you. We need no "coalition" to prosecute this purpose. You have filled us with our own coalition … it is called the people of the United States, and if you thought your petty, veiled threats would alter us from this purpose, you are again sadly and fatally mistaken."

"Zenim, you have admitted your cold blooded, calculated butchery to the world, and tried to call it good. History will judge you the same way it did Hitler, and the same way it did Mao, at least in the free, civilized world where the truth of tens of millions of dead is allowed to be discussed for the genocide it is."

"I make a commitment before the citizens of America and before God. We will not rest, we will not stop, we will never, EVER GIVE UP! If it takes us three years, or if it takes us ten years, our nation will overcome your dastardly and cowardly attack. We will produce aircraft carriers like the ones you sank by the dozens, we will produce technology to defeat whatever you may throw at us. We will produce weapons and methodologies that you will never conceive of in your closed, collective society."

"To our allies I say, STAND WITH US."

"We may have been knocked to the ground, but you can count on us getting back up stronger than before, filled with a righteous indignation that we will pour out on our enemies."

"STAND WITH US."

"We will not forsake you. The United States of America makes a solemn commitment and promise to return to liberate any who fall under the blight that is now spreading. We shall return! There will be no iron curtains at the end of this fight, the governments currently prosecuting these invasions and this tyranny will cease to exist every bit as much as Nazi Germany and Imperial Japan did."

"STAND WITH US."

"And we will stand with you to the end. If you choose not to, then all we ask is for you to stay out of the way, we will do this with, or without help."

"To our forces who are fighting on in Asia in the face of monumental odds. Who fight with the knowledge that our relief efforts have failed and that relief is far off, I say. "

"FIGHT ON."

"Fight this enemy wherever you may find him and out of whatever circumstances you may find yourself. Take to the hills if you must, take to the streets ... take to the night. They are the enemies of all we believe in and all we as a people stand for. "

"FIGHT ON. "

"With your weapons, with your fists, with stones and clubs if you must. Fight with your words, fight with non-compliance, fight with your silence. Like an American Hero from the Vietnam War, Rocky Versace. When they captured him and beat him and ultimately marched him off to execute him, he was singing "God bless America". "

"FIGHT ON."

"And never give up. We will make every effort to come for you soon, but if we cannot, do not despair. As surely as the sun rises in the east, we are coming. The time will arrive when like at Normandy on June 6th, 1944, you will look out and see the sea and the sky filled with the innumerable host of your comrades come to liberate the captive and put down the tyrant."

"To the American people I say, take heart! Yes, armies of tyranny and coercion are on the march in the Middle East and now ominously in Asia. Yes, many of our own have died at the hands of these tyrants. Yes, some of our friends will undoubtedly fall under the control of these tyrants, but our fathers and grandfathers faced the same threats. The fight for liberty has always been so tested. Like them, America will rise to the challenge and again be the vanguard for liberty for the world. We will liberate the captive and destroy the despot."

"In the mean time, WE HOLD THE COURSE."

"We will hold new elections to replace those who have fallen."

"WE HOLD THE COURSE."

"We will submit new names for the heads of those agencies to congress for approval where the former leaders have been taken from us."

"WE HOLD THE COURSE."

"We will establish, in keeping with the brave example from Idaho that yesterday saved tens of thousands of lives, a national Homeland Defenders program. This program will be established at the local level, allowing any American to sign up and defend infrastructure in this nation in the best traditions of local militia and deputized civilians defending their own."

"WE HOLD THE COURSE."

"I announce today, two national goals associated with the war effort, from which we will not step back even after we win this war."

1. We will be TOTALLY energy independent within eighteen months
2. We will build and deploy and effective anti-ballistic missile shield for the entire United States within three years.

"WE HOLD THE COURSE AND THAT COURSE IS LIBERTY!

"It is individual liberty, morality, accountability and responsibility. These are the key ingredients of our success as a people and our way of life. "

"To punctuate this, let me close with the following two quotes. From the Declaration of Independence: "

> *"We hold these truths to be self evident. That all men are created equal, that they are endowed by their Creator with certain unalienable rights, that among these are LIFE, LIBERTY and the PURSUIT OF HAPPINESS."*

"The other is from Patrick Henry. "

> *"We shall not fight our battles alone. There is a just God who presides over the destinies of Nations, and who will raise up friends to fight our battles for us. The battle, Sir, is not to the strong alone. It is to the vigilant, the active, the brave. Besides, Sir, we have no choice. If we were base enough to desire it, it is now too late to retire from the contest. There is no retreat but in submission and slavery! "*

"So my fellow Americans, WE HOLD THE COURSE. Though we have been injured, though we have been grievously hurt, we do not bow, and WE DO NOT COWER. "

"Millions who have gone before have purchased our right to stand now. Millions who are yet to come are depending on us. We shall overcome this darkest day in American history, and when we do, with the help of God we will find the bright lining that rims every dark cloud. "

"Thank you all, Keep the faith, and may God bless America in this, the hour of our greatest need!"

THE END OF VOLUME I

About the Author

Jeff Head is a forty-five year old father of five children, three of whom are now grown, who lives in Emmett, Idaho. He and his wife of over twenty-three years recently became the proud grandparents of Braedon, born to their oldest daughter Katie and her husband, Nathan.

Mr. Head is a member of the Sons of the American Revolution and a member of the U.S. Naval Institute. He has worked as an engineer for the last twenty-three years in the defense, nuclear power and computer industries. Mr. Head has been involved with a number of defense projects over the years, including the A-7D attack aircraft program, the MLRS (Multiple Launch Rocket system) program and THAADS (Theater High Altitude Air Defense System).

While working at Structural Dynamics Research Corporation at a Director level, Mr. Head was involved with consulting efforts at Thiokol to help their practice and operations in the years following the Shuttle Challenger disaster. As a result of that effort, Mr. Head was presented a Vice President's award from Thiokol Strategic Operations in 1992 for his efforts in the Computer-Aided-Engineering and Design (CAE/CAD) area.

Since 1995, in both a program management and consulting role, Mr. Head has traveled extensively overseas. This has included visits to the Far East, India and portions of Eastern Europe on behalf of U.S. firms.

Printed in the United States
3819